Goodbye, My Princess

Goodbye, My Princess

Fei Wo Si Cun
translated by Tianshu

NEW YORK AMSTERDAM/ANTWERP LONDON TORONTO
SYDNEY/MELBOURNE NEW DELHI

An imprint of Simon & Schuster Children's Publishing Division
1230 Avenue of the Americas, New York, New York 10020
For more than 100 years, Simon & Schuster has championed authors and the stories they create. By respecting the copyright of an author's intellectual property, you enable Simon & Schuster and the author to continue publishing exceptional books for years to come. We thank you for supporting the author's copyright by purchasing an authorized edition of this book No amount of this book may be reproduced or stored in any format, nor may it be uploaded to any website, database, language-learning model, or other repository, retrieval, or artificial intelligence system without express permission.
All rights reserved. Inquiries may be directed to
Simon & Schuster, 1230 Avenue of the Americas, New York, NY 10020 or permissions@simonandschuster.com.
This book is a work of fiction. Any references to historical events, real people, or real places are used fictitiously. Other names, characters, places, and events are products of the author's imagination, and any resemblance to actual events or places or persons, living or dead, is entirely coincidental.
Text © 2010 by Fei Wo Si Cun
English language translation © 2025 by Simon & Schuster, LLC
Previously published in China in 2010 by New World Press as *Eastern Palace*
Jacket illustration © 2025 by Zijing
Jacket design by Laurent Linn
All rights reserved, including the right of reproduction in whole or in part in any form.
SIMON & SCHUSTER BOOKS FOR YOUNG READERS
and related marks are trademarks of Simon & Schuster, Inc.
For information about special discounts for bulk purchases, please contact Simon & Schuster Special Sales at 1-866-506-1949 or business@simonandschuster.com.
Simon & Schuster strongly believes in freedom of expression and stands against censorship in all its forms. For more information, visit BooksBelong.com.
The Simon & Schuster Speakers Bureau can bring authors to your live event.
For more information or to book an event, contact
Simon & Schuster Speakers Bureau at 1-866-248-3049 or
visit our website at www.simonspeakers.com.
Interior design by Hilary Zarycky
The text for this book was set in Nyte.
Manufactured in the United States of America
First Edition
2 4 6 8 10 9 7 5 3 1
Library of Congress Cataloging-in-Publication Data
Names: Fei, Wo Si Cun, author. | Tianshu (Translator), translator.
Title: Goodbye, my princess / Fei Wo Si Cun ; [translated by Tianshu].
Other titles: Dong gong. English
Description: First edition. | New York : Simon & Schuster Books for Young Readers, 2025. | Audience term: Teenagers | Audience: Ages 14 up. | Audience: Grades 10–12. | Summary: Now married to the heartless crown prince, princess Xiaofeng lives a secret life outside the manor until a stranger reveals a past she cannot remember, and she must recover her memories of love and betrayal.
Identifiers: LCCN 2024029449 (print) | LCCN 2024029450 (ebook)
ISBN 9781665971041 (hardcover) | ISBN 9781665971058 (paperback)
ISBN 9781665971065 (ebook)
Subjects: CYAC: Kings, queens, rulers, etc.—Fiction. | Romance stories. | Memory—Fiction. | China—Fiction. | LCGFT: Romance fiction. | Novels.
Classification: LCC PZ7.1.F4427 Go 2025 (print) | LCC PZ7.1.F4427 (ebook) | DDC [Fic]—dc23
LC record available at https://lccn.loc.gov/2024029449
LC ebook record available at https://lccn.loc.gov/2024029450

Note from the Translator

The position of crown prince is always fraught, but it is especially so in the history of the various states that have constituted the history of China, where it is conferred not by accident of primogeniture but as a political calculation by a father who has survived the contention for the throne himself. The Chinese title for this novel, set in a fictional dynasty, is 东宫, *The East Court*, the name for the residence of the crown prince. The east, where the sun rises, is also the direction of spring, of new beginnings, of ascendancy—but it is an ascendancy that necessitates his father's decline.

The relationship between a crown prince and the crown is existentially tethered—because a crown prince cannot be crowned until his father dies, he poses a mortal threat to the king. Yet a king who intends his kingdom to survive cannot be without an heir. They are family, but more than that they are lord and vassal, their relationship framed by power, politics, and state.

Crown princes have been the source of major political upheaval and succession crises throughout history and have fueled more than one rumor of legitimacy (or lack thereof). Crown Prince Liu Ju famously died after he was forced into rebellion by ministers who spread rumors that he was employing witchcraft against his father. Though his grandson would reinstate his line to the throne, and despite his own father's grief and eventual regret, Liu Ju would never be king.

More than seven hundred years later, Li Shimin, who is otherwise considered a sage ruler, ambushed and assassinated his elder brother, Crown Prince Li Jiancheng, and aided in the assassination of his younger brother, Li Yuanji, in the Xuanwu Gate Incident. Within days of their deaths, Li Shimin was named the new heir and within months, his heartbroken father abdicated in his favor.

Nearly 1,100 years after that, the succession crisis caused by the Kangxi emperor's death would fuel speculation and spawn countless rumors, novels, films, and television shows. It serves as the most succinct example of both the advantages and the pitfalls of this method of choosing a crown prince—in personally appointing his heir, the king can ensure that only someone truly deserving of the throne may sit on it. But it also fosters competition, backroom politics, and hostile takeovers. Nine of Kangxi's twenty living sons were deadlocked in a struggle for the title, and his initial successor, the second prince, attempted to force an abdication by staging a coup d'état. Disgusted, the Kangxi emperor deposed the second prince and did not publicly appoint another heir, which caused his other sons to form allegiances with the fourth prince and the eighth prince, his two most likely candidates.

The Kangxi emperor placed the name of his successor in a box to be opened upon his death, but even that was not enough to quell gossip and unrest. His heir, the fourth prince

Yinzhen, is widely speculated to have doctored the document, changing 传位十四子 (*the throne to the fourteenth prince*) to 传位于四子 (*the throne to the fourth prince*).

Though this rumor has no basis in reality (legal documents of the time were written in Manchu and Mongolian, in addition to Chinese), the conspiracy theories surrounding his right to rule had significant ramifications on Yinzhen's reign, despite his general reputation as a hard worker, and many of his brothers lived the rest of their lives under house arrest.

Princes, then, had to be calculating if they wanted to inherit the crown, and ruthless if they wanted to live long enough to wear it. As Li Chengyin says, "The only place more dangerous than the palace is the crown prince's manor, and the only thing harder to be than a king is his heir."

It is not an easy environment for someone who is as naive, carefree, and impetuous as the titular crown princess to survive. Her encounters with the immovable machinations of imperial power are not ones that lay bare the best of humanity, for even good kings are cruel people—in fact, they must be in order to effectively wield the absolute power they are given. When you are a political institution unto yourself, is there anything of your personal life that politics does not taint?

This is the foundational problem of the narrative—a boy enmeshed in the games of power and a girl who cannot receive his personal affections separate from his political performance—and indeed, his cruelty is intended as a demonstration of his love, an attempt to protect her from the harms his position may bring. But at what point does the fact of the performance cease to matter, when all you receive of it is the real, lasting pain? Can intent be separated from impact? What is the value of love when it can only be filtered through abusive, dehumanizing systems? What is the value of feelings when they are not acted upon, only spoken of, or felt?

Is there room for love in a monarchy?

Note on the Translations

Chinese palaces are cities more than they are palaces in the European sense, composed of the "outer" ceremonial palace and the "inner" domestic palace, where the emperor, his wife and consorts, and his young children lived. The inner palace is divided into a series of interconnected courts over which higher-ranking or senior members of the family were given a level of administrative authority. The crown prince sometimes lived outside the palace in a residence of his own but more often lived as the head of his own household in the east of the palace. The palace is subsequently enclosed by the imperial city, which hosts the governmental and administrative buildings necessary for the day-to-day running of an empire.

For expediency, "manor," "mansion," and "Court of Spring" are used to denote the household of the crown prince, while "palace" is used to denote the household of the emperor, and "imperial city" is used to denote the entire palace complex.

O, THERE IS A FOX,
HE SITS UPON THE DUNE.
SOAKING IN THE SUN,
WAITING FOR THE GIRL
TO RIDE PAST

Goodbye, My Princess

PART ONE:

正直
Upright

I've fought with Li Chengyin again.

Every time we argue he ignores me for ages and won't let anyone else talk to me either. So, like always, I slip out into the city with A'du.

I'd go out alone if I could, but A'du shadows me everywhere, even to the privy. Not that I mind her—she's a little uptight, but she can fight, which comes in handy more often than not.

Today, we decide to go to the teahouse to hear some stories, but the man telling them is not that good, and his spittle flies everywhere as he expounds on a swordsman who can take someone's head clean off from a thousand paces away.

I lean close to A'du. "Is that possible?"

A'du shakes her head.

I didn't think so either.

I've seen A'du use her gold-inlay dagger and she's quicker than lightning, so there definitely are master swordsmen in the world, but from a thousand paces away? That sounds like horseshit.

As we leave, I spot a circle of people at the other end of the street. I'm a born busybody, so of course I'm squeezing through the crowd faster to watch my fill.

It's a girl in mourning robes, kneeling in front of a ratty bamboo mat. Two feet stick rigidly out from beneath it, and as she cries, the bystanders sigh and shake their heads, tutting at the length of white cloth she's spread out. The words *will sell body to pay for father's burial* are written across it in stark black ink.

"What a devoted daughter!" I say. "How much money do you think you're worth, miss?"

Everyone turns to glare. I've forgotten that I'm still dressed like a man, so I shrink back and wet my lips nervously. A'du tugs at my hem, and I know exactly why she's worried. She's always fretting that I'll get into a scrape again, but I swear, except for that time with the startled horse and the time with the hooligans and the very few other times we've chased after pickpockets, I *do* try to mind my own business.

I sneak around the crowd, taking measure of the body. Plucking a bit of loose straw from the mat, I squat down and twirl it against the bottom of the corpse's foot.

Slowly, slowly, around and around.

I'm patient. I wait until the corpse can't control himself anymore. He starts shaking, violently shaking, and people finally realize that something's wrong. Some point at the mat with a shout, their teeth clattering so loudly I can hear them, while others yell, "Dead man walking!" But most are stunned into wide-eyed silence.

I don't let up, not until the corpse stops resisting. He flings the mat off and leaps up, screaming, "Who's the bastard tickling my feet?"

I needle him and he lunges, kicking at me. A'du darts

between us in a flash and I'm safely behind her, making faces at the swindler.

He flies into a rage. He and his accomplice run toward us, and A'du, who doesn't like to make a scene, grabs me by the hand and drags me away.

She's such a wet blanket sometimes. Halfway through doing anything interesting, she always makes a deserter out of me. But her hand is a steel trap I can't wriggle out of, so I have little choice but to follow after until, before a teahouse, I lock eyes with someone.

Someone beautiful. His eyes, crow-dark and piercing, are a sharp contrast to his moon-white robes. My heart pounds, though I'm not sure why.

A'du doesn't let go until we reach the archway at the end of the avenue, and when I turn to look back, the stranger is gone.

She doesn't ask what I was looking at—it's what I like most about her, that she hasn't too many questions. But then, I've been distracted all day. It's all Li Chengyin's fault. He never wins our fights, but that doesn't mean he doesn't have other ways of tormenting me, like telling people to ignore me. Sometimes I feel like I hardly exist. If I didn't sneak out for the occasional breath of fresh air, I would have died of boredom a million times over.

I kick aimlessly at a pebble, which skips and rolls like a ball in a cuju match. He's a brilliant player, Li Chengyin. Between his feet, the small leather ball is a living thing. Not that I'd know much about it, because I can't play. I've asked to learn, but no one's bothered to show me, because not only has Li Chengyin refused to teach me, he's refused to let anyone else do it either. He's petty like that.

With some force, I kick the pebble into a dark pool of water. The splash startles me out of my reverie, and when I look up I realize that I've wandered into a narrow alley. The walls of other people's homes rise up on either side of me, capped by strangely shaped grotesques. They build so high here. I shiver, hair standing on end. There's no sign of A'du when I turn.

I call out, but the empty alley echoes my words back. A'du hasn't left my side once, not in the three years since we've been here, and now she's disappeared. Terror rises in my throat.

Then I see him, the man in the moon-white clothing. He stands at the end of the lane. In a panic, I yell again for A'du.

I'm certain I don't know him, but he'd looked at me oddly. He's *looking* at me oddly.

"Hey," I call. "Have you seen A'du?"

Instead of answering, he comes closer. The sun scatters across his face. It's a nice face, handsomer than even Li Chengyin's. His brows are straight and sharp like swords, his eyes glisten blacker than gemstones, and his nose is tall. Though his lips aren't full, his mouth is well shaped, and the whole effect is pleasant.

He stops in front of me and bursts into a smile. "What's this A'du you're looking for?"

"My A'du, of course," I say, impatient. What other A'du is there? "Have you seen her? She's wearing a yellow tunic, like a little oriole."

His smile turns lazy. "Wearing a yellow tunic, like a little oriole . . . now that you mention it, I *have* come across such a person."

"Where?"

"Right here, of course." He's close to me, too close—I can catch the glint in his eyes. "Is that not you?"

I drop my eyes to my own top, pale yellow and cut in a man's style, like A'du's.

He continues, "Xiaofeng, it's been a long time, but you haven't changed a bit."

Xiaofeng is my milk name. No one's called me that since I arrived in Shangjing. I blink at him. "Who are you?"

His lips thin. "Of course, you don't know who I am."

"Did my father send you?" A'die had promised he would send people to visit me and bring me treats from home, but no one's ever come, the liar.

He doesn't answer this either. "Do you want to go home?"

Of course I do. When I dream, I dream of home.

"Did my brother send you, then?" I press, curious.

That smile again. "You have a brother?"

I have five. My fifth brother is the one who loves me most; before I left he cried and cried and made such a scene, lashing at the ground with his whip, but it was only because he couldn't bear the thought of my leaving him for such a distant place. If this man doesn't know that much, then my family can't have sent him. Disappointment trickles through me. "How do you know my name, then?"

"You told it to me."

I? Did I know him? I can't remember him at all. But he

5

doesn't strike me as a liar, because no liar lies so conspicuously. I crook my head and consider him. "Who are you really?"

"Gu Jian." He doesn't explain further, like these words are answer enough. But I've never heard that name.

"I'm going to find A'du," I inform him.

He calls after me. "I've been looking for you for three whole years and that's all you have to say to me?"

What? "Why were you looking for me? Did we know each other?"

"You ran away from home three years ago," he says, "because of me. I've been looking for you all this time. But you say you don't know me anymore."

He's an unconvincing liar. Forget three years, I can recall things from *thirteen* years ago as if it were yesterday. Like once, A'niang gave me sour jam to eat, and I spat it out because I hated the taste. Or the time she held me in her arms and we watched my lord father ride back, lit by a blazing sunset. It had looked like he was wearing a suit of molten gold armor.

I'm no longer interested in this conversation and go in search of A'du, but I can't help glancing back. Gu Jian stands right where I left him. He smiles when he catches me, but the smile is strained.

What a strange person. I wouldn't know anyone like *that*.

When I come to the end of the alley, A'du is sitting on the railing of a small bridge. "Where were you?" I ask her. "I've been worried sick."

But she doesn't move, not even when I shake her.

Gu Jian reappears. He unseals A'du with a casual flick of

the finger. She leaps up, pulling me behind her with one hand and unsheathing her dagger with the other.

"You fought me once, three years ago," Gu Jian drawls. "I immobilized you just now. If it really came down to it, do you think you'd be the one to stop me?"

A'du glares up at him. When she gets like this, she looks like a mother hen protecting her chicks—she'd glared up at Li Chengyin like this once too, when the fighting got bad. I can't fathom anyone being able to immobilize A'du. Most people can't get close enough to touch her, much less paralyze her completely.

I gape at Gu Jian.

But he lets out a long breath. He looks between us one more time and, finally, walks away.

I stare after him until he disappears and the alley is empty again. Then I turn to A'du. "Are you okay? Did he hurt you at all?"

A'du shakes her head and signs something to me.

She wants to know if I'm sad.

But why should I be?

No one is behaving normally today.

As the day dims, I lead A'du to Wenyue Tower. We always dine here when we're in the city, because their roast duck is the best in all of Shangjing. By the time it's brought to our table, old Uncle He and his daughter, Fujie'er, have come to sell their songs. Uncle He is blind, but he can still play his huqin, so we order a ditty or two.

Fujie'er slips into a familiar curtsy when she sees us. "Master Liang."

I ask her to sing me something, and she and Uncle He begin to play a song called "Picking Mulberry."

Roast duck, warmed wine, Fujie'er's voice—I can't think of a better way to spend the evening.

Meat sizzles on the grill when A'du flips it, and she dips the cooked slices in sauce before setting them on my plate. As we eat, a rowdy group of men storm up the stairs, completely oblivious to the dirty glares thrown their way.

I'm less subtle in my disdain. "What a bunch of assholes."

A'du doesn't understand what I mean.

"They might be in their civvies," I explain, "but look at their riding boots and swords. They're used to cavalry footwear, and by their wrist and thumb guards, they're used to archery, too. They're wearing weapons in public and they're made up like a bunch of useless dandies. Who could they be but the Yulin Guard?"

A'du nods emphatically. She's no fan of the Yulin Guard either.

As the troops settle into their seats, one of them calls, "Hey you! Come sing us 'Dreaming of My Love'!"

Uncle He is trembling and apologetic. "This young man has paid us for two songs, sir, and we've just finished the first. We can attend to you gentlemen once we're done."

"Heavens, who gives a fig if you're finished or not?" The guard slams his fist against the table. "You'd better come over here if you know what's good for you, you blind old bat."

Another guard glances my way and guffaws. "Get a load of that one. Scrawnier than a girl, but he's handsome enough, don't you think?"

The first one looks me up and down. "He's prettier than the singing chit, at least. Why don't you join the boys and me for a round?"

I sigh and put my chopsticks down. I hadn't wanted to brawl, but it looks like I'd only been delaying the inevitable. "What a shame," I drawl. "This used to be such a nice establishment before they let in a herd of wild animals to spoil everyone's fun."

"What did you call us?" the guards snap.

I smile sweetly. "Beg pardon. Are you not fit to be even that?"

The first to have opened his mouth is also the first to lose his temper. Whipping his sword out, he lunges at us. A'du slams a hand against the table, but nothing moves except the canister that holds our utensils. She plucks out a single chopstick. Before the canister drops, the guard's blade flashes, inches from our faces.

A'du plunges her hand down.

A terrible scream trills through the room. The sword clatters to the ground. The guard's hand is nailed soundly to our table, leaking blood. Wailing, he tries to free himself, but he's stuck fast.

His friends unsheathe their own weapons, but A'du pins them in place with a cold stare, hand coming to a rest atop the canister.

The one on our table howls like a stuck pig. I pluck an osmanthus cake from the platter and shove it into his mouth. He gags around it, but at least he's gagging in silence.

I look around. "Who wants to drink?"

No one dares breathe too loud. I rise to my feet and take a step forward. The guards take a step back. I take another step forward. They take another step back, all the way to the doorway and the staircase beyond it.

Someone yells, "RUN!" and the whole hive buzzes back downstairs.

No one here is any fun at all. I don't even get the chance to point out that, unlike A'du, I can't shove a chopstick through anyone's palm.

The guard is still pinned to our table when I return to finish my duck. The gamey smell of blood lingers, rancid, in the air, and I wrinkle my nose. A'du understands immediately. She wraps a hand around the chopstick and pulls it free, kicking the guard away.

Cradling his injured hand, the man all but crawls from the room, leaving his sword behind. A'du picks it up and offers it to me. Back home, you have to surrender your weapon if you lose a fight—A'du's lived in Shangjing for the last three years, but she remembers our old ways.

But as I see the crest on the blade, all my excitement falls away, and I refuse it. "Give this back."

By this time he's reached the stairs, so A'du flings the sword. It lands with a thunk in the column next to him.

He gives a shout and scrambles off, too scared to look back. He tumbles cleanly down the steps like a cuju ball.

We leave Wenyue Tower when the moon has risen, a sliver of silver that hangs in the trees like a plump rice cake someone's taken a bite out of, radiating a gauzy glow. But I can't think about food. I've eaten too much. I inch down the street, bloated and uncomfortable. Based on my current crawl we probably won't make it back until daybreak, but A'du waits ahead for me, as patient as ever.

A crowd of people floods out from a dim alley as we approach the corner, each armed to the teeth. Someone shouts, "That's them!"

I realize too late that it's the Yulin Guard—the Yulin Guard, and they've brought backup.

Why must every romp end in a brawl? I swear I'm not someone who goes around picking fights. I sigh over the sea of black heads. There probably aren't actually hundreds of them, but it feels that way. A'du drops a hand to her dagger and looks to me, asking what we should do. My appetite for a brawl went the way of the roast duck the second I saw the seal and, absent that, we have one option: to run like hell.

A'du and I spring out of there. We aren't the best warriors in the world, but I think we could lay a claim to being the most accomplished escape artists. In three short years, we've cultivated a network of shortcuts and side streets specifically for losing people in.

But the Yulin Guard are good. They're close on our heels, and though we run in circles trying to shake them, they refuse to stay gone. I'm on the verge of hurling when A'du pulls me from the small street into a wider avenue—right into the path of another platoon.

I double over, hands on my knees, breathing hard. I don't see a better way out—we may have to fight whether we want to or not.

The clamor grows as the bastards chasing us draw closer.

But so too do the troops ahead and their swaying lanterns, and I realize with a start that I know the man who is leading the retinue.

"Pei Zhao!" I yell, delighted. "Over here!"

He doesn't pay me any mind, so I call his name again, waving my arms until the lantern bearer at his side takes a step forward, illuminating my face.

Pei Zhao blanches and immediately dismounts his white horse. "You—"

I don't give him the chance to finish that word. "We're being chased," I say. "Help me!"

"Of course." He draws his blade, calling his men to attention. They unsheathe their weapons just as the guards chasing us burst from the alley, stumbling to a stop when they see the ocean of bobbing lights and Pei Zhao with his longsword out. Their ringleader forces out a smile.

"G-General Pei—"

"What do you think you're doing?" Pei Zhao's face is dark.

His official title is the Jinwu General, which means he is the commander of the Yulin Guard, and they are in a world of trouble. While everyone is distracted, I grab A'du and slip away.

We have to jump the gate to get back. Thank the heavens A'du is good at qinggong—she makes no sound at all as she carries me over the high walls. It's late, later than I expected, and frighteningly quiet. Though I'm not sure why I'm surprised; it's always quiet here. Quiet, and vast, and empty.

The two of us slip in, silent as mice. A smatter of distant lights is the only thing that breaks the pitch of night, and when we get back to my rooms, I feel for my bed, my wonderful bed, yawning, "I'm so tired—"

A'du leaps up, startling me from my comfort. Light floods the room as a mess of people burst in, some lighting candles, others carrying lanterns, but all of them led by Yongniang, who flings herself tearfully to her knees.

"Your Highness, please, just execute me—it's easier than the torture you're putting me through!"

I hate the kneeling. I hate Yongniang. I hate being called *Your Highness*. But most especially I hate all these people constantly moaning about how I'd better sentence them to death already because I was going to drive them to it someday.

"I'm back now, aren't I?"

It's the same dog and pony show every time. Yongniang may not have bored of it, but I have. Her tears are gone as quickly as they'd come and she orders the ladies-in-waiting to prepare me for bed. They peel away the soft clothes I have on and wrap me back in my shroud, layer upon layer of heavy fabric, until I'm swaddled into a human layer cake—the kind you have to dig through forever to unearth a single peanut.

At my ear, Yongniang mutters, "Don't forget, my lady, that tomorrow is the Honorable Lady Zhao's birthday. You have to at least make an appearance."

But I'm so tired I can't stand straight. Servants crowd me, washing my face, running combs through my hair, like I'm a puppet they're arranging for a play. Whatever Yongniang is nattering on about goes in one ear and out the other, because I've already fallen asleep.

It's a sweet sleep, a good sleep, a dreamless sleep, the kind you sink into when you're worn out and comfortably full. But right as my sleep is at its soundest, a *bang* startles me awake.

It's light, and Li Chengyin is storming into my room.

Yongniang and her retinue of ladies-in-waiting fall to their knees.

My hair is a mess and my face is crusted over, but I push myself to my feet. Not because I'm intimidated by his presence, mind, but because it's impossible to win an argument while you're horizontal. It undermines your authority.

And he's clearly here to argue.

"You can rest?" He glares down at me.

I luxuriate in my yawn. "Why shouldn't I?"

His eyes are shards of coldest ice burrowing deep into my skin. "Stop playing the innocent," he says. "We both know what you did."

This isn't the usual script. I pause. "What?"

"You know exactly what. Lady Zhao ate the birthday noodles you sent over, and now she's taken ill. Don't you ever disgust yourself?"

"I didn't send any birthday noodles," I scoff. "It's not my fault if she has the runs."

"So you have the nerve to do it but not the courage to own up?" He burns with contempt. "I didn't realize girls from Xiliang were so shameless."

He knows just how to provoke me. "Girls from Xiliang only own up to the things we've actually done," I retort. "Why would I admit to something I haven't? If I had quarrel with your precious Lady Zhao, I'd take a knife and stab her;

I wouldn't poison her. You, on the other hand, throwing out baseless accusations—is that what Shangjing boys do?"

"Don't think I won't depose you," he warns. "I'd sooner lose my title than put up with a viper like you."

"Do it then," I say. *"Do it."*

He turns on his heel and stalks from the room.

I'm too angry to go back to bed, and my stomach has started aching again. Yongniang falls to her knees, trembling with terror. "Don't mind him," I tell her. "He threatens to depose me every year. He's meeting his quota, that's all."

But this doesn't comfort her.

"My lady, I'm the one who sent noodles to Lady Zhao. This is my fault."

My eyes widen, but she doesn't stop.

"I swear to you I didn't put anything untoward in there. I only thought—it's Lady Zhao's birthday today, and if Your Highness didn't favor her with anything, it might seem a little—a little—and you were sleeping so soundly, so I went ahead and had someone send it over, but I hadn't imagined—"

"If we didn't tamper with the food, then it's not our fault," I say. "Now get up, your kneeling's going to be the death of me."

Yongniang rises, but her eyes are damp. "My lady, you shouldn't use that word. It bodes ill."

Another rule I've forgotten about. They'll be the thing that kills me if Yongniang doesn't get there first. It's only a word. Who on this Earth doesn't die?

Since Lady Zhao's birthday is thoroughly spoiled, Li Chengyin ends up making a fuss up at the palace. He can't depose me—if his father doesn't step in, the ministers will—but it doesn't mean I escape punishment entirely. Li Chengyin rats me out to his great-grandmother, the grand-empress, and she has people send me copies of *The Woman's Manual* and *The Woman's Guide*, along with orders to copy them ten times in their entirety.

I'm confined to my rooms copying books from dusk till dawn when news comes that Li Chengyin's gotten a maid pregnant.

I bet the Honorable Lady Zhao is pleased.

No one's been pregnant yet since I've been here, so there's nothing I want more than to go see the spectacle, but Yongniang puts her foot down.

"My lady, you mustn't," she begs. "They're all saying that His Highness only spent the night with that girl because he was inebriated, so if you visit her today, Lady Zhao will think you're doing it to spite her."

But why should she? It has nothing to do with her. The logic in the Court of Spring goes around in circles and I can make neither heads nor tails of it, but if Yongniang says that that's how Lady Zhao will take it, then perhaps she really will. I can't afford another argument with Li Chengyin. If he goes to his great-grandmother again, she'll sentence me to execution by pen.

That night, the empress summons me into the palace.

I'm rarely alone with her. Usually, I accompany Li Chengyin when he visits, but the most she ever says to me is *rise* or *sit* or *you are dismissed*. She hasn't summoned him this time—only me—and Yongniang, ill at ease, insists on coming.

A'du isn't allowed into the empress's residence because she refuses to give up her dagger, so she waits for us outside the doors to Yong'an Court.

The empress is as beautiful as Li Chengyin, but she's not his birth mother. His birth mother was the Lady Shu, who everyone says was as learned as she was lovely. The emperor had adored her. But she'd died giving birth, and as the empress hadn't any children of her own, Li Chengyin was brought to her court to be raised, which is why he'd been the natural choice when it came time to appoint an heir.

The empress says a great many things, but in truth I understand very little. I'm barely fluent in the language of the Central Plains to begin with, and she speaks so formally that I'm lucky if I catch one word in three. She must see my expression, for she lets out a long breath.

"The trouble is, you're still young, but why can't you pay more mind to what goes on in your manor?" she says. "Never mind, I've ordered people to clean out a quiet courtyard in the palace for this Xu girl. As for Lady Zhao, you should spend some time with her, comfort her, and take some pressure off Yin'er."

This, at last, is something I can comprehend, but she turns immediately back to address Yongniang, and I lose the thread of it again. I understand the gist, though, for Yongniang's face is carefully blank and all she says is "It's my fault, Your Highness."

I stare down at the carpet. It's a tribute gift from Tuhuolu, with long soft shag that feels like stepping onto a fresh snowfall. I trace a circle with my foot, and the print turns into a patch of white. I smooth it back, and the print is back, too. And when I draw another circle, it turns white again and—

The empress coughs. I snap my head up to see her staring at me. I sit up straight, slipping my foot guiltily under my skirts.

As we leave, Yongniang says, "Please, Your Highness, won't you think of me a little before you get into any more scrapes?"

"I know, I know." I wave her away. "But I've been locked in my rooms for days. How could I possibly get into any trouble?"

"Yes, yes," Yongniang concedes. "You've been very good. But since the empress raised the matter, I think it's best to do as she asks."

I huff. "Li Chengyin told me I'm not allowed near that woman. I'm not going to visit her; it'll only upset him."

"It's different this time," Yongniang says. "You're acting on Her Majesty's orders, so you're well within your rights to go. You can take this opportunity to make peace with her—she's still angry about Miss Xu, and if you extend her a hand now, she'll be grateful. And if you can get her on your side, it won't matter whether the child in Miss Xu's stomach is a boy or not."

I don't know what Yongniang spends her time thinking about, but I'm sure it must be clever, because she was once the grand-empress's most trusted lady-in-waiting. When I was made princess consort, the grand-empress sent her to teach me etiquette for the wedding ceremony.

Back then, Li Chengyin liked to pretend that I didn't exist. His servants had followed suit, for I was a newcomer, a foreigner, and I had no power to do anything to them. They all mocked me, including the scullery maids. I missed home, missed it like mad, and all I could think to do was cry until I cried myself sick.

He told everyone I was faking it. He didn't let anyone send for the physicians and kept it from the palace. It had been Yongniang and A'du who sat by my sickbed, forcing down spoonfuls of medicine long after I could neither eat nor drink. They were the ones who dragged me bodily from the clutches of Lord Yama. It was the worst time of my life, and Yongniang spent it by my side.

So while I don't understand Yongniang, I try to humor her.

"I suppose I'd better see her, then," I say.

"Not 'see her,'" Yongniang corrects. "You ought to bring her a gift, try to win her over."

I don't know what *a gift* entails, but after some careful consideration, I select a bow and quiver—tributes from Gaochang—two chess sets made from precious stone, a few pairs of knucklebones to play jacks with, and a tankard of tribute wine from Baiyi. Yongniang pales when she sees what I've chosen.

I peer at her, trying to gauge her reaction. "What's wrong?"

Yongniang takes a breath. "Why don't I prepare something?"

She ends up gathering a set of gilded jade bangles, an ornament made from gold and kingfisher feather, a set of coral hairpins, and a pearl-inlaid necklace in addition to tallow cream and jasmine powder and an assortment of sickly sweet-smelling things. I worry that nothing looks interesting enough, but Yongniang assures me that "Lady Zhao will appreciate the thought you've put into this."

I *am* looking forward to seeing Lady Zhao, whatever the circumstances. I've met her just once, the day after the wedding, when she was made an honorable lady and had come to pay her respects to me. She had worn pale chrysanthemum-colored robes and had been perfectly mannered under a roomful of scrutiny, but she'd been standing too far away for me to see her face. I still can't say exactly what she looks like.

He likes her though. Everyone says she's the reason Li Chengyin had been such an unwilling groom. He'd only agreed to our wedding because the empress promised he could take Lady Zhao for a mistress if he married me, which is why he despises me—he's constantly worried I'm going to do something to hurt her, so he won't let her come to my court and doesn't let me visit her, either.

I don't know where he heard that Xiliang girls are dangerously jealous, but whoever told him that also told him that we poison and hex, too. So when we fight, all I have to do is mention his Honorable Lady Zhao and he'll scamper away like a dog with its tail between its legs.

Girls from Xiliang may not be especially jealous, but I admit I sometimes am. I want someone to care that deeply for me. I want my family by my side. Yongniang is kind, but there are things I can't say to her, things she can't understand. How can I explain the way you could take a horse all the way into the heart of the desert, and the night wind would rustle the grass? The way the sky would press low, so dark it was nearly purple, as limpid as grape jelly, sour and cold against the tongue. Yongniang hasn't even seen a grape.

A'du understands, but she doesn't respond. All she ever does is stare calmly, quietly back at me, no matter how excited I am.

I miss Xiliang, my lively, noisy Xiliang. And the more I miss it, the more I hate Li Chengyin's cold, desolate manor.

I visit Lady Zhao on a lovely clear afternoon, accompanied by Yongniang and twelve ladies-in-waiting. Some carry censers, some wave large fans, and others hold the brocaded boxes we prepared. With such a procession snaking through the manor, it's no wonder Lady Zhao's doors are flung wide open to greet us when we arrive.

She's planted fragrant oranges in her courtyard. The trees are bursting with tiny green fruit, like a bush of colored lanterns. I've never seen their like and crane my neck to see, but the moment my attention drifts, I step on my own hem and pitch forward.

Lady Zhao rushes forward to help me up, looping her arm through mine. "Jiejie, are you hurt?"

In truth, I am the younger by two years, so if anything, I should be calling her jiejie, but I'm in too much pain to make a fuss. She doesn't let go until we're inside her rooms, where she orders someone to draw up a steep of tea. I sit gingerly on her daybed, trying to keep as still as possible. I'd fallen hard, and if I so much as twitch the pain scalds through me.

Yongniang takes my silence as an opportunity to order the ladies-in-waiting to bring in the presents. Lady Zhao rises to her feet and curtsies low. "Thank you, Your Highness, but this is too great an honor."

I freeze, casting about for the appropriate response.

Thankfully, Yongniang steps in again and helps her up. "Please, Lady Zhao, there's no need to stand on ceremony. Our princess has been meaning to call and was only waiting for the right time. Now that the servants are busy preparing to bring Miss Xu to the palace, Her Highness worried you might feel neglected, so came by specially to visit. If you find yourself in need of anything at all, please do not hesitate to ask—you are the princess's right hand here in the manor, so you mustn't feel a stranger."

"I understand Your Highness *completely*."

I'm not sure *I* understand. I only feel suffocated. Lady Zhao is not as beautiful as I imagined, but she is agreeable and her voice is soft. I can't bring myself to like her, but I don't dislike her either. In fact, I spend the entire afternoon with her. She seems quite pleased with Yongniang, smiling behind her sleeve as Yongniang talks and complimenting me on my accomplished attendant.

I run into Pei Zhao as we're leaving. He's on duty today and is clearly surprised when he sees whence I'm coming, but if he has any thoughts he keeps them to himself as he kneels to make courtesy.

"You can get up," I tell him, adding, "Thank you for the other night." It wouldn't have been the worst thing in the world to get into another fight, but I'd recognized the insignia on the weapons. They'd been Li Chengyin's guards. I would have been in hot water if they remembered me.

Pei Zhao's face is expressionless. "I'm sure I have no idea what you're talking about, Your Highness."

Yongniang pulls me away before I can respond and begins to lecture me as soon as we're safely back in my rooms. "It isn't proper for you to spend so much time with outside men. My lady, you should stay away from the Jinwu General."

If Yongniang knew how much time I spent with "outside men," she might faint.

There's a bruise blossoming on my thigh, so A'du goes to brew me some medicine to drink. I've finally finished the books I was sentenced to copy, and the old restless itch takes over—I'm dying to go into the city again, but Yongniang's been keeping a tight watch of late. I toy with the idea of sneaking out after she's gone to bed, but before I can do anything about it, Li Chengyin pays me a visit.

He's never come after dark, so no one's ready for him. Yongniang is fast asleep in her room, the attendant on night duty is dozing, and A'du and I are playing cards—the loser has to eat a whole orange. A'du has won four hands in a row, so I've eaten four oranges in a row, and my stomach churns with sour bile, which is when he makes his entrance.

If I remember correctly, it's my job to prepare for his arrival. I'm supposed to lay out his clothing, light the incense, spread balsam in the furnace, and brew tea for both the nighttime and morning rinse—at least, according to all the tripe I was forced to memorize before the investiture. Of course, the attendants have to do the actual work, but I'm supposed to supervise.

But then Li Chengyin didn't come, so even Yongniang's let things slip.

I've just drawn a good hand when I catch sight of him. At first, I think I must be dreaming, but when I lower my cards and look up again, he's still there.

A'du gets to her feet immediately. Li Chengyin and I have never gotten along, and a few times it very nearly got physical, so she reaches for her dagger as soon as he steps into the room, her face pinched in warning.

His is acrid as he settles himself on my bed.

I stare blankly at him.

"Shoes," he says coldly.

The attendant on duty has startled awake. She'd frozen when she saw the crown prince. At his words, she rouses herself and rushes forward, but Li Chengyin prods her away with his foot. "Tell your mistress to do it."

I help her up. "What the hell is wrong with you?"

"I'll kick her if I want. I'll kick you if I want, too," he snaps.

A'du unsheathes her dagger. Frostily, I ask, "Have you come just to fight?"

He smiles oddly. "I haven't come to argue. I've come to sleep." He points to A'du. "Out."

I don't know what he has planned, but it's clearly nothing good. The commotion has woken nearly everyone, including Yongniang, who is happy and alarmed all at once—alarmed because of the annoyance plain on his face, and happy because she probably thinks his being here is a good sign, whether or not he's come to upset me.

Her arrival cools us both, and soon she's busy directing

water to be drawn, a washbasin prepared, and his nightclothes brought out from storage. My rooms explode into a bustle of activity, and I am surrounded by a crowd of people who wipe my face and comb my hair and stuff me into a nightgown. By the time I struggle free, Yongniang is tugging A'du away.

She resists at first, but Yongniang leans forward and says something that makes her face burn red, and she follows obediently after. Then she is gone, and I'm alone in a room with Li Chengyin.

I haven't been alone with a boy in my nightclothes before, but I'm too cold to be shy and am tired from all the fuss, so I crawl into bed, pull up the covers, and try to sleep. As for Li Chengyin . . . his bedtime is his own business.

Sometime later, I feel him crawling into bed behind me, bumping my foot with his as he tugs at the blanket. "Move over."

Docile in my doze, I offer him some of my blanket. He curls up in it, turning away from me.

I don't get much rest though. I'm not used to sharing my bed, and he's a fitful sleeper. Halfway through the night, he steals away my portion of the sheets. I wake up shivering, kicking him away and snatching them back, which is how we end up angry again at midnight.

He huffs. "I wouldn't even be here if it weren't for Sese."

I think I see him soften when he uses Lady Zhao's bower name. Then I remember what she said this afternoon, and also what Yongniang said, and I wish I hadn't because when I put it together it only makes me sad. It's not like I cared, back when he didn't come. But now that he has, all it does is remind me of everything I'm missing.

It's not like I don't know married people are meant to share a bed. It's just that I also know that he's never thought of me as his wife. He's only ever wanted *her*. I went to visit her today, and I brought her presents, and she pities me. That's why she told him to come.

I don't need anyone's pity. I'm a Xiliang girl.

"You can go," I say, sitting up.

"Don't worry," he says. "I'm leaving as soon as it's light." Then he turns and falls asleep again, and there's nothing for me to do but get up and put on a robe.

There's a lamp on my dressing table. The candle within is dimmed by its cover, but light seeps warmly out. Something is seeping from my heart, too. I miss A'die and A'niang. Miss my brothers, my little red horse. My home.

I'm so lonely here.

A pale shadow falls across the window.

My heart leaps into my throat, and I push open the pane. No one. Only a scatter of icy moon across the ground. Night's brisk wind pierces me through, but as I'm closing the screen, I catch sight of a figure in white standing in a distant tree. When I squint, I can see the outline of a man.

I'm too surprised to react. The Court of Spring is the crown prince's manor—how could an assassin have gotten into one of the most heavily guarded places in Shangjing?

I stare at him. He stares back.

The night is so silent that you could hear even the gentle breath of the moving breeze. The lamp on my table flickers. And he stands on a bough, gazing down. The leaves rise and fall. He rises and falls with them, bathed in a wash of light. Behind him, the bright wheel of the moon illuminates the billow of his hair and sleeves, as though he were caught inside of it.

I recognize him.

Gu Jian.

But he's gone before I can be sure I'm not wrong, or dreaming, or both.

True to his word, Li Chengyin is gone by morning. Yongniang is delighted by the whole affair—her eyes light up every time she brings it up, and she brings it up *a lot*. I don't have the heart to tell her the truth, that nothing happened. I may be young, but A'du and I have been to pleasure houses. We may not have eaten their pork, but that doesn't mean I've not seen pigs run.

Grateful for Lady Zhao's show of goodwill, Yongniang brings her over the day after to play cards with me.

I lose every round.

It's one thing to lose to her in love, but to lose at gambling? Yongniang beams, clearly under the impression that I've taken her advice at long last and am doing it on purpose to make Lady Zhao happy.

It must work, because from that day on, Lady Zhao comes often to play cards. She's charming, and she knows what to say to make people happy—like when she compliments my short boots, saying, "We don't have leather as fine as that in the Central Plains."

I'm so pleased I promise her on the spot that I'll have

someone bring a few pairs for her the next time A'die sends a caravan to Shangjing. But Lady Zhao looks down at her cards. "Your Highness," she says. "When will you go see Miss Xu?"

I look at her, confused. Miss Xu is doing perfectly fine. The empress has a whole fleet of attendants looking after her, she doesn't need *me* to visit. And anyway, Yongniang told me that Lady Zhao and Li Chengyin fought terribly over the Miss Xu affair, and that she cried until he swore he wouldn't look at the girl again, no matter whether she had a son. So I don't understand why Lady Zhao would bring it up and pretend to be so generous when everyone knows how much she hates Miss Xu.

Yongniang answers for me. "Miss Xu has been invited up to the palace, so without Her Majesty's summons, even the princess consort will find it hard to visit."

"Oh," says Lady Zhao carelessly, as though she doesn't give two figs.

Luck favors me today and I win some money, so I'm in high spirits when Lady Zhao leaves. But once she's gone, Yongniang pulls me aside and says, "My lady, you must be more careful, lest you become the arm Lady Zhao uses to wield her sword."

I puzzle at that turn of phrase.

Yongniang explains, "Lady Zhao is going to find a way to stop Miss Xu's child from being born. Whatever her plans, Your Highness can by all means look the other way and let the chips fall where they may. But you must be careful not to get caught in her snares yourself."

But the child is already in Miss Xu's stomach. What could

GOODBYE, MY PRINCESS

Lady Zhao possibly do to stop it from coming out?

"There are ways," Yongniang says darkly when I prod. "But you are a good person, my lady, so you shouldn't go around asking questions like that."

She must say these things on purpose, because while I'm not especially good, the words guilt me into dropping the subject.

When the weather turns cool, I find my opportunity to slip from the manor.

I don't realize how stifled I've been all summer until I'm in the city again, where the streets are full of people and carriages and horses. We go to the teahouse to listen to stories, but the old storymaster has been replaced by a new one, who has abandoned swordmasters in favor of recounting the Li dynasty's westward wars decades ago.

"After such a terrible loss, and being cowed by our courageous generals, Xiliang got to their knees and acknowledged our emperor as their lord and ruler. Our emperor Xuan is a benevolent man, so he arranged for a treaty marriage to seal the accord. He sent his own sister, the Princess Mingyuan, to marry the khan of Xiliang, and the two kingdoms lived in peace for ten years.

"But when the old khan died, the new khan proclaimed himself emperor. He was a foolish man and a coward, and he tried to attack our troops, starting a war he couldn't finish. Little did he know our mighty army would soon arrive at his border, and when he saw them he couldn't bow quickly enough, offering up his own daughter for a new treaty marriage. With his groveling, he convinced our emperor to give him a second chance."

The audience roars with laughter, but A'du leaps up, hurling a cup to the ground. She's usually the one who stops me from getting into trouble, but today I pull her from the teahouse, worried she might hurt someone.

The bright sun flashes outside.

I remember Princess Mingyuan. She'd been so beautiful, but though she lived in Xiliang for decades, she always wore her own clothing and plaited her hair the way girls in Shangjing do. A'die had been heartbroken when she fell ill and passed away. He'd treated her well, because he said that, through her, he was treating the Plains well.

That's the way it is in Xiliang—we repay kindness with kindness. It's nothing like here, where people are constantly scheming, saying one thing to your face while doing another behind your back. Three years ago, I would have been as angry as A'du, but these days I'm too tired to care.

A'du and I rest beside a bridge, watching sails fill with wind on the canal. A captain raises his long pole and plunges it into the water, slowly backing his vessel away from the port.

We didn't have boats back home, so when I first arrived I thought they were carriages that could walk on water, that bridges were rainbows someone constructed from stone. We have rivers, but none so wide, nor so deep and murky. Our waters are clear and shallow, like a sheet of gauze laid across the grasslands, and you can cross all of them on the back of a horse.

I've seen so many beautiful new things since coming to Shangjing. None of it makes me happy.

A distant splash catches my attention.

"Someone help! My gege's fallen into the water!" A girl, about seven or eight, is sobbing as she shrieks, "Save him, please!"

A little head bobs beneath the surface of the canal. I jump in after him, only remembering when I start to sink that I don't know how to swim either. By the time I grab hold of his arm, I've lost count of how many lungfuls of water I've swallowed, and it dawns on me that I've gotten myself into real trouble this time—I'm not going to save the child, and I'm going to drown, too.

I wouldn't mind dying so much if it weren't for A'du, for there won't be anyone to look after her if I'm gone. I don't know if she remembers the way home on her own. I choke and sputter as I descend. I'm seconds from losing consciousness when someone fishes me out.

A'du sets me down on a large boulder by the shore, and I cough up a stomach full of canal water. Her clothes are soaked through. She looks like she might burst into tears.

"Where's the boy?" I manage blearily.

She lifts him up so I can see. He's dripping too, and fixes me with a pair of dark eyes.

I push myself to my feet, my head spinning. People gather around to watch the commotion. It's strange to be the person on display for once, instead of the person watching the fun. As A'du and I squeeze the water from our clothes, a man and a woman barge through the crowd, crying, "My son! My baby!"

They cling tightly to him, weeping loudly while their daughter stands to one side, rubbing her eyes.

My heart warms at the sight of them. All day long the teahouse masters tell stories of courageous champions, and now it's my turn to be the hero. I'm relishing the thought of it when the boy bursts into heaving sobs. "A'die, he pushed me into the canal!"

He points straight at me.

I stare at him.

"I saw it happen!" the little girl chirps in a sweet, childish voice. "He pushed Gege into the water!"

Almost immediately the crowd surges forward to berate us.

"What could a child possibly do to deserve that?"

"I guess you can't judge a book by its cover!"

"We won't let you get away with this!"

I look at A'du, but she's as confused as I am.

"Take the child to a clinic," someone says. "Have a physician look at him, make sure he doesn't catch cold."

"You should pay for the trouble you've caused," says someone else. "You owe them that at least!"

"But we're the ones who saved him," I protest. "How can you accuse us of pushing him in?"

"If it wasn't you, why jump after him?"

I gape at them. What kind of logic is that?

The boy's mother gathers herself up. "Look at the state of him! You'd better hope you can afford a miracle worker."

"That's right!" one of the bystanders says. "We should send for someone and make sure he's not hurt."

"He seems fine to me," I say. "And even if he isn't, I'm the one who rescued him—why should I pay?"

"Fine," the mother huffs. "If you don't want to give us

money for a physician, we can take this to the magistry."

"Take them to the magistry!" the crowd roars. They're so loud my ears ring.

I am fuming. If they want to bring this to a magistrate, then *fine*, we'll take it there. If my body's upright I needn't fear a crooked shadow, and if I'm in the right, no one can make me believe I'm wrong. We spill into the streets, attracting a great deal of attention. "Come see how wicked the world's become!" the boy's parents wail. "How bold the liars are!"

A'du and I shield ourselves from the fruit rinds that are thrown at us, as we duck globs of spittle. She pulls me away from the line of fire, but the harder the crowd tries the angrier I become.

By the time we arrive at the Wannian County magistry, my temper's cooled somewhat. Finally, a place where we can all be sensible. Because we're in one of the two counties under the jurisdiction of Shangjing, court opens with great ceremony, first with the constables lining up and calling for order, and then with the magistrate himself striding in, taking his time to get settled before instructing us to report our case.

This is how I learn the family's name is Jia, that they live on the banks of the Grand Canal, and that they sell fish for a living. When it's my turn, I give them a fake name—Liang Xi, the one I always use outside the manor. But then the magistrate asks what I do for a living, and I'm at a loss for how to answer.

One of the constables interjects. "Then you're without employment?"

It's not far from the truth, so I nod.

After he finishes interrogating the couple, the magistrate turns to question their children, who parrot their parents' every lie. Then he turns to me. "Do you know how to swim?"

"I don't."

The magistrate nods, considering. "It might have been an accident, but you nearly cost a child his life. What do you have to say for yourself?"

"I jumped in the canal because he was *in* the water—why would I push him?" I'm so angry that I stamp my foot. "What would I be pushing them for?"

"You don't know how to swim," says the magistrate slowly, "yet you went after him. If you weren't the one who did the pushing, why would you risk your own life to save him?"

"It's not like I thought too much about it," I retort. "I saw him drowning, so I jumped."

"You expect me to believe that?" he asks. "Man is selfish by nature and considers his own life precious above all. If, as you say, you don't know him, what could your willingness to enter the water be but an expression of guilt? And if you weren't the one who pushed him, why should you feel guilty? Since you clearly felt guilt, there can be no doubt you *were* the one who pushed him."

There is a wooden plaque behind him that reads CLEAR MIRROR, HIGHLY HUNG. I bore holes in it with my eyes as my temple throbs, and with every pounding beat of my skull, the urge to roll up my sleeves and hit the magistrate grows stronger.

He mistakes my disbelief for affirmation. "I understand it was an accident, but you've caused the Jia a great deal of distress. Therefore, it is within my purview to sentence you to a fine of ten strings of copper, to be paid to the family as remuneration for their ordeal."

I'm incredulous. "Is this how you hear crimes?"

"You think me unjust?" the magistrate says.

"Of course you're unjust! You refuse to listen to anything I say despite the fact that anyone with eyes could tell you *I wasn't the one who pushed him!*"

"And have you any evidence to corroborate this claim?"

I glance at A'du. "A'du saw me. He was the one who helped us both out of the canal."

"Then have him step forward and give testimony."

"He can't." I swallow my annoyance. "He doesn't speak."

The magistrate bursts into laughter. "So you want a *mute* to testify for you?"

It's over the minute he opens his big mouth to laugh. A'du draws her dagger, and if I hadn't pulled her back, the magistrate would have been short two ears. She glares at him as the constables object around us. "You can't bring weapons into the magistry!"

But A'du is faster than they are. She barely moves—the tip of her dagger flashes, and then she draws her hand back into her sleeve. A sharp crack splits the room. The bamboo canister where the magistrate keeps his sentencing qian splits open, spilling the flat pieces of wood across the ground. Every last one is cracked from end to end, reduced to splinters.

Everyone gapes down at them. Onlookers crowding the magistry doorway murmur that this must be sleight of hand, but the court attendants know it's no trick. It's skill.

The magistrate's face is ashen, but he swallows and forcibly composes himself. "How dare you bring arms into a court of law? G-guards!"

A few of the constables are brave enough to step forward, but I stop them short. "If you come any closer, I can't be responsible for what happens next."

"*This is the magistry of the capital city,*" the magistrate hisses. "What you are doing is treason!"

"Your Honor," I start, "you misunderstand—"

"I'm warning you, if you don't want to be prosecuted for contempt, you'd better hand over—" But then he catches A'du's glare and withers beneath it. "You'd better put away your weapons!"

Seeing the dagger safely sheathed, the magistrate lets out a breath and exchanges a look with his secretary. The secretary walks over from the dais, saying softly, "My lord, do you have a patronage?"

I roll my eyes. "Say what you mean."

The secretary swallows his temper and presses his voice lower still. "His Honor sees that your technique is impressive, and you look like you've had some training, so he is wondering if you were in the service of a lordship."

I fight to conceal a smile. The bully's scared of other bullies, then. Rather than getting us into bigger trouble, our little display has convinced him that we have powerful backers—he probably thinks we're errant swordsmen, sponsored by a wealthy family. I consider this. If I use Li Chengyin's name, he probably won't believe me, but—

"My lord is the Jinwu General, Pei Zhao."

"Of course." The secretary dips into a shallow bow, hiding his stark white face. "No one but the Yulin Guard could be so remarkable."

I hardly want to be lumped in with them, but I'm also not going to say that out loud. They have a saying in the Plains: a wise man doesn't try to beat his odds.

The secretary returns to the dais to murmur something to the magistrate. I watch the magistrate's face curdle slowly until he slams his gavelwood down. "If they're the Jinwu General's men, then he should be the one to deal with them!"

My heart pounds. The magistrate is wilier than I gave him credit for—if Pei Zhao's on duty in the manor today, if he can't come, if he sends someone who doesn't know who I am, the water I've been treading is going to come to a boil. I try not to jump to worst-case scenarios, but the image of us fighting our way out of the courtroom and fleeing fugitive into the night does flash through my mind.

Afterward, Pei Zhao tells me that though the magistrate of Wannian County is a mere seventh-rank title, it's a difficult office to fill because of its proximity to the seat of imperial power. Anyone who can sit on that bench is as slippery as a snake. Since we embarrassed the magistrate by making such a to-do in his courtroom, he sent for the general in order to resolve the whole affair and come out of it with his dignity intact. Pei Zhao spends ages trying to explain the politics to me, but I still don't understand.

Luckily, Pei Zhao isn't on duty, so when they ask for him, he comes.

Today he is wearing a set of heavily embroidered court robes I haven't seen before, looking as soft and refined as a gentleman scholar. Pei Zhao has been on duty and in his light armor the handful of times we've met, so it takes me a moment to recognize him when he walks in.

If he's surprised to see me and A'du, he doesn't show it. The magistrate rises from his seat and steps off the dais in welcome, smiling wide enough to split his own face in two. "My apologies for having disturbed you, my lord. I would not have done so if I had any other choice."

"I heard that two of my men had pushed a child into the canal," says Pei Zhao. "Of course I had to come see for myself."

"Naturally, naturally. Please, General, sit up on the dais."

Pei Zhao declines. "This is your courtroom, Your Honor. Please, continue your investigation. I can stand to the side and listen."

So the magistrate starts the whole ordeal over.

It bores me to death, especially when he starts repeating the bit about how *man is selfish by nature*, and I roll my eyes.

The children keep insisting, and I keep denying.

Finally, the magistrate, discomfort artfully displayed across his face, looks at Pei Zhao. "General Pei, as you can see..."

"May I ask the children a few questions?" Pei Zhao says.

"But of course."

"Then please see the girl to the back rooms," he says, "and give her some sweets. She can come back when I've finished talking to her brother."

The magistrate agrees, and when the girl's been led away,

Pei Zhao turns to the boy. "You were playing by the shore when this man pushed you in, is that right?"

He doesn't hesitate. "Yes."

"Then you were pushed from behind?"

"Yes."

"But you don't have eyes on the back of your head, so how could you tell who pushed you?"

The boy opens his mouth to speak but can't find the words. Then his eyes brighten. "I remembered wrong. He pushed me from the front—I fell backward into the water."

"I see." Pei Zhao turns to the magistrate. "Your Honor, this child needs a set of dry clothes; I fear he may catch cold if he stays in his own much longer."

The magistrate sends the boy away, and Pei Zhao has the girl brought back out. Pointing to me, he says, "You saw this person push your brother into the canal?"

"I did."

"And how was your brother pushed?"

"He just—just pushed him. He pushed my brother and my brother fell."

"But did he push his front or his back?"

The girl pauses. Then she says, with certainty, "The back."

"You're sure? Think carefully."

"Well, if it wasn't his front then it was his back. My brother was sitting there and then this person came up from behind and pushed him."

Pei Zhao turns back to the magistrate. "Your Honor, I've finished my examination. As their stories don't align, I ask you to investigate further."

The magistrate's face has gone all blotchy. "Of course, my lord." He bangs his gavelwood and orders the boy back.

The boy denies everything at first, but when the magistrate threatens him with a caning, he bursts into tears and lets the cat out of the bag: His parents live by the river, and this is a ploy they often use to extort money. Without any evidence to prove their innocence, most people pay up. They hadn't expected I would drag them all the way down to the magistry.

"Now that the truth is out and my men are cleared of the charges against them, I ought to take my leave," Pei Zhao says.

Looking slightly ashamed of himself, the magistrate says, "As you wish, my lord."

But I'm not finished. "I have something to say."

Pei Zhao shoots me a reproving glance, but I've already stepped forward. "You said that people are selfish, that we only value our own lives, that the only reason I would want to save a child is if I was the one who pushed him. But you're wrong. I risked my life for him because he's a child and I was scared he was going to drown. And that's the way the world should be.

"Just because you're selfish doesn't mean everyone else is, and punishing me for helping is going to stop good-hearted people from stepping up in the future. I'm not saying I did anything impressive, but at least I don't have any regrets. And I'd do it again if I had to."

When I turn to leave, the people crowding the door begin to clap. Some even cheer for me, and I smile wide, feeling pleased with myself.

I have to run to catch up to Pei Zhao. I perk up when I see his steed. "General Pei, can I take your horse for a ride?"

Now that we've left the magistry, Pei Zhao has returned to being exceedingly deferential. "My lord, this horse is ill-tempered. Perhaps I could find you another—"

I swing onto it before he can finish the thought. It lays its ears flat and whickers gently, docile under the reins. Pei Zhao is surprised.

"You're a fine rider, my lord. My beast is headstrong to a fault—it doesn't usually let anyone else near."

"This is one of our tribute horses from Xiliang," I tell him, running a hand through its long mane. "I have a lovely red one exactly like it back home—it'll be seven years old this year, I think."

Pei Zhao orders two additional mounts to be brought to us—one for him and one for A'du. I watch him climb on, admiring his horsemanship. In Xiliang, men are judged by how well they ride, and he's better than most.

There's no room to gallop in the busy streets, so I'm reduced to meandering through the crowd. Shangjing is beautiful at the height of autumn, when the air is brisk and clear and the streets bustle with noise. Pei Zhao had been riding behind me and A'du, but the horse I'm riding is too sweet on its owner and refuses to outpace him, so in no time at all he catches up to us.

"What a day," I sigh. "I can't believe those people."

Pei Zhao smiles wanly. "Human hearts are hard to read, my lord. You should take more care in the future."

"Couldn't be me," I say breezily. "You all keep too much bottled up inside. Xiliang girls wear our hearts on our sleeves—I couldn't act like a Shangjing girl if my life depended on it."

Again, that faint smile. Did I say something wrong?

"But you're not like the rest of them, General Pei," I hasten to add. "You're a good egg, I can tell."

"You flatter me."

A gust of wind billows past, cutting me off. My robes have all but dried in our long detour to the magistry, but my smallclothes are still damp, so when the breeze passes, the cold pierces my bones. I sneeze.

"There's an inn up ahead," says Pei Zhao. "If you have no objections, my lord, I can buy you something to change into. It's easy to get sick wearing wet clothes in weather like this."

This reminds me that A'du was soaked too, so I agree.

Pei Zhao walks us to the inn, where he books a luxury suite and, in no time at all, comes to deliver us a set of clothes. "I've sent all my people away," he says, "so take as much time as you need. I'll be outside if you need me."

He closes the door behind him. A'du locks it as I open the bundle. Everything's there—from smallclothes to jackets, right down to socks and shoes folded neatly inside. Once we've changed, A'du helps me tie my hair up, and I can feel clean again.

I open the door.

Pei Zhao stands at the far end of the long hallway. In the short time we've been apart, he's changed into civvies, and with his hair tied back like that he looks more like a gentle scholar looking absently down at the street below than he does a commander of imperial guards.

"General Pei!"

He turns when I call.

He must have been quite deep in thought, for his gaze is odd when he sees me and A'du, and he glances quickly away. "I can escort you home," he says.

"It was so hard to sneak out," I grouse, slumping against the windowsill and following his gaze to the crowd below. "Come on, let's stay out a little longer and go drinking. I know a place that sells this sorghum wine that will get you drunk so quickly—"

"I have duties, my lord," says Pei Zhao. "Please, it really would be best if we returned to the manor."

"You're not on duty today," I point out. "So you're not the Jinwu General. And I don't look like a princess. My day's been bad enough, can't you let me have a drink or two to ease my nerves at least?"

"It would be best if you allowed me to escort you back," he repeats.

I huff, turning away from him, and pretend not to hear. My stomach gurgles—loudly—and I remember that I haven't had lunch today. Pei Zhao must hear it too, for his face burns. He's standing a few paces away, but I can see his blush clearly, and I smile—I haven't seen a grown man glow quite that shade of red before.

"*Now* can we go eat?"

Pei Zhao sighs. "Yes, my lord."

I'm not fond of his serious tone, but truth be told, he's already saved us twice and I'm pretty grateful.

A'du and I lead him through the winding, narrow alleys until we arrive at Miluo's tavern. Miluo rushes forward in a cloud of tinkling hairpins and golden bells and pulls me into a laughing embrace. "I saved some of our finest offerings specially for you," she says to us.

She peers behind me to give Pei Zhao a once-over. Miluo has bright green eyes, so people are always caught off guard the first time they meet her, but Pei Zhao doesn't seem surprised at all. It makes sense when I think about it—the Pei are a prominent Shangjing family, and they're often invited to state banquets for foreign dignitaries. Not to mention that Shangjing attracts people from all over the world. Of course he wouldn't find her eyes strange.

Miluo's tavern is known for two things—their wine and their beef—so she has servers cut us a plateful of the latter. As she seats us, the sky outside opens up.

Autumn showers are melodies that linger, pattering softly against the roof tiles. A group of merchants from Bosi sits at the table next to ours, and one takes out his metal flute and starts to play. The flute is wailing and the tune is unlike anything I can remember hearing. Accompanied by the staccato of the rain, he fills the room with wonder.

Moved, Miluo sets down the jug of wine she's holding and steps barefoot onto an empty table. Her figure is soft and full, and as she moves, she looks nearly boneless. The sound of the bells around her wrists and ankles is a hoarse twin to the rush of the rain as she twists, enchantingly snakelike.

The merchants clap, cheering her on. Leaping lightly from the table, Miluo approaches, circling us with her dance.

I haven't laughed like this since I left home. Miluo is agile and lithe, like a ribbon of silk winding around me, like a butterfly that flits this way and that. I trace after her steps, but

I'm not graceful like she is. A'du draws a reed flute from her lapels and stuffs it into my hands. I thrill at the chance to play again.

And I do—at least until the smell of beef drifts over to us, and then I shove it at Pei Zhao, saying, "You go!" and pick up my chopsticks to attend to the plate.

I hadn't actually thought he'd know how to play, but he does—and he does it well. The reed flute is a melancholy instrument, while the metal flute is vibrant and strong, so together the two form a beautiful duet. At first, Pei Zhao is playing the harmony, but as he slowly takes over the melody, the tune takes on a passion that wasn't there before.

It's like a drift of desolate smoke from beyond the Yumen Pass. I can almost hear the chime of distant bells, see caravans as they crest endless dunes and fade back into the horizon. Then the tune erupts into life, like the gates have been flung open and a storm of soldiers is streaming through bearing rippling banners—bellowing—horses thundering—armor clanging—the wind—

The song races faster, faster, and Miluo dances faster, faster, spinning until she is a golden moth flitting all around me and I am dizzy from watching her.

Then the music takes a bleaker turn, and I'm reminded of the way an eagle soars up, up through the ninefold heavens, looking down at the soldiers and the horses from above. Rising as a gale whips up gusts of sand. By the time I'm finished eating, the eagle has flown to the top of the highest icy peak. When it sweeps past, a single feather falls from its massive wings, wafting down, floating in the wind, until it lands in front of a blossom of snow lotus. It lies there, half buried in the ice, as the breeze curls loose scatters of white over it. The petals tremble, and the desert sand comes to a halt at the summit of that mountaintop.

The tune drifts to an end, and the tavern is so quiet we can hear every raindrop. Miluo collapses against the table, unable to catch her breath, her green eyes bright and watery.

"I can't—I can't anymore," she says, but the Bosi merchants burst into smiles. Someone pours her a cup of wine and, though she's breathing hard, Miluo tosses it back in one gulp, turning to Pei Zhao with a winsome smile. "You play well."

Pei Zhao says nothing in response, just uses alcohol to wipe down the flute, returning it to A'du.

"I didn't know you could play," I say. "Not many people in Shangjing can."

"My father was once an envoy to the west," Pei Zhao explains, "and when he came back, he brought a flute with him. I had too much free time as a child, so I worked it out."

"I know!" I clap in delight. "Your father is General Pei Kuang. My a'die's fought him—he said your father was a good leader."

Pei Zhao demurs. "The khan is too kind."

"My lord father doesn't compliment just anyone," I assure him. "If he says your father is a good leader, it's because he means it."

"As you say."

With that dull response, he's managed to kill all my interest in the topic.

The merchants at the next table have begun to sing, a soft and melancholy tune that's wonderfully moving, though I don't understand the words. Miluo translates in her lisping accent:

> *The moon here is boundless*
> *Far from my hometown*
> *It waxes and it wanes*
> *But I cannot go back now*
> *The stars here burn bright*
> *Far from my homeland*
> *The Silver River is shining*
> *But I cannot go back again*
>
> *The wind here is gentle*
> *Billowing my old country robes*
> *The sun here is dazzling*
> *And shines on the old country, too*
>
> *Know you, o know you,*
> *Beneath which mountain I will die?*
> *Know you, o know you,*
> *In whose land I shall lie?*

I try to sing along, but their sorrow dampens my spirits. Absently, I sip at another cup of wine. Pei Zhao nods sympathetically but says, "If they miss it so terribly, why not go back?"

"Not everyone's like you," I sigh, "lucky enough to not need to leave home. Who knows how much of a choice they had?"

Pei Zhao is silent for a long time. When I ladle myself another cup of wine, he interjects. "You've had too much to drink, my lord."

With great feeling, I recite, "*O, who can distract me from my sorrow? Only Du Kang!*"[1]

He looks impressed, but I'm quick to put a stop to that. "Don't think too well of me yet," I say, holding up three fingers. "I know this many lines of poetry total."

Finally, he breaks into a smile.

Miluo's wine turns out to be quite formidable, and I turn out to have drunk far too much of it, for by the time we leave the tavern, my steps are faltering, as if I were walking on slips of desert sand. It drizzles still, and the sky is darkening. Distant fog rises into curls of white mist, embracing the hundred thousand homes of Shangjing, its canal-spanning bridges and its riverside pavilions a suggestion in the rain. Wind blows thin drops across my flushed cheeks, easing their heat. I stretch a hand out to these tiny gemstones and they pitter against my palm, unexpectedly ticklish.

Faraway lanterns bob and flicker while, along the road, the taverns and teahouses bloom into brilliance to meet the oncoming evening. In the riverhomes that float atop the Grand Canal, strings of fat red lanterns illuminate the passengers' cooking smokes, which vanish into the fog.

Shangjing in the mist and the rain looks like a painting, though the artists in Xiliang couldn't come up with such a sight—its splendor, its warmth—no matter how talented they

---

[1] From "A Short Song," by Cao Cao.

are. This is a divine city, blessed by the gods, the capital of the empire, the liveliest corner of the universe, with a thousand vassals and a million citizens, but it can't replace Xiliang in my heart. Shangjing is lovely, but it is not home.

Pei Zhao accompanies us all the way back to the crown prince's manor, leaving once he sees us slip in through a side door. In the quiet, a wave of dizziness washes over me and I double over, retching. A'du pats me gently on the back. We squat there in the garden until the breeze clears my head enough that we can sneak back to our rooms.

Yongniang is waiting for us.

She offers no reproach for sneaking out, nor any rebuke for reeking of drink. She doesn't even fault me for wearing men's clothes. She only looks at me bleakly and says, "Your Highness, something's happened."

"What is it?" I ask.

"Miss Xu lost her child."

My eyes widen, but Yongniang's expression doesn't change. "I took it upon myself to send someone to comfort her, but I fear Her Majesty may summon you for questioning."

My brain hasn't caught up to what she's saying. "What would she want me for?"

"Her Majesty is the head of the imperial household, so anything that happens in the inner palace is her domain. Your Highness is the head of the Court of Spring. Miss Xu is under your care, so of course Her Majesty will want to question you."

I haven't so much as met Miss Xu—what answers could

I give her? But Yongniang hasn't been wrong before. If she says the empress is going to summon me, then the empress is bound to do just that.

"Quick," I yelp. "Quick, draw me a bath! Someone brew me a tonic!" I can't show up drunk in front of the empress.

My attendants hurry to prepare. This is the fastest I've ever run to the washroom, and I leap in as soon as the water is heated. Watching me trip over myself, Yongniang can't resist commenting, "If Your Highness only abided by the rules, you wouldn't be in a position to hurl yourself last minute at the Buddha's feet."

Hurling yourself last minute at the Buddha's feet is an apt phrase. "I'd suffocate," I tell her. "If I have to hurl myself at His feet, then I'll hurl myself at His feet. I trust Him to look after me."

Yongniang's face is as serious as ever, but her mouth twitches like she's suppressing a smile, so I tug at the corner of her skirt with a dripping hand. "Yongniang, you're a good person; you have to put in a good word for me when you pray. Thank you ahead of time!"

"Emituofo, how could you joke about the Buddha like that?" Yongniang folds her hands together. "Forgive us, Rulai."

She *says* that, but her grin tells a different story entirely. When the tonic arrives, she brings it to me. "Drink up, or it'll get cold and sour."

It's sour when it's hot, too—I have to pinch my nose to get it down. Yongniang has people scent my clothing with incense so that I'm almost finished dressing by the time the empress's ministresses arrive at the manor. I tell Yongniang to smell me for any lingering trace of alcohol. She does so carefully and sprays me heavily with flowerdew, sticking a perfumed pill between my lips. It's bitter going down, but my breath does smell nicer.

I learn then that the empress has summoned me and Li Chengyin both.

It's the first time in days that I've seen him, and for a moment I think he must have grown taller again, but it's because we're going to the palace, and so he's covered his hair with a coronet. He's wearing his court clothes, his fine jade pendants, his ornaments made from gold. He steps into the waiting carriage without a glance my way.

It's the empress who tells me the full story.

Miss Xu had taken ill, and the physicians who examined her said she must have eaten something to induce labor. The empress ordered everyone who served Miss Xu locked up and had all the food and drink sealed into evidence and delivered to the Bureau of Investigations, who confirmed that Miss Xu's miscarriage had been caused by a dose of something in her meal.

Every one of Miss Xu's attendants was interrogated. Under duress, one servant cracked and revealed they were acting under orders.

The empress's voice is as serene as ever, but her words are chilling. "I moved Miss Xu into the palace because I did not want anything to happen to the mother of my first grandchild. Never did I imagine she'd be attacked under my very nose. Hundreds of years has the Li family ruled this kingdom, and nothing like this has ever happened."

Her tone is soft, but her voice is hard, and she has never sounded like this before. I hold my breath for fear of being too loud. I suspect everyone has the same thought, for the court is utterly still.

"Do you know who the servant accused?"

I look at Li Chengyin, and Li Chengyin looks straight ahead. "I don't, Your Highness" are his only words.

The empress turns to one of her ladies-in-waiting. "Read the testimony to the crown prince and princess."

And as she does, my shock turns into horror. "Your Highness, I had nothing to do with this!" I protest. "I didn't bribe anyone to drug Miss Xu's food."

"All the evidence and the witnesses point to you," says the empress calmly. "If you wish to contest it, you must provide me with proof."

"Why would I hurt her?" I ask. "I don't know her, I don't know what she looks like, I don't even know where she lives."

Someone must really have it out for me today.

The empress turns to Li Chengyin. "Yin'er, what say you?"

He looks at me at last and then kneels at his mother's feet. "I await your verdict, Your Majesty."

"The crown princess is entitled to certain privileges," says the empress. "And she is a princess of Xiliang besides. But if this is her doing, then perhaps she does not have the judgment needed to manage your court."

Li Chengyin does not say anything.

I'm shaking, but it's not because I'm scared. "I said I didn't do it, and I'll keep saying it all the way to the execution block if I have to. I don't give a fig about being the head of any court, but I won't be accused of doing something I didn't do."

"The testimony is all here," the empress says. "Yin'er?"

"I await your verdict, Your Highness," he repeats firmly.

The empress's smile is tight. "They say it takes one hundred years to forget a single night of marriage. You do not seem to be having any such trouble."

In a low voice, Li Chengyin says, "It's because I must, Your Highness. A kingdom has its laws, and a family has its rules. They must all be followed, whatever our feelings may be."

The empress nods. "Good, good. I am glad to hear you say it." She turns to a lady-in-waiting. "Have Lady Zhao demoted, and escort her from the Court of Spring immediately."

I'm afraid I've broken my brain trying to keep up with this, and Li Chengyin is more at a loss than I am. "Your Highness!"

"The testimony was real," the empress explains. "And the servant who gave it took her own life, thinking that the trail would go cold with her death. But the Bureau of Investigations is nothing if not thorough. The maid was deeply indebted to the Zhao. A confession like hers could have implicated her entire family, but she was an orphan, with only a godmother who raised her. Would you like to know what we found buried beneath her godmother's floorboards?

"Fifty pieces of imperial silver. The nice thing about imperial silver is that there are records of their provenance. I had the godmother brought in for interrogation, and she admitted they had been sent over by the Zhao. Your Honorable Lady certainly knows how to strike her birds and use her stones. Keeping a wretched woman like that in your court is a stain on this family and its heirs."

"Your Highness," Li Chengyin starts. "Please—there must be some mistake. Someone *must* be framing Lady Zhao. We ought to investigate more thoroughly and not rush to conclusions—please, Your Highness!"

It would have been better if he'd kept quiet. This isn't stoking the flames—this is adding oil directly onto the fire.

"You have been utterly bewitched by that—*vixen*!" the empress snaps. "*She* was the one who made a fuss over Miss Xu, and *she* was the one who tried to frame your wife for poisoning the girl."

But he just won't shut up. "Please, Your Majesty, you must be rational—Lady Zhao is not that kind of person. Please, you have to look into it—"

"What is there to look into? Tell me, who has your child hurt that Lady Zhao would find it such a thorn in her side? Allowing her to stay in your court is inviting calamity in through our front doors." The empress's rage is like a rising storm; it thickens with every word.

"You did not have a single word of defense to say on your wife's behalf, but now that you have heard the truth, you claim that that temptress was framed? You are the crown prince. Someday, you will be king. *How* could your reason be so easily swayed? *How* can I allow this to stand? No, that girl must be put to death. If she is not, who knows what ruin she might bring to this kingdom? If she asked you to give up the throne for her, would you do it?"

Li Chengyin looks so terrified that, however reluctant I am to do it, I bring myself to kneel next to him. "Your Highness, Lady Zhao made a rash decision when her judgment was impaired, but if you sentence her to death, then—then—"

I hadn't really thought about how I could continue, but Li Chengyin is more than ready to plead her case. "Your Highness, Lady Zhao's father and brother are both ministers, and His Majesty relies heavily on them. Please, on that account, you must reconsider."

The empress's laugh is cold. "You said it yourself—a kingdom has its laws; a family has its rules. You said you would abide by them, no matter your feelings."

His face is ashen. Li Chengyin doesn't protest anymore. He kneels there, a single plea on his lips: *"Your Highness."*

"It is not my place to meddle in the princess's household affairs, but I have no other choice. So allow me to be the villain here and bear the brunt of the blame." She turns to an attendant, ready to issue her decree.

As a last resort, I clamber forward and cling like a child to the empress's skirts. "Your Highness, can I say something? You're right that the Court of Spring is my domain, and I know I haven't done a very good job running it, but I want to speak."

The empress softens. "Go on."

"His Highness loves Lady Zhao, and if you sentence her to death, I don't think he would recover. It's true he has never found favor with me, but we've been married for three years, so I know His Highness well enough to know he cannot lose Lady Zhao. If he did, he would hate me forever. And—and she helps run the household—I don't understand any of the ledgers or the account books, so if it wasn't for her, nothing would be running at all."

I look back at Yongniang. "Yongniang, you tell Her Majesty."

"Yes, my lady," she says, and pays her courtesies to the empress. "My queen, what the princess means to say is that Lady Zhao has been by His Highness's side for many years, and she hasn't misstepped once. She's respectful to the princess and aids her in the day-to-day running of the manor. It's true she was in the wrong, but as it was a momentary lapse, the princess hopes you will be merciful."

The empress considers this. "Lady Zhao cannot stay in the palace. There will be no end of trouble if she does." She sighs. "I remember the day the two of you were married. The emperor himself commented on what a fine pair you made, how lucky this family is to have you. But it has been three years, and there has not been so much as a whisper of an heir—and then this mess. How am I to be easy?"

Li Chengyin's eyes may stare fixedly enough at the ground, but his mouth is quick to say, "It's my fault, Your Highness."

"If you really thought that you would spend more time with your wife instead of that Zhao girl."

"Yes, Your Highness."

I open my mouth to say something, but Yongniang tugs on my skirt to warn me not to. The corner of Li Chengyin's mouth moves slightly, but he doesn't speak.

"Why don't you get up," the empress suggests. But he remains resolutely on his knees, so I have little choice but to follow suit. The empress ignores this. "Do not be upset about Miss Xu. You are young, after all."

He stays wisely silent. I don't think he's upset about Miss Xu at all; if anything, he's more upset about Lady Zhao.

"Miss Xu has had a rough couple of days," the empress continues. "Why don't you raise her by a few ranks so that she can stay in the manor with you?"

"I don't want—I don't think it's proper for me to keep so many women in my court, Your Majesty." Li Chengyin looks defeated.

I know why he's so resistant—he'd promised Lady Zhao when he married me that she'd be the only other woman in his court—so I'm not surprised when the empress is annoyed.

"You are next in line for the throne, do not be so immature." To me, she says, "Come, child, stand. Will you go sit with Miss Xu and comfort her on my behalf?"

I know when I'm being gotten rid of, so I leave Li Chengyin to his lecture. A page boy leads me to the out-of-the-way courtyard where Miss Xu lives, and it's there that I meet her. She lies in bed, her face pale and worn, but beautiful. When her attendants announce my arrival, she struggles to push herself upright, and Yongniang hurries forward to ease her back down.

Not knowing how to comfort her, I repeat the empress's words: "You needn't be so upset; you're young yet."

Tears slide down her face. "Thank you, Your Highness, but all I can hope for is a quick death."

"Don't say that," I say, a little embarrassed by her agitation. "Look at me! I'm trudging along, aren't I?"

Yongniang coughs delicately. I've said something wrong again.

Last time I was sick, the empress had people check in on me, and they wouldn't stop asking if I wanted anything to eat, if I needed anything to be sent for. But what would I need that I didn't already have? Now I realize they were probably trying to show their concern. "Do you want anything to eat?" I ask. "I can have something brought over."

"Thank you, Your Highness," Miss Xu says, but this doesn't seem to comfort her much—she's ashen and dull eyed, as though she has nothing more to live for. Yongniang steps forward to console her, but that doesn't stop her tears. By the time we leave, she still hasn't stopped weeping.

When we get back to Yong'an Court, the empress has begun proceedings to promote Miss Xu. Li Chengyin's face is dark. As we walk through the gates, I can hear the empress saying, "It's better for everyone if your court can work together, but the princess is childish still, and there are many things she doesn't know how to handle. It's not a bad thing to get an extra pair of hands." She looks up and, seeing me, gestures that I should enter.

I step forward, ready to make courtesy, but she snags me by the arm and helps me up. A thrill shoots through me—the empress is invariably dignified, and aloof. Her rare affection catches me off guard.

"Lady Zhao may escape execution, but she shall not escape punishment," she says. "I want her demoted immediately and confined to her quarters for three months. The crown prince is not to see her. If he does, I will have her banished from the Court of Spring."

Li Chengyin's voice is tight, but as usual, he defers. "Yes, Your Highness."

The second we leave the inner court, before we've even left the palace, Li Chengyin strikes me.

I have no warning—just the shock that stuns me into place. A'du rips her gold-inlay dagger from her belt and presses it to his throat as Yongniang shouts, "Don't—!" but before either of them can do anything, I step forward and slap him back. I may not have any real training, but that doesn't mean I'm going to stand here and be bullied. If he takes my eye, I'm taking his too.

Li Chengyin sneers. "Go ahead and kill me, then." He jabs an accusing finger at me. "I know it was you. I know you were the one who poisoned Miss Xu and framed Sese for everything."

"How dare you?" I'm shaking with anger.

"All you know how to do is play the innocent for Her Majesty. Acting like you're so naive, like you have no idea what's going on. Don't think I don't know you complain to her about how I neglect you. Don't think I don't know how much you envy what Sese has. You're a poisonous snake, and if *anything* happens to her, you won't get away with it. I can't wait to depose you the second I'm king."

"Do it, then," I say. The blood rushes to my head as I push A'du away to step right up in his face. "Depose me. You think I *wanted* to marry you? You think I *wanted* to be your consort? There are a million men back home who'd die to marry me, and every one of them is better than you. What do you know how to do besides recite some stupid poems? You can't shoot as well as me, you can't ride as well as me—if you lived in Xiliang you couldn't find a wife!"

Li Chengyin storms away in a tornado of fluttering sleeves. My heart is pumping frost straight into my veins. I've gone cold. I knew he disliked me—we've been bickering on and off for three whole years—but I couldn't have imagined he actually *hated* me. Loathed me. Thought so poorly of me.

Yongniang helps me into the carriage. "Don't take it to heart, my lady. His Highness is lashing out because of Miss Zhao."

I know. Of course I know. He thinks Lady Zhao was wrongfully accused, and he's taking it out on me. But I haven't done anything wrong, so what gives him the right to treat me like I have?

He claims I envy her—and I do. I envy that she has someone who's good to her, so good that he believes her no matter when or where or why. Someone who trusts her, who protects her, who looks after her. Apart from that? I don't envy anything she has, and I wouldn't do anything to hurt her.

I've always thought of Lady Zhao as a kind, gentle person. She's clever—I know that from playing cards with her—but I hadn't thought she could be so cruel. Not that the empress's punishment seems like much of a punishment—at least, not if she intended to punish Lady Zhao. Miss Xu is so fragile—whether she is made a proper member of Li Chengyin's household or not, the most she'll be is another pitiable soul haunting the halls of the Court of Spring.

I'm too preoccupied to fall asleep that night. Sick of tossing and turning, I fling back my blanket and get out of bed.

"Do you think Lady Zhao is a bad person?" I ask A'du.

A'du nods—then reconsiders, shaking her head.

"I can't understand what these Plains girls are thinking," I say. "Men in Xiliang can marry lots of women too, but no one has to *stay* together if they can't get along."

A'du nods again.

"And anyway, what's so good about Li Chengyin? He's handsome, but his temper is so ugly—and he's *so* petty!" I lie back down. "If I'd had a choice, I wouldn't have married him."

If I'd had a choice, it wouldn't have come to this: forced to marry a boy who loved someone else. If I'd had a choice, I wouldn't have a husband who hated me, but I didn't, and since Lady Zhao's been confined to her rooms, I'm sure he resents me more than ever. If I had a choice, I wouldn't be miserable. I don't want to be chained to someone who can't stand the sight of me.

I would rather have married an ordinary man, a man from Xiliang. He would like me, and he would take me riding, take me hunting, play the flute for me. We would have a pile of chubby children, and every day would be happier than the last. But that life only exists in my dreams.

A'du grabs my hand to point out the windows.

I push them open to see someone sitting atop the glazed tiles of the building opposite mine. He's dressed in pure white, striking against the black roofline. I know him—Gu Jian.

I hesitate, unsure if I should raise the alarm—but then he slips from the roof like a great bird riding a billow of wind to light at my window.

"What are you doing?" My eyes are wide.

He says nothing, just stares at my face. I draw back,

self-conscious. It's a little swollen where Li Chengyin struck me. Yongniang had iced it for me earlier, but it hasn't stopped smarting. Not that I lost to him—my palm tingles from how hard I slapped Li Chengyin, and I'll bet his face is at least as red as mine.

"Who hit you?" His voice is careful, but there's an undercurrent I can't quite place.

I rub my cheek. "It's nothing. I returned the favor."

But he won't let it go. "Who did it?"

"Why are you asking?"

His face is blank as he answers, "To kill them."

He scares me with his answer, but my alarm doesn't deter him. "Who would dare hit the crown princess? Is it the emperor? The empress?"

I shake my head. "I'm not going to tell you anything, so you'd better stop asking," I say.

To his credit, he does change the subject. "Will you come away with me?"

I scoff, shaking my head. He's mad. I go to close the window, but he darts a hand out and catches the casement. "Are you still angry?"

"Why should I be?" I want to know.

"So you don't blame me for what happened?"

"I really don't know you," I tell him, looking him dead in the eye. "You should stop coming here in the middle of the night raving about things that make no sense. This is the crown prince's manor, and if anyone caught you, they'd use you as target practice, understand?"

Gu Jian smirks. "I wouldn't be scared if this were the palace itself, much less a crown prince's measly manor. I go where I want when I want. Who could stop me?"

I'm annoyed by his arrogance, but he does have a point—he probably does have the skill to come and go as he pleases. "What do you *want*?"

"I wanted to see you again," he says, and then asks again, "Will you leave with me?"

I shake my head.

"But you're miserable here." He grabs my hand, clearly angry.

"Who said I was miserable? And even if I were, it doesn't have anything to do with you."

He reaches out for me again, but I pull away, hissing, *"Let go!"*

A'du rushes forward, but he forces her back several paces with a flick of his sleeve. Without waiting for her to recover, he grabs me and tugs. A lightness overtakes me as I'm pulled through the window. We flutter along, lighter than air, and I'm aware of nothing but the wind roaring in my ears until we find solid footing again on cold, slippery tiles. He's taken me to the summit of the main hall, the highest point of Li Chengyin's manor. It extends around us in a maze of silent edifices and splendid halls—the soaring, layered eaves, the ceramic beasts walking the ridges of the rooflines, all of it sunk in the sea of inky night.

I shake him off, catching myself so I don't stumble. "What do you think you're doing?"

Again he doesn't answer. He points instead to the walls beneath our feet. "Look at this place, Xiaofeng. All these high walls, the way they close you in like a well that lets no sun in. How can you stand it?"

I don't like the way he says my name. "That isn't any of your business."

"What will it take to get you to leave with me?"

I roll my eyes. "Nothing. I'm not doing it. You're not invincible just because you're a good fighter. If I start screaming, the Yulin Guards' arrows will pierce you all the same."

His face pinches into a smile. "Have you forgotten who I am? As long as I have a sword in my hand, all the Yulin Guards in the world could not stop me from doing what I wanted."

Gu Jian's arrogance sparks a flash of brilliance. "You must be unrivaled," I wheedle. "I bet you haven't lost to anyone before."

He smiles, a real one this time. "That's not true. Three years ago, I lost to you."

My mouth falls open. "*Me?*" I point at myself. "You lost to *me*?" I can't fight at all—I can barely lift a sword. I couldn't win against his pinky finger.

"That's right." His face is peaceful. "The prize was the rest of our lives. If I lost, then I would marry you, protect you, cherish you until the end of our days."

"And if I lost?" My mouth is wide enough that I could swallow a whole egg.

"If you lost . . . if you lost, you'd have to marry me and let me protect you and cherish you until the end of our days."

I shake him off again. Heavens, this is not how you tell a joke.

"I didn't let you win," he continues, "but I had no defense against you, so the result was much the same."

"But it doesn't matter what the outcome was," I remind him. "I don't remember any of this, and I don't know you, either. You can't fool me so easily."

Gu Jian pulls a pair of jade pendants from his sleeve. "When we were promised to each other, we split these yuanyang pendants in two. You kept one, I kept the other, and we arranged to meet on the fifteenth, right when the moon was roundest. I would wait for you outside the Yumen Pass and take you to my home."

I inspect the pendants. Xiliang isn't far from Hetian, where jade is mined, so I've seen hundreds of thousands of pieces of jadeware in my life, and since I've been in Shangjing I've seen hundreds of thousands of rare artifacts too, but no jade I've come across has been so pure, so white, so luminous.

High-quality lamb fat jade has the clarified translucency of a dewy complexion, and under the moon it radiates a soft light. "I don't know what these are," I tell him, but I *am* curious. "Why am I here then, if we were supposed to elope?"

Slowly, he lowers his hand. "It was my fault," he says, his voice small. "Something came up and I couldn't make our meeting date. By the time I arrived, three days had passed, and all I could find of you was your pendant."

I crook my head, considering him. The regret on his face is real enough, but I've lost interest in his story. "If it was your fault, then there's nothing more to say, is there? I promise I'm not lying—I really don't know who you are. You've got the wrong person. And you'd better not come here anymore—

you're going to get me into trouble if you're caught, and I'm in enough hot water as it is."

The eyes on me are intent. "Xiaofeng, do you blame me?"

"I don't care about you," I say honestly.

He gazes at me for a moment longer. Then he sighs and digs into his lapel to pull out a whistling arrow. "Here. Use this to call me if you're in danger."

What danger could I get into while A'du is by my side? But when I don't take the arrow, he shoves it into my hand and, without asking, swings me over his shoulder. Before I can gather my wits enough to protest, he's deposited me on the ground in front of my bedchamber, and by the time I turn to look after him, he's far away. When he arrives at the summit of the main hall again, he glances back at me and finally, mercifully, disappears into the dark.

"That Gu Jian's certainly impressive, but he's nuts to think we know each other. I don't think I'd forget, do you?" I close the window, passing his arrow to A'du.

She looks at me with such soft pity. I crawl back into bed with a huff, wishing she could speak to me, wishing I knew what she was thinking.

Sleep is not restful, and I have unsettled dreams.

Someone plays a reed flute lowly, close to me but just out of my grasp. I want so badly to approach, but he's shrouded by thick fog and I can't see his face. I wander endlessly until at long, long last, I find him. But as I fly toward his open arms, I stumble and fall, fall into the deepest valley.

Despair overtakes me, but then he is there, catching me, pulling me into the warmth of his embrace. Cold air rushes past as we plummet down, until the sky is falling all around us, the stars coming down like sheets of rain, and all I can see between heaven and earth are his eyes—

His eyes, which are full of me.

I'm intoxicated. It's *him*, I know it's him, and I know I love him and he loves me.

As long as he's here, all is well.

The sky is light when I wake. I've had this dream before, but it doesn't leave me with anything more than melancholy. I never catch so much as a glimpse of his face.

There is a sprig of flowers, damp still with dew, on the pillow next to me. I start—A'du sleeps by my bed, and no one gets past her but Gu Jian. I fling my blankets off and rush to the window, but of course it's empty. Gu Jian's long gone.

I stick the branch into a vase, feeling somewhat cheered.

It doesn't last long.

Yongniang rushes in to tell me that Li Chengyin spent all of last night drinking, that he's dead drunk, raging in his rooms. It's pathetic.

If I were him, I wouldn't throw any tantrums. I'd sneak out to see my Lady Zhao, because as long as she's alive, I'd find some way to be together. *So long as the green mountains remain, we need fear no kindling to burn*[2] and all that.

I ignore him and tell Yongniang to do it too. Let him drink himself to death for all I care.

For three days straight that's exactly what he does. On the fourth, he falls ill.

---

2 Idiom from *Slapping the Table in Amazement*, a collection of vernacular stories by Liang Mengchu.

Li Chengyin doesn't let anyone see him intoxicated and forces his entire retinue out of his rooms whenever he's drinking, so by the time word gets out, his cold has turned from a cough to a fever. There's an entire manor between our two courts and not much movement between them, so I don't hear anything until he's already dangerously ill, though no one from the palace knows yet.

"His Highness is refusing to take his medicine, and he won't let anyone inform the palace," Yongniang murmurs. "He's upset with Her Majesty about Lady Zhao."

I don't know if I'm amused or annoyed. "Is he avenging Lady Zhao by punishing himself?"

"His Highness is good and kind, and he is much favored by the king and queen, but I fear he may be . . ." Yongniang is forbidden to say anything bad about Li Chengyin though, and she lets her words hang.

So I do agree to see him—not because I care if he dies, but because I don't care to be a widow.

He must be on death's door when I arrive, for he doesn't have the energy to work up a temper. Usually, he'd have me chased out like vermin if I approached, but when the attendants pull back the curtains today, his face is redder than steamed crab. I hadn't had crab before I came to Shangjing—the first year I was here, they'd been served to everyone at the Chongjiu banquet. I'd gaped and poked, unsure where to start eating the big insect, and Li Chengyin had mocked me about it for ages after, saying that I was a bumpkin from Xiliang who hadn't even seen a crab.

I press a palm against his brow. It's boiling.

"Li Chengyin," I call.

But he doesn't respond.

As I'm about to withdraw, he darts out a hand to grab mine. It burns to the touch too. His breath comes in labored gasps and his lips are cracked. I can just make out what he's saying: *"Mother. Mother!"*

It's not Her Majesty he's calling for—he doesn't call her *mother*. She's the empress and he's the royal heir, so they are exceedingly, unfailingly polite to each other. She doesn't treat him all that much different from how she treats me, I realize—apart from saying *rise* or *sit*, all she really does is lecture him.

I'm startled by the pity I feel.

It's tiring to be princess consort—there's so much I can't do, so much I can't say, and I'm forced to attend a million different ceremonies every year, dressed head to toe in layers of jewelry and stiff robes and heavy golden coronets. The empress looks after me because she says I'm young and from far away, but it's a chore all the same.

I imagine it must be a thousand times harder to be the heir, because he has to memorize the same books that give me a headache just to read. He has to write well and draw well, ride well and fight well, and I don't think his childhood could have been nearly as happy as mine.

He's clutching me so tightly that I can't free myself. The servants arrive with trays, which Yongniang brings over, murmuring, "Your Highness, the medicine is here."

Not sure what to do, I shake him slightly, trying to rouse him. "Li Chengyin," I call. "Your medicine is here."

His only answer is to pull me closer. Yongniang has people come with pillows to prop him up against, and she tries to feed him, but his mouth remains resolutely closed. For every spoonful we manage to get in, nearly half spills down his shirt.

I watch for a while until I can't take it any longer. "Give it here."

Li Chengyin has my right hand captive, so I hold the bowl with my left and turn to call A'du. "Block his nose."

A'du pinches it tightly. As he opens his mouth to take a breath, I press the bowl up against his lips and tip the medicine down his throat. He swallows instinctively, but I'm pouring too quickly and he chokes, coughing against my hand. Those eyes open at last. *"Burn,"* he gasps out. *"It burns."*

Better burned than dead, I say.

I signal to A'du that she can let go, though Li Chengyin makes no similar effort—with my hand caught in his, he turns over and is quickly asleep again. Yongniang brings me a stool to sit on, but it doesn't take any time at all for discomfort to set in, so I call A'du over to take it away again and move onto the bed, where I don't have to lean so far over or extend my arm quite as much. That doesn't last long either, for soon my arm goes numb. I try to draw it away, but the second I move, his grip tightens around me. A'du unsheathes her dagger and gestures at his wrist, but I push her away, shaking my head furiously. If she chops his hand off, I'd be surprised if his father *doesn't* send troops against mine.

I miss Lady Zhao with a vengeance. It would never have fallen to me to look after Li Chengyin if she were here. It wouldn't have been my hand he grabbed, no matter how sick he got.

At around the two-hour mark, when my whole arm is tingling, I start planning a prison break for Lady Zhao, dreaming about making her take over this thankless work.

By four hours in, I've lost feeling in half my body and can't bear it anymore. I call softly for Yongniang.

She comes in and bends down so I can whisper in her ear.

"Yongniang," I stammer. "I need to use the privy."

"I'll have someone bring the chamber pot," she says, and is gone quicker I can call her back. Soon enough she has a screen unfolded and the room cleared of people. I stare up at her, pained.

"Yongniang, I don't think—"

"I can help you, Your Highness."

"But Li Chengyin is right there!"

"His Highness isn't just anybody," Yongniang reassures me. "He's asleep, and it wouldn't matter even if he wasn't: he's your husband. They say couples are two halves of the same being, so there's no need to be shy."

I'm not in the mood to endure her lecture, but to ask me—in front of Li Chengyin—in front of *any* man—I'm hot with embarrassment. "Yongniang, please," I beg, "you have to think of something."

She ponders on it but, despite my pleas, can't come up with anything better.

"Never mind," I sigh. "Can you at least come here and block me?"

Yongniang slants herself between us, but because Li Chengyin's still holding my hand and she isn't allowed to turn her back to either of us, it accomplishes very little.

Tentatively, I untie my laces, poking my head out every so often to peek at him. A'du unfastens my robes and unwraps my skirts, but just as relief overtakes me, Li Chengyin shifts.

He opens his eyes.

I shriek.

A'du leaps into action, her dagger sliding easily from its sheath. Yongniang starts, alarmed by my screaming, but A'du shoves her out of the way to press the sharp of her blade to Li Chengyin's neck.

"Stop—don't—!" I yell, gathering up my skirts. I scramble to retie the laces, but Plains clothing is so fussy that I can't tell which string pairs with which on a good day—and that's when I have ladies-in-waiting to do it for me. I fumble through the knots. "A'du, stop! He startled me, that's all."

She retreats.

Li Chengyin stares at me, and I stare at Li Chengyin. He looks unfocused, eyes glassy and glazed as he glances around at the folded screen, the stunned Yongniang, and then at my chamber pot at the foot of the bed, my hand that's tightly twined in his, and my tangled laces. The corners of his mouth twitch.

In three years of fighting I've not once been at such a disadvantage. My face burns with humiliation. "If you laugh," I hiss, "I'll have A'du stab you through the heart!"

But no matter how I glare, he can't suppress his glee. He bursts out laughing, harder than I've ever seen him, until the whole bedchamber echoes with its sound. Half of me simmers with rage, and the other half would like to crawl into a hole and die.

Yongniang sucks in a sharp gasp when I snatch A'du's dagger and pummel Li Chengyin with the back of its blade.

"You think I won't hit you?" My voice is high. "You think I'll go easy on you because you're sick? I'd kill you if it weren't for the fact that your a'die might send troops against mine!"

Yongniang hurries forward to stop me, but A'du steps between us. I'm using the dull of the blade, but I'm sure it hurts, though he doesn't lose his temper the way I expect him to—not that he takes it lying down, either. He snatches at the dagger and chases after me when I duck away. Catching the glint of light off its blade, Yongniang calls, "My lady, please don't hurt His Highness. Your Highness—Your Highness, be careful!"

I can't afford to be distracted when Li Chengyin's attempting to disarm me. "A'du, get her out of here!"

There's no fight to be had with Yongniang trying to stop it.

A'du sweeps Yongniang from the room. My hair's a mess. A gold pin slips from a braid and catches on my baby hairs. I only lose focus for a moment, but Li Chengyin manages to steal away my dagger.

I lunge, ready to snatch it back, but he leaps to his feet, raising it above his head. He's much taller than I am, and even on my tiptoes I can't reach. When I jump for it, he swaps hands.

"Jump higher," he crows. "Higher!"

I see red. Specifically, the red of his girdle under the yellow silk of his sleeping robes. In a spark of genius, I grab it and jerk him toward me.

"What are you doing?" Li Chengyin stammers.

With one hand firmly on his girdle, I kick—hard—at his knee. He lands heavily on it, and I grab his wrist, twisting the dagger neatly from his hand.

Just then, A'du walks back in and lifts the curtain to reveal me sprawled out over Li Chengyin, hand buried in his clothing, and her face reddens. She turns on her heel and runs out faster than I can explain myself.

"A'du!" I jump up to call her back, but Li Chengyin grabs for the dagger and we tumble from the bed to the ground. How have I not noticed how nimble he is? He's usually more restrained, and we're usually pulled apart before we really start going at it. He may be sick, but he's as hardy as a camel, and I have no real advantage over him, especially once my strength starts failing. He snatches the dagger from me, and when I pry at his fingers, he drops it and kicks it out of both our grasps.

I lie there, trying to catch my breath. Li Chengyin has both my wrists in one of his hands. From this close, I can see the individual drops of sweat beading his forehead. Now that he's worked it up, the frost in his body will probably dissipate soon.

The two of us are snarled in a deadlock, twisted in the blanket—him unable to let go, and me too tired to push him off. Eventually, his gaze drops to the sash that's keeping my skirt up, and he extracts a hand from the tangle to tug at it.

My heart turns over. "What are you doing?"

Sloppily, he begins to bind my hands together, and a new fear overtakes me: What if he wants me restrained so he can have the upper hand?

"Hey!" I say. "You have to play fair, or else I'll call A'du in and have her chop you to pieces!"

"Be quiet," he advises me.

"A'du!" I shriek. "A'du, help!"

He probably is a little scared of A'du—he can't best her the way he can me. He looks about the empty room for something to gag me with, but the bed is a twist of blankets, and the pillows are strewn all over the floor—there's nothing close at hand. He may have tied my hands, but my legs are free, so I twist and struggle like a just-caught fish. Seizing my chance, I yell, "A'du, come and rescue me! A'du!"

Panicked, Li Chengyin seizes me by the hand and tugs me toward him. For lack of anything better to silence me with, he stops my mouth with his own.

I freeze.

He smells of sweat and agarwood, of medicine and something else I can't place. His lips are warm and soft, and I'm reminded of my favorite roast duck, only roast duck isn't so yielding. All I can see is his face, those eyes.

We can't look away from each other.

I can't breathe.

He's forgotten to also.

I open my mouth to yell, but his arms unexpectedly tighten, pressing me closer, and when my lips part, his tongue slips in.

Disgusting, I remind myself. My skin is a map of raised gooseflesh.

But his mouth is insistent, and his hands fumble with my laces. If it wasn't for the fact that they're tied so tightly, who knows what would have happened to my robes, and then I *would* have to perish.

The instant I get my wits back, I bite down. As hard as I can, and kick him for good measure, too.

He doesn't move again after that, but I fly up and snatch A'du's dagger, making short work of my restraints. "Li Chengyin, I'm going to *kill you*!"

He blinks lazily up at me, and then down at the blade. I press it closer. "If you tell *anyone* what happened today, I'm going to have A'du murder you."

Li Chengyin sits there, leaning carelessly back against his palms as though the blade at his neck is no sharper than a child's toy. "And what, exactly, happened today?" he drawls.

"You kissed—and—and then—in any case, if you breathe a *word* of this to *anyone*, I'll run you through right here."

But he offers up his neck. "Do it then, if you want to be known as a husbandkiller. The second I'm cold in the ground, His Majesty will send troops to raze your Xiliang."

He's the *worst*.

I do hesitate, unsure if I should actually stab him or if I should get A'du to teach him a lesson later.

"If I'm in a good mood," he says, "maybe I'll pay closer attention to what I say, lest anything *untoward* slip out."

I peek at him. "And what would put you in a good mood?"

Li Chengyin strokes his chin. "Let me think . . ."

"What's there to think about?" I snap. "Either way, I'm going to have A'du kill you if you talk—"

"Kiss me."

"*What?*"

"If you kiss me again, I won't tell."

I squint at him. Is it the illness? He hasn't been acting like himself all day. Whenever we used to fight, he would be spiteful and vicious, but today he's acting like a naughty child.

I steel myself. "You promise?"

"A gentleman never goes back on his word."

Slowly, I set the dagger down and screw my eyes tightly together to kiss his cheek. I kiss hard enough to leave tooth marks, and he sucks in a sharp breath. I'm gathering my skirts up to leave when he tugs me back to him. I stumble and fall, straight into his lap.

He kisses me again.

And he doesn't stop, not for a long time, not until I can't catch my breath, until my lips are swollen and tingling like I've accidentally bitten into something spicy. Then he brushes my mouth with a thumb, saying, "*That's* how you kiss somebody, understand?"

The urge to stab him rises again, and if it wasn't for the fact that it would start a war—that it would plunge our people into violence, into bloodbath, then—so I swallow it all down. "Thanks for the lesson," I scoff.

"You're welcome." His grin is crooked and widens across his face. "Since you've had it, why don't you demonstrate?"

"Didn't I just do it?" I push myself off him. "Liar!"

"No, that was *me* kissing *you*. You didn't kiss me."

I tell myself to grit my teeth and bear it. For peace.

I grab him by the lapels and jerk him toward me, moving my mouth the way he'd done, kissing him viciously. By the time I let go, he's flushed from neck to ears, eyes bloodshot, breath ragged.

"What is it?" I ask. "Are you feverish again?"

"No," he says, too quickly. "No, you can go."

So I straighten my clothes, smooth down my hair, and pick up A'du's dagger for good measure as I sweep from his chambers.

There's no one waiting for me outside, and I don't spot a single one of my attendants until I'm back in my own rooms. They're so astonished to see me they forget to curtsy—and you must know that every member of my retinue was hand selected by Yongniang, and every one of them is exactly like her, perfectly proper at all times.

It's not until I catch sight of my own reflection that I realize what's wrong—despite my best efforts, my hair is a tangled mess, my clothing is rumpled, and worst of all, thanks to Li Chengyin, my mouth is noticeably red. The ladies-in-waiting hurry to help me into new clothes, mercifully holding their tongues. If I have to tell anyone what happened today, there's no way I can live in this manor with a shred of dignity left.

I still haven't stopped seething when an attendant knocks at the boudoir door to report that Li Chengyin has sent a page over with a present. My ladies-in-waiting exchange glances—they're all well aware of how the crown prince feels about me.

I'm apprehensive. I know him—when we fight, he's capable of ignoring me for days on end. Today's argument was worse than most, and he sends . . . presents?

"Let him in, then," I say. I'm not about to be cowed.

So the little page boy comes marching in, a tray held aloft between his hands. Whatever present sits atop it is covered by a sheet of red silk. Because he was dispatched by the crown prince, the page stands very straight, a somber expression on his face, looking for all the world like he's delivering an imperial edict straight from the mouth of the emperor himself.

"HIS HIGHNESS SAYS," he begins, "THAT HE DID NOT MEAN TO RIP YOUR HIGHNESS'S GIRDLE. HE WAS OVERCOME WITH EMOTION AND FEELS VERY POORLY ABOUT IT, SO HE WANTED TO DELIVER THESE LOVERS' KNOTS AS AN APOLOGY. HIS HIGHNESS SAYS HE SHOULD HAVE COME TO HELP YOUR HIGHNESS WITH THESE PERSONALLY, BUT AS HE HAS BEEN WORN OUT BY THE EXERTION AND FEARS THAT THE SWEAT WILL MAKE HIM SUSCEPTIBLE TO COLD, HE WILL KEEP TO HIS OWN ROOMS. HIS HIGHNESS ALSO SAYS THAT HE WON'T BREATHE A WORD ABOUT WHAT HAPPENED TODAY TO ANYONE, SO YOUR HIGHNESS MAY BE AT EASE."

I'm going to *kill him*. I am. Not a single person in the room looks at me. Some are staring very resolutely up into the rafters, some are boring holes into the earth, and some are biting down hard on their lips. Others, though, can't stop themselves from giggling, and their shoulders are shaking with the effort of holding it in. Every last one of them pretends not to have heard, but their attempt to spare my feelings doesn't make things any better.

Fine. You've won this round, Li Chengyin. If this is his version of *not telling anyone*, I shudder to think what "telling" would look like—all that's left is to put up a public notice.

And to phrase it like *that*—it's on purpose, I *know* it. I'm never going to live this down.

Between gritted teeth and a smile that hurts my cheeks, I force out, "Do thank His Highness on my behalf."

The page boy kneels and bows, raising the tray above his head. Gingerly, I lift the covering to find, as promised, a set of richly embroidered girdles, wound cheerily into the two halves of a single heart. I could vomit. One of my ladies-in-waiting hurries forward to take the tray.

I'd known Li Chengyin wouldn't let me be, but I didn't expect him to stoop so low. A'du comes back to my chambers at around sunset, bringing Yongniang with her. Yongniang's not halfway through a cup of tea before someone opens their big fat mouth to tell her about the girdles. Yongniang knows better than to ask questions, but she's smiling wide, and when she sees my swollen mouth, she orders soup for dinner. At this point I doubt if anyone in the manor is unaware that I left Li Chengyin's bedchamber with my hair wild and my clothes disheveled or that he'd gifted me a set of girdles to replace the one I lost.

A *lovers' knot*. The thought of accepting such an intimate gift makes my skin prickle. I wouldn't think it strange if he'd sent me three yards of white silk to hang myself with, but *girdles*—it can be nothing but some harebrained scheme he's cooked up.

Not that anyone else sees it that way, least of all the girls in my court. Every one of them struts about, giddy, as if they truly believe I've somehow conquered his heart at last.

"Emituofo, His Highness has finally seen the light."

GOODBYE, MY PRINCESS

"See how good His Highness is to our lady now that Miss Zhao is locked away? I wouldn't be surprised if she'd conjured some witchery to enchant him."

"You're right—our lady is so beautiful, there'd be no justice in the world if His Highness didn't favor her."

"You didn't see the way Her Highness looked when she saw the girdles—she was blushing!"

"I'd blush too! I can't believe he would be so bold, delivering something like that in the middle of the day."

"That's not the boldest thing he's done. You didn't see what Her Highness looked like when she came back—her hair was all scattered and her clothes were torn, like His Highness—His Highness—"

They dissolve into giggles.

I leap to my feet. I want to tell them that my face was red because I was angry—that my clothes were torn because we were fighting—that it isn't what they think.

Li Chengyin doesn't like me like that, not really. He only ever wants to torment me.

No, not merely torment. Scapegoat, too.

I realize this three days later, when the empress summons me again. She is stern when I pay my respects and doesn't call anyone to help me to my feet the way she normally does, nor does she tell me to rise and be seated. Instead, she launches into a long lecture, the vast majority of which I don't understand, but the sum of which I take to be a berating, though she's as tactful as always.

All I can do is kneel there and listen.

It's not like she's never lectured me, but it's different this time. She used to only do it when I'd done something bad, like forgetting the rules during a ceremony, or saying something improper at a sacrifice. And she hasn't had me kneel like this either.

She opens with a long treatise on *The Woman's Manual* and *The Woman's Guide* before bringing the monologue around to the famously virtuous Zhanghui empress. She goes on and on until I'm bored to death and my knees ache, but I'm too scared to move.

I think she knows, though, that I can't make heads or tails of anything she's saying, because at long last she heaves a long sigh. "You are the princess consort," she says. "Mistress of the Court of Spring. You are meant to be a model for all of the women in this kingdom to follow. Yin'er may not act his age, but you should encourage him to be more mature, not join him in his childishness. Never mind that you are a member of the royal family, even a commoner's wife should know to be modest."

It dawns on me why I've been called here, and I protest. "It wasn't me, it was *him*—"

The empress glances coolly at me. "I am aware he started it, but do you not know to not indulge him? He is still sick; what will you do if he takes a turn for the worse after this? You will be queen someday. You will be keeper of the Six Courts, the standard of the inner palace. How will you convince people of your authority if you continue to behave like this?"

I want to crawl inside a hole and die. She's all but calling me shameless for dallying with Li Chengyin while he's sick, and Heaven alone knows that I *haven't*. But who would believe me if I told the truth?

The empress catches sight of my face and must decide that I've been berated enough, for she says, "You may rise. I am saying all this for your own good. You know how bad it will be if this gets out. Of course young couples should be intimate with each other, but you have to be more circumspect. These Plains are not like your Xiliang. A careless word here is sharper than a knife, especially in the palace, where rumors are poisonous enough to kill."

My eyes sting. "I won't ever be good enough at being princess consort," I say. "I don't want this title anymore."

But the empress acts as though she hasn't heard me, turning to address Yongniang instead. "Look after the princess," she says. "She is young and has many responsibilities. I do not want her to risk her own health by bringing the prince any more medicine. Have her copy *The Woman's Manual* ten times."

I purse my lips, trying to bottle up my annoyance. She's warding me off like I'm some kind of nine-tailed vixen, and I understand the trap Li Chengyin's sprung.

Stupid girdles. They're more dangerous than white silk. Copying *The Woman's Manual* out ten more times—it's a punishment worse than death.

By the time we get back to the manor, I'm so mad I could pick up a knife and storm Li Chengyin's chambers right then and there. Plot against *me*? He must have tired of breathing. I almost do it, too, but Yongniang isn't more than two steps behind me the whole time, and she has ladies-in-waiting preparing sheafs of paper and grinding me ink, so there's little I can do but swallow my rage and start my copying.

The words are difficult, and every time I finish one, I silently curse Li Chengyin. By the time I've written a measly five lines of text, I've buried him a hundred times over in my head.

I stay up that night. I stay until the air is quiet and the people are still, and I crawl out of bed to slip my clothes on. A'du pushes herself blearily up from her bed mat when she hears me get up, and I murmur, "A'du, give me your dagger."

She doesn't know what I want to do with it, but she hands it to me anyway. I slide it carefully into my lapels and pull a robe on over my nightclothes. Without A'du, I can't avoid the Yulin Guard, so I bring her along as we scuttle through the shadows toward Li Chengyin's rooms.

But when we come to the corridor, A'du stops short.

Yongniang, carrying a censer in her hands, is heading straight toward us.

Of all the nights for a coincidence. I've forgotten it's the fifteenth of the month, when Yongniang goes to worship the moon. I'm contemplating whether I should have A'du incapacitate her when she catches sight of us and starts. I freeze, ready for her to summon the Yulin Guard to take us back into custody, but she glances toward where we're headed—Li Chengyin's rooms, glimmering faintly with light.

I turn, ready to tell A'du to knock her out, but she glides past, silent but for the soft flutter of her sigh.

For the life of me I can't understand why she lets me off

so easily until she pauses to say, "The night wind is frigid, my lady. Don't stay long, lest you catch cold."

She thinks I'm going to a *dalliance*. Injustice burns in my chest. I take A'du and storm to where Li Chengyin lives. A day I don't avenge myself is a day I have to live in humiliation, and I intend to knock every tooth out of his head.

A'du helps me onto the wall, but then I hear a shout: *"Assassin!"*

The vibration of fletchings leaping their string is the last thing I feel before the sky fills with arrows hurtling toward us like a rain of locusts that blots out the sky. Lanterns flare to life, and A'du dives, knocking the bolts from the air, but she can't hold out for long. I try clambering back to the other side, but my foot slips and I fall. Had the wall been so high before?

Wind rushes past my ears. All I remember thinking is that I'm going to turn into mincemeat at the bottom of this wall.

I fall backward, catching a glimpse of A'du's panic-stricken face. She grabs for me. Behind her is a receding night, scattered with a fracture of white stars. The moon disappears behind the wall. I'm falling too quickly for her to reach me in time, but someone else grabs me around the waist, catching me in his arms. Through the tangle of hair I can see a silver flash of armor reflecting back pinpricks of torchlight, like little red flowers that bloom across the metal. The red flowers bloom in his eyes, too—eyes that stare intently into mine.

It's like that familiar dream—the wind, the stars, the eyes that gaze at me—that gaze only at me.

I'm sure this must be the person I've been dreaming about. It has to be—

"Your Highness."

The ground startles me awake. The bright armor, the straight brows and bright eyes, the proud bearing—is it him?

Pei Zhao bows low. The arrows have long since clattered to the ground, but it's only when he puts me back down that I realize how tightly I'm clinging to his arm. A'du rushes up to inspect me for injury. I stand, a little awkward, and wonder. Pei Zhao is handsome, and a capable soldier, but I would know, I think, if the man I'm dreaming about is him. I sneak a glance, my ears hot. The night I'd planned is going disastrously—first Yongniang, now this.

Pei Zhao signals, and the guards disappear. I feel like I should say something to fill the silence they leave behind. "General Pei, I'm impressed—"

"Please forgive us, Your Highness." Pei Zhao clasps his hands and dips into another bow.

"It's not your fault," I fumble. "A'du and I shouldn't have come over the wall. It's no wonder you thought we were assassins."

"Is there a reason you're here tonight, Your Highness?" His voice is polite.

It's not like I can tell him I'm sneaking in to take revenge on Li Chengyin, so I force a smile. "Can't say."

Pei Zhao looks as he always does. The only acknowledgment of what I say is a lowered head and a "Yes, Your Highness."

I breeze past with A'du, trying to look like I haven't just

humiliated myself in front of the Yulin Guard, but Pei Zhao calls me back. "Your Highness."

"What is it?"

"His Highness's chambers are this way."

Haven't I suffered enough? I glare at him, but as his eyes are respectfully lowered, I don't even get that satisfaction. I have no choice but to turn around and slump back toward Li Chengyin's rooms. When we arrive at the door, I tell A'du, "Stay here, and don't let anyone else in."

A'du nods and signs that she understands.

The attendants haven't retired yet. They're playing riddles under the dim candlelight, so I slip quickly past them, hidden by the dark. No one notices when I enter the inner chamber.

Inside, the candles are lit. Flickering flames cast hazy shadows onto the canopy, dancing like soft dapples of water. I creep toward the bed, drawing the curtains back slowly, careful not to make a sound.

Something darts through the air, passing close to my face. I flinch back, but then the world spins and I'm pressed to the bed, the cold gleam of a blade to my throat, inches away from slitting it. I stare up, skin icy with sweat. He's a different person in the dark, face hard in a way that is wholly unfamiliar.

Why would a crown prince need to wear a weapon to bed?

"You?" He stares down at me, drawing the dagger away. As he slides it back into its sheath, he also slides back into the Li Chengyin I'm used to, the one who says, lazily, "What are you doing here in the middle of the night?"

"Me?" I stammer through my answer. I'd been planning to tie him up like a giant zongzi and beat him within an inch of his life, but it's not like I can *say* that. "I'm not doing anything."

"*I* know why you're here," he says, glancing sidelong at me. His mouth isn't smiling, but his eyes are. "You missed me, so you came to visit me."

I remember why I'm angry now. The girdle. The lecture. *The Woman's Manual*! I draw the dagger at my waist and point it at him. "You're right," I grit. "I've missed you plenty."

But he doesn't look intimidated by me at all—in fact, he starts laughing. "Is this how Xiliang girls miss people?"

"Stop laughing!" I put the dagger to his neck. "Hand the knife over."

He scoots forward. "Why should I?"

"Don't come any closer—" But I don't get the chance to finish my thought because his arms tighten around me and his mouth is on mine again. The kiss is softer this time, and slower, like he's savoring it.

I'm reminded of the fastidious way he eats crab at the banquets we've attended, the way he disassembles them with more care than girls take with embroidery, the way you can reassemble their anatomy with the shells he leaves behind.

A'du's dagger is in my hand, but I can't bring myself to actually hurt him. If I do, our kingdoms might really come to blows, and my a'die's getting older—I don't think he has the energy to wage any more wars.

So I let him kiss me until he pulls back, but before I can catch my breath, he moves to my neck. I squirm away, discomfited by the sharp pinch of his teeth, and he shifts to nip at my earlobe. His breath is a soft tickle against my ear, and I have to suppress the urge to giggle. I'm limp beneath him, and when he plies the dagger from me, it clatters across the room. Only when he moves back to reclaim my mouth do I realize that his other hand has found its way beneath my robes and is wound about my waist, pinning me in place. I push him off me, yelping, "You—let go of me or else I'm calling A'du!"

"Call her then." Li Chengyin grins. "I don't mind. In fact, why don't you call the entire court to my rooms? I'm not the one who snuck into your bed."

Snuck into bed—why does everything sound so nasty when he says it? Put like that, I couldn't clear my name if I washed it in the Yellow River. I'm contemplating whether I should go through with stabbing him and teach him a lesson when wind blows the curtains back.

Li Chengyin shoves me to the other end of his bed. I turn in time to see a cold flash of light piercing straight toward him. In the moment it had taken him to push me to safety, Li Chengyin has lost his own chance to escape, and the sword sinks deep into his chest.

I scream. A'du comes running, but not quickly enough to prevent the man from attacking again. She'd given her dagger to me, so she grabs a candelabrum from the desk and throws it.

The assassin ducks and it clatters to the ground, but I'm calling for the Yulin Guard, who storm the room. A'du exchanges blows with the assassin as the din outside grows louder—and I don't know when the tears start, but it must be sometime between when the assassin leaps through the silk screen window, A'du hot on his tail, and when I look down to see Li Chengyin crumpled in my arms, covered in an obscene amount of blood. I'm worried—I'm scared—but he's looking up at me, asking, "Are you hurt—?"

He doesn't finish the thought because he's interrupted by a bout of coughing. Red splatters across the collar of my nightclothes and the sob I've been swallowing back bursts in great breathless shudders as I call his name. But he doesn't hear me.

I've despised him, but I don't *really* want him to die.

In my panic I cling to his hand, but he smiles up at me through lips wet with blood. "I've never—seen you—cry," he gasps. "What, scared of being—a widow?"

The fact that he's smiling makes me cry harder. I press my hands fruitlessly to his wound but the red seeps through my fingers, warm and slick, nevertheless. How could he survive losing so much of it? My heart pounds in my throat.

His handmaidens have rushed into the inner chamber, but a few shriek and collapse at the sight of us. The court is a confused mess, but I can hear General Pei giving orders, and when he enters, he's a lifeline thrown to a drowning man.

"General Pei!" I scream.

He immediately calls for someone to send for a physician, then comes back and seals Li Chengyin's pressure points to stem the tide of ceaseless bleeding. "Your Highness," he says, seeing how tightly I'm clutching at Li Chengyin, "if you let go, it will be easier for me to check the prince for injuries."

I'm grateful to have someone else telling me what to do. I let go and Pei Zhao peels back the soiled clothing, frowning. I don't know what it means until the help he'd sent for arrives, along with half the Ministry of Imperial Physicians.

Though it's late, the palace has been alerted, and the emperor and empress have come personally. One of the ministers approaches them and, in a low voice, says, "Forgive me, Your Majesty, but—the crown prince's injuries are deep, and I fear . . . I fear he is in grave danger."

Though the empress is crying, she makes no sound. Her only motion is to wipe her tears away. The emperor's face is severe. I'm worn out from weeping and sit silently instead, waiting for A'du to return. Pei Zhao sent men after the assassin, but I don't know if they've caught him yet or not. I'm worried for Li Chengyin, but I'm worried too for A'du.

She doesn't return until nearly dawn, carried in by Pei Zhao's men. She's badly injured, and when I call her name, she opens her eyes weakly to look at me. She tries to lift her hand, but manages only a slight twitch of the fingers. I follow her eyes to my lapels, which are stained with blood—Li Chengyin's.

"I'm okay," I say, though my voice is wobbly.

A'du lets out a breath. She shoves something into my hands, then passes out. I stare down at it. Li Chengyin is hurt because of me. A'du is injured too, and it's my fault, all of it—I was the one who told her to give me her dagger, the one who let her chase after an assassin without a weapon. A'du, who's been with me all these years, who's guarded me with her life. It's always me, always my messes that make her suffer. I collapse, stifling my sobs with my hands, but there's no one around to comfort me, for they are all occupied with Li Chengyin. Li Chengyin, my husband, who is almost dead.

PART TWO:

春容
Springtime

I cry until Pei Zhao comes over. "Your Highness," he calls softly, "the assassin was gone by the time my men arrived, so they brought Miss A'du back first. But the city gates have been closed and Shangjing is locked down—there's no way out. The Yulin Guard is searching the streets as we speak. He'll be caught soon."

I hear the words, but they don't register. My attention is fixed on the thing A'du had shoved into my hand: a block of wood, carved with an unfamiliar emblem. I hold it out.

"A'du gave me this." I sniffle. "Do you think it has anything to do with the assassin?"

Pei Zhao sucks in a sharp breath. Clearly, he recognizes it.

"What?" I ask, curious.

But he doesn't answer. He retreats a step and gives it back to me, saying, "It may be better if you gave this to His Majesty yourself, my lady. I'm afraid this is beyond my authority."

I think so too—the king is the will of Heaven incarnate, the sitting emperor, the person who rules over all, and—more important—he is Li Chengyin's father. If someone wanted to kill his son—to kill A'du—he should want to know. So I dry my eyes and find an attendant.

Li Chengyin's parents are seated in his room, waiting to

see me. I walk in and pay my courtesies, sinking to my knees. "Your Majesty."

I don't often get to see the king, and when I do, it's usually from a distance. I can tell that he's near my a'die's age, that his hair is also threaded through with gray. He's very cordial and tells his attendants to help me up.

But I refuse.

"My lord," I say, "my attendant A'du took this from the assassin. I don't know what it is, but please—I'm sure it has something to do with this." I raise the wooden plaque above me as I press my forehead to the ground.

One of the attendants steps forward to take it. The emperor's face changes the instant he sees it, and he turns on the empress. "Meiniang!"

The name, I realize, belongs to the queen.

She leaps to her feet, pointing at me. *"You!"* she snarls. "How *dare* you!"

I blink up at her, but I've yet to work out what's happening when she sinks to her knees. "Your Majesty, this must be some trick. I brought Yin'er up myself, I've poured all of my heart's blood into him—I should never hurt him."

And then she turns on me. "Where did you learn to slander me thus?"

I'm barely fluent in Plains. I can't read what's carved into the wood, and I've never seen it before, so I stare blankly back at her, not sure how to defend myself.

Finally, the emperor speaks. "Meiniang, she doesn't know what this is. How could she use it to slander you?"

"Please, Your Majesty," she begs, "you can't believe these

lies. Why should I hurt Yin'er when he's as good as my own blood-born son?"

"Your own blood-born son?" the emperor says dispassionately. "Perhaps."

"You are breaking my heart." Her voice falters, and tears well in her eyes. "Aside from carrying him nine months, what have I not done for him that a blood mother would? He was three moons old when I brought him into my court. *I* am the one who spent the last nineteen years raising him. *I* am the one who taught him to read. *I* am the one who urged you to name him your heir! I spent my whole life raising him, why would I hurt him? I am innocent!"

The emperor's smile is cold. "Miss Xu was innocent too. Why would you hurt her?"

She jerks her head up.

I do too.

"I may not ask about what happens in the inner courts, but don't mistake that for my not knowing. Meiniang, this is consequence. Why would you use Miss Xu to depose Lady Zhao if you truly wanted Yin'er to rule in peace? Why go to such lengths to incriminate a girl whose father and brother have two armies between them if you had no desire to separate him from power? What are you afraid of?"

"I—I don't understand what you're saying, my lord," the empress stammers. "What have I to fear?"

"That's right." The emperor looks down upon her. "What *have* you to fear? After all, his mother's death has nothing to do with you."

The blood drains from the empress's face.

But her husband is not done. "You were too hasty," he says. "What harm could it have done you to wait another twenty years? Wait until I'm dead, until Yin'er deposes the crown princess in favor of Miss Zhao. Wait until Xiliang inevitably declares war, because even if we win, our enmity with them will only grow, and there will never be peace again—the people would be bound to revolt. If we lost . . . I'm sure you could find reason enough to have him deposed.

"It must have crossed your mind when you advised me into the treaty marriage. So tell me again—*what's the hurry now?* Have Yin'er and Xiaofeng been growing too close lately? Is that inconvenient to your plans?"

"Thirty years of marriage," the empress says, almost to herself, "and this is what you think of me."

"Not what I think of you," the emperor corrects. "What you've become. Have I ever asked you to answer for Lady Shu's death? For Miss Xu's miscarriage? For Miss Zhao's confinement? I've understood that what you do, you do out of self-preservation. I've always thought that any son of mine who couldn't handle a few of your tricks wasn't worthy of being heir.

"But you've wronged too many people, my dear, and it's caught up to you. You've taken leave of your reason, and I can turn a blind eye no longer. Even a tiger knows better than to hurt its own cub. Yin'er may not be yours by blood, but you've been his mother for almost twenty years. How could you have the heart?"

"But I didn't." The empress's tears drip down her cheeks. "It doesn't matter if you don't believe me, I wouldn't."

My heart is so cold. I'm too frightened to believe my ears—the empress hasn't been anything but kind. She's so gentle and so refined, and I couldn't believe her to be so conniving.

"You know exactly what you've done. Must I order you to a magistrate and force you to account for your crimes beneath the eyes of the world? If you confess, I can at least keep you from death—on account of those thirty years."

Her tears patter against the ground like rain. "But I'm innocent," she keeps protesting. "I am."

"Swallow the second half of the prescription then, if you want to exonerate yourself. The one you laced Lady Shu's medicine with twenty years ago. It's still hidden in the secret compartment in your wardrobe, isn't it? I'm happy to send guards to check."

The empress slumps to the ground.

I feel like I've weathered a thunderstorm tonight, struck by bolt after bolt of lightning. When the emperor waves me to him, I inch tentatively forward to kneel at his feet. He smooths a hand over my hair, saying, "Don't be afraid, child. I won't let you come to harm. The empress wasn't the only one who wanted Yin'er to marry you, you know; I know how kindhearted Xiliang girls are.

"Take good care of Yin'er," he continues. "He lost his mother so young. That boy would dig his own heart out for anyone who was good to him."

I don't need him to remind me of that. The fear that is settling into my gut is not fear of him—his hands are as gentle as my a'die's hands, and his face is Li Chengyin's face, which I am never afraid of. What scares me isn't the might of the palace—it's the shadows that hide inside a human heart.

For three whole days, Li Chengyin does not stir.

I keep watch by his bedside, but he takes a turn for the worse when the wound becomes infected. He runs a high fever, refuses to eat, and it's a chore to force medicine down his throat. There's a moment one day when I think he really might not make it, but my eyes are dry. I've made up my mind—if he dies, I'm going with him.

Xiliang girls don't waste our time on tears. I've already wept for him, so there's no reason to cry any more.

Li Chengyin often mutters under his breath while he sleeps. I scoot closer, leaning in to his lips.

"*Mother*," he breathes, like he'd done last time. I can't help feeling sorry for him. He might be the heir to the throne, but he's also a boy who's never known his mother, who was raised by the same woman who killed her. He'd be sad, I think, if he knew.

He's attended to by physicians all day, and I discover that the emperor has issued the edict to depose the empress. It was a massive shock at court, but because the list of her crimes was so long, and because Li Chengyin is hovering at death's door, there's little the ministers can say about it.

Among themselves, though, the attendants whisper that the empress comes from a powerful family, and that her relatives have gotten every minister under their control to raise official objections. I hadn't realized that even the emperor can't do whatever he wants.

I spend mornings with Li Chengyin and afternoons with A'du. She's bruised all over, but that's nothing compared to the internal injuries she's sustained. It makes no sense to me—she's A'du, the best fighter I know. Who could be strong enough to hurt her so badly?

Because her medicine has to be changed out so often, the physicians have peeled away her bloodied clothes and laid out the trinkets in her pockets on a side table: a bird-shaped clay whistle, a red velvet flower—all things I'd bought on a whim. She keeps them close in case I want to amuse myself.

My A'du, my best A'du.

This is all my fault.

There's a whistling arrow set out neatly among her things, and a thought strikes me. I palm it and slip from the room—since everyone in the manor has gathered in Li Chengyin's courtyard, the gardens are eerily hushed. I shoot the arrow into the air and wait.

Gu Jian lands like a gentle sweep of wind.

He takes one look at me and says, "What's wrong?"

I know I look wretched. My eyes are red and swollen, and I haven't slept at all, so my complexion is sallow too. But I ignore the question and tell him what's happened instead.

He's quiet. "So you want me to kill the empress?"

I shake my head. I don't know if the empress deserves to die, but I know the emperor will sentence her. She might not be executed, but she'll definitely be deposed, and having to live out the rest of her life under house arrest seems like justice enough.

"I want you to save A'du," I say. "Will you?"

"How odd." Gu Jian smiles. "You don't ask me to save your husband, but you do ask me to save your maid. Is it because you don't like him enough, or because you like her too much?"

"Li Chengyin's injuries are external," I explain patiently. "There's nothing you can do for him. But A'du . . . A'du only went after the assassin because I told her to, and her worst injuries are internal, so I know you know how to save her."

His face curdles. "You're right, I do. But why should I?"

"You were the one who said you'd help me if I needed you to."

"Yes," he says. "If *you* were in danger. I didn't say it applied to anyone else."

"But A'du's life is my life, and she risked it for *me*. So her injuries are my injuries too, and if you won't save her, then—" I raise her dagger to my neck. "My life is over too."

He lifts two fingers and flicks the blade. Tremors jolt through the dagger and into my arm. I lose my grip, and the knife clangs to the ground. I rush to pick it up, but he's faster, snatching it away with a whirl of his sleeve. Angry, I strike him, but he catches my wrist before I skim the corner of his tunic. My eyes sting.

"*Fine then*. Don't save her. But if you don't, then you'd better leave, because I *never* want to see you again."

He considers me, and then sighs. "Don't be angry," he relents. "I'll help—I'll help, okay?"

It's easy enough to find an excuse to dismiss all the attendants in A'du's room, and then I beckon out the window. Gu Jian slips through the frame, noiseless and graceful. He walks to the bed and examines A'du.

"Whoever hurt her was brutal," he says. "They very nearly maimed her."

My heart stutters, but then he continues: "I can save her." He eyes me. "How will you repay me if I do?"

"How could you ask that at a time like this?" I snap. "If you can save her, I'll give you as much money as you want."

"What would I do with your money?" He scowls. "You think far too little of me."

"What do you want then?"

"I want... I want you to kiss me."

And *I* want to roll my eyes. Why are boys *like* this? First Li Chengyin, then this Gu Jian? But needs must. I grit my teeth and stalk over, seizing him by the shoulders, and press a rough kiss right onto his lips.

But he shoves me away. "Who taught you to do that?"

"What?"

"You only used to kiss my cheek," he says. His face darkens. "Was it Li Chengyin?"

I'm afraid he won't want to save A'du if I argue with him, so I keep my mouth shut, but that makes him more sour.

"Do you let Li Chengyin kiss you?"

Why shouldn't I? He's my husband.

For a single, horrifying instant, I am frightened of Gu Jian, frightened that he'll storm to Li Chengyin's bedchamber and finish the assassin's job. His whole body is wound up tight, and he glares balefully at me.

My temper flares.

"*You're* the one who said you kept me waiting for three whole days," I snap. "*You're* the one who said you didn't show up. It doesn't matter if I remember anything you're claiming, I still married someone else. I can't force you to save

A'du if you don't want to, but if you want me to apologize for marrying Li Chengyin, then I'm telling you that I won't do it. Xiliang girls may not care about that *faithful in death* nonsense that Plains girls are taught, but *he* is my husband. And it doesn't matter what we used to be, because right now? We are nothing."

Gu Jian retreats half a step, and, though there is an angry shine to his eyes, there is an even greater—sorrow? Regret? But I've said what I said, and I've been wanting to say it for a long time. Because whether Li Chengyin is kind to me or not, it's Xiliang I married him for, not myself, and he saved me from the assassin besides. For all of that, I shouldn't be faithless.

"You can go," I sniff haughtily. "I shan't ask for your assistance again."

He gives a sudden, soft smile. "So this is the karma I've wrought."

And then he pulls A'du up and seats himself behind her, pressing a palm to her back. He sits with her until sundown, passing his own energy to her. I guard the door, worried that someone might interrupt, but it's been days since I've had a good night's rest, and I begin to doze—only for short spurts of time though, for I'm jarred awake as soon as my head bumps against the column I'm leaning against. I look up to see that Gu Jian has walked from the room.

"How is she?"

"Alive," he says. "She'll recover."

When I see the color in A'du's cheeks, I let out a breath and turn to Gu Jian, thanking him over and over, but he acts like he doesn't hear, reaching into his lapels to pull out a small jar instead. "Take it. For Li Chengyin's injuries."

Why's he being so nice for a change? I eye him. He sees the hesitation on my face and barks out a laugh. "What, are you afraid I'm going to poison him? Give it back, then."

I snatch the jar away. "I'll thank you when he's better."

He laughs again, devoid of humor. "Don't thank me. I'm not doing this out of the kindness of my heart. I'm doing this because I don't kill the defenseless."

I pull a face. "You're bluffing. Look, when he recovers, I'll buy you a round of drinks, okay?"

Gu Jian doesn't bother to acknowledge this. He's gone in a flutter of sleeves.

Despite what I tell him, I give the little jar to the physicians. They scoop out a little to examine, but no one has any idea what it could be, so they're all too afraid to use it. To tell the truth, I am too, and I spend all day waffling over whether or not to give it to him. Finally, I sneak some when no one's looking and smear it over my own arm.

It's cold, but not much else. And when I wake up and wash it off the next morning, the skin underneath seems normal—if more supple—and I feel more at ease. Masters like Gu Jian always come with a miracle elixir or two, so who knows, maybe it *is* what he claims. Later, when I'm sure no one is watching, I take a smear and dab it onto Li Chengyin's wound.

I don't know if it's the poultice or the physicians' prescriptions, but near sunset on the fourth day, his fever breaks.

Everyone attending to him lets out a breath, so I'm sent

back to my rooms for rest. But I'm not asleep for long when Yongniang rouses me, her face drawn. "It's His Highness," she says. "He's not doing well."

There's a crowd gathered by the time I rush over, and when the physicians see me, they clear a path to his bedside. His face is stark white, his breathing labored, and the laceration is leaking yellow pus. Though the fever is gone, he hasn't woken.

"It's his lung," a physician informs me softly. "It was badly damaged, and the infection has spread to his blood. These next days—they will be dangerous ones."

My first thought is of the poultice, whether I had been wrong about it, but I don't have much of a chance to ponder it too deeply, for the emperor has sent someone to check in, and the physicians are at a loss for what to report.

I, however, am utterly calm. I sit on the footrest next to his bed, folding his cold hands in mine, warming them with my own heat, ignoring the officials who murmur among themselves. When night falls, when the court empties, Yongniang brings me a cloak. I'm leaned against the bed when she arrives, staring unblinkingly at Li Chengyin.

He's so handsome. I've thought that since the first time I saw him. His brows are dark and full, his nose is sloped just so, and his skin glows like Hetian jade. He's not pale and rosy the way pretty girls are—there's a refinement to his complexion, a gentleness that isn't as rough or as rugged as the boys back home. Li Chengyin's looks are like the water here, like the mountains here, like Shangjing itself—mild and pleasant.

I call Yongniang.

"Have someone let Lady Zhao out of her rooms," I say. "She'll come sit with him."

It should be *Miss Zhao* since she's lost her title, but I'm not used to calling her anything but *Lady*. Yongniang furrows her brow.

"I'm afraid . . ." she starts, "I'm afraid that might not be proper. Miss Zhao is confined by order of Her Majesty, and without an order from His Majesty . . ."

I'm rarely angry anymore, but I snap at her now. "He's almost *dead*, Yongniang. Li Chengyin loves Lady Zhao best, so why shouldn't she be allowed to see him? Especially when we know she was framed?"

It's also not proper, but Yongniang is used to me calling Li Chengyin by his given name. What she isn't used to is me ordering her around, so she hesitates. But I glare, and she relents.

Lady Zhao is thinner. She is haggard and has lost the plumpness that made her pretty. Since she's been stripped of her title, she's only allowed to wear plain clothing, so she has extra pathos and is extremely affecting. She lowers herself to her knees to greet me, and I say, "His Highness is badly injured. You should go sit with him."

She snaps her head up to look at me, her eyes red with tears. I don't know why my throat is so tight. "You'd better go in," I manage. "But don't cry."

"Yes, Your Highness," she murmurs, wiping her tears away.

She sits in his chambers for a long time. I can't make out what she says, but I can hear that she wasn't able to contain her tears after all—she wails the entire time, until I'm well and sick of hearing her. I walk outside to sit on the front steps of the court, gazing up at the sky.

It's dark and velvety. A few cold, lonely stars wink against the empty.

I'm in the middle of a wonderful bout of self-pity for how much like an interloper I feel when someone interrupts my thoughts.

"Your Highness."

The chime of his plate armor is clear and resonant, but I don't feel like talking to anyone. But it wouldn't be right to pretend I didn't hear—he *has* saved me more than once. So I force out a smile. "General Pei."

"Night wind is cold, Your Highness. You'd best not sit in its path."

He's right. I pull my cloak higher around my shoulders. "Do you have a wife?"

"N-not yet, my lady." He seems taken aback.

"You Plainsmen care too much about what other people say," I tell him. "In Xiliang, all you'd have to do is shoot down a wild goose and give it to the girl you like. As long as she is willing, even her parents can't stop her from marrying you. General Pei, when you wed, you should find someone you love—otherwise, you're only hurting their heart and your own."

Pei Zhao says nothing in response to this sage advice.

I look up at the stars, and it's hard to stifle a sigh. "I miss home."

It's not that, exactly—it's that I'm upset, and when I'm upset, I miss Xiliang.

Pei Zhao's voice is gentle. "Your Highness, the wind is rising. You should go inside."

"I'm not going back there," I grumble. "Li Chengyin wouldn't want me disturbing him and his Lady Zhao. Let her stay—if he knew she was here, maybe he would heal faster."

So Pei Zhao stops trying to persuade me and retreats a few steps. Bored of conversation, I rest my chin on my palm and let my thoughts wander. Li Chengyin will be happy to hear that Lady Zhao was framed, I think, and once he hears that, he'll want to give her her titles back. And once he gives her her titles back, I'll be the most hated person in the manor again.

At least, I'll be the person *he* hates the most.

I'm frustrated, but I don't know why I should be. I trace the ground with the tip of my shoe. Yongniang approaches.

"Miss Zhao shouldn't stay so long," she murmurs. "It's not proper. I've asked someone to escort her back to her quarters."

I sigh again.

Yongniang seems to understand what I'm thinking. "Don't worry, Your Highness. I was there the whole time. Miss Zhao didn't say anything untoward. She only cried."

I don't care what she says to Li Chengyin. It doesn't *matter* what she says—he'd like her regardless.

Pei Zhao bows, clasping his hands before him. "Your Highness, these are extraordinary times. Please do take care."

I rise lazily. "Fine, fine," I tell him. "I'll go in."

He bows again. I turn toward the door. The winter wind blows past, and I shiver. How did I forget how cold it is? But then I realize Pei Zhao had put himself in the path of the wind, taking the brunt of it.

Surprised, I glance back—and meet his eyes. He probably wasn't expecting it, for he's staring straight at me. He quickly averts his gaze, looking like he's been caught doing something he shouldn't have.

Not that I'm in the mood to think about Pei Zhao's odd behavior, for all the long faces in Li Chengyin's rooms make me sober too. He's still unconscious. The physicians tiptoe around the truth, but I understand the words they don't say: *If he doesn't wake soon, he likely never will.*

I don't know what to do, what to say to make it better. Someone's placed his hands atop the brocaded blanket, but they are deathly white and bloodless. When I smooth my fingers against his, they are freezing.

Too many nights have passed with too little sleep, and I'm bone tired. I sit on the footrest and, not sure why I'm doing it, begin to talk—about anything, about everything. I haven't spoken so many words in a row to him without shouting before.

When had I first seen him?

It must have been on the night of our wedding, when he'd lifted my veil. One moment I'd been suffocating under the heavy cloth, and the next the world burst into a dazzle of candlelight, illuminating the planes of his face, the contours of his body, dressed in richly embroidered black robes.

In the months leading up to the wedding, Yongniang had spent every waking second teaching me a book called *Rites and Rituals*, so I'd know what he was wearing and why—

He'd been in his formal court clothes: a black tunic with a crimson skirt, both adorned with the Nine Ornamentations. Five had been patterned onto the tunic: the adaptable dragon, the steadfast mountains, the tranquil phoenix, the passionate fire, and sacrificial wine cups, a symbol of faithfulness. The remaining four were sewn onto his skirts: the pure pondweed, the bountiful grain, the just axe, and 亞, the ability to distinguish right from wrong.

Beneath, he'd had on a sheer muslin undershirt with dark trim, and over, he'd worn a leather belt with gold clasps above a white waistband with a red border. Atop his head sat a crown with nine strings of white pearl tassel fixed beneath his chin with black silk cord and secured into his hair with a rhinoceros horn pin. His skin was as smooth and lovely as whitest jade, and he looked every inch a royal prince.

I must have fallen for him even then. Even at first sight.

But he hadn't liked me.

Because after lifting the veil, he turned on his heel and left without so much as touching our nuptial wine.

Honestly, I'd been relieved to see him go. I'd never had a stranger in my bed. Instead, Yongniang spent the night with me, afraid I'd be homesick, afraid I'd be angry. She'd made excuses for him, saying he must have caught cold, that he probably didn't want me to catch it either.

Some cold he'd had. It'd lasted three long years.

I'm so lonely here. I've come from thousands of miles away, alone but for A'du—and A'du doesn't speak. If it wasn't for Li Chengyin picking fights, I think I'd be lonelier.

And now he's dying.

I tell him everything. Everything I do and don't remember, because I'm scared that if he dies he won't know what I want him to hear. There's so much I thought I'd forgotten that I remember—all the angry words we've said to each other, how furious I'd been, how I forced myself to pretend not to care because that was the only way I'd win.

I tell him how everyone saw the lovers' knots he gave me, how they all giggled, and how the empress lectured me about them. I don't know why I should tell him any of this. Maybe I'm worried. Maybe I'm terrified of him leaving.

The night is quiet. Distant candlelight casts shadows on the bed curtains. His rooms are so large that everything seems separate from us, retreating into a layer of lacquered night, divided by thick, impenetrable silence. Mine is the sole voice in the dark.

I'm scared of being a widow. Widows have to marry their husbands' brothers in Xiliang—the Princess Mingyuan had been married to my uncle first, before she'd married my lord father. They don't have any customs like that here, but I'll be more miserable than I am already if Li Chengyin dies. I force myself away from this, force myself to say something idle and insignificant.

I don't dislike him as much as I'd believed—not really. We don't have much to argue about, except when he picks a fight about Lady Zhao. We haven't had more than a handful of calm words to say to each other in over three years, but sometimes, it feels strange to *not* argue with him, like when I'm confined to my rooms and forced to copy out books.

As much as I hate it, I have to admit that my writing's gotten better. I've practically memorized *The Woman's Manual* and *The Woman's Guide*, but—a secret I haven't shared with anyone else—I hardly understand a word. When I copy it out, stroke by stroke, it looks like I know what I'm writing. Like the *yin* in *Chengyin*—the first time I saw it written I mistook it for *qin*, like *industriousness*. Of course, I've since learned how to write it, but I haven't figured out what it means.

"Yinzhou..."

"What? What's a yinzhou?" I ask reflexively.

"The founder of the kingdom . . . his holdings were in Yinzhou. East of Zhongzhou . . . south of Liangzhou . . . the place where the dragon was born . . . so I am the successor of the legacy of Yin."

My mouth falls open. His breath is shallow and his voice is soft, but the words are clear and he looks sensible, though he struggles to keep his eyes open. I freeze—and then I scream.

Everyone descends upon the room. The attending physician pushes ahead of everyone else, yelling, "What's happened? How is he?"

I point. "He—he—he—"

The *he* in question is staring at me, expressionless.

The physician bursts into tears. "His Highness is awake! His Highness is—go, someone go tell the emperor!"

And then the court bursts into action. Everyone bustles, for the physician has said that as long as Li Chengyin can wake up, he should make a full recovery. The Ministry of Imperial Physicians are beside themselves with joy, big bright smiles beaming from their faces as they take his pulse, and measure out new prescriptions, and buzz back and forth like bees. The attendants look like they're about to celebrate the New Year and spread the news wherever they go.

I'm not sure when I doze off, though I do remember the lull of the physicians' voices droning on and on . . . but when I wake, I'm sprawled out across Li Chengyin's bedside, a blanket laid over my shoulders. My leg is stiff and my joints crack every time I try to move. But I slept well and I slept deeply, and I've left a splotch of drool on Li Chengyin's sleeve—his—sleeve? I must have slept on his arm all night.

The room is empty except for us, and he is looking at me, eyes full of amusement.

It's that expression that convinces me he is going to be fine. With some effort, I get my stiff leg back under me, but it's no use—I can't put any weight on it, so I'm not going anywhere anytime soon. And my back . . . my back is as sore as if someone had run over it with a carriage all night. I'm never, ever sleeping in that position again.

Using the edge of his bed, I make one last effort to push myself to my feet but can only limp a few steps forward on my good leg, not sure if I should call someone over or if I should wait for the numbness to subside on its own. I haven't had a chance to make up my mind yet when Li Chengyin speaks.

"Where are you going?"

"Back to my own court to get some rest," I say, but my tongue's gone numb too, and I almost bite it.

"Who told you to spend the night here?" he laughs. "I couldn't even wake you this morning. Pigs are more selective about where they sleep, did you know that?"

I resist the urge to roll my eyes at him. Of *course* the first thing he does is antagonize me.

He pats the bed next to him.

"What?"

"Didn't you say you wanted to rest? The bed's big enough for the both of us."

He's not wrong. The bed's big enough to fit most people's entire bedchambers, much less two measly people. But that's not the point. The point is—"You want me to sleep with you?"

He sniffs. "It's not like you haven't before."

That's not wrong, either.

And I *am* tired.

So I climb on. Li Chengyin offers me half of his blanket, but I'm scared of jostling him, so I grab the one I'd been sleeping under and crawl beneath it.

The next thing I'm aware of is Yongniang's voice calling me softly. I rouse, pulling my cloak silently over my shoulders to join her outside. She tells me that the empress's deposition has been made public at last, but that the grand-empress has stepped up to keep the inner courts calm.

Alongside the deposition comes another edict—this one reinstating Lady Zhao.

Li Chengyin is fast asleep, his face pale and bloodless. He's lost so much weight that his eyes look bruised.

"Have someone summon her to attend to the prince," I tell Yongniang. The place next to him hasn't been mine to claim, and I've occupied it for far too long.

I leave without waiting for her reply, calling for a palanquin to bring me back to my own rooms. The tiredness has dissipated by the time I return, and I pause to appraise myself in the looking glass. If I were prettier, would he like me more?

Not that I would admit to it, but I *do* care if he likes me. I *want* him to like me. Because as he was hovering dangerously close to death, I came to an important realization. I love Li Chengyin.

But Li Chengyin loves Zhao Sese.

And it is agony.

I don't want to eat. I don't want to sleep. I just sit there, all day, staring at nothing.

Lady Zhao's moved back to her old rooms. The grandempress sends her a veritable army of bequests in apology, and with her father's recent promotion, there are more people than ever who want to get on her good side, so her courtyard bustles with activity. When I pass by, I can sometimes hear laughter, and music, and song.

Li Chengyin's recovered too. I know because, though I haven't seen him, I once heard the sound of his laughter wafting from her rooms.

He sounded so happy.

Two things happen the day of the blizzard.

First, we hear from the palace that the emperor has betrothed Pei Zhao to Princess Luoxi. Then, we get news that Miss Xu is coming to the manor.

Pei Zhao comes from a good family. His mother is the emperor's sister, which makes him Li Chengyin's cousin, so Yongniang tells me, "General Pei was born to be a prince consort."

This is a Central Plains custom, cousin marriage.

I'm unexpectedly disappointed. Once he becomes a prince consort, I doubt he'll stay the head of the Yulin Guard for long, and once he gets promoted out of the Court of Spring, I might not meet with him again. I can't see Li Chengyin, and now I won't see Pei Zhao, either.

Yongniang prepares a courtyard in the west of the manor for Miss Xu. She claims it'll be a good place for Miss Xu to rest, because it's quiet, but I think she's been put there because the rooms are far from Li Chengyin's.

"Lady Zhao will be on the rampage, so you'd best avoid her if you can, Your Highness," Yongniang advises.

I feel trapped.

Thankfully, A'du's more or less recovered too, so we slip out of the manor again.

After two months of us being cooped up inside, the air is much colder and there is snow fresh on the ground, but because it's almost the New Year, the streets bustle. There are people everywhere, and merchants are calling out from their stalls—some sell snow willows, others red streamers, street food, picture scrolls. Acrobats and puppeteers, tightrope walkers and people setting off firecrackers clog the avenue. I love the city when it's so noisy, and I often drag A'du through the throng, wandering from stall to stall.

Not today, though. Today, I can't summon the interest, so I decide to bring A'du to Miluo's tavern, which is as busy as always. From afar I can hear the chime of Miluo's laughter, as clear and crisp as a bell.

When I duck below the bamboo awning, I realize that the person she's laughing with is Pei Zhao.

I'm taken aback. This isn't the sort of place I would have expected to find the dutiful General Pei, and I don't know what to say. He's surprised too—it's probably not the place you'd think to find a princess consort, either. He's in his civilian clothes, so I greet him with a "Master Pei."

He responds in kind. "Master Liang."

Every other table is full, so I wave A'du over to sit with him and order two tankards of wine.

How did that line go? *The wine washes away melancholy.*

I don't have much melancholy to wash away—just my own boredom and listlessness—so my spirits perk up after a few cups. I pluck a pair of chopsticks from their canister and drum them against the cup, humming a folk song from Xiliang:

> *O, there is a fox,*
> *He sits upon the dune.*
> *Sits upon the dune,*
> *Watching the moon.*
>
> *No, not watching the moon—*
> *He's waiting for the shepherd girl*
> *To come back.*
>
> *O, there is a fox,*
> *He sits upon the dune.*
> *Sits upon the dune,*
> *Soaking in the sun.*

> *No, not soaking in the sun—*
> *He's waiting for the horseback girl*
> *To ride past.*

A few people clap, but it doesn't cheer me any. I sigh, tipping back another cup and turning my attention to the lamb. A'du tugs at my tunic, telling me not to drink so much, but I ignore her. I'm about to dig in again when I hear the rasp of a flute. It's Pei Zhao.

A'du must have handed her reed flute to him at some point, and he's lost in his playing. The tune is melodious and sweet, and I prop my chin up on my hands, listening. It's the melody of the song I'd been singing. His playing is jerky, but he does hit most of the notes, and once he's fumbled through it once, it flows much easier the second time. It's supposed to be a funny song, but for some reason all I hear is sorrow.

He sighs too and puts the flute away.

I down another cup of wine. "Can you do me a favor?" I ask.

Pei Zhao is as courteous as ever. "Of course."

"Can you sneak me into Vermillion Tower? I haven't been up there."

He looks uncomfortable. "Forget it," I mutter. "Pretend I didn't ask."

But he surprises me. "I can't sneak you into the tower, but there are other ways. Though I fear that it might be . . . unsuitable, Master Liang, as you will need to disguise yourself as my attendant."

My eyes brighten. "That's all?"

So A'du and I do just that and follow General Pei brazenly to the tower gate.

Vermillion Tower is the highest point in Shangjing—higher than the Jeweled Pavilion in the imperial city. Because it's the city's south gate, it's heavily guarded—every three steps a guard, every five steps a sentry. But Pei Zhao only needs to show them his seal to be allowed up.

Because the guards are concentrated at the bottom of the tower, there's no one patrolling the very top. At this height, the wind is sharper than a knife, but I can see the gridded streets ablaze with light. The buildings in the east and west markets look like they're made of crystal, scintillating and refractive.

And then, farther in the distance, the shadow of the imperial city grazes the distant skyline, an ocean of ceramic roof tiles disappearing dimly into the horizon.

Pei Zhao points. "There's the Court of Spring."

Truth be told, it doesn't matter to me where the manor is. I stretch to my tiptoes, casting my gaze beyond the city walls, but no matter how high up I am, I can't see Xiliang.

I lean up and over the battlements, raising my face to the wind. "Do you ever miss home?" I ask.

Pei Zhao considers his words. "I was born and raised here," he says carefully, "and I've never left the capital for long, so no, I don't miss it."

I deflate. Maybe I *am* childish. I glance at him, somewhat embarrassed. He's standing on the opposite end of the tower, his robes flapping in the high winds, his face recessed in the shadow of what few lanterns swing up here, expression utterly unreadable.

"Play something for me," I say.

A'du offers the flute to him, and slowly, he plays—it's the same song I'd sung in the tavern. I rest on the parapets and hum along: "O, there is a fox, he sits upon the dune . . ."

But I know the fox isn't waiting for any girl. He's homesick.

I'm not sure how long it is until I stop humming, but the sound of the flute stays with me for a while. The familiar tune eases me, and though we sit in the cold, a small sliver of warmth thaws my heart. It's the sound of Xiliang, the breath of Xiliang, the one morsel of love I feel in this entire city.

A blanket of yellow clouds presses low on the city. The moon and the stars are nowhere to be found, just the wind, the cold wind, the whistling wind, which scrapes me raw. I snuggle, yawning, into A'du. Ice pricks at my face. I look up, startled. *Snow.*

The flurry drifts lazily from the heavens. The wind calms, and the only thing left in all the world is the fall of white flakes, unending and impenetrable. They blossom like crystalline flowers, scattering through the air. It snows like the sky has broken, billowing ceaseless flakes down in every direction. The lanterns flicker valiantly against the dark, but the snow is a heavy curtain that buries all. Pei Zhao puts the flute away, fighting a cough—he must have been playing this whole time. What a silly boy—just because I didn't say stop doesn't mean he had to keep playing.

"It's snowing, my lady," he says. "I should take you back."

A flake has caught in his lashes. He blinks and it's gone.

"I'm not going back," I inform him.

"Your Highness—"

"Don't call me that."

"Yes, my lady."

I glare, annoyed, and change the topic. "Do you love Princess Luoxi?"

He looks away.

I pat him consolingly on the shoulder. "I figured as much. I didn't think you'd be forced to marry someone you didn't love, too. You Plains boys have such sad lives, not that I'm in any position to pity you. If even a crown prince can't marry who he wants, why should you?"

I've never been the most eloquent, and I think I must have made him uncomfortable, for he says, placidly, "Of course."

"Don't feel bad!" I say. "I'll treat you to a round of drinks with some pretty girls for company, how's that?"

Pei Zhao chokes on something and coughs.

"There's a girl at Mingyu Lane who likes me very much," I proclaim, in the spirit of generous sharing. "You'd be lucky to go with me!"

"Your Highness—"

"Don't call me that!" I tug his sleeve. "Come on."

Madame Wang's face splits like a ripe melon when she sees me, and she comes up to welcome us. "Master Liang, how lovely to see you again!" she says, pulling me forward. Pei Zhao clearly didn't expect me to be a regular in a place like this, and he's taken aback. "Girls, Master Liang is here!"

Madame Wang is a plump and genial woman, but her voice is piercing. In no time at all, Mingyu Lane comes to life as a crowd of colorfully dressed girls flutters down the stairs, calling, "Has Master Liang come?" and "Master Liang, you haven't visited in *so long*," and "Master Liang, we thought you'd forgotten us!"

I'm swept into their flock.

"Nothing like that." I laugh, trying to explain myself. "In fact, I was passing by—"

"*Hmph!* Yueniang was saying the other day that if you didn't come soon, we'd drink that nice wine we kept for you ourselves, didn't she, girls?"

"That's right! *And* the snow we buried under the plum tree—she was keeping it to boil for your tea!"

"Oh! It's snowing today; why don't we use that to warm the wine?"

"Yes, yes!"

I'm dizzy from their chattering. "Speaking of Yueniang, where is she? I don't see her."

"Yueniang's sick!"

"Sick?" I'm surprised.

"That's right! *Lovesick!*"

"Lovesick?" I repeat.

"The day before last"—this in a hushed, excited whisper—"someone *important* came to take some tea and listen to us play music. And then—when he left—Yueniang started *longing for* him!"

"What kind of person could make *her* sick with longing?" I wonder.

"Well, he looked like he was from some nice scholarly family. He was handsome—"

"—and well-spoken!"

"—and dignified!"

So Yueniang has no chance with him. I must have sat through hundreds of stories in the teahouses, and all the people who get secretly engaged are wealthy young masters and well-bred misses, not the girls who sell their own company for a living. And Yueniang is the most sought-after girl here. The soldiers who have surrendered to her colored skirts are too many to count—how can she be careless enough to lose her heart?

Yueniang and I are bosom friends, so I bound up the stairs to visit her in her room. She hasn't yet gone to bed, but she's leaning weakly against the brazier, cradling her cheek in a hand, gazing at the red candles on her vanity.

"Shiwu!" I call her by her pet name.

She looks up when she sees me but doesn't look any livelier for my troubles. "You've come?"

I look her up and down. "You haven't really fallen in love?"

"Silly girl," she sighs. "You wouldn't understand."

"But *you* were the one who told me that a girl can't fill her stomach on a man's beauty," I remind her.

"He's not simply beautiful," she protests. "He's well-spoken and a gentleman." Yueniang clasps her hands dazedly. "Heaven willing, I'll see him again."

"And what if he's a girl pretending to be a boy?" I can't resist cutting in. "You said you knew me to be a girl because I treated you like a gentleman."

Yueniang brushes this off. "He couldn't possibly," she says. "Not from his manner."

"But . . ." I lower my voice. "But I brought *Pei Zhao* with me today. Didn't you say you wanted to avenge your family?

Why don't you seduce him and make him do it for you? His a'die has a whole army, and he's the Jinwu General. There are not many people more powerful than the Pei."

But Yueniang shakes her head. "It's no use," she says. "Gao Yuming is the most powerful person in this city. He's been prime minister for more than two decades, and he has allies all over court. Even the Pei won't be able to take him down—especially not when the Lady Gao is going to be named empress soon."

"Lady Gao?"

"That's what all the girls are saying—that the emperor deposed Empress Zhang to make way for Lady Gao."

I'm a failure of a princess, I am. I'd had no idea who the popular candidates for the next empress were. I've seen Lady Gao twice—both times when I was visiting Empress Zhang. I try very, very hard to recall, but I have no idea what she looks like.

"If you could just meet with the emperor," I muse. "Then you could ask him to open the case yourself."

Yueniang's family used to be ministers at court, but Gao Yuming framed them for some crime and had her whole family put to death. She'd been six or so at the time—lucky enough to have escaped in the fray, but not lucky enough to escape being sold into indenture.

All these years, all she's wanted is revenge.

Yueniang sighs softly. "I doubt it would make a difference. And anyway, I don't care if I see the emperor or not—the only person I want to see is *him*. . . ."

She's gone mad with love, she really has. I leave her to

bring Pei Zhao upstairs. There are braziers lit everywhere, so the second I open Yueniang's doors, the warmth washes over us and we're pulled inside by a gaggle of girls.

I shoo them all away because Pei Zhao looks awkward and uncomfortable in their presence. Yueniang accompanies us as we drink. It's been a long night, and I'm hungry, and the chefs at Mingyu Lane are famous across the city, so we order a meal. I feast until I'm full, until I've eaten away the strange misery that had overtaken me atop the gate tower.

Yueniang holds her pipa, plucking lazily at the strings as she hums a soft tune.

> *No one knows what longing is*
> *Until they long and feel its ache;*
> *No one knows what longing is*
> *Until their body is a wisp of a cloud,*
> *Their heart is a sliver of willow,*
> *Their breath a strand of gossamer about to break.*[1]

Her voice is the thing that sounds like a strand of gossamer about to break.

I look at Pei Zhao. "Aren't you going to eat?"

"I'm not hungry," he says.

He's made some great strides forward, I think—at least he doesn't call me *young master* this time. I point at him with

---

[1] Adapted from "To the Tune of Moon Palace: Thoughts of Spring" by Xu Zaisi.

my chopsticks. "You should try the fish, at least—they flavor it with spices all the way from Bosi, it's the best in Shangjing. You're sure you don't want any?"

I push the plate toward him, and he has a few bites.

"That girl earlier . . . is she a descendant of the Chen family?" Pei Zhao asks as we walk back to the manor.

I nod and tell him her story, careful to describe it as pitiably as I can. Whether or not Yueniang thinks he can help, he is a Pei. But when we're within sight of the manor walls, Pei Zhao stops and turns.

"Your Highness," he starts, "I don't know if it's my place to say this, but . . ."

"Spit it out." I hate how people dance around things here.

He takes a moment to gather his thoughts. "Your Highness, I'm sure your heart is in the right place, but His Highness is next in line for the throne, and it's not safe for either of you to misstep. It could make things—difficult—for him if you keep associating with people in Miss Yueniang's position, and I think, perhaps, it would be best to avoid her in the future."

"I won't stop seeing her because you tell me to," I snap. I'm more annoyed with him than I've ever been. "I know you noblemen like to look down on people, but I'm not like you. I don't make friends just because people are powerful and influential. I'm sorry I tarnished the virtuous General Pei's name by making him consort with *fallen women*, but you needn't worry—I have no intention of bringing you with me anymore, so you can go off and be your prince consort without worrying about ruining your reputation."

And then I ignore him all the way back to the manor. The

tromp of our horses' hooves is the only sound that breaks the silence. The manor is on a main road—a king's road—so it's paved with wide slabs of stone, slick with still-falling snow, and the going is slow.

I didn't know then how many things were going to change.

Because it's almost the New Year and we are short a queen, much of the holiday planning falls to me. I have to arrange the palace ladies' audiences with the emperor and organize the feasts because though Lady Gao is now the highest-ranking woman in the palace, she is a consort, not a wife, and isn't entitled to do anything more official than oversee the inner court. Yongniang tells me, though, that people are wondering if the emperor will let her host the New Year's Day liturgies.

"Will she be the new empress, then?" I ask.

"I should not speculate," Yongniang says. She's too careful to speak out of turn about something like this, and she warns me also. "It would be best if you didn't comment on it either, my lady. It's not the kind of thing a daughter-in-law should ask."

Not that I have time to gossip about the next queen anyway—there's plenty to occupy my time closer to home: Lady Zhao is docking Miss Xu's annual stipend.

Miss Xu comes to me in tears. She's not the type to make a fuss, but her attendants hadn't been as easy to bully as their mistress. When they complained, though, Lady Zhao's attendants accused them of stealing from the coffers and demanded that they be expelled from the manor. I do my best to comfort her, but they are dismissed anyway, and all I can do is ask Yongniang to find new girls to look after her.

And then we get news that the grand-empress has taken ill. It's nothing serious—just a cold—but as she's in her seventies, everyone holds their breath for her recovery, and I am summoned daily to attend to her.

Lastly, Li Chengyin twists his ankle playing polo. He's not badly hurt, and he can walk fine, but because he got himself injured again so soon after the attempted assassination, the emperor orders him to the palace in a rage, furious at his carelessness.

I'm not sure what happened after, but I do know that once he came back, Lady Zhao said something to anger Li Chengyin, and the rumor is that he struck her.

It's their worst argument yet. Lady Zhao won't stop crying, and it takes the combined efforts of all their attendants to talk them down, but Li Chengyin's temper being what it is, he's shut himself in his own rooms and refuses to visit hers.

Yongniang urges me again and again to see him. I know what she wants me to do, but pay it no mind.

In the end, he's the one who comes to see me.

Because it snowed earlier, the night is freezing, but we light so many braziers that my entire court is drowsy from warmth. By the time Li Chengyin arrives, I'm sound asleep.

He's brought only a single attendant, so if it wasn't for A'du rousing me, I don't think I would have noticed him. She shakes me awake, and when I see him, I have to rub the bleariness from my eyes for a clearer look.

"What are you doing here?"

"Sleeping!" He's ill-tempered and seats himself on the edge of my bed so that the attendant can pull off his boots and overrobe before being dismissed with a wave of the hand. A'du's slipped off somewhere too.

I nod and yawn, snuggling myself back into bed, and if Li Chengyin hadn't tugged at the blanket, I probably wouldn't have woken again.

Groggily, I offer him half of my blanket, and he crawls in next to me. I don't know who helped him undress the rest of the way, but he's wearing thin silk underclothes. Boys must run hot, because he's nice and toasty, especially when he slips an arm beneath my neck to draw me toward him. It's pleasant, but something nags at me.

"Can you stop breathing down my neck?"

His answer is a kiss pressed to my nape.

I squirm away. "Stop it," I tell him. "I can't sleep."

He says nothing, moving up instead to nip at my earlobe. It tickles, and I start to giggle, and when I giggle I slacken against him—until a tug at my waistband wakes me up.

"What are you doing?" I mumble.

He leans forward to press his mouth to mine. Suddenly I realize what he wants—and shove him away with a shriek. Li Chengyin very nearly tumbles off the bed—he's tangled in the canopy and has to twist free. He glares at me. "What was that for?"

"You—you—go find your Lady Zhao if you want to do *that*!"

It doesn't matter if I love him, I won't be *her* stand-in.

Li Chengyin chuckles. "Are you . . . jealous?"

"Jealous of who?" I roll my eyes. "Stop lying on yourself."

"Lying *to* yourself," he corrects.

"So you admit it? That you're lying?" I force out a laugh. "Go find your Lady Zhao and your Miss Xu. I bet they're in their rooms, *yearning* for you."

"And you don't? *Yearn* for me?"

"I already have someone I like!" I say as my heart gives a sour little twist. Because the person I like doesn't like me, and instead of being sweet and pleasant and winning him over, all I know how to do is make myself thornier and more contrary. "I wouldn't care if you brought *dozens* of other women back to the manor. You can do what you want."

A shadow crosses his face. I haven't seen him look this way, not even when I used to provoke him by bringing up Lady Zhao.

"Don't think I don't know this is about Pei Zhao," he says, none too pleasant.

I gape at him.

"Don't forget," he huffs, "you *have* a husband. Just because your Xiliang doesn't have shame enough to care that their princess is embarrassing them by sneaking out and dallying with him all day—"

"So what if I sneak out?" I snap, chagrined. I didn't know he was aware of how often I slip into the city, nor has it occurred to me that he might find out about my drinking with Pei Zhao. "So what if I go drinking sometimes? You have one consort after another, and it's not like I've done anything untoward—"

Li Chengyin surprises me by laughing. "I doubt he has the

nerve! He's about to marry my sister, and our Plains princesses aren't like you Xiliang girls—"

I go to slap him, but he ducks away and I catch him on the chin. "What's wrong with Xiliang girls?" I'm shaking. "You bring all *kinds* of women into the manor, and have I *ever* said anything? Pei Zhao and I have only drunk together a few times—what gives you the right to lecture me? Just because your family is more powerful than mine—do you think my a'die would have sent me so far from home if your father didn't force him into a marriage treaty? Do you think I *wanted* to be your wife? Any Xiliang boy is worth *ten* of you, and the person I like—the person I like is a hundred, a thousand times better than you. You aren't worth a single strand of his hair!"

And then the person I like really does get angry, pushing himself off my bed and storming over to the chamber door without so much as putting on his overrobe. "Don't worry," he says, turning back to look at me. "I won't disturb you again. You can go dream about your true love in peace!"

He stalks out, barefoot, into the ice and snow.

I pull the blanket up over my head and groan. Knowing that I picked the fight on purpose doesn't make it feel any better. I'm not so bighearted, not so giving that I'd bed him when I know he'd rather be with Lady Zhao. I'd rather he keep ignoring me.

Girls are the saddest, sorriest, most pitiable creatures on earth. I think so, anyway. It took so little for me to fall in love. It's a good thing he's not kinder, because then maybe I'd never be able to leave his side. I'd be like one of the girls from

Yongniang's stories, mooning after him day and night, pining for him to look my way.

And I certainly don't want to be reduced to that.

It's late by the time Yongniang rouses me. She dresses me quickly, and we rush into the palace to visit the grand-empress. She's recovering well, and her spirits are high when she greets me, ordering someone to go fix up a bowl of the same porridge she's eating.

I don't know what's in the porridge, but it tastes odd. My stomach turns when I force down a few bites.

Yongniang sees my face and rushes over with a cup of tea. My stomach is cramping so badly that the tea is unappetizing, and I murmur to Yongniang, "I think I might throw up."

The grand-empress's ears perk. "You want to throw up?"

And then a crowd of attendants is surrounding me, holding rinse basins and pitchers of clear water and kerchiefs, rubbing my neck and lighting incense to settle my stomach. But the empress uses ambergris, which I don't like, so when the smoke hits my nose, I retch again, bringing up nothing but bile. Yongniang comes over with flower-infused water for me to rinse with.

The grand-empress looks worried and has someone fetch a physician.

"No—" I start. I must have caught cold yesterday—I hadn't been able to go back to sleep for a long time after Li Chengyin left. I sat up all night without a blanket, and then I woke with a stomachache. "It's something I ate."

"The physician can tell us when he comes," the grand-empress says cheerily. "It'll be good news, I'm sure of it.

Come, there's no need to be shy—flowers will bloom and trees will bear fruit, it's the most natural thing in the world! We should let the Bureau of Astromancy know so they'll have plenty of time to calculate what name would be best. . . ."

I want to sink into the earth and perish. The grand-empress obviously thinks she's about to have a great-great-grandchild, but I haven't done anything to give her one.

After a thorough exam, the physician tells her roughly the same—that it's nothing more than a cold, combined with the venison porridge, that's unsettled my stomach. The grand-empress sulks.

"Where's the crown prince?" She poses this question to the room.

"Fasting, Your Highness," is the answer.

This does not please the grand-empress at all. "What's he fasting for? Doesn't he know that his duty is to continue the family line? He's almost twenty—at his age, his father had *three* sons, and he hasn't had *one*! That Zhao girl is always mincing after him and hasn't laid so much as an egg, and Miss Xu—well. Does he not want me to hold great-great-grandbabies? Does he want to drive me to my grave?"

The whole roomful of people sink to their knees at this, but the more they try to wheedle her down the more she works herself up. "Summon me Li Chengyin! If he's any use at all he'll give me a baby to hold by this time next year."

The grand-empress is the one other person I know who calls Li Chengyin by his name instead of his title. But she's calling him here to yell at him, which means he'll probably think I've said something to her, which means he'll probably argue with me again, which means—well, it doesn't matter what it means, because I'm happy to fight if he picks one. Who's afraid of him?

But the grand-empress is more devious than I gave her credit for, because she doesn't raise her voice at all when he enters. In fact, she smiles, all benevolence. "You've washed and gone to make your offerings?"

These are the things you do in preparation for going to the south of the imperial city to take fast. Li Chengyin, not knowing what happened, answers her truthfully. "I have."

"Good, good," the grand-empress says. "Well, you're in luck today, because there's no need to worry about all of that anymore; the ancestors don't care about that nonsense anyway." And then she addresses the room: "Take the crown prince and princess to Qingyun Court, and don't open the doors until I say otherwise!"

Before I can protest, we're dragged out to Qingyun Court by a hive of attendants, who throw us in and slam the door behind us. I bang on the wood, trying to force it open, but it doesn't budge.

Li Chengyin glares at me, and I glare back.

He grits out a single word: "You!"

"How is this *my* fault?" I snap.

"Would we be stuck here if you didn't go tattling to the grand-empress?"

I turn away with a huff and storm over to the table to drop onto a cushion. It's thankfully warm, and I pick at my fingers, which is at least better entertainment than dealing with him.

We're left alone for half the day. Once the sky darkens, a

servant comes with dinner and tea, which she passes through the window. I open my mouth, but she slams the window shut too quickly for me to get a word out. The grand-empress's orders, I'm sure.

I frown down at the tray, but there's no use in starving when there's food on the table. The grand-empress has sent some of my favorite dishes, so I scoop half the rice into my own bowl and eat while Li Chengyin sits on the other side of the room, unmoved. He gets hungry eventually though, and the soup that accompanies our meal is his favorite, so he walks over to the table and eats his dinner, docile.

I pace around until I'm bored enough to pick a few pebbles from the potted miniature in the outer rooms and play chess against myself. It's diverting enough for a while—but then the braziers start burning out, one after the next.

Thankfully, the fires in the inner quarters are burning, so I move myself over to the bed to continue the game—until the candles burn out.

Remembering that there are candles in the outer chambers, I shiver through the cold to venture outside, clutching a blanket tightly to me. Li Chengyin's sitting where I left him. I *want* to mind my business, but it slips out: "Aren't you cold?"

He doesn't look at me. "No."

Then why does his voice shake?

One hand around my blanket and the other around a candle, I creep closer to him. When the light catches on his face, I have to stifle a gasp.

Despite the freezing winter air, his forehead is covered in a sheen of sweat, and his face is bright red.

"Is it the fever again?" I ask.

"No."

But he's shivering. I place the candle carefully back onto the table and press the back of my hand to his forehead. If he really is sick, the grand-empress will *have* to let us out.

He groans when I touch him and then tugs me into his lap. His lips are burning against my mouth, his breath short against my cheek as he kisses me so thoroughly that I gasp for air. And then he pushes me away from him, panting. His voice is strangled. "There was something in the soup."

Something in the soup? Poison?

But no, Li Chengyin is his great-grandmother's darling. She wouldn't feed him anything untoward.

The bowl is on the table, so I scoot over to sniff at it, but it smells—like soup.

He envelopes me from behind, pressing fluttery little kisses to my ear. "*Xiaofeng* . . ."

Maybe because he's kissing me or maybe because he's calling me by my name, my knees go weak and I sink back against him.

Li Chengyin has never called me by my name. I hadn't known he knew it.

He cups my face and turns me to him to continue his assault on my lips, holding me so close, it's like he wants to consume me. He's roiling hot beneath my hands, like a cauldron of bubbling water.

And it hits me at once what was in his soup.

Grand-empress—!

An elder! Should have! More *dignity*—!

He starts working at my waistband, his mouth never once leaving mine as he pulls me to the bed. I try to push him off, but he's much stronger than I am, and I'm hit with a wave of sadness—if he doesn't stop now he'll regret it when he wakes up tomorrow. If his Lady Zhao finds out, she will cause such a row, and then I really will be the most pathetic crown princess on this earth.

Once he's done with my clothing, Li Chengyin starts tugging off his own. I have a tough time getting out of male robes, but he makes short work of it, and then I'm face-to-face with his bare chest. I haven't seen him beneath all those layers before.

His smile is a wicked thing. "Like what you see?"

"You're a bully and a brute," I proclaim, sticking a finger to his chest. "What's there to see? Don't think—don't think I haven't seen it all! I may not have eaten pork but I *have* seen pigs run!"

He doesn't bother arguing with me. He leans in, his lips by my ear as he murmurs, "Then . . . would you like a taste?"

I suck in a sharp breath.

"But Sese," I remind him.

Someone should present me with an official acknowledgment of my strong-mindedness.

"What Sese?"

"*Your* Sese!" I grab his arm. "Think of your Lady Zhao—you can't betray her! She's the one you love, remember?"

"*You're* my wife. *You're* the person I married. How am I betraying her?"

"But you don't like me."

"But I do." His voice is patient and insistent. "I like you."

"Only because you had a philter."

"I'd like you even if I hadn't, Xiaofeng. I like you so much."

Men are beasts and this proves it. A little supplement in his stew and he's gone puppy eyed, all thoughts of his Lady Zhao tossed to the back of his mind.

I shake his arm, trying to rouse him. "You're the crown prince. You're the heir presumptive. You're supposed to be stronger than other people. You have to be calm, and resolute, and you can't—can't—something step and a lifetime of regret!"

"*One false step will lead to a lifetime of regret*," he corrects.

"Yes, that, so you have to resist. For Lady Zhao's sake you have to defend your chastity—"

"I don't want to be chaste!" He's pouting. He's *pouting*. "You're so cold-blooded, so heartless, so cruel!"

"H—?" I rub at the gooseflesh that prickles my arms. "How am I cold-blooded? How am I heartless? How am I cruel?"

"How are you not cold-blooded? How are you not heartless? How are you not cruel?"

"Show me where," I retort.

"Here," he says, and darts forward to kiss me. "And here. And here."

Heat floods into my cheeks.

The arrow is on the bow, waiting for the archer to loose.

But I grit my teeth. I am resolved. This is for his own good. I fumble for a porcelain pillow and bring it down with a mighty thunk. He doesn't see it coming at all and slumps, unconscious.

He ends up with a massive knot on his head. For lack of better options, I press the porcelain against it, a trick Yongniang taught me the last time I bumped my head against a door. But it's there when he wakes up in the morning and turns to me, annoyed. "Why did you tie me up?"

"It's for your own good, so you'd better learn to bear it," I tell him, patting his cheek comfortingly. "Do you need to flip over? I can help you."

He's probably stiff from being tied up all night, but because his arms and legs are secured with the curtain tethers, it's hard to turn him. I push and push to little effect, though apparently, it takes no effort at all to upend myself when I slip, falling on top of him, my hair hooked to the tethers.

"Can you not climb all over me?" Li Chengyin says, casting me a glance.

"Sorry," I say. I tug at my hair, trying to untangle it, but my predicament seems to be no hindrance at all to him—he kisses my shoulder, then my neck. The feel of it is intoxicating, raising an unfamiliar flutter in the pit of my stomach.

"Untie me," he murmurs. "I promise I'll be good."

"Only a fool would believe you," I inform him. We've been at each other for years. I might not be a genius, but it doesn't take one to figure out what he's trying to do. I untangle my hair and push myself off him, shooting him a dirty look. "Stay put!"

"I think—"

"Don't think."

"I want—"

"Stop wanting!"

"Will you listen?" he snaps. "I need to use the privy. You have to let me go for that, don't you?"

I think back to last time, when I was trapped in his rooms, in bad need of a chamber pot, and how I'd almost been driven to tears by it.

So I unfasten him.

He's just returned when the doors slam open and a squadron of attendants descends upon us, their faces pink when they catch sight of our clothes strewn all about the floor, looking askance at Li Chengyin when they see the bump on his head.

They've brought water to wash with and a fresh change of clothes, but like a thunderclap, they are gone again, locking the door behind them, before we realize what happened.

I stare after them, stunned. Do they mean to make us spend another night here?

Li Chengyin's discovered more philter in our food. "Great-grandmother," he calls out the window, "are you trying to murder me?"

If she doesn't want us to eat, then fine. I won't eat.

Li Chengyin doesn't touch the food either. He must love Lady Zhao very much, I think, to go hungry in order to stop himself from repeating last night's mistake. The two of us retreat to the bed, the warmest place in the court, accompanied by our gurgling bellies. The grand-empress is more ruthless than I'd given her credit for—she hasn't so much as changed out the braziers.

The hours crawl by. Without anything better to do, we start playing chess, but he grows bored of winning all the time and gives it up, declaring that it's not fun to keep besting me. By the time noon rolls around, when I'm so hungry I hardly have the energy to speak, he tugs at my arm. "Sing me something."

"Why should I?"

"Because if you don't . . ." Li Chengyin pushes himself up on one arm and makes like he's getting off the bed. "If you don't, I think I might go see how the food tastes."

"I'll do it, I'll do it!" I pull him back. But, not knowing all that many songs, I hum the only one that comes to mind: "O, there is a fox . . ."

He says I'm not a good singer, so after I finish the song twice he makes me stop. The two of us flop back onto the bed, staring up at the canopy. And then we start to talk.

Some strange alchemy of boredom and cold and hunger has given us something to say to each other for the first time in three long years. Li Chengyin tells me how the Court of Spring was given its name, tells me of having once been a naughty child who snuck up behind his uncle Pei and yanked the old man's beard. I learn that his favorite nursemaid passed away last year, and he mourned her for a long time after. That he once got into a fistfight with the Prince of Zhong's son.

He passes on palace gossip, too—things I hadn't had a chance to hear, like how his brother, the Prince of Chu, actually likes boys, and why his sister the Princess Yongning is forever begging to be sent to a nunnery.

I tell him about the things I've seen in the streets of Shangjing, things from outside the palace and the royal court that even he doesn't know about. He listens eagerly, gasping when I need him to gasp and laughing when I say something funny.

Then he suddenly asks, "Where exactly have you seen pigs run?"

"What?"

"You said you may not have eaten pork, but you've seen pigs run. Where have you seen pigs run?" His face looks sour.

"Oh!" I sit up excitedly to tell him about Mingyu Lane, my hands dancing as I describe its aura—ethereal—and its girls—spritely—who know everything from music to song to poetry—

"So you often visit brothels?"

"Not brothels," I correct him, "Mingyu Lane."

"The princess of a kingdom, a model of her people, going to a *brothel*!"

Heavens above, his voice is so loud. I shove a hand over his mouth, hissing, "Stop yelling! I was curious; it's not like I *did* anything!"

Li Chengyin eyes me. I can just make out his muffled words. "Unless you . . . then I . . ."

Does he want me to kiss him again?

Do boys think of anything else?

"You kissed me so many times yesterday." I pout, withdrawing my hand. "I think that's plenty. Whatever I owe you, my debt's been paid."

He opens his lapels to show me the scar over his heart, fresh and pale and shiny. "And this? What about this debt?"

I feel like the air's been let out of my indignation. "That was the assassin, not me."

"But I was the one who rescued you! If I hadn't pushed

you out of the way, he might have gotten you too."

It's hard to argue against something true. "What do you want then?" I snap, mostly because I'm stubborn and I don't want to admit I'm softening.

"Next time you go, take me with you."

I stare at him. And then I take a breath. "THE PRINCE OF A KINGDOM, A MODEL OF HIS PEOPLE, GOING TO A BROTH—"

It's Li Chengyin's turn to shove his hand over my mouth. "Stop yelling! I'm curious, it's not like I want to *do* anything!"

"But we're stuck here," I say, deflated. "And we're probably not going to be let out anytime soon. Your great-grandmother will keep us locked in here until the New Year if she has to; how are we supposed to go?"

"I have an idea," says Li Chengyin. But it's a terrible idea. He wants me to fake an illness, and I'm not that good of an actor. I've been as sturdy as a horse since I was young, and other than that first time when I'd just arrived in Shangjing, I have never been seriously sick.

So then he tells me to pretend to faint, but I'm not good at that either. I lie there, trying to keep still, but the giggles keep bubbling up. Frustrated, he finally says, "If you can't do it, I will."

He's a better actor than I expect. He collapses back against the bed, limp and unmoving. I call out the window. "*Help!* Someone help! The crown prince has fainted! *Help!*"

An entire phalanx of servants comes barreling inside. They rush to summon a physician, and the grand-empress is notified.

The physician examines Li Chengyin and comes away saying that both his pulse and his body are weaker than they should be.

You'd be weak too if you'd missed your last two meals, but that's not what the grand-empress thinks. She thinks he's been *worn out*. So though she's a shameless old coot, she doesn't try to shut us into Qingyun Court again.

I'm sent back to the manor, but Li Chengyin isn't so lucky—he's sent straight back to his fast, because tomorrow is when the court will offer sacrifice to the Heavens. Not that it means I have much of a break, because I discover that Lady Gao hasn't been named host of the New Year festivities—I have.

Which is how I end up having the worst holiday season yet.

Busyness aside, the thing I'm most worried about is the New Year's Day ceremony. Even with Yongniang and Lady Gao, I'll have to remember the program of events and attend all of the feasts and celebrations that follow.

I'm so tired that most nights I fall asleep at the dressing table while my attendants wipe the powder and rouge from my face, and every morning before the sun's up Yongniang and her fleet of maids pull me out of bed to put it all back on again. When the empress was here I didn't have to bother with any of this, and now I'm suffering for it, spending all day meeting with people while they pay me their respects, repeating the same few holiday wishes over and over again.

The only fun is on the fifth, because that's when wives are expected to visit their parents, so all of the married princesses are called back to the palace for a feast in their honor.

The emperor's aunts sit at the center table, flanked on either side by his sisters—Li Chengyin's aunts. The eldest of them, the Pingnan Princess, leads the others in toasting me, for though they are my elders, I have become the highest-ranking woman in the royal family.

I empty the cup. Yongniang steps forward to help the Pingnan Princess to her feet, and I remember with a jolt that she's Pei Zhao's mother.

They don't look anything alike.

I scan the crowd for Princess Luoxi. Li Chengyin has no shortage of sisters, and I don't see them often, so I haven't paid enough attention to be able to tell them apart. This time though, I pay her extra mind, because I'm curious about what Pei Zhao's bride will look like—pretty, and graceful, and bearing a resemblance to her aunt.

The younger generation is expected to entertain at banquets by composing poems—something that would confound me if Yongniang wasn't so smart—she's found someone to do the work for me ahead of time. All I have to do when my turn comes is recite the three lyric poems they've written to the tune of "Song of Tranquility," and the ordeal is over. Then Princess Luoxi steps up, reciting a poem to the tune of "Song of Brightness and Peace" that uses so many complicated words that I can't make sense of it.

Everyone is quick to compliment me, saying that Luoxi's poems are second only to mine. I look carefully at her. She seems like the kind of wife that boys would want—gentle, and talented, and from a good family. She and Pei Zhao will make a fine couple, I think.

Maybe I'm too tired, because the rest of the holidays are dreary. I haven't seen Li Chengyin in days, and the rumor is that he and Lady Zhao have made up, that they're getting along sweeter than ever, which ruins whatever's left of my mood. The one thing I'm looking forward to is Shangyuan, on the fifteenth.

It's my favorite part of living in Shangjing.

Ten miles of splendid lights, the ninefold city walls, fireworks in all eight directions, the Seven-Star Pagoda blazing with light. Six lanes of celebration, the Wufu Temple bells ringing, the four directional gates opening, the Sanyin Mountains ringing with sound. Coming and going in pairs, the city is one in harmony—that's how they describe Shangyuan in Shangjing.

There's more than a week until the fifteenth, but the city streets are already decorated with colored lanterns—the main thoroughfare is bright with them. There are lamps fashioned into the shapes of birds and beasts, people and landscapes, dazzling and clever and twinkling as far as the eye can see. And on Shangyuan night, when they lift the restrictions on fireworks, the most famous workshops in the city compete against one another atop Seven-Star Pagoda in stunning displays of light. Because it's constructed of brick and built on high ground, half the city can see their work adorning the heavens when they do battle.

Even ministers' daughters will be let out of their deep bowers, so the streets will be flooded with beautiful girls.

They will ring the Taiping Bell inside Wufu Temple and fling the city gates wide open to let people in from the countryside to enjoy the festival. There is a lovers' shrine atop Sanyin Mountain—or so they say—so throngs of unattached people will climb up to seek love, for no one who has received a piece of red string on Shangyuan night will remain alone for long.

As for "coming and going in pairs"—that's another Shangjing custom—if a couple is married, they will go see the lights together, and if they haven't . . . secret trysts and rendezvous are implicitly allowed for this one night.

I lost a shoe last year when I climbed Sanyin Mountain with A'du to see the lights. I heard later I wasn't the only one, because the Daoists who sweep up the temple ended up donating thousands of pairs to the needy afterward, carrying them down the mountain box by box. This year, I resolve to tie the tops of my boots with leather straps so they won't fall off if someone steps on my heel.

By the fourteenth, all of the audiences and the banquets and the rituals come to an end, and I can afford to be lazy at last. I have every intention of sleeping in and resting up for Shangyuan the next day, but I'm started from my dreams by Yongniang.

"What's happened?" I yawn, so tired I can't sit straight.

"There was a talisman under Miss Xu's bed," Yongniang says. "Lady Zhao's birth date and horoscope were written on it, so she's brought Miss Xu to see you, my lady."

I'm tired and sleepy and annoyed. "So what? It's just a wooden thingy, why's she making such a fuss? Miss Xu wouldn't be stupid enough to do that during New Year's, and anyway, she can't *really* believe she could curse Lady Zhao with a few scraps of wood, can she?"

Yongniang frowns at me. "Witchcraft is forbidden, my lady. Ten years ago, Minister Chen's entire family was killed because he tried to use witchcraft against His Majesty. The first queen of the dynasty was deposed for it, and her son was stripped of his titles . . ."

I'm too groggy to listen to Yongniang yammer on, so I force myself out of bed and have my attendants wash me up before crawling into my clothes for the day.

"This whole affair with Miss Xu . . . there's something off about it, my lady. You must be careful," says Yongniang.

"What do you think I should do, then?" I ask.

Yongniang sighs. "It would have been best if you could avoid it altogether and refer it to the empress for her judgment. But the inner court has no leader, and we're in the middle of the holidays . . . we shouldn't bring ill omens into the palace. I think . . . I think this is perhaps a matter for His Highness."

But if I kick this over to Li Chengyin, this Miss Xu is going to be found guilty for sure. She's been a thorn in his side for so long that he'll seize this opportunity to be rid of her, no matter what the truth may be. Miss Xu is so sad, and so alone—it's not like he likes her any better than he likes me, and the last time I visited her, all she could do was cry. She couldn't prove her own innocence if she tried, and I can't bear to hand her over to the mercy of Li Chengyin.

Seeing me silent, Yongniang presses. "My lady, this is a pool of muddy water. It will be hard to keep yourself clean."

"Well, I'm not going to toss Miss Xu to the wolves, if that's what you mean," I say. I can tell she wants to keep trying to convince me, so I straighten my clothes and order, "Call Lady Zhao and Miss Xu in."

Yongniang doesn't know what to do with me when I play the part of princess consort—but she's been serving in the imperial city for ten years, and she knows the rules, so she has no other choice but to obey.

Lady Zhao is polite enough, curtsying prettily when she sees me. I have Yongniang help her up and invite her to take a seat.

Miss Xu, on the other hand, remains kneeling, her face blotchy and her eyes red like she's been crying.

"Why hasn't anyone helped Miss Xu?" I ask the room.

The attendants don't dare disobey, so they rush over to pull her to her feet.

"The weather's nice today," I say lightly. "Have the two of you come for a holiday visit?"

Lady Zhao's face sours.

She's supposed to visit me every New Year's Day in her formal robes to pay me respects, but in the three years since I've been married to Li Chengyin, he's never let her be alone with me, so she's never bothered to come. She thinks I'm saying it to vex her, but the truth is that I've been too busy to observe all of these useless traditions, so even Miss Xu has been excused from it this year.

This isn't something I realize immediately—Yongniang tells it to me later—because all I think at the time is that it's because I'm being nice to Miss Xu. So I have the talisman brought over for a look.

Because it's Unclean, Yongniang refuses to let me touch it, and has it placed on a tray instead. I examine the birth chart inscribed upon it, but it doesn't provide answers. A thought crosses my mind. "Why look under Miss Xu's bed all of a sudden?"

Lady Zhao's face darkens.

Her lapdog had gone missing, apparently, and her attendants went looking for it everywhere. Someone said they saw it enter Miss Xu's courtyard, which is why Lady Zhao's servants went inside to look. They didn't believe Miss Xu when she said she hadn't taken it, fighting her attendants when they objected, and that was how Lady Zhao's people found the talisman.

"Your Highness," wobbles Lady Zhao most piteously. "I throw myself at your mercy."

I turn to Miss Xu. "Where did this come from?"

Miss Xu sinks back onto her knees. "I don't know, Your Highness. I beg you to look into this further."

"Get up, get up," I tell her. I hate when people kneel at me for no reason. To Lady Zhao, I say, "Why would Miss Xu curse you out of nowhere? I don't think this is as clear-cut as it seems."

"The evidence is here," says Lady Zhao. "Your Highness, surely you must see what is just."

Her voice is calm, but none too polite, and her eyes are accusing.

Yongniang answers before I can respond. "Her Highness was making an observation. I assure you, Lady Zhao, that she has no intention of favoring anyone, so please do be careful what you imply."

Lady Zhao rises abruptly and curtsies at me. "Then I shall await Your Highness's judgment and hope that the truth will out. I will take my leave." And then she sweeps from my rooms without waiting for my answer, taking her people with her.

Yongniang is furious. "How dare she? Who does she think she is?"

But it's only natural for Lady Zhao to hate me—it's not like I like her either.

Miss Xu, on the other hand, still kneels on the ground, gazing timidly up at me. I sigh and pull her to her feet. "Why don't you tell me everything that happened, from the beginning?"

She hesitates. Yongniang has someone bring her a cup of tea. She drinks it slowly, and starts to recount the day's events—

Her rooms may be far from the rest of the manor, but it's the new spring, so all three of us have received gifts. Nothing more than a few trifles really, and not of much worth to either Lady Zhao or I, but for Miss Xu, these are rare treats. She's a meek girl, but good to people who are good to her, so she decided to share the cakes and pastries she received with her attendants—but because it's bad form to regift things from the palace, they ate their sweetmeats quietly, behind closed doors.

So when Lady Zhao's people came, Miss Xu swept the crumbs guiltily under the rug and refused to let them search her rooms for fear that they might uncover her impropriety. But Lady Zhao's attendants had insisted. They turned her rooms upside down looking for the lapdog—and found a talisman beneath the bed instead.

Some of Lady Zhao's people had gone buzzing, like a nest of kicked wasps, back to their own hive to report their findings, while the others stayed back to prevent Miss Xu from leaving. Once Lady Zhao saw the talisman she went white and shaky and dragged Miss Xu all the way to me to make her answer for it.

"I don't know where it came from, I swear," Miss Xu sobs. "Please, Your Highness, you have to investigate, you have to clear my name."

But how am I supposed to do that? They're both singing their own tunes, and I don't know what to believe. The one thing I know for certain is that the talisman couldn't have fallen from the sky.

"It was under your bed," I say. "Are you sure you don't know who could've put it there?"

Miss Xu mistakes my question for an accusation. She falls to her knees with a heavy thud, clutching at my skirt. "My lady, I know who I am and where I stand. I know His Highness won't ever favor me—why would I try to curse Lady Zhao?"

"I'm not saying you did," I rush to reassure her. "I'm saying that it can't have been easy to put something there without anyone else knowing, especially because you don't leave your rooms and you're surrounded by your attendants. I want to know if anyone suspicious has visited lately, or if you remember anything strange happening."

Finally, Miss Xu relaxes. "I can't think of anything, my lady."

Forget it, I won't make any headway with Miss Xu. She's about as calculating as I am. I try to comfort her, telling her to go back to her own rooms while I investigate. "The tide always recedes to reveal the rocks," I say. "It's a question of when. Don't worry, there will be plenty of time after the holidays to figure things out."

I try to seem solemn and capable as I say this, and she must buy it, for she curtsies and then is on her way.

"My lady, are you sure you know how to handle this?" Yongniang asks.

"Of course I don't," I yawn. "What plan could I have? I couldn't figure this out if you gave me a hundred years."

Yongniang looks pained. "Then how do you plan to resolve the matter with Lady Zhao?"

"Well, I wasn't the one who cursed her. Why should I resolve anything with that woman?"

Yongniang looks like she doesn't know if she should laugh or cry, and immediately launches into a lecture about my responsibilities as a princess consort, most of which I don't catch because I am, at long last, drifting into sweet, peaceful slumber.

A slumber I'm unceremoniously jerked out of when someone drags me from my bed.

I flail, opening my eyes to see that Li Chengyin is the one who's pulled me up by my collar.

"You can *sleep*?"

Shit, shit, shit.

Lady Zhao must have gone and tattled.

"Why shouldn't I! I told her I'd investigate the thing with

Miss Xu, didn't I, and I'll do it when I get to it—no amount of badgering from you is going to make me go any faster!"

He knits his brow. "Has something happened to Miss Xu?"

I gape. He doesn't . . . know? So Lady Zhao didn't tell him?

"No, nothing." I plaster on a bright, shiny smile. "Did you want something?"

"Shangyuan's tomorrow."

"I know that." Of course I know that, why else would I be trying so hard to get some rest?

Seeing that my expression hasn't changed, he continues, "I'm going to Chengtian Gate with His Majesty tomorrow, to celebrate with the people."

"I know that too." They go every year, standing atop the gate and waving to their citizens while the citizens shout *long live* from below. He calls it *celebrating with the people*, but what it *actually* entails is standing out in the cold for half the night while the winter wind blows at you. Thankfully, girls don't have to come, or else I would have to go be frozen into an icicle instead of seeing the lanterns.

"What did you promise me?" He pouts, glaring at me.

What was that phrase? *To make your bed with kings is to lie beside a tiger.*[2] Well, to make your bed with the king's son is like lying beside a tiger cub—I can never tell what he's thinking.

"What . . . did I promise you?" I ask, nervous.

"I knew you'd forget!" He raises his voice. "You promised to take me to a brothel!"

---

2 Idiom originating from the novel *Tales of the Huyan Family Generals*, by an anonymous author.

I leap at him, covering his mouth with my hand. *"Shut up!"*

Yongniang picks this moment to enter. She probably doesn't trust us to behave and came to attend us personally when the others told her we were left alone together, only to see me affixed to Li Chengyin's front side like an eight-legged crab, my hand over his mouth. Having picked me bodily out of bed, his hands are fastened around my waist, and I look like a monkey climbing a tree—we could not have been in a more compromising position if we tried. She ducks back out immediately.

A'du last time, Yongniang this time. Their timing is *impeccable*.

But it doesn't affect Li Chengyin's mood at all. "Hurry up and get dressed," he says. "I've prepared our clothes. Once Shangyuan ends, we won't have another opportunity as good as this one again."

I'd assumed that after he and Lady Zhao made up, he'd have forgotten our deal.

He has someone bring over a big bag of clothes. I haven't seen him in commoner clothing—it's discomfiting in a way I can't describe. Not bad, just nothing like himself.

"Should we paste on fake beards?" he asks excitedly, digging through the pile and fishing one out to show me. "No one would guess it's us.

"Or camouflage, should we wear that?" He digs dark robes from the pile also. "Then we can escape into the night if we need to."

And then, pulling out a bottle, "I have sedatives if we need them—it'll make our lives easier—"

I can't bear to watch any longer. Your Highness, we're going to a *brothel*, not on a *crime spree*.

"Bring enough money," I say, cutting him off.

And he is not hurting for it. Not that I need to point that out. He digs out a bag of gold nuggets, enough to buy the whole of Mingyu Lane outright.

Li Chengyin grins when he sees me in male clothing and keeps grinning until I threaten not to take him. He arranges his face easily back into its usual expression.

But when I call A'du into the room, Li Chengyin objects.

"I'm not used to not having her," I say.

He's stubborn. "You have me, isn't that enough?"

"But what if . . . ?"

"What, do you not think I can protect you by myself?"

I sigh. To be honest, I'm still feeling guilty about the assassin, so I don't press the issue, though I sign to A'du that she should follow us from a distance, just in case.

So Li Chengyin and I slip out of the manor. Yongniang probably thinks we're in my bedchamber, and there's no one else around to take note of us, so I'm in a good mood. I'm going to enjoy myself, whether or not I have to bring the spoilsport along.

Once we leave the manor gates, I realize it's raining. A fuzzy, frosty kind of rain, sharp enough to bite into bone, and a nagging worry starts to plague me—if the rain picks up, tomorrow's lantern fair is bound to be disappointing. Two years ago there was a storm, and though they'd built awnings to keep the lanterns dry, it hadn't been half as pretty as a lantern show with clear skies, and a white moon, and lights as far as the eye could see.

The clop of our horses is crisp against the wet street. The willow trees have long since lost their leaves, their bare branches a scatter of wet hair shadowing the stalls on either side of the avenue, which have begun to ignite their lanterns. With the last of the holidays coming up, restaurants and teahouses are flooded with people, and carriages ribbon through the streets in a stream. There's a strange, calm anticipation to all this splendor, like an expectant bride sitting at her mirror, about to depart for her new life, waiting for tomorrow.

There is a boy ready to stable our horses by the time we dismount at Mingyu Lane.

It's more crowded than usual tonight. The first and second floors are crammed with people. We're damp from the rain, but Madame Wang beams when she sees me, about to call up for the girls when I stop her.

"Madame," I say, "is there a room available for us to change out of these wet clothes? My friend here is a first-time guest, so he's shy."

Madame Wang gauges Li Chengyin, her eyes lingering on the pearls in his cap. Her mouth curls into a grin. "Of course. Come with me, Master Liang."

"Where's Yueniang?" I ask as we ascend the stairs.

"Yueniang's entertaining a guest."

I'm curious. Yueniang played two listless songs for me the last time I was here, and we've been friends for years. She's not just the most celebrated performer in Mingyu Lane, she's a music teacher in the Royal Academy, too—she's been before plenty of high-ranking officials and noble peers and she hasn't once been so flustered.

"What guest has put her to all this trouble?" I ask.

"Which other?" Madame Wang laughs. "The same one as last time, of course. He's certainly kept our Yueniang waiting."

Oh?

I badger Madame Wang to let me go see, but she's hesitant. "It wouldn't be proper to interrupt. . . ."

I wheedle and ply, but she stands firm. She's a businesswoman first and foremost, so I suppose she doesn't want anything to sully the reputation of Mingyu Lane. Instead, she leads us to a lavishly decorated room and gifts us two sets of richly embroidered robes, calling for a pair of maids to change us into them as she goes to prepare our meal.

As soon as she's gone, I shoo the maids from the room and change into the dry clothes myself.

"What are you planning?" Li Chengyin asks in a low voice.

"Planning?" I shoot him an innocent smile.

"Don't pretend, I know you have a plan to find out who this guest is."

"Well, obviously. Me and Yueniang are like sisters. I have to go see this 'favored guest'—what if he's a bad man?"

Li Chengyin snorts. "And pray tell, what do *you* know about which men are bad and which ones are good?"

"I know plenty," I retort, sticking a finger in his face. "You, for example. You're a bad man."

His face sours. "Who is a good man, then?"

My a'die, of course, but if I say that he's going to continue bickering with me. I spark with an idea. "His Majesty is," I say.

His face sours more, like he's swallowing something back, but it's not like he can tell me his own father is a bad man, so he falls silent.

I lead him from the room, navigating the halls with ease and slipping into another set of chambers. It's dark inside, a wall of black so solid I can't see my fingers when I stretch them out. I feel for the lock, latch it, and then fumble for Li Chengyin's waistband.

He stiffens but doesn't push me away. After a long while, he asks, "What are you doing?"

"Shhh! Did you bring a flint?"

He slips it from his belt and presses it into my hand, slightly huffy. But then, he's always huffy, so I ignore him and light the candle on the table. "I'm going to disguise myself," I inform him, "and go take a look at Yueniang's guest."

"I want to go too," he insists.

"You can't." I open a trunk and pick through it.

"Why not?"

I smile, pulling out jars of powder and rouge. "Because I'm going dressed as a woman. Interested?"

As I expected, he deflates, but as I'm lowering myself down at the dressing mirror, he says, "I can do it."

I fall to the ground, heavily, right onto my backside.

Li Chengyin pulls me up. "In any case, I want to stay with you."

I stare up at the rafters, speechless. "*I'm* going to go look at a handsome man. What are *you* going there to do?"

"You were the one who told me Yueniang's face could put the moon to shame."

I don't know why my temper takes such an ill turn. I'd known he was a scoundrel, I suppose, but I hadn't known he was a scoundrel with such principled conviction. *Death beneath the peonies makes for a happy ghost* indeed![3] I glare at him. "Come here then."

"What for?"

In the mirror, my smile is vicious. "To make you pretty, of course."

The maddening thing is that he really is.

I braid his hair, securing it firmly with a pin, and paint his face, taking care to dust yellow powder between his brows. Then I dig through the dresser and trunk, looking for a skirt long enough to put him in. The robes are airy and gossamer thin, and when he turns, he looks like an immortal transcendent. It reminds me of a snatch of poetry, something about the spring that is laden with rain—[4]

Worst of all is when I catch sight of us standing side by side in the mirror, because he's much prettier than me. His skin is soft and smooth to begin with, and when he's dressed like this, all of the sharp corners and deep shadows of his face are rounded out, softened.

The only thing that can't be hidden is his height. He mightn't be mistaken for a *dainty* girl, but it's enough. A few of the guests go so far as to wave at us when we walk down the stairs back onto the main floor. I force a smile, and we duck and weave through the crowd. We're almost at the back

---

3 Idiom adapted from *The Peony Pavilion* by Tang Xianzu.
4 From "Song of Everlasting Regret" by Bai Juyi, "Like a sprig of pear blossoms laden with spring rain," describing female beauty.

door when a man staggers out to block our way.

He drapes a heavy hand on my shoulder, saying, "Come sit with me, sweetling!" His breath is heavy with the sharp reek of liquor.

I'm too stunned to react, but Li Chengyin isn't. He slaps the man across the face.

The man clutches his cheek, startled.

I smile. "There was a mosquito."

And then I grab Li Chengyin and we make a run for it. We hurtle through the crowd as quickly as we can, and it's not until we make it through the doors that separate the outer quarters from the inner courtyard that I hear the man, squealing like a stuck pig. The waitstaff rush over to croon over and comfort him, but by comparison, the inner yard is calm.

The building that sits in the yard is connected to the main building by a covered bridge and is where important guests are received. The soft strain of sweet melodies billows through the air, and the occasional whisper seeps from the gauzy windows. The drum of the rain is soft and mild, like a beat that accompanies the music playing in pleasant rushes of sound.

Madame Wang has had flowers and trees planted in the garden, but it's too early in the new spring for any of them to have bloomed. In the calm, the only sound is the rustle of branches.

I pull Li Chengyin over the bridge after me. How strange it is for the two of us to be here, our skirts sweeping across the wood grain, the jade pendants we wear chiming with every step. Scattered lanterns dot the garden, a hazy suggestion of light that seems at once very close and very, very far away.

The hand entwined in mine feels like a stranger's, and I realize with a start that this is the first time I've held it like this. My ears burn, though I can't say why. His hand is soft, and warm, and firm around my own. I'm scared to look back at him, but again I'm not sure what I'm scared of. Thankfully, the bridge is short, and in a moment's time I've pulled him into the other room.

It's tastefully decorated, lit with red candles and scented with sweet incense. A red wool rug covers the ground, soft like stepping into a fresh fall of snow. This is where Yueniang entertains her favored guests.

I hold my breath and tiptoe forward.

Through the screen I can make out a male figure. Yueniang sits to one side, plucking her pipa and singing a tune called "Forever Joy." But the curtain blurs away the visitor's face, and I can't get a good enough look.

Footsteps startle me from my nosiness. At first I think it's the drunkard again—but it's Youniang and a troupe of the other girls. She's surprised to see two strangers inside the door, but I tug at her sleeve, pressing my voice low to say, "It's me!"

She presses a hand to her mouth and retreats, suppressing a grin. "Master Liang! I didn't recognize you dressed up like that." She glances behind me. "And what lady is this? She doesn't look familiar."

I smile. "I heard Yueniang's special guest had come, so I wanted to see what all the fuss was about."

Youniang presses her lips together to hide her smile. "Of course."

I step forward to whisper into Youniang's ear. Her face

GOODBYE, MY PRINCESS

looks strained, but I hurry to reassure her: "It'll just be for a few seconds, I swear. Don't worry, nothing will happen."

Apart from Yueniang, Youniang is the person I'm closest to here, and she's too gentle and yielding to hold me off for long. Finally, she assents. I turn to Li Chengyin, asking gleefully, "Do you know how to dance?"

I'm sure he must be dying of consternation, not that he shows it. "Which dance?"

"One of the peasant step-songs."

Internally I'm urging him to say that he doesn't, and then I can be absolved from his company and leave him here, but his answer is a crisp, "I do."

Oh, but I'm a dummy. I must be, to forget that the crown prince is the one who performs the peasant dances every year during spring ablutions. I'm the biggest dummy in the world.

But I'm a stubborn dummy. "This is a *female* step-song."

"I've seen it danced a hundred times," he says. "It's the same principle."

Well . . . if that's the case, he might as well come along.

Yueniang's pipa quiets, and the accompaniment picks back up. There must be an entire troupe of musicians in there, playing a tune that's meant to announce the arrival of dancers. The beat is slow, steady, graceful.

I suck in a deep breath, taking the fan that Youniang passes me, and enter the room with Li Chengyin.

Yueniang sings us in: "You are like the moon in the sky...[5]"

Her voice is as full as a pearl, as supple as jade. My heart

---

[5] From "Written on Behalf of My Wife" by Li Bai.

crashes in my chest, curiosity driving my steps eagerly forward. I trail after the dancers, smiling enchantingly when they smile, turning when they turn, lowering my fan when they do—and freeze.

I'm not the only one who freezes.

As the others dance, Li Chengyin and I are rooted to the ground, half turned, all rigid.

Because I know the guest. Because Li Chengyin knows the guest.

And we don't just *know* him—heavens—

I want to be swallowed into the earth.

It's the emperor.

The dancers' sleeves flutter in time to the music, sheets of gauzy white that billow like snowflakes in the wind. And we are scarecrows, standing stock-still in a rustling field of grain. Youniang is trying desperately to catch my eye, but I can't seem to move my feet. I pinch myself, hard, and pinch Li Chengyin too. Is this a dream? It must be.

But His Majesty is His Majesty, and as the two of us gape, he gazes placidly back, lifting his teacup to take a sip as though his presence here is nothing earth-shattering at all.

Li Chengyin startles back into himself and pulls at my sleeve, returning to the step-song. I've never danced with such fear in my heart, and when I turn to face front again I see that Yueniang has noticed me. Her eyes are wide. I wink, and she glares, scared I'll disturb her guest's mood. I want to tell her that I wouldn't *dare* pull anything untoward in front of this particular guest.

When at long last the music ends, Yueniang rises with a smile. She's about to say something when the guest remarks, "This step-song is quite something."

"The dancers are trainees," Yueniang says tactfully. "I fear they may not be the best accompaniment for the music. Why don't we dismiss them, and I can play you something on my pipa."

He nods. "As you say."

Yueniang has just let out a breath when he lifts a finger. "Have these two stay behind."

He is pointing straight at us—first Li Chengyin, and then me. Yueniang looks close to fainting; her smile is strained to the point of breaking. "Why . . . why those two?"

"Their dancing was splendid. I'd like them to sit for a drink with us."

Now that he's said it, how can she refuse? Yueniang looks guiltily at me, I look guiltily at Li Chengyin, and Li Chengyin looks guiltily at his father. His father . . . well. He gazes guiltlessly back at all of us.

In any case, everyone else leaves the room, including the accompanists. We are the only four remaining, left to glance shiftily at one another.

It's the emperor who breaks the silence. "Yueniang, why don't you ask the kitchen to prepare some food?"

Yueniang furrows her brow. She glances between us, but he is unmoved, and I am violently fluttering my lashes at her. She doesn't understand what I'm trying to convey to her, and before her guest notices anything amiss, she curtsies and retreats from the room.

My knees go weak. I collapse to the ground, kneeling—more from tiredness than from fright, to be honest. The dance had been so long, and Youniang's troupe is made up of the best dancers in Shangjing. I'd gone mad trying to keep up with them.

Li Chengyin sinks to his knees beside me.

The atmosphere in the room is strange, unsettling.

His Majesty won't make me copy out books, will he? I've made a big mess of things this time—I didn't just bring the crown prince to a brothel, I've also gotten us both caught by the emperor himself. If I have to copy out *The Woman's Manual* thirty more times, it might really be the death of me.

But then—His Majesty's come to the brothel too. And if we're all equally guilty, there won't be a need for punishment, will there?

At last, His Majesty speaks. "Yin'er, what are you doing here?"

I slide my eyes toward Li Chengyin. His Majesty's question is a sly one, but if Li Chengyin throws me under the carriage then I'll make sure he never hears the end of it.

Thankfully, he doesn't. "I was curious," he says, lifting his chin defiantly. "I wanted to see what all the fuss was about."

"And her?"

"She was curious too, so I brought her with me."

I owe him for this.

"Oh," the emperor says, deliberately casual. "How well-matched you are, to share so many interests."

Li Chengyin's face is blank. "And may I ask, Father, why *you* are here?"

My mouth almost drops wide open. I'd have *never* expected Li Chengyin to be so bold—and in any case, since all three of us have been caught here, there's no need to spell things out so explicitly. But the emperor surprises me by laughing.

"*The secret to good governance lies in not offending your able ministers*[6]—you are my heir. Surely you understand this principle?"

"Of course I do. But I also recall you saying that the last dynasty fell because of factionalism. That the power of its ministers overwhelmed the power of the throne, and the king could get very little done. By the time the locust plague came, they'd utterly lost the loyalty of their populace."

I don't comprehend a word they're saying. Why is it that even a visit to a brothel can turn into a debate about politics? But it doesn't matter that I don't get it—the emperor seems to understand perfectly fine. He smiles. "And today—how do you intend to handle things?"

"By reopening the case. By reversing the verdict."

The emperor shakes his head. "The case is ten years old. The witnesses, the evidence—all of it is gone. Tell me, how will you reopen it?"

Li Chengyin is not discouraged at all, in fact, he's smiling too. "There is plenty of evidence. And as for witnesses . . . if there weren't any, I doubt you'd be here in disguise, Father."

The emperor sighs fondly, sounding every bit like my a'die does when I demand a ride on my little red horse. "Oh, you!"

The feeling I understand. The words, I do not.

---

[6] From *Mengzi*, Book *IV*, Part *I* by Mengzi.

Someone comes running down the hall—a song girl I know, who knocks at the door and calls to me. "Master Liang, come quick!"

The emperor and Li Chengyin are both looking curiously at me. I clamber to my feet. "What is it—what's happening?"

"Someone's forced their way into the building. They're saying that Youniang owes money, and they're going to take her hostage!"

"Don't worry," I say. "Take me to her."

Li Chengyin catches my arm. "I'm coming with you.

I look back at the emperor. "But you should stay with His Majesty."

The Majesty in question cuts in: "You two go. I have people to guard me, don't worry."

So we rush back over the covered bridge, all the way back into the main hall, accompanied all the way by Madame Wang's piercing voice: "Don't you *dare* touch one of *my* girls!"

"It is perfectly legal to collect a debt!" The person speaking is a man, plump and fair, with a long, wispy mustache and shifty eyes. My temper flares when I see him.

"Back again, Sun Er?"

Sun Er is a loan shark. Last time we met, it was because I'd beaten him up for harassing a widow and her son for money. He'd been picking his teeth up off the ground after that, and since then he's been chastened enough to not try anything while I'm around. He blinks owlishly, trying to place me.

"Master Liang! What are you doing dressed like that?" He cackles.

Drat. I'd forgotten what I'm wearing. I slam a foot down on a stool, tucking the hem of my skirt into my belt. "And what about it? You think I can't handle you in women's skirts, is that it?"

Sun Er is frightened into sobriety. "Not at all, Master Liang—I'm here to settle a debt, that's all. Nothing wrong with that, is there? Youniang isn't an orphan or a widow, and she's not sick or destitute—I'm well within my rights to ask her to pay me back."

"Why do you owe him money?" I turn to Youniang.

"What money do I owe?" Youniang says. "An acquaintance from back home brought his wife to Shangjing to do some business a few months back. His wife fell ill and died, and he needed money for her medicine and her funeral, so he went to Sun Er to borrow some. But Sun Er said he wouldn't lend money without a guarantor, and my friend didn't know another soul in the whole city, so of course I helped him out. But he's taken the money and gone home without paying it back, so Sun Er is demanding that *I* pay it instead!"

"What kind of acquaintance would leave you to settle his debt?" I'm so angry I could hop.

Sun Er unfolds the receipt. "Master Liang, if she was an orphan or a widow I could forgive the debt, but as no good deed goes unpunished—"

Li Chengyin bursts into laughter.

Sun Er jumps up. *"Who's laughing!"*

"Would you like to repeat that?" Li Chengyin's face is dark, and I can't stop him from advancing on Sun Er.

But Sun Er turns instead to me. "Master Liang, I'm afraid

things might get ugly if I don't get my money back today."

"She's merely the guarantor. If you want your money, go find the person who actually owes it to you." Li Chengyin's laugh is cold. "The law clearly states that you can only approach the guarantor when the debtor is dead or imprisoned, escaped, or incapable of payment."

"You don't call this escaping?" Sun Er sneers, but he is clearly surprised that Li Chengyin wants to talk of laws.

"Is it? According to this lady, he's simply gone home, so you know his location. Why are you harassing his guarantor instead of going after him?"

"Well, how the hell would I know where he's from?"

"Why don't you ask?" Li Chengyin nudges Youniang forward.

Youniang is so startled she trips over her words. "D-Dingzhou, Yonghe Prefecture, County Qing, in the village of Xiaowang."

"And now you know where the debtor is. If you want your money, go there instead of coming here and causing a scene."

Madame Wang bustles forward to add her voice to Li Chengyin's. "That's right—if you want your money back, go find the person who owes it to you. None of the girls at Mingyu Lane have anything to do with it. Out, out!"

And as she speaks she steps forward, shepherding Sun Er and his gang out of Mingyu Lane, shooing them right out the front door. Sun Er's friends start yelling abuse, but Madame Wang pats Li Chengyin on the back, saying with some satisfaction, "Good girl, standing up for your old Mother Wang like that. Are you one of Youniang's dancers? Your spending money is on me this month!"

My sides hurt from how much I'm laughing. Sun Er seethes with anger, but there's nothing he can do about it. He raises a hand and beckons at his crew, who crowds in close to listen to him speak and then disperses.

"I think Sun Er might be up to something," I say.

"Close the doors!" Madame Wang calls to a young servant. "Don't let them in again. Oh, and bring the Bosi glass lanterns inside—they're expensive, I don't want them damaged—"

But as she speaks, Sun Er and his band of ne'er-do-wells come storming back, bamboo canisters in hand. Madame Wang spots them first and gestures her attendants over to the doors. They've closed them halfway when the men open the canisters and fling them toward us. Muddy black liquid splashes all over an attendant too slow to dodge it, and over the onlookers—including Madame Wang.

"This is a new skirt!" she shrieks. "I'm going to kill you—"

She orders the doors opened again so that she can go out and give the men a piece of her mind, but by then Sun Er and his friends have absconded, pulling faces at her from halfway down the street.

Youniang steps forward and inspects the stained skirt. "Mother, don't work yourself up—it's just ink. It'll come out if we soak it with vinegar before washing it—come with me, let me help you . . ."

Madame Wang follows Youniang obediently, leaning on her arm, muttering all the while, "Let them come to my establishment next time and I'll kill them, I swear—"

Then she orders the boys to take the doors out of their frames to wash.

But the beech doors are new enough that they've only been treated with lacquer once, so it's hard to get the stains out. Madame Wang is frantic, but I have an idea. Turning to a serving girl, I say, "Bring me some rouge and eyebrow powder."

Youniang peers at my face and smiles. "Master Liang, you're already prettier than all the girls here without all of that. Why do you need it?"

I grin, pulling Li Chengyin from the crowd. "This one's even prettier than me. Quick, this is the one it's for."

Annoyed, he shakes me off, but the serving girl's come back with jars of pigment. I shove the tray into his hands. "Here!"

He stares at me. "What do you want me to do?"

"Last time, when your Sese ruined her white silk fan by killing a fly, you used the bloodstain to paint a butterfly. If you can decorate a fan, you can decorate these doors."

Li Chengyin huffs, clearly reluctant. I rise on my tiptoes and grab his lapels, pressing my lips close to his ear. "If you don't, I'll tell everyone what's happening in the back rooms."

"You wouldn't!" He's glaring.

"Everybody come look, the emp—"

He silences me with a hand over my mouth. And then he starts. He doesn't use a brush or any water, but dips his fingers straight into the soft powder to draw a large circle onto the door, dotting it onto the ink stains. I never get the chance to watch him draw, much less with his hands. The people around us are impressed too, calling out with encouragement and delight.

The scene is quickly revealed: the stains have been transformed into layered mountain ranges, given depth by hazy blankets of fog. Patches of trees dot the peaks, veiled in a gauzy shroud of mist, while a red sun rises over a perfect, splendid landscape.

Madame Wang is ecstatic. "This is better than the painter I was planning to hire!"

Of course he's better—he's the crown prince. Since he was a child he's had the best artists to teach him to draw, the best poets to teach him to write, the best lyricists and musicians and calligraphers to teach him how to compose. There's nothing he doesn't know how to do, not that he's unaware of this fact, for he looks exceedingly pleased with himself, clasping his hands in acknowledgment of everyone's praise. Picking up the pot of eyebrow powder, he titles his work. Ink-Stained Doors, he writes, the words dancing across the panels. I don't much know how to appreciate calligraphy, but I can tell his work is extraordinary.

Yet it feels incomplete, and after some contemplation, he adds the words *by the fifth son of the family Li of Shangjing* in smaller writing beneath. Placing the powder back onto the tray, he calls for water to clean his hands.

Madame Wang could not be happier and goes to draw the water personally. I feel a bloom of pride, too. A'die might not have wanted to send me all the way here to be married, but he did find me an impressive enough husband, one who is good at everything except for riding horses and winning fights.

After we wash up and get changed, Madame Wang has the kitchen bring us some appetizers, all the while looking quizzically at Li Chengyin. I'm worried those eyes might see something they shouldn't, and I'm opening my mouth to distract her when we hear the whistle of fireworks from the courtyard in the back.

Unlike other fireworks, these shoot high into the heavens, straight and unwavering, a streak of white light against the endless pane of night. The whistle is high, piercing, and loud. They rise until they can rise no farther and explode into a shatter of golden sparkle, cutting open the darkness with their brilliance. Sparks linger in the air long after the explosion, lightening the sky.

Li Chengyin's face goes pale. He turns and runs for the back rooms. I don't have time to ask what's going on, I just follow after, though his legs are long and it's hard to keep up. It isn't until I'm at the bridge that I realize something is wrong—it's deathly still in the yard, and there is a dark lump beneath the bridge that is seeping out rivulets of blood. Why is there a body here?

There's no time to think too much about it. I yell for A'du.

But she doesn't respond.

I call her three times, which is twice more than I usually have to. Has something happened to her? My heart thunders in my chest.

Li Chengyin kicks the door down.

We haven't been gone for longer than two steeps of tea, but the room has changed so completely. Everything carries the gamey scent of blood. Eight or so corpses are strewn about the floor, every one of them wearing the same black robes as the man beneath the bridge.

Li Chengyin flips over the screen that shields the rest of the room from view. The curtains are in tatters. The tea table atop the settee has been knocked to the ground. The column beside it bears scars from someone's blade, and there are more bloodstains. There are the dead—and there is one person who draws breath in shallow gasps, leaning up against the column. Li Chengyin lunges forward to help him up. His face is covered with blood, his eyes wide and shocked, his shoulder so badly injured I can see bone.

"Where is the king?" Li Chengyin asks.

With his remaining hand, the man grabs Li Chengyin's lapels and pulls him close. He gurgles in a few labored breaths and grinds out, hoarsely, "His Majesty—His Majesty—"

"Who hurt you? Where is he?"

"He was—masked—an assassin—too strong, I wasn't able to—" With what seems like all his effort, the guard raises a hand to point out the broken window, the light in his eyes beginning to dim. "His . . . Majesty . . ."

Li Chengyin wants to ask something else, but the guard's hand slackens, falling motionlessly into a pool of blood.

He lifts his eyes to look at me. They are bloodshot. His clothes, too, are streaked with red. Bodies lie all around us. We weren't gone very long—how could someone, anyone, kill this many people so quickly? Kill this many royal guards? It scares me—but Li Chengyin picks up a blade and plunges out the window without hesitating.

"A'du!" I scream, but she doesn't come. I conjure up horrible images of the last time A'du met with an assassin—and it occurs to me that if a swordsman is powerful enough to overcome a room full of the emperor's best men, it would be nothing at all for him to take care of Li Chengyin. So I pick up one of the scattered swords and follow him out the window, resolving that, if it came down to it, I would hold my own for as long as I could handle.

There is a small yard out back, with a tastefully curated garden of rocks at the center, all transported from the faraway south and stacked artfully to support the flowers and the trees. But the weather has yet to warm, and the shrubs are bare. Li Chengyin disappears behind the rock garden and stops abruptly, pushing me reflexively behind him when I catch up. Pressed against the rock, I can see nothing but the back of his head, remembering that the last time we'd met with an assassin, he'd done just this. My heart tightens with a sudden, sharp pain, sweet and sour all at once. I stand on my tiptoes to peer over his shoulder.

Several black-robed royal guardsmen are tangled in a battle with a masked man. Their commander is a powerful fighter, but clearly no match for the assassin, who wields a sword with one hand and has the other tight around the throat of the king. Though he's at a disadvantage, his technique is impeccable, every strike drawing a hiss of pain. By the weak moonlight I can see dark drops of blood splattered across the rockery. Something like thunder rolls in the distance. The assassin presses his sword to the emperor's neck.

No one moves.

No one breathes.

We can only stare.

"Let go of him!" Li Chengyin's voice is swallowed up by

thunder, but I can distinguish his every word. I'm frightened—more frightened than I've ever been, but it's not because of the corpses or the assassin. I'm frightened of something I can't quite place.

The noise grows louder and louder, and as it approaches I realize that it isn't thunder after all, but the beat of horses' hooves against stone, echoing in the cavernous air, bearing down on Mingyu Lane like a wave of floodwater.

In the grasslands, when A'die led charges of men across the plain, the horses hadn't been so loud, so overwhelming. I'd been able to hear the din of Mingyu Lane at first, the hubbub of the front quarters, but it's been drowned out by the most terrifying kind of tide, which always rises and never sinks. The buildings shake on their foundations. The sound surges toward us like a sandstorm, towering and boundless, and there is nowhere left for us to escape. We are caught in its power.

The assassin does not speak. He forces the emperor back with him as he retreats.

No one dares move until the emperor speaks. "Zeng Xian, kill him!"

The commander of the guards is Zeng Xian, then. I've heard of him, the commander at large of the Shenwu Army, who rumor has it can singlehandedly fight off hundreds of enemy troops. He is advancing on the assassin, blood dripping down his arm. The blade is sharp and bright against the emperor's throat. My back is damp with sweat. But Li Chengyin is calm. He smiles.

"Do you know who I am?" he asks.

The assassin's face is covered with cloth. His eyes peer out over it, impassive as he gazes upon Li Chengyin.

"The Shenwu Army has arrived. You are surrounded. If you try and escape, you'll be shot, but if you put down your weapon now, I can ensure that you keep your life."

Light dances in the assassin's eyes. He hesitates. Li Chengyin presses his advantage. "If you don't believe me, take me hostage. I can be your captive until you feel safe."

My palms are slick with sweat. The sword I hold is slipping from my hands. I step out from behind Li Chengyin. "If you need a hostage," I say, "you can take me. I'm just a girl, so you don't need to worry about me trying anything."

Li Chengyin whips around, glaring furiously. But I glare back. I know what he's trying to tell me, I understand this isn't a game, but I won't watch him be taken hostage by an assassin, I just won't.

The assassin is silent. He stands there, cold as ice, while Zeng Xian and his men hover, too afraid to get close, but unable to retreat, either.

Li Chengyin stands there, motionless, as the sound of horses quiets. After a long moment we hear footsteps coming down the hall. I tense—*accomplices?*—and Li Chengyin reaches for me. His hands are dry and hot. Strangely, it settles me.

My ease is interrupted when a squadron of soldiers comes rushing into the yard. Their leader, a man in silver armor, looks startled to see the assassin and the guards in a deadlock. Yet he is the picture of calm when he drops to one knee. "Forgive me, my liege. I am late."

GOODBYE, MY PRINCESS

"Rise." Though there is a blade against his neck, the emperor is unfailingly composed. "Bring my orders to the gate guard—the entire city is to be locked down, effective immediately. I want the nine gates closed at once."

"Yes, sire."

"I want the Shenwu Army to aid the Yulin Guard in searching the city for this man's accomplices."

"Yes, sire."

"Don't breathe a word of this to anyone. I don't want undue alarm."

"Yes, sire."

"Go, now!"

With a bow, the general retreats. I can hear the soft murmur of voices in the hall, and then footsteps as the Shenwu Army disperses to carry their orders. But then the general comes back, saying, "Your Highness, please return to the manor. We have the situation under control."

Li Chengyin shakes his head firmly, his eyes fixed on the assassin and his hand in mine. "Take me," he says. "Let my father go."

"No," I protest. "Take me."

Li Chengyin whips around again. *"Shut up!"*

This is the most hostile he's sounded in three years of fighting, but I am resolute.

"I'm much more valuable than either of them," I call. "You must have done your research. You must know I'm not merely the princess consort. I am a treaty bride, and the peace of two kingdoms rests on my shoulders. You might have the emperor hostage, but he won't be intimidated by the likes of you. He'll order the guards to shoot you into a million pieces, and if he's killed he still has an heir. The crown prince won't be threatened by you either—if worse comes to worst, the emperor has plenty of other sons. I'm different. If I die, Xiliang will revolt. There will be war. So I promise you, if you take me, you will leave here alive."

"A pack of lies!" Li Chengyin spits. "Someone, drag her back to the manor!"

But I ignore him. "Think about it," I say. "I'm right, aren't I?"

Finally, at last, he nods.

"Good! Then let the emperor go, and I'll come with you."

"You come here first." I'm surprised by his voice. It's flat and toneless, the way I sounded when I first learned to speak Plains.

"Let the emperor go, then I'll come."

His response is to press his blade closer to the emperor's neck.

"Stop! I'll come, I'll come."

Li Chengyin lunges forward to stop me, but I swing my sword at him. He ducks reflexively away, losing his chance, and the assassin grabs me. From somewhere high above, a volley of arrows flies down, but the assassin knocks them straight out of the air, bending at angles I didn't know a human body could. In the confusion, the emperor twists out of his grasp and I raise my sword, piercing toward the assassin, but he's faster than I am and knocks it from my hand. As he does, I shove the emperor back toward Li Chengyin.

Zeng Xian catches him and pulls him out of range. The

assassin's hand is freezing against my throat, but colder is the glint of his steel against my collarbone.

"Xiaofeng!"

I lift my gaze to Li Chengyin and see the misery welling in his gaze.

I won't forget the way he looks. I'll carry it with me until my dying day, though it may be today. The emperor wouldn't let this assassin escape, whatever the cost, because I'm not that important. Xiliang is not that important. I see his face and I know we both understand that I was lying.

The Shenwu troops rush forward to circle the emperor and Li Chengyin. I smile at him, even if I know it must be ugly. I smile even if it hurts, because if this is the last time we see each other, I want him to remember me smiling.

Shoot, I mouth at him. *Shoot.*

There must be archers stationed all around us. As long as they aren't stingy with their arrows, they can turn the assassin into a porcupine in no time. And he's killed so many people; he's so powerful—if he's not eradicated he'll only fester.

But Li Chengyin ignores me.

"Nobody move," the emperor cautions.

Li Chengyin grabs an arrow from Zeng Xian's quiver. "If you touch a single hair on her head, I will make mincemeat out of you if I have to spend the rest of my life doing it. Let go of my wife and I will guarantee your safety. If I go back on my word, then I swear to the Heavens I will be like this arrow—" He cracks the wood shaft in two and throws it at the assassin's feet. "Let her go!"

The assassin sneers. He turns the sword around and brings

it hilt-first down on my head. I slump. The world darkens.

I am hungry and cold when I wake, and my hands are bound. It takes a second for me to gather my wits and remember that I've been taken hostage, that Li Chengyin had begged for my release, but where am I? It's light, and if I open my eyes I can see pine trees and cypresses blotting out the blue of the sky, but I have no idea how long I've been unconscious, or where the assassin has gone, or where I am.

The rush of trickling water accompanies the freezing howl of the wind. I crane my neck—a patch of wilted grass sprouts from the hard ground on my left, a cluster of rocky soil to my right. Hunger aches hollow in my stomach, and I am dizzy with it. Shangjing is so big that no matter if the Shenwu Army seals the city and combs it block by block, it might take days, weeks, for them to find me, and if I starve before they do, I'll be the most tragic girl there ever was.

A flutter of skirts catches my eye—the assassin. I'm surprised he hasn't left me to make his escape, but perhaps the gates are too tightly guarded. Perhaps he's afraid that the Shenwu Army or the Yulin Guard will find him, so he's keeping me around to ensure his own safety.

Desperate he must be, and seasoned he is, and a new fear overtakes me: How will he torture me now that I've landed in his clutches? But there's nothing fear can do to save me, so I squeeze my eyes shut, resolving to be strong.

Nothing happens.

After a long while, I smell something. Something tantalizing. Despite my best efforts, my eyes pop open, and I crane my neck for a glimpse of the source—a carton of mutton stewed with milk vetch. It's nothing special—peasant food that you can find anywhere on the streets—but after sleeping all day and going without dinner, I'm starving. My stomach growls.

But I'm a Xiliang girl, and we don't bargain with our enemies.

To my surprise, the assassin walks over to loosen my ties himself and then lopes away. I struggle to push myself to my feet and, by the light of day, get my first good look at him. His face is still covered, and he sits against a tree, sword in his arms as he stares at me.

We're in a field near a stream that's covered with patches of yellowed reeds. I can hear the squawk of water birds in the distance. Wind rustles through the trees, cold enough to pierce your heart. I eye the meat, swallowing back saliva and rubbing my wrists. He doesn't seem likely to kill me soon, or else he wouldn't have wasted money on food, but I don't think I could free myself regardless.

As though he can tell what I'm thinking, the assassin speaks. "If you try to escape, I'll cripple you." His voice is as flat and toneless as it had been earlier. The accent is unpleasant and discomfiting in a way I can't describe, but I do understand what he's saying.

Well, *I'm* not scared of him. I glance over, pulling a face. What's that saying—? Life and death are governed by fate; wealth and poverty are ruled by heaven. There's only so much I can control, and one thing I can is choosing to have some mutton. At least then I won't starve to death.

So I start eating. Maybe I'm too hungry, because the flavor is so good it reminds me of the mutton that the royal kitchen makes. Everything tastes delicious when you haven't had anything to eat. I'm so engrossed that the assassin can't help a cold snort.

"I don't know what you're laughing about," I say, chewing. "I might look ugly when I eat, but that has nothing to do with a criminal like you. And anyway, we don't care about these little things where I'm from. Don't think that I'll forgive you because you fed me, because I'm telling you, you're in big trouble. Do you know who my a'die is? When Xiliang finds out that you've kidnapped me, they'll chop you into pieces. You'd better stay inside the Yumen Pass if you want to live, because once you enter our territory, you're dead. And you'd better watch your back inside the pass too, because His Majesty is also my father. Do you know how many people die because they angered a king? Of all the people to offend, really. And my husband—my husband is the crown prince. Do you know what a crown prince is? He's the future emperor! He might not be as scary as his father, but he's impressive enough."

Between eating and bragging I've lost the plot a bit, but the assassin makes no sound. He doesn't speak. I glance at him, taking in his plain black robes and his unadorned sword. There's nothing to identify him by, and no reason I can tell why he would want to kidnap the king.

But something does occur to me.

Sun Er can't be innocent. He distracted me and Li Chengyin away right before the emperor was kidnapped—but how could a low-life good-for-nothing know an assassin? I'm missing something.

The eyes on me are frigid as I try to put it together, but

I won't be intimidated. The emperor has plenty of capable men, and Li Chengyin isn't stupid either. Of course he'll think of Sun Er and use Sun Er to trace us. This man may be a stranger, but Sun Er is notorious enough, and his whole family lives in Shangjing—the monk can run but the temple won't leave with him, and sooner or later they'll find clues. Sooner or later, they'll get me out of here.

The assassin has to have come from somewhere. Someone has to have trained him. He must have some peer to make him peerless, someone who taught him to use Sun Er to sneak in and capture the king. The clamor had been enough to lure us from the room—but what if it hadn't? Wouldn't we be corpses on the ground too?

The thought chills me, and for the first time I realize how difficult it's been to stay alive. If it wasn't for A'du . . .

I jump up. "Did you kill A'du?"

The assassin doesn't answer.

I'm no match for him, but if he did anything to her, I'll kill him. I tell myself that he can't have, he won't have, for if he did overpower her she would at least have injured him. She's like me in that way—it might cost us our lives, but we'll bring our enemies down with us. And since he's unharmed, A'du must be alive.

The logic is not very sound, but I can come up with nothing better.

The assassin picks up his sword. "Time to get going."

So that was my last meal. Like a convict, given one final feast ere the execution block. But there's no use in begging. I raise my chin.

"Kill me if you want. My a'die will avenge me. And His Majesty, and Li Chengyin, and A'du. If she's alive, she'll chop your head off and send your skull to my lord father to use as a drinking cup."

As the assassin continues to glower, I remember another name. "And I have an old sweetheart—if you kill me, he won't let you live either. He's a better fighter than you, and his sword is faster than yours, you'll see!"

But he is utterly unmoved.

I sigh. Fine. If I die full, at least I die without regret. I only wish I knew how A'du was.

"Any last words?" the assassin asks.

"No," I say, sighing again despite myself. "If you're going to do it, do it fast, that's all."

Something stirs in his eyes. "You're loyal," he says. "I'll give you that. Not many girls would be willing to die for their husbands. I'll let you go easy."

"I'm not dying for him," I protest. "You kidnapped the emperor, not my husband. And anyway, I owe him. This way we'll be square."

The assassin goes for his blade.

"Wait!" I cry. "If I'm going to be dead anyway, can you at least take the mask off so I can see your face? I don't want to not know who killed me. I won't know who to haunt."

The assassin looks impatient and draws his sword out a few inches.

"Wait!" I say again. "Before I go, can I at least play you a tune? In Xiliang, if you don't play a song before you pass, you won't be reincarnated."

I don't count on him believing a word of my lies, so I'm surprised when he nods.

My head is all muddled, but I don't have any better ideas. Surviving one minute more is better than surviving one minute less, so I delay as much as I can, rooting around in my sleeves for my little reed flute. I can't locate it, but I do find something else, which I palm and fling at him as quickly as I can.

It's the rouge powder, light as gossamer, but it never reaches him. He whisks his sleeve and the breeze carries it yards away. Real poison wouldn't catch him off guard either. But this is what I wanted. While he's distracted, I shoot the whistling arrow Gu Jian gave me. It whizzes through the air, sizzling and sharp.

I didn't lie, I do have an old sweetheart. I don't know if we were sweet or how or why or when, but he is the best swordsman I know. He gave me a flare and I've only used it once, to save A'du. Now I'm the one at death's door in need of saving.

I haven't seen Gu Jian for ages. I don't know if he'll come in time. I'm sticky with sweat despite the cold, but the assassin pays the flare no mind. He picks me up by the waistband and lifts me with a single hand. And then he throws.

I am like a kite who has lost her tether soaring through the air. I scramble to grab for something, anything, but all I can clutch at is the formless, shapeless wind. Before I understand what's happening, I plunge into frigid depths.

I don't know how to swim. The assassin's tossed me far, and I've fallen into the heart of the river. I sink, sink, until all around me there is nothing but the bone-piercing current. Above me the light refracts off perfect crystal waves.

I open my mouth only to swallow a lungful of water—and think back to the last time I was drowning, when A'du had to come fish me out. I think back to Pei Zhao looking kindly in his civilian clothes.

Then the image of Li Chengyin floats to mind. Our little length of fate has concluded, and I'm struck by how unfair it is that it should end right when I like him and he likes me—and he does like me, he must, or else why would he have taken an oath on his own life? For the first time, I think how lucky it is that he has Lady Zhao. At least when I die he won't have to mourn for too long, and he can forget me in due time and live happily.

Water gushes in through my nose and my mouth. I choke on it, struggling for breath, for consciousness, as the wavering lights overhead rise farther and farther from me and I sink deeper and deeper into the abyss. The light dims, and I think I can feel the wind rushing past, the arms that hold me close as I descend. He found me, he saved me, and the two of us are tumbling into a free fall, spinning until the sky full of stars looks like rain coming down around us. There is nothing between heaven and earth but those eyes—those eyes that are full of me.

I'm drunk, I'm intoxicated in his arms. I know him, I know I love him, and I know he loves me. As long as he's here, I'm safe.

I must have dreamed of falling a hundred, a thousand times, but in the end, it's the water that takes me.

And he never came.

My hero never came.

Neither did Li Chengyin.

PART THREE:

变化
Changes

I'm a steelyard weight, slipping into the deep.

I don't know how long I sink. It could be for years, or it could be for the space of a bad dream, but then a painful pressure against my chest forces the water from my lungs.

I don't know how much river I spit up, only that it's a lot.

I lie there, half conscious, entirely dazed, as the sun pierces my eyelids. With a huge effort I turn my head away. Nothing there but wilted grass. I turn the other way. Nothing but rocks and dirt.

And the edge of the assassin's robes. After all that, I still haven't drowned. And he's the one who fished me out.

Every time I open my mouth to speak, I spit up more water. Coughing, I manage, "Kill me then—"

But he pays me no mind. With the hilt of his sword, he tips my face away as I retch again, throwing up enough to fill a small stream.

I close my eyes—and sleep.

In my dreams, I'm in the manor again.

In my dreams, I am fighting with Li Chengyin.

Who asked you to save my father? he shouts. *Did you think I'd be grateful?*

I'm angry. I retort that I don't need his gratitude, that I was returning a favor, but I'm crying when I say it, and my heart hurts for no reason I can understand. I don't want him to see me cry, so I hunch over a brazier, but it's hot and I can only rest upon it for a little while without burning my face.

I raise my eyes, which are puffy, and lean away from the flame, but my cheeks are boiling. Yet my body is cold, so cold that I shiver. *Is it snowing?* I ask A'du, and A'du goes to fetch my little red horse, for A'die isn't here and that's the best time to slip away and go riding. It's wonderful to gallop across the grasslands when it's snowing, because your nose goes bright red and the sand dunes are covered in white, the needlegrass looking like A'die's whiskers—A'die, who will lecture me for sure when he finds out where I've gone.

Li Chengyin hasn't seen my little red horse. He doesn't know how fast it can run.

But why am I forever thinking about him? He's not good to me. He doesn't pay me any mind. My heart burns, acid shooting through my veins.

It's not true—he's not *unkind*, it's just—what I want is for him to care about me, to look at me, to look *only* at me. Why did Lady Zhao have to get here first?

I heard the way he called my name when he broke that arrow. If I really don't make my way back, he'll be sorry, won't he? At least for a time.

I wish I knew how long.

When I force my eyes to open, I find that I'm no longer by the riverbank, but lying in a room, not too big and not too small. Moonlight seeps in from outside.

It must be Shangyuan already, bustling and busy and beautiful, the holiday I have waited all year for. I'll have to miss it now. I'm cold, and I can't stop shivering. There are furs wrapped about my shoulders—sheepskin, but the wool is thick and warm. Or, at least, it should be—but I've realized that I'm running a fever. There's a winter blanket draped over me too, but beneath it, I'm shaking.

As my eyes adjust to the dark, I start to see the boxes stacked all over the room—a storeroom, I think. The assassin is sitting quite close and watches as I wake. Without speaking, he nudges a bowl toward me. It's hot to the touch.

"Ginger tea."

I flick my eyes up but can't muster the energy to say that I'm too weak to pick it up. This is the second time I've been sick, and it's as terrible as I remember. Perhaps this is what happens when you're not often ill—when you do succumb, it is to the serious kind. I make two attempts to pick up the bowl, but my hands shake and I can't muster any strength.

I'm surprised the assassin would brew me ginger tea. Surprised he'd bring me indoors, even if it's to a storeroom. At the very least, it's warmer than the shore.

He walks back toward me and takes the bowl in one hand, helping me up with the other. My throat hurts too much to think deeply about what that might mean—steadying it with my fingers, I drain the tea in a few large gulps. It is spicy—and it burns on the way down—but I do feel better, like my blood has come alive again. But the nausea hits immediately.

I cough and cough until I'm flushed. The assassin takes the bowl away and proceeds to thump my back. I suck in a long breath and, faster than he can move, pull the cloth from his face.

He could have ducked.

In fact, I'd been counting on it. If he had, I would have gone crashing back against the boxes, but I was hoping I could smash the bowl in the process and snatch a shard to arm myself with. But he didn't. He let me unmask him.

The moon is white and pure, and the face it lights is familiar.

Gu Jian.

The blood rushes to my head.

"Why?" is all I can think to ask.

He doesn't answer, just lowers the bowl.

So I ask again. "*Why?*"

Why him? Why kidnap the king? Why kill so many guards and take me captive? Why any of it?

I must be stupid.

How many people in the whole of the world could have rivaled him? Why didn't it occur to me, considering the assassin's skill, that the two men could be one and the same?

And I'd been waiting like a fool for him to rescue me.

"There isn't a reason," he says.

"But you killed so many people!" I'm shouting. "Why? Why abduct the king?"

Gu Jian stands, and the light slanting through the window falls from his face to his shoulders. His voice is calm. "I'll kill who I want to kill, and it's not my concern if you have a problem with it."

I clutch at his sleeve. "What did you do to A'du? If you hurt her, I swear—"

"I haven't done anything to her. Believe me or don't believe me, take your pick."

I let out the breath I've been holding. "Then let me go," I wheedle, softening my voice to coax him. "I won't tell anyone, I promise. I'll say I escaped on my own."

Gu Jian smiles, but it's bitter. "Why, Xiaofeng?"

"Why what?"

"Why are you so good to Li Chengyin? Why can't you stay away from him? He uses you. The women he's brought into the manor bully you. He pushes you around. Don't you understand? Once he's crowned there will be more women, more people who will take advantage of you. Why do you care about him? You're willing to sacrifice your own happiness, spend the rest of your life inside that cold, empty palace, and for what? For Xiliang?"

I stare at him. "Xiliang is Xiliang," I say, "and I've made my choice. Besides, he doesn't treat me badly."

"You think that still? Don't you know what he's thinking? Don't you see how deeply he plans? Xiaofeng, you won't win—not against those women, and certainly not against Li Chengyin. They keep you around for the time being because of Xiliang, but once you're no longer useful, you'll be tossed aside."

"You're right. I'm not smart or clever or cunning. I can't win against anyone. But he is my husband, and I will not desert him."

"And if he deserts you?" Gu Jian sneers.

"He wouldn't," I say, but I shiver.

He'd thrown himself in front of a blade to save me. He'd

pushed me behind him in the garden. Every time we've faced danger, he's put himself between me and it—and he would not abandon me.

"How much do you think you're worth, compared to an entire kingdom? Hearts harden and blood freezes on that throne, Xiaofeng. Did you hope your Li Chengyin would save you? Did you think he would rush over? But today is Shangyuan, and the gates are open, and they will pretend all is well so their citizens can enjoy the festival. You're not worth more than that—you'll see. They'll be celebrating atop Chengtian Gate whether you're dead or alive, and if I were a real assassin, I could kill you and escape tonight. In a week, in two weeks, the Yulin Guard will find your corpse. Li Chengyin will cry a few days to show people how sad he is, and then he'll make Lady Zhao his wife. Do you really think he'll remember you?"

I lower my head but don't speak.

Gu Jian takes my hand. "Leave. Come with me. We can be free of this place, of all the scheming and plotting. We'll leave the Plains altogether, and we can herd horses or raise sheep."

I tug my hand from his. "I don't care if Li Chengyin is good to me or not. I chose this. My a'die chose this. I can't leave, and Xiliang can't either." I look deep into his eyes. "Let me go, *please*."

Gu Jian searches my face for something he won't find. Then, after a long while, he says, "I won't."

I'm tired and I'm sad. My already-sore throat hurts from all the talking, and I lean carefully back against the crates, holding a hand to my feverish neck.

He'd been about to say something else but can't bring himself to anymore.

"Do you want to eat?" he asks.

I shake my head.

"I could get you roast duck from Wenyue Tower," he offers.

I start to say no but change my mind halfway through. He brings the blankets up around my shoulders and tucks me in, saying, "Rest here then. I'll be back soon."

I close my eyes.

And then, in about the time it takes for a stick of incense to burn down, I open them back up again. The room is dark and quiet. Silver light seeps through the latticed windows, their shadows projected hazily onto the ground. I push myself up to look—it's the fifteenth of the month, when the moon is at its fullest. The streets must be busy tonight.

Wrapping the furs tighter around myself, I stagger to the doors and test them. But they're locked from the outside. I look around. There's no need for windows in a storeroom, so the only ones that exist are placed high up, for ventilation. I couldn't reach them if I stretched.

But where there's a will . . .

I drag a trunk over and find another to stack on top. I don't know what's inside, but thankfully the trunks aren't heavy, because by the time I maneuver them all over with my feverish limbs, I'm soaked through with sweat.

The windows don't budge when I climb up and push against them, so I stagger back down, looking for something to help. Flipping open a trunk reveals bolts of silk in different colors and weaves. This could be a wealthy family's household, or a silk merchant's warehouse. Not that that would be any use. Disappointed, I close the trunk. And then my eyes land on the ginger tea.

I smash the cup, digging through its shards to find one with a nice sharp edge, and clamber back to the window, but all of the lattices are carved into the frame, and I must saw through each individual length of wood. The porcelain cuts into my finger, drawing blood.

Hopelessness nearly drowns me. Maybe I'll still be stuck in here when Gu Jian returns. He might not kill me, but he could shut me inside forever if he wanted to, and then I would never see A'du again—or Li Chengyin.

Yet like a tide the feeling recedes, and when it's gone I draw myself up and begin again.

I don't know how long it takes, but I hear a crack as the lattice on the bottom corner breaks away. My spirit soars, and I start on the other corner. Once they're both detached, I tug with all my remaining strength. The window comes free—

And I find I've celebrated too early. The window is too high up. From one of the trunks beneath my feet, I pull out a bolt of silk. I secure one end beneath the trunk and fit the other through—and out—the window. Grabbing this makeshift rope, I navigate through the window and carefully down.

My arms are weak and achy though, and the silk is slippery, so I wind it around my wrist. The whole of my weight is concentrated on that loop, and the silk is pulled taut to the point of burning. But I try not to think about that. I'm thinking about what will happen if I slip and fall.

Slowly, step by step, I inch closer to the earth. When I'm close enough to the bottom that I can extend a foot to the ground, my knees go weak and I crumble.

Someone is standing in the distance, I realize, pushing myself up and dusting myself off. He has been here the whole time.

Gu Jian.

He's watching wordlessly, a platter of food in his hands.

I force myself to smile at him.

And then I run.

In three steps he's on me, one hand yanking me by the wrist and the other tight around the roast duck.

"Let me go," I beg. "What's the use of locking me up? I'm not going to leave with you."

Gu Jian laughs coldly. "Fine. I can let you go—but only if you let me take you somewhere first. You can leave then, if you don't change your mind."

This must be some trick. "Where do you want to take me?"

"You'll know soon enough."

I hesitate, narrowing my eyes suspiciously, but he shrugs. "If you're not brave enough, then you can certainly choose to stay here forever. All the better for me if you do."

"And you'll keep your word?"

He smiles. "As long as you keep yours."

"Fine then. Let's go."

Gu Jian pauses. "You won't regret it?"

"There's nothing to regret. Unless *you* regret it."

"There's nothing to regret," he echoes and then opens the lid to the roast duck, saying, "Finish this, and then we'll leave."

I'm not much hungry, but I can tell he won't take me unless I eat, so I pick up the chopsticks and bring the food to my lips. My throat hurts and my tongue feels like it's made of unsanded wood, but I finish everything. "Come on, then."

"Was it good?" Gu Jian asks, examining me.

I force an enthusiastic nod. He doesn't say much else, just lifts his head to observe the round wheel of the moon lifting up from the horizon. He wraps the fur around me, bringing it so high onto my shoulders that it hides half my face. Only then does he say, "Okay. Let's go."

Gu Jian's qinggong is as impressive as ever. The trees blur as we speed past, rising and falling upon the roofs until we come to a wall.

A familiar wall.

He pulls me up so that I can stand atop it beside him, and the world is spread out beneath my feet.

The ceramic tiles, the layered eaves, the carved beasts that walk the roofline. All of the courts that I could not be more familiar with because every time I sneak out, they are the first things I see. The manor. *We were in the manor this whole time.*

"Yes," says Gu Jian when he sees my dumbfounded look. "We've been in your Court of Spring."

I bite my tongue to keep from saying anything, but I'm admonishing myself. I should have shouted. Should have yelled loud enough to bring the entire Yulin Guard to me. No matter how powerful Gu Jian is, he couldn't possibly snatch me away from thousands of guardsmen. I could be safe if I'd thought to yell.

Not that regret is of any use, for he pulls me off the wall and onto someone else's roof. We turn and weave our way across their building, slipping into a garden through a side door and stepping out into the bustle I'd dreamed about all year.

Lights flood streets that are teeming with laughter. It feels like everyone has come out to celebrate, all the lanterns in the world on display. The moon is a distant mirror in a sea of inky black, like a nugget of sweet rice, white and milky, the kind with honeyed filling inside. It reflects off the thin frost that glazes the roof tiles, and the night seems brighter and clearer for it.

Despite this, it's not cold. The wind blows the acrid smell of spent fireworks, the perfume of powders and rouge, the aroma of food drifting from street stalls—blended together, the scent colors the air with festivity. Lanterns hang from every available rafter and beam, in the trees, atop awnings and beneath them. Dancers perform dragon dances and lion dances, and on the canals, people row boat-sized lanterns in lantern-sized boats.

We walk into this sea of radiance through a dizzying, flashing, spinning array of yellows and pinks, blues and purples, reds and greens. Carousel lanterns, embroidered with different stories, spin in the heat of candle flames. Glass lanterns from Bosi flicker, piercingly bright, while scaffold lanterns are built into massive patterns and words, and lantern riddles beckon with prizes for whoever can solve them. Biggest of all is a lantern maze that replicates battle formations, inviting people to lose themselves inside, though, judging by the peals of laughter floating through the air, none of the lost seem to want to be found.

Last year, last week, last night, I would have been delighted by it all, but today I lower my head and let Gu Jian take my hand and lead me through the streets until he is forced to stop by a crowd of people that has formed to watch a crew of dragon dancers. In their arms, the dragon ducks and weaves, winding its way toward us. A spout of sparks explodes from its mouth.

Everyone startles away. I flinch back too. The retreating crowd pushes me back, and I am caught in their tide. I nearly fall, but Gu Jian steadies me. When I open my eyes again, I realize that he's pulled me into his chest and is using his sleeve to cover my face.

I push him away. Thankfully, he doesn't fight it, just catches me by the arm and continues onward.

As we pass the city's southern market, we hear a shrill whistle, which then pops in midair. Everyone raises their head to see threads of golden light, woven into a giant flower, so bright it outshines the moon—the fireworks competition has begun in earnest. The entire street looks up to watch. Even Gu Jian is transfixed. The cold wind of early spring billows through his hair, blowing back the ribbon he's tied it with, and every time another firework flares through the air, the flash catches on his face. Every time it dissipates, he disappears back into the shadows. I watch him, sundered by dark and bright.

What I'm thinking as I watch is that if I escape, he may not be able to catch me. There are so many people out today.

If I can lose him in the crowd, he won't be able to find me again.

But his hand is tight around my arm, and I don't think I can wrest it free.

On either side of us, vendors are calling out their wares—trinkets and banners and flowers, all of it signifying the New Year, jangling and jingling and dizzying to look at. My head pounds. I peer through half-lidded eyes, unable to stomach any of it, but we're stopped by a clueless merchant who shoves his things in our faces and says, "Young master, why don't you buy a pin for your wife's hair? Only a beautiful flower could match such a beautiful bride—and we're selling them at ten coppers for two!"

Gu Jian lifts a hand, and at first I think he's going to wave the man off, but he pays the merchant instead.

"Lower your head," he tells me.

"I don't like these fussy things," I say, but he doesn't listen and slips them into my hair—first one, then the other.

Because he's close, I can feel his breath on my cheek, warm and ticklish, and smell the perfume on his clothes. It's not the fragrance I'm used to—ambergris and agarwood—but a faint, unfamiliar scent—like Xiliang muskmelon, a cold, pure sort of smell.

Then he steps away, taking my hand and inspecting me carefully as if he's scared he put them in unevenly. He's never looked at me so intently before, and I squirm in discomfort, ears burning.

"Let's go," I say.

I don't know where we're going, and he doesn't seem to

know either. We walk in starts and stops, carried by a current of traffic that sets our pace.

Then we turn—and Chengtian Gate is there, rising high. The street, usually reserved for royalty, is flooded with commoners tonight. In the distance, the tower gate is ablaze.

I'm afraid, suddenly.

Afraid of why he's brought me here.

"What?" Gu Jian's smile is a hard twist of the mouth. He turns back to look at me. "Are you scared?"

His smile hadn't looked so mocking the first time I saw it. He'd been wearing a moon-white robe then, standing under the eaves, watching me and A'du run past.

Why has he changed so much?

"What exactly do you want?" I ask, though I know the answer.

"There's nothing more tragic than a deadened heart."[1] His voice is casual, like he's discussing nothing at all of importance. "My heart has died, so I want to see yours do the same."

I don't really hear what he's saying. I'm staring uneasily at the soaring tower. Red muslin lanterns hang from the battlements, strung together by lengths of smaller, multicolored ones, and the edifice looks stitched together with layers of light, like the jade palaces where gods are supposed to live. The closer we walk, the more I see. The crimson curtains that flutter in the breeze. The high coiffures of royal attendants. Their willowy shadows are cast upon the fabric as they pass to and fro, and I am reminded of a shadow puppet show I once

---

1 From *Zhuangzi*, attributed to Kongzi.

saw. At that height, from this distance, everything above us is like that puppet show—and everything is out of my grasp.

Music floats faintly down.

When people begin to cheer, I look up to see that the curtains have been drawn back and that the attendants are throwing something down at us—gold coins, I know, prepared by the palace as a reward for its subjects. They chime against stone tiles as they fall, a thunderstorm of riches.

The kingdom is wealthy. Its people are at peace.

Everyone bends down to grab the gold—everyone except me. I am upright, looking at Chengtian Gate.

Because I've finally seen Li Chengyin. I'm far away, but I recognize him at once. He leans against the railing. Behind him, wind stirs the jade tassels of the embroided canopy to melody, and stirs up his long sleeves too. All around me, people fall to their knees, calling, "Long live the emperor! Long live the king!"

The imperial family are wealthy. They preside over an epoch of peace.

And none of it has anything to do with me.

Lady Zhao draws toward the front of the gate dressed in her ceremonial robes, and though she doesn't step out from behind the curtain, I recognize the shape of her shadow. She drapes a fur cloak around Li Chengyin's shoulders. When the wind rises, whipping his robe about, I see its crimson brocade lining, the gold embroidery shimmering in the candles. He turns and I cannot see his face. But I imagine him smiling at her.

I've never been let up to Chengtian Gate. I've never spent

Shangyuan with Li Chengyin. And I've never known it was because he spent it with Lady Zhao every year, looking down at the blazing city. Tonight. Tonight is the night you're meant to spend with the person you love.

I thought things were different. Stupidly. I thought that, after last night, things were going to change. I'd seen the way he looked at me. I'd heard the way he called my name. The way he swore an oath on his own life for me. And I'd let myself believe. But it's only been a day and he's already standing there with someone else, like nothing happened. Like everything is the same. He's savoring the beauty of the night, accepting the adulation of the crowd.

I'm missing.

I could be dead.

I am his wife.

Someone calls my name.

I turn to look dazedly at Gu Jian. I smile at him and open my mouth to say something, but the cold wind whips up again, stealing my words from me. I choke on the air. My throat had been sore, and now it hurts like it's been torn in two. My head aches. Sharp pebbles rattle inside my skull like the pebbles that have lodged themselves in my larynx, fighting me for breath. I curl up into myself as though my coughing could dislodge the pain from my heart.

I'm cold, I tell myself, *and I'm sick, which is why I'm feeling so poorly.*

Gu Jian helps me to my feet, but I stumble. Something has broken irrevocably. My voice is hoarse as I say, "It's nothing."

But his brows are knit and he draws his hand over my lips.

When he takes it away I can see the blood on his fingers and splattered all over his sleeve, little pinpricks of red. I feel faint. I can't stand for much longer. He holds me, whispering, "Xiaofeng, you can cry. You'll feel better once you let it all out."

I shove him away. "Why should I cry?" I rasp. "*You brought me here. You wanted me to see this, you wanted to make me cry, so you don't have to pretend to give two figs. You said you'd let me go if I came here with you, and I want to go.*"

"Xiaofeng—!" He steps forward to steady me again, but I scurry back, though it takes all of my effort to remain upright. I rip the pins from my hair and fling them at his feet. "*Don't touch me. If you try and follow me, I'll kill myself right here.*"

Maybe because of my threat, he does stop following.

I walk as far as my feet will take me, pushing through the people, the lanterns, the light. I clutch at the fur around my shoulders, cold again—so cold my teeth chatter violently against each other. I'm feverish, I'm unsteady, and I stand beneath the displays, gazing at all the happy people. In the distant heavens, fireworks bloom from the brick pagoda. Happy Shangyuan, beautiful Shangyuan, but where am I supposed to go?

There is nowhere left in heaven or on earth for me.

Where are you, A'du? Let's go home. I miss Xiliang.

A carousel lantern spins, its bamboo panels animated with the dancing silhouette of a beautiful girl, and I know I'm delirious, but she looks like Lady Zhao, and she is covering her face daintily as she giggles, and she's asking, *Did you think things would change? Did you think you had any place in his heart? Did you think he would pity you because you saved his father?*

I was only ever deluding myself.

I lean against a tree for steadiness. The bark grates against my forehead, but the pain is comforting, because it distracts me from the pain in my chest. A'du is gone. I'm all alone. *Where am I supposed to go?*

Could I walk to Xiliang? If I didn't make it home in a month, I'd walk another two; if I didn't make it in six months, I'd walk another six. Whatever it takes.

I raise my head. The moon shines tenderly down on Shangjing, illuminating everything in its gentle, quiet glow. How many times have A'du and I slipped through the wide avenues and narrow alleys? But this isn't where I belong.

Slowly, I turn. Xiliang is west, so I should leave the city through Guanghua Gate and aim west, straight west. When I see Yumen Pass, I will have reached it.

I will have reached home.

Then I hear startled shouts.

"Fire at Chengtian Gate!"

At first I think I must have heard wrong. I look to the south. Chengtian Gate emits a faint glow. Beneath the stacked eaves thick black smoke rises. People gasp, watching as flame swallows the tower. The red muslin, the strands and strands of lanterns, all devoured by a ravenous fire that burns brighter and brighter, aided by the wind, until it becomes an inferno.

The streets burst into activity.

Some run, others shout, but no one knows what to do. Dozens and dozens of soldiers burst from an alley. They shout as people rush aside, their horses tearing down the road like the wind. A fire brigade streams out from behind them, every man hauling wooden water cannons and carts of water that skip and slosh over the uneven pavement as they are dragged along.

Shangyuan is a dangerous time for a fire—with fireworks and oil reserves all over the city—so the fire troops have plenty of water prepared. There have only been small fires, though. Never a conflagration. The Shenwu Army streams in to surround Chengtian Gate and, not long after, escorts a ceremonial carriage back toward the imperial city.

I shouldn't feel so relieved. It shouldn't make a difference if everyone atop that tower died tonight.

The thing I *should* do is return to Xiliang. I'll tell A'die I'm back, and then I'll ride my little red horse out onto the grasslands like I've done a thousand times. I'll go back to my life as the ninth princess.

I draw myself up and turn west again. But a horse carrying a Shenwu soldier flies past. I hear the thwack of a riding crop, and then someone yells, "By order of the emperor, close the gates!"

The people around me descend into confused speculation. Nothing like this has happened before. In the distance, the fire is dying down at last. White dragons dance from the water cannons to Chengtian Gate and a fine mist clings to the air alongside the smell of burned wood.

"We won't be able to leave the city tonight if the gates are closed, will we?"

"Don't worry too much; they're probably trying to get

everything under control. Once they've fully extinguished the fire, they'll reopen the gates...."

I'm too tired to pay this any mind. Breathing feels like burning, like an ember has lodged in my throat, dry and scorched and aching. I sit by the side of the road, trying to tamp down my temper, and lean back against a tree.

I'd only meant to rest a little while, but tiredness overwhelms me.

When I was small—no bigger than a toddler—and my a'die took me out hunting, I would fall asleep as he rode. He'd bring me all the way home like that. I slept so soundly against him, and when I woke, I'd find that I'd left a patch of drool on his tunic.

Pinpricks of light circle blearily around me, overwhelming my vision. They look like the shooting stars that dotted summer skies back home. They say that if you knot your waistband and make a wish when you see one, it will come true, but I was too clumsy and always forgot.

There are so many comets tonight—if I make a wish, would it come true?

With some effort I lift a hand. I'd meant to knot my belt, but it's too heavy and my hand slumps back to the ground. Never mind, then.

Never mind.

I close my eyes and slip into sleep.

I don't know how long I'm out. It feels like a lifetime. My slumber is deep, but shallow at the same time, because there is a carousel lantern in front of my eyes, spinning and spinning and spinning, glinting gold and too bright to look at.

Someone whispers in my ear. They won't stop talking. *Why won't you let me sleep?* I want to scream. I must be sick, because I'm hot and cold by measures, and when I'm hot, my teeth chatter still.

I think I say something—about how I want to go home, how I want my a'die, my A'du, my little red horse. I want the life I used to have, because the thing I want now is not mine to want anymore.

And I'd known that when I hunched over coughing under Chengtian Gate.

My chest is tight, and I slip back into a daze.

In my dream, I gallop into the desert, looking for something, looking all around. Perhaps I am crying, for I hear myself sob.

But what is there to cry about? I'm a Xiliang girl. We don't cry over trifles.

Once I wake, I find that my body aches. My eyelids are tight, so heavy I can hardly open them, but when I do, A'du is here, her eyes red as she looks down at me. It is dark, but there are stars overhead, illuminating us in their tepid glow. We're in an abandoned temple, but how did we get here?

A'du helps me up and raises a bowl of water to my mouth. The burning in my chest has mostly abated, and I clutch at her hands, croaking, "A'du, let's go home."

The words are so garbled even I don't quite understand what I'm saying, but A'du nods. She presses her cool hands against my forehead, a welcome relief against the heat. Thank heavens she came. Thank heavens she found me. I don't have the strength to ask her where she'd gone. She must have been worried, but I feel much better since she's returned to my side. A'du is back. We can leave.

My eyes droop, and I want to sink back into sleep, but with some effort, I wrest them back open when A'du leaps to her feet. She's heard something—then I hear it too, a roll of distant thunder.

Horses, coming for us.

She bends to help me up, but there's no strength left in my bones.

I hope it's not the Shenwu Army or the Yulin Guard. I don't want to see them. Don't want to see Li Chengyin, and I fear A'du has no way of keeping me away if they come.

The temple gates are kicked open.

A white shadow slips from the rafters above, floating down like a mammoth bird. A bright blade pierces toward the door, and there is a scream.

It's Gu Jian. And by their uniforms, the people outside are the Shenwu Army. I sway. I may not want to see Li Chengyin, but I don't want Gu Jian to kill anyone either.

A'du palms her gold-inlay dagger as Gu Jian tangles with the Shenwu Army. I pull the blade from her hands and, befuddled, she looks at me as I creep closer to the fighting.

The soldiers must think I'm in league with Gu Jian, for they rush toward me, but he doesn't let them close. His movements are sharp. Every time his blade flashes, another person falls. Blood splatters hot against my face, and more people collapse at my feet. It's like these men have had the fear of death trained out of them, for they rush unrelentingly toward that flash of white, only to be ceaselessly buffeted back.

I swallow down the lump in my throat. I want to scream, *stop it*, but my voice is hoarse when I do. No one seems to hear me anyway. So I grip the dagger. And I plunge it toward Gu Jian.

He disarms me easily.

A great groaning sound splits across the sky, like a giant boulder hurtling toward us. Instinctively, I look up. A'du is soaring toward me, but it's like an earthquake, and I fear the little temple will collapse from the might of it.

A'du's hand is inches from my own.

Gu Jian is reaching for me.

But he is stuck on the other side of the Shenwu Army, and the roof is collapsing.

A searing pain cracks against the back of my skull, and I am plunged into bottomless darkness.

Splash!

I fall into the water and sink.

The cold is like a knife, cutting my flesh from my bones, but I don't struggle. I let myself fall into it, like an infant who longs to return to the womb, like a flower floating down to the earth it sprouted from. This, I know, is the most tranquil kind of return.

FEI WO SI CUN

The River Oblivion will wash all my love away.

"O, there is a fox, he sits upon the dune. Sits upon the dune, watching the moon. No, not watching the moon—he's waiting for the shepherd girl to come back."

"No, sing another one!"

"But this is the only song I know!"

I will forget you. In this life and every life.

I sat on the dune, watching the sun sink inch by inch below the horizon. My heart sank with it until it disappeared behind a sloping edge of sand and was gone.

Annoyed, I hurled the pendant into the sand and mounted my horse, urging it away from where I'd been waiting.

Stupid shifu. *Bad* shifu. The worst shifu in all the world.

He'd promised to be my matchmaker, promised to find me the most handsome boy in the world to marry, but then he didn't come, though I waited three whole days.

Diplomats from the Central Plains had reached my lord father last week with a marriage proposal from their emperor: their crown prince had turned sixteen, they said, and they hoped he'd be able to marry a Xiliang princess in order to secure the treaty between our two kingdoms. They'd sent a princess to us once, a very long time ago, so it was our turn to return the favor.

Two of my elder sisters had wanted badly to go. They'd heard the Plains were beautiful. They could wear splendid clothes, sail on real boats, and they wouldn't have to put up with the wind or the dust or the fact that we had to move often from place to place looking for fresh water. But the diplomats tactfully declined. Because the princess consort was going to be the empress of the Plains someday, they explained, they were hoping for a trueborn daughter, the daughter of the queen of Xiliang, not the daughter of a mere consort, whether they were royal or not.

I didn't know what kind of rule that was, but it left me. Only me, for my a'niang was the queen of Xiliang, and she had no other girls.

My sisters had been jealous, but honestly, I couldn't see what the fuss was about. I'd seen Plainsmen—silk merchants mostly—and each was more delicate than the last. They didn't know how to shoot. They didn't know how to ride. And their crown prince had been raised deep inside a palace, where all he learned was how to recite nice poetry and draw pretty things.

I had no desire to marry someone who couldn't so much as hold a bow. I'd fought with my lord father for days until finally he said, "I know you don't want to wed the crown prince, but I can't very well refuse the proposal without good reason. If you have someone in mind, I can troth you to them and tell the envoys to pick someone else. They can't find fault with us then, can they?"

But I was barely fifteen. Every boy I knew saw me as their baby sister. They never took me hunting, never brought me singing, never let me go anywhere with them—I wouldn't find anyone in the royal city who'd agree to marry me.

When my shifu found out, he'd thumped his chest and promised he'd find me the handsomest boy in the world. They called that *matchmaking*, he said, in the Central Plains. He'd arrange for us to meet, and then if we liked each other, and if we could get our parents' permission, we could be engaged.

You couldn't tell much about anyone from the way they looked, but the fire had been close enough to singe my eyebrows, and I needed *some* way to avoid the crown prince. So I agreed.

He told me to wait atop the biggest dune, three miles outside the city, and handed me a jade pendant—the boy with its twin would be the person he chose. He told me to look closely, and make sure I liked him.

But then I waited—three whole days and three whole nights—and not only did the male suitor not show up, I didn't see so much as a male fox either.

He'd been teasing me. I should have known. All he did was make fun.

Last time, he'd tricked me into believing that the River Oblivion was behind Yanzhi Mountain, and I snuck out on my little red horse with a bag of food. I'd ridden for a week and a half, climbing all the way to the top of the mountain—to find a wide field of grass. Never mind a whole river—there hadn't even been a puddle.

It had taken twenty days to get back. I'd gotten lost winding down the mountain path and had to ask an old shepherd for directions. A'niang thought I'd gone missing, that I was lost forever. She'd hugged me close, sobbing, but my lord father had been so angry, he locked me in the palace for days.

I asked later why he'd lied, and shifu said, "Why did you believe me in the first place? Don't you know how many liars there are in the world? You can't believe everything people say. I was trying to teach you a lesson, otherwise you'll be taken advantage of."

I'd looked into those shiny eyes of his and longed to give him a shiner.

But I never learned, and I didn't know why I didn't, because I must have fallen for his tricks a dozen times or more. I might have spent my whole life schooling myself on his "lessons" and I still wouldn't be the clever sort.

Dropping the reins, I let my horse take me back at its own pace. As it munched on the grass, I wondered if I should tell my lord father that it was my shifu who I liked, and to please engage me to him. He'd played plenty of terrible jokes on me; the least I could do was get even.

It was a stroke of genius. I perked up and picked up the reins again, humming a ditty as I urged my horse back toward the capital.

"O, there is a fox..."

I was approaching the refrain when someone behind me called, "Miss, I think you dropped something."

I turned to see a boy sitting astride a white horse.

Shifu once said that not all boys on white horses were princes, that more likely they were monks, traveling westward over the merchant roads on a pilgrimage to retrieve sutras. But this boy wasn't wearing red kasaya. He wore white and looked handsomer in that color than anyone I'd seen. The Bosi merchants who passed through Xiliang sometimes dressed in white too, but theirs was a warm melon white. This—this was a white as clean and bright as the moon in the sky.

And he was beautiful, too. Eyes shaped like crescents, smiling though he wasn't, skin as fine as the best jade in the Hetian quarries. His hair was tied up in the Xiliang style and he spoke our language well, but I could tell at once he was a Plainsman, because no one here had a complexion like that.

His posture was strangely imposing—like A'die storming the battlefield, wielding his blade, looking proudly down on his troops to protect his land.

This boy looked like that too, like he was the only lord under all of heaven and upon all the earth.

My heart skipped a beat. His eyes were as fierce as sandstorms, as though they could swallow everything in their path. When he looked at me, I couldn't think of anything else. A piece of white jade lay on his elegant fingers—the same one I'd thrown away in my tantrum.

"Isn't this yours?"

But my temper flared again when I looked at it. "No," I said sourly. "It's not mine."

"There's no one else around." He offered it to me again.

I gestured at the land around us, though I knew I was being contrary. "Who said there's no one else around? The wind is around, and the sand, the moon, the stars—"

He smiled. "And the you."

I must have been possessed, for my face burned bright and hot. I didn't flirt, but I could tell he did, a little, and I regretted coming out alone. It occurred to me that I was a girl who didn't know how to fight, and he was right about us being the sole people around.

"Do you know who I am?" I proclaimed loudly. "I'm the ninth princess of Xiliang. My lord father is king here, and my lady mother is a princess of Jieshuo, daughter of the Tie'ergeda Chanyu, the fiercest man in these lands and the rightful ruler of the north. Vultures fear landing when they hear his name, so you'd better not pull anything funny, or my lord father will have you killed to death."

"Killed to death, is it?" His smile unfurled wide and lazy across his face. "What's a proper girl like you doing going around and threatening people? Do you know who *I* am? I'm the fifth son of the Gu family. My father owns a tea emporium, and my mother is the lady of his house, the daughter of a farmer. My lineage may not be as impressive as yours, but if you really did kill me dead, your Xiliang wouldn't have any more tea to drink."

I pouted. We just started importing tea, and there was very little more valuable than it here. My lord father loved tea from the Central Plains—everyone loved tea from the Central Plains—and if he wasn't lying, then I was in big trouble.

He looked at me, laughter twinkling in his eyes.

Someone behind me laughed too, and laughed loudly.

My shifu. I didn't know where he'd sprung up from, but he was making fun of me again.

"How dare you show your face?" I yelled. "I waited *three days* for you! Where's the handsome boy you promised?"

Shifu pointed. "He's right there!" he called.

I turned back around to see the boy on the white horse, a mischievous smile dancing on his lips. He extended his hand again. Not one, but a pair, I realized, his pendant a perfect match for mine.

For a long minute, I didn't know what to do.

I didn't want to marry *him*. He was *so* handsome, but too sharp-tongued, and he hadn't let me win our dispute. I huffed and turned my horse back to the city with every intention of ignoring them both. But shifu and the Gu boy rode behind me, chatting.

"I thought you weren't coming," shifu said.

"I got your letter; of course I came," said the Gu boy.

There was an easy camaraderie between them, and I realized quickly they were old friends. They talked the whole way back to the royal city—shifu told him all about Xiliang, our customs, our people, while the Gu boy listened carefully and asked questions—and didn't seem to mind at all that I could hear everything they said. As the subject meandered from the traditions to the trade routes, I yawned. Shifu had never said quite so many words to me.

Thankfully, the silhouette of the city was rising in the distance.

Constructed from stone, the city walls were a mountain range that soared up into the sky, growing taller the closer we came. Xiliang was arid, so there weren't many other large cities, and until a hundred years ago, we'd been primarily nomadic. Then a khan arose to bring together the tribes of the western grassland, levying their power to build this marvelous city and unite them under a single banner: Xiliang. Over the years, we formed marriage alliances with neighboring kingdoms, became a tribute state to the empire of the Central Plains, and, because we were right on the path that merchants took between the Plains and the caliphates farther west, we became wealthy.

Our kings had always been good leaders, our men brave warriors, so slowly, though we didn't expand, we strengthened—until even the Central Plains didn't dare underestimate us. Under the fabric of the purple-black sky, the walls seemed more towering, more impressive. The lamp that swung from the gate tower was a twinkling star that danced below those more distant cousins that sparkled like frost up to the very border of heaven.

I patted my little red horse smartly, and it started to trot. The bell I tied to its neck chimed crisp and merry, a pretty duet with the camel bells that clanged in the distance. Merchants, probably, taking advantage of the cool of night to press forward to their next destination, which is why we didn't close the city gates.

I came to them first.

The well keepers inside the gates recognized me and waved, tossing a string of grapes. I caught it. The merchants gave it to them, and they kept the sweetest ones for me.

I grinned at them, plucking a grape and popping it into my mouth. Then I turned to shifu and the Gu boy. "Hey! Do you want some?"

I didn't call shifu *teacher* or *master* or any of that, because he only became my shifu by tricking me. At the time, we were strangers, and I hadn't known how good he was at swordplay. He'd goaded me into fighting him by promising that the winner could take the loser on as an apprentice. To no one's surprise but my own, I lost terribly. But he didn't have the dignity of a shifu, so I didn't act like an apprentice, either.

Absent-minded, he shook his head. He turned to the Gu boy and said something. He'd taught me a little from the Plains books, like:

> *But I have seen the one I love*
> *And my heart at last is easing.*[2]

and

> *The best of all the gentlemen*
> *Is mild and modest as jade.*[3]

He'd stuffed my head full of nonsense, and all that talk of jade made me think that gentlemen ought to *look* like jade too, with fair skin and wearing all white. Shifu also wore white, but he wasn't a gentleman. He, I thought, was a scoundrel.

The Gu boy's name turned out to be Xiaowu. He'd decided to stay in the royal city for a while and was living with shifu, for shifu's rooms were clean and well-ordered and didn't lodge any smelly camels. I visited shifu often, and eventually, I got to know the boy too. Most of his business was conversation, I discovered, and there was always fragrant tea to be had in his quarters. Pastries too, all the way from the Central Plains. Best of all, he shared his curios with me—odd little knickknacks that delighted beyond measure.

But every time we saw each other he asked the same teasing question: "Ninth Princess, when's our wedding?"

It was all shifu's fault. If he'd been a more responsible teacher, I wouldn't have landed in this mess. I would tell Gu Xiaowu I'd rather resign myself to marrying the crown prince

---
[2] From *The Book of Songs*, "The Odes of Zheng: Wind and Rain."
[3] Popular saying used to describe male beauty.

than be wed to a hooligan like him, and he would laugh.

I didn't want to marry anyone, though. I wanted to stay in Xiliang. Why would I ever want to leave?

But the diplomats had begun to badger my lord father about the proposal in earnest. And that wasn't all—once the Mohu heard that we were hosting Plainsmen, they sent their own envoy, loaded down with gifts, lumbering to Xiliang.

Mohu was one of the biggest kingdoms in the region and was home to tens of thousands of well-trained archers—not anyone my lord father would dare offend. So he met with them. When the attendant I'd ordered to eavesdrop on their meeting returned, she whispered that they had also come with a marriage proposal—on their chanyu's behalf.

The chanyu of Mohu was in his fifties, and his wife had been a Jieshuo princess—my a'niang's older sister. She died two years ago, but her position was empty because his other consorts were busy jostling for it among themselves.

A'niang was furious when she heard. I was too. We weren't blood relations, but he was my *uncle*, and his beard was white besides. He wanted to be my husband? I certainly wasn't about to marry a man as old as that.

Stuck between offending Mohu and offending the Plains, my lord father could do little more than continue to stall. But the envoys all boarded within the city, and it was getting harder and harder to hold them off.

So I decided to slip away and see my grandfather.

Every autumn, the aristocrats of Jieshuo went to Tiangen Mountain to hunt. A'weng invited me over to amuse myself whenever he could, especially now that his health was starting to give him problems. He said that seeing me was like seeing my a'niang, which made him happy.

Jieshuo custom forbade married women from returning to their childhood homes unless they had been renounced by their husband's family, so A'niang was all too happy for me to go and send her love. She hadn't liked the idea of sending me off to the Central Plains and despised the idea of my going to Mohu, so when I told her my plan, she prepared some rations and some water, and when my lord father left the city on an outing, she snuck me out too.

I rode my little red horse toward Tiangen.

Mountains surrounded the royal city—the range that rose from its west to its north was called Yanzhi. It had sinuous, soaring peaks that circled it like the sheltering arms of a colossus, shielding it from wind, from sand, and from cold, so that the land at its base was a green oasis in a barren desert.

Tiangen Mountain was a lone, high peak to the east, half lost in clouds, the kind Plainsmen painted onto their screens. Its peak was perpetually covered in a sheet of snow, and I once heard that no one had summitted. Past that were the endless grasslands, lush and verdant, of my a'niang's homeland.

Before I left, I wrote a note for shifu. He'd been busy since Gu Xiaowu came to stay, and if I left for Jieshuo I probably wouldn't be back until winter. In the note, I reminded him to feed A'ba and A'xia, the two little gerbils who lived in his courtyard. I'd been the one to catch them, but my lord father hadn't let me keep them in the palace.

The weather was nice and cool when I left with the merchant trains. They snaked endlessly out of the royal city, heading west. I was the only rider on the eastward path.

Desert nights were quiet, the velvet sky so dark and heavy you could touch it if you stretched. The stars were big and bright, like the dew that sat fat on grape leaves, and just as cold. I climbed over an ocean of sand dunes and noted sparse patches of grass, making sure I wasn't going the wrong way. I took the same path every year, but before, it had been with A'weng's troops escorting me.

My little horse cantered after the Big Dipper's tail, and I started to imagine what I would do when I saw my grandfather this time—perhaps I'd ask him to get his bond servants to catch me a songbird.

I was dead tired by the time the red sun started showing signs of rising, shooting through the eastern half of the sky with purple sunrise. The stars had disappeared long ago, and the sky revealed light beneath the ashen gray. Thin curls of predawn mist hung in the air. I had to find a place to rest. Noontime sun was strong enough to kill a person, and you didn't want to be caught on the road then.

When we'd waded through a small, shallow river, I found a shadowed little hill and dismounted, leaving my horse to graze. Fashioning myself a pillow from some scant tufts of grass, I lay upon it, falling easily into sleep. I rose when the sun slanted west and let loose its heat on my face.

I dug out some rations, along with half a skin of water. I took my time eating, filling the waterskin back up as I whistled for my horse.

In but a moment I could hear the beat of its hooves as it bounded joyfully toward me, whinnying. It pulled up short, nudging my hands and licking them. I smoothed its mane, saying, "Are you full?"

It's a pity the horse couldn't talk back to me, but it could look at me with those bright, dewy eyes. I patted its neck, but it startled, nickering.

How strange. My little red horse pawed and stomped the grass, clearly distressed, and I wondered if there were wolves around.

Grassland wolves were terrifying. They roved in packs and were fierce enough to fight lions. It was an ever-present danger to meet them alone, but this was autumn, when the desert was at its most fertile and there were plenty of gazelles and wild rabbits out. They should have had enough to eat. There was no reason for them to be near—they didn't usually descend from their dens up in the craggy peaks of Tiangen unless they were starving.

But my horse *was* distressed, and it wouldn't be agitated for no reason. I hoisted myself back into the saddle. Tiangen Mountain was straight ahead, and past the foothills lay the border between Xiliang and Jieshuo. A'niang had sent word, so there would be people stationed there waiting to meet me. It would be safer to head forward instead of turning back.

I urged my horse on, but it didn't take long for me to catch the sound of hoofbeats behind me, so I pulled us to a stop, balancing atop the saddle so I could see farther into the distance. Could A'die have sent people after me so quickly?

There was a battalion drawing closer, but I couldn't make out their flags. There was nothing to do but ride as hard as I could to the border.

My horse shot forward like an arrow, galloping at full speed across the grasslands. But the flatness of the terrain worked against us—there was nowhere to duck, nowhere to hide, and the battalion was gaining on me. Sooner or later, they would catch up.

I glanced back. The riders were close and must have numbered in the thousands. A'die wouldn't have been able to muster a force like this one with ease, and he wouldn't have sent such a large number of men for such a little thing. *Where had they come from?*

It didn't take long for my little red horse to reach the foothills, and from far away I could see a black speck on the horizon, singing a lingering, carrying song. A Jieshuo herding song, familiar and warm.

A'weng's people, I thought, and urged the horse faster, faster.

They must have seen me too, for a man rose in his stirrups to wave wildly at me.

I waved furiously back. The armored riders were on my heel, inching closer with every league we traveled. But I was nearing the white flag of Jieshuo, its tail unfurling in the sunset wind, like a fish soaring among the clouds. As I neared, I realized that I knew the man—it was Heshi, A'weng's favorite archer, who, when he saw the dark line of riders that chased me, planted the flag into the earth and raised his bow.

"Stop!" I called. "I don't know who they are!" We should

know that at least, lest we do something we couldn't take back.

I blazed past Heshi, coming to a stop a hundred or so feet beyond his horse. There were dozens of archers with him, their arrowheads dazzling in the bright afternoon sun. They rode up to me as they took aim, closing ranks around my little red horse. Heshi smiled. "Little princess, how have you been?"

I wasn't a daughter of the royal house of Jieshuo, but they all called me *princess* because of A'niang. I was so relieved to see them that I nearly forgot the people on my tail. "I'm good!"

But my pursuers made themselves known as they approached, hoofbeats as loud as thunder. Less than two arrow lengths from us. Heshi's smile widened as they approached.

"So many," he exclaimed. "Are they looking for a fight?"

He raised his bow as he spoke, nocking an arrow to the string. The white flag of Jieshuo flapped beside him. Everyone on these grasslands knew that if they saw this flag, the armies of the Tie'ergeda Chanyu were near. They knew if they crossed it, Jieshuo's armies would flatten all their encampments, kill all their people, and seize all their herds. Outside the Yumen Pass, no one dared disrespect this flag.

But the horses pressed forward, unrelenting. The honeyed glow of sunset refracted off their armor, scattering orange light across the plain. I sucked in a sharp breath.

The light armor, the livery, the helmets—these were Mohu troops, though they didn't carry the Mohu flag. I'd never been there, but I *had* been to the Anxi Protectorate and had seen them train—their horses were fine horses, their armor distinct, their bows quick and piercing.

Heshi recognized them too, and he shot me a glance. "Princess, ride east. Go around Binli River. The chanyu has settled to the east for autumn."

"I'm not going to leave you here to fight them all alone," I protested.

He sighed, resigned, and passed me a blade. I took it from him, but my palms were damp. The Mohu troops were fierce, and they outnumbered us, pressing down like a black mass that shook the mountains. Heshi was an excellent archer, but we had only a few dozen men.

The blade was no better than a lump of metal in my hand. I hadn't thought of myself as being less capable than my brothers in anything, but I hadn't stepped foot on a battlefield.

Our flag whipped in the wind. The sun sank slowly, slipping beneath the very edge of the world, and the grass undulated like waves, like the dunes that shaped the horizon. A chill set in. I blinked away the sweat that stung my eyes.

The cavalry slowed as they approached.

"I am Heshi of Jieshuo!" Heshi called. "Your horses trespass on our lands. Turn back if you don't want war."

Heshi had a reputation. His fame as an archer was known to all—in the language of Jieshuo, *heshi* meant arrow. If he wanted to shoot out the left eye of a great goose, the right would not be touched. He was a favorite of the Tie'ergeda Chanyu, my a'weng, and the riders must have known that, for a ripple shuddered through their ranks at his name. One man rode forward to parley.

I didn't speak Mohu, but Heshi did, and he translated. The Mohu claimed they'd been chasing after an escaped bond servant. They claimed Tiangen Mountain was neutral territory, ungoverned land, since it sat on the border of Mohu, Jieshuo, and Xiliang—if we insisted it was Jieshuo land, no one would support our claim.

"An escaped bond servant?" I repeated, confused. The Mohu general raised his whip to point at me and continued to speak.

Heshi drew himself up, suddenly furious. "Princess, he's saying that you're the missing slave."

"What?" My temper flared. "Rubbish!"

Heshi nodded. "It's all pretense."

The general spoke again.

"What did he say?" I demanded.

"He says that if we don't hand you over, they will take you by force, and that if war does rise, it will be our fault for harboring a fugitive."

I laughed in disbelief. "How *dare* they?"

"Yes, Princess," said Heshi darkly. "But we're outnumbered, and you're their target. It would be best if you went on ahead to the royal encampment and asked them to send a relief force. If we can't hold them off, at least they won't have a chance to ambush the chanyu."

So Heshi meant for me to escape alone. I was scared, but not a coward. I drew myself up, saying, "Send someone else— I'm not leaving you!"

"Princess, there aren't enough men that I could spare one to protect you," Heshi said patiently.

And as much as I hated to admit it, he was right. I'd be getting in the way if I stayed. I was a good shot, but I hadn't been tested in battle, and I was surrounded by seasoned warriors.

"Okay then." I tightened my grip on the blade. "I'll let them know Mohu is coming."

Heshi nodded and handed me the waterskin at his side. "Ride east a hundred leagues. If you can't find the chanyu's tent, head north—the prince's people should be no more than thirty leagues from there."

"I understand."

With the broad of his blade, Heshi smacked my horse's rear, and it took off galloping.

The Mohu riders clamored at the sight, but by then I was far away, my horse a red streak of lightning that carved through the grassland. I kept looking back, worried, but though Heshi and his men were surrounded, they managed to pick off the riders who tried to come after me. Mohu soldiers tumbled to the ground and I pulled farther away, out of their reach. The fighting disappeared into the horizon until the only thing I could make out was that white flag. Then the sky darkened, and night descended.

I galloped on.

The night was suffocatingly humid, and there were no stars out nor a moon to light my way. I'd not seen weather like this, not ever, and I feared it would rain. Nothing would have been more dangerous. The sky was dark and inky, like someone had taken an iron bowl and capped it overhead, and without the stars, it was hard to tell where I was or where I was going.

I rode blind for half the night, terrified that the Mohu troops would find me. They didn't, but neither did Heshi's troops. I nearly cried, but my tears were interrupted by a crack of purple light that split the night in two. The low rumble of thunder roiled in the distance. Despite all my hopes, it was going to storm. I had to find a place to shelter.

Lightning struck again, darting through the low clouds like snakes. By their borrowed light, I saw a group of craggy rocks ahead. I'd been galloping along the edge of Tiangen Mountain all night, but I was still in its shadow.

Finding a boulder to shelter under was better than getting soaked to death, so I brought my little red horse up to the mountain. It leapt lightly over the rocks but, worried that the scattered pebbles would get lodged in its hooves, I dismounted to lead it by the reins instead. It was beginning to pour. The rain whipped past, fast and heavy and painful against my skin. It soaked me through, dripping from my hair to my eyes, coming down in streams that I couldn't blink away quickly enough. Finally, I found an overhanging rock large enough to shelter under.

I led my horse to the overhang and the two of us ducked beneath. The rain came down in sheets, and I worried about Heshi. My little red horse half knelt on the stone. It licked my palm as though it understood. I clutched at its neck. "How do you think they're doing?" I muttered.

The water was like a white curtain flowing from the rock. Fog rose, seeping through, like another little rainfall.

I don't know how long the storm lasted, but it did stop. The water burbled like a river off the stone, but as the wind swept past, it cleared the sky of clouds, revealing a sliver of clean, radiant moon.

My robes stuck to my skin, and it was cold in the breeze. I sneezed. But the fire starter in my lapels had been ruined, and there was no dry wood to build anything from.

When the water trickled to a halt, my little red horse snuggled in close to me, lapping at my face with its warm tongue. Now the storm had ended, it was time to get going again.

The moon had just about set by the time we climbed down the mountain. My horse had been sullen, annoyed when we'd been forced to shelter beneath the rock, but now it was bounding with excitement to be galloping toward where the horizon was beginning to pale. The sun was about to come up, I thought, or else why would I be so hot?

I was growing bleary, the reins slipping from my hand. Rocking back and forth atop the horse felt like being swayed in a cradle and, after a long night without rest, tiredness overtook me. I didn't know how long I was half conscious—perhaps it was a little while and perhaps it was a long time—but I was startled forcefully back into wakefulness when my horse splashed across a shallow little stream, spraying cold water all over me.

Under the great, vast empty I was the only person in all the world. Tiangen Mountain was far behind me, a giant who held up the sky and wore a crown of snow that never melted. The stream we forded was snowmelt that ran off from the mountain.

In my tiredness I remembered that I hadn't eaten since I left Xiliang. But my rations were secured behind the saddle, and I couldn't work up an appetite when my mouth tasted drier than wood. I was thinking about whether I should dismount and drink something when the flash of a black shadow on the horizon caught my eye. *A rider.*

I stared, terrified it was the Mohu cavalry again, but it was a single person astride a very fast horse.

If it was the prince's scout, I would be in luck, but . . .

With some effort, I drew the saber at my back. If it was the enemy, I'd fight for as long as I was able—that was my last thought as everything went black.

Everyone in Xiliang had been taught since childhood to ride and shoot. I'd grown up on horseback, knew my way around a saddle before I took my first steps, and if anyone found out their ninth princess had fallen from her steed, I'd be the laughingstock of the entire city.

The blade was still in my hand when I woke. I blinked blearily. The sky above me was bright blue. Fluffy white clouds hung so low that they seemed within reach, and I was lying on the soft incline of a grassy hill that blocked the heat of the sun. A cool breeze billowed past, carrying the familiar sound of my little red horse's whinny.

I breathed a sigh of relief.

"Awake?"

The voice was familiar. My head spun as I pushed myself up, disbelieving.

Gu Xiaowu sat lazily on the grass, gnawing at a piece of beef jerky.

"Why are you here?"

"I was passing by," he shrugged. Only a fool would believe that.

My stomach gurgled. I remembered then that I was carrying rations. I whistled, and my horse trotted over—but it wasn't wearing a saddle. My head snapped back to Gu Xiaowu, who I realized too late was sitting upon it, and the jerky he was eating—wasn't that mine, too?

"Hey!" I snapped. "Where's my food?"

"There's one left," he said around a mouthful of beef. He waved the last half strip of jerky at me.

One left? There was one *bite* left.

Not even that—I watched him stuff it into his mouth.

"You ate it *all*?" I yelped. "What am I going to eat?"

"You'll have to go hungry then." He drank a mouthful of my water. "You were running a fever earlier, so you shouldn't be eating this junk anyway."

Liar. I leapt to my feet. "Give me back my food—I want it back."

"It's in my stomach." He laughed. "I can hardly return it."

I fumed and looked around for my sword. Seeing me stamping around in circles like a furious ant, he said, "If you come back to the royal city with me, I'll give you an entire cow to make up for it."

I rolled my eyes. "Give me one reason."

"Your lord father is offering a reward for your return. One hundred pieces of gold to anyone who brings you back to the city." He eyed me. "*One hundred!* Do you know how many cows that would buy?"

Now I was angry for real. "He posted a notice for me?"

"Why would I lie?"

"And I'm only worth *a hundred* pieces of gold?" I was

disappointed in my a'die, I really, really was. "I'm worth *at least* a hundred times that! And—and—he should offer to make you a marquess and give you as many bondmen—and as much livestock—as you wanted!"

He'd always claimed I was his favorite little princess, and he'd posted a reward of only *a hundred* pieces of gold? Stingy! That was the word for it.

Gu Xiaowu erupted into laughter. I didn't know what he thought he was chortling at. I eyed him balefully. He gazed at me as he smiled, as though I were his prize money.

"I'm not coming back with you," I announced. "So you can stop dreaming."

"Then where are you going to go?" Gu Xiaowu asked. "The Mohu diplomats have been angry since you left, you know, saying that your father let you leave to avoid them. They sent troops after you. You'd be in trouble if they found you out here."

I thought so too, because they already had.

And then I leapt up with a gasp—I'd very nearly forgotten Heshi and his men. I had to get to A'weng.

"What? What is it?"

I hadn't intended to tell him anything, but the grasslands were big, and he was the one person I knew out here. I eyed him. Shifu was a good fighter; maybe Gu Xiaowu would be too.

"So the chanyu's a hundred leagues from here?" he asked, once I'd told him what happened.

I nodded.

"And the prince is within a thirty-league radius of the royal encampment?"

I nodded again.

"But Jieshuo are nomads," he said. "How will you find them?"

"I hadn't thought too much about that," I admitted.

Gu Xiaowu furrowed his brow. "Distant rivers can't save a nearby fire," he said. "The Anxi Protectorate is closer. Can't we borrow their soldiers?"

I fumbled for words. Anxi was an outpost that guarded the Plains Empire's western border, and they rarely involved themselves in outside conflicts, no matter how bad the fighting got. Our battles were our own to fight. Like when arguing with your brothers—you wouldn't call in an outsider. It didn't matter if it *was* someone you were all tributaries to.

"We can't, not about something like this."

"Why not?"

I didn't know why not, only that no one did. "We just can't," I said. "And anyway, our fighting here has nothing to do with the Plains or its emperor."

"*Under the heavens there is nothing that is not the emperor's land. Within the oceans there are none who do not act as the emperor's hand,*"[4] he said. "As long as it's beneath that sun, it has something to do with the emperor. Not to mention that the outpost was erected here to keep the peace, which Mohu has disturbed. Why not teach them a lesson?"

This was all too abstract for me. He pulled both our horses over, saying, "If we head south, Anxi is less than half a day's ride away. Come on, I'll go with you."

---

4 From *The Book of Songs*, "Lesser Court Hymns: North Mountain"

I hesitated. "Is that . . . okay?"

"Do you want to help Heshi or not?"

"Of course I do!"

He lifted me onto my horse. "Then what are you waiting for?"

It wasn't until we'd been riding for hours that I thought to ask: "How did you find me, actually?"

The noon sun was high overhead, illuminating his jadeite face. He smiled wide. "Luck!"

He'd been right about the length of the ride. By sunset we could see the moat that surrounded the city, which had been built over a hundred years ago to guard the strategic pass between the Central Plains and the western kingdoms. Merchant caravans often stopped here after the royal city, so the protectorate was about as prosperous as Xiliang.

I'd been worried that we might be brushed off—we were just two people, after all—but to my surprise, Gu Xiaowu brought me straight to the city magistry and started to beat the signal drums that stood outside.

I didn't know it at the time, but there was a ritual to these drums: sometimes, they were called *sleeping*, and other times, *waking*. Striking them was a signal that war was coming. Soldiers rushed from within to sweep us in front of the magistrate, who was seated in his courtroom, fierce with his thick black beard and gleaming suit of armor. Of all the Plainsmen I'd seen, he looked the most like a warrior.

He spoke to us in a deep voice, but I didn't know much Plains, so I glanced to Gu Xiaowu. He motioned for me to start talking—the magistrate could speak Jieshuo.

"Why did you strike the drum, child?"

I spoke Jieshuo because of my a'niang, and I told him all about Mohu bringing armies past the border, about Heshi, who badly needed rescue.

The magistrate hesitated. I supposed that it was because the Plains had only gotten involved to quell revolts, and because Jieshuo was more powerful than Mohu. Bringing a Mohu army past the Jieshuo border did sound unlikely.

Indeed, what he said after we finished speaking was "Jieshuo's cavalry is renowned for their skill. Why would they need to send for aid instead of fighting Mohu themselves?"

I told him about how the chanyu's encampment was migratory and how, though the prince might have been closer, it would take time to find him. Heshi had just a few men with him. He wouldn't be able to hold off the Mohu army for much longer. And the longer the magistrate deliberated, the more frantic I became.

Gu Xiaowu stepped forward.

He said something in Plains, something that astonished the magistrate, who rose from behind his desk. Gu Xiaowu walked forward, bowing deeply. Their voices were low—I couldn't hear anything, and I wouldn't have understood it either way—but the magistrate nodded.

And then he gave us two thousand cavalry.

I was overjoyed. "How did you convince him to give us so many people?"

Gu Xiaowu looked like a fox when he smiled. "Secret."

I pouted.

The Plains army was disciplined. They rode in neat lines

through the night. No one spoke, and there was no noise except for the horses and the armor and the roar of their torches. Those torches were made of wood wrapped with fire-oil-soaked cotton, a special export from the lands beyond Tiangen Mountain. Shepherds used it to light their cooking fires sometimes, but it didn't burn clean—it was smoky and pungent—so no one used it inside the royal city. I wouldn't have thought to use it for torches, though. Plainsmen were so canny. They were forever finding surprising uses for things.

We rode all night, catching up to Mohu's cavalry near daybreak. They'd long since retreated to their own borders.

And by the time we found them, the white flag of Jieshuo had disappeared. My heart pounded—what if Heshi and his men were already dead?

Gu Xiaowu spoke to the battalion leader in Plains. Then the man gave an order and his riders dispersed into a formation, circling around the Mohu cavalry, which was more than twice as large as the one we rode with.

My lord father once said that Plains armies were adept at using formations, which gave them an advantage against stronger forces. The Mohu general pulled his horse around and called out—I didn't understand what he was saying, but Gu Xiaowu had spent time all over the grasslands selling his tea, so he did.

"He's asking why we brought troops into Mohu territory."

"But they brought troops over the Jieshuo border yesterday," I protested. "And they claimed it was over a lost slave. Where do they get the nerve to act like they're in the right?"

Gu Xiaowu turned to address the Plains commander, who in turn ordered someone to bring word to the Mohu.

"I told them we're bringing the princess of Xiliang back to her kingdom," he smiled. "We're just passing by and have no intention of fighting them."

If Gu Xiaowu said that he was the second most shameless man in the world, I don't think anyone could claim they were first. His face was perfectly straight as he lied, and I wondered if all Plains people were like that—shifu liked to lie to me too.

Both sides shouted back and forth for a time, and as they did, the Plains commander had his troops use the autumn morning fog to hide the fact that they were circling around the back of the Mohu troops. By the time the Mohu general realized what was happening, it was too late. The vanguard was charging.

Victory was decisive. The Mohu troops were caught in the formation, and half were sundered beneath the quick edge of Plains blades. Seeing that they couldn't hold out for much longer, the Mohu finally lowered their bows and surrendered.

Gu Xiaowu looked on unflinchingly. I didn't think tea merchants saw much fighting, but he didn't seem scared at all, watching impassively as though the killing were nothing more than a game. The Plains commander oversaw the surrender, leading his army of two thousand and their new captives back east.

I rode into the cavalry, looking for Heshi. The Mohu general was brought to see the Plains commander, who was very polite and turned him over to Gu Xiaowu. I nudged Gu

Xiaowu to interrogate the man, but the man was tight-lipped and refused to say a word.

Very placidly, Gu Xiaowu asked, "Why keep him around if he won't talk?"

So the commander ordered the Mohu general's execution. They brought me his head, dripping with warm blood that landed on the grass like blooms of red flowers.

I didn't have the stomach for it. I hadn't eaten anything in a day and a half either, and swayed on my feet.

Seeing the color drain from my face, one of the aides brought me a waterskin, but I couldn't keep the water down. I heard Gu Xiaowu asking for another Mohu soldier to be brought in. They showed him his general's head first, and then asked where Heshi was.

Mohu warriors may have been brave, but no one was that courageous when they were taken captive and their general was dead. He told us everything.

They had forced Heshi to retreat all the way to Tiangen Mountain, where the small band of men had mounted a resistance with rocks as cover until they'd run out of arrows. But the Mohu hadn't hurried to kill them. Instead, they took Heshi's horses and left him and his men in the mountains.

I shuddered at their ruthlessness. There were wolves up there. Without horses, without arrows—Heshi was defenseless.

We set off for Tiangen Mountain immediately, but that wasn't enough to calm me.

"The people of Jieshuo aren't that easy to kill," said Gu Xiaowu.

He said it to comfort me, but it vexed me to hear.

We circled the mountain until sunset, until I'd lost nearly all hope. Tiangen was vast—when would we find Heshi?

On one hand, I was afraid he'd been eaten—if he had, my a'weng would be heartbroken. On the other, I couldn't believe that the greatest warrior in the grasslands could be killed by wolves. No matter that he had no horse, no arrows, he was Heshi, and he would survive.

Without the sun to warm it, the wind carried a sharp chill. The soldiers who rode on ahead of us began to yell, and I tightened my grip on the reins, pulling my horse to a stop. "What is it?"

The soldiers were calling out in Plains. Then Heshi climbed out from between the crags, a boulder in his palms. His right arm was crusted with blood, and there were others behind him, coming out to stand atop the rocks. Though they were covered with dust, they were as fierce as ever, glaring down at the soldiers.

I called out, hurling myself off my horse to run to him and throw my arms around him. I must have jostled his wound, for he winced as he smiled wide. "Little princess!"

Everyone's spirits seemed lifted, including those of the Plainsmen, who looked happier than if they'd won a war.

We made camp that night under the shadow of the mountain. What few tents the soldiers had brought were being used as makeshift shelters for the wounded. Heshi had broken his right arm, so the commander applied medicine for him, which he endured without complaint.

Now that we had found him, my whole heart felt lighter,

and I all but inhaled my flatbread. Gu Xiaowu sat opposite me, watching me eat. I was stuffing my face happily until I caught him looking, and the last bite got stuck in my throat—I could neither push it down nor bring it back up. He cackled so hard he didn't bother passing me a waterskin.

I found my own and tilted it back, gulping down mouthful after mouthful to wash the bread down. When I had composed myself, I asked, "What did you say yesterday to get the magistrate to agree to send aid?"

Gu Xiaowu smiled brightly. "I told him that if he didn't, he'd not have any good tea to drink again."

Yeah right.

The stars shone brightly tonight. I raised my head to look at them. They were like lanterns that hung in the distance, winking down at us. A belt of milky white crossed the sky—the place where Heaven himself bathed, it was said, a river made of stars, and I wondered if Heaven could dip his hand into it and scoop the stars out as easily as I could scoop a palmful of sand. Would they seep through his fingers the way sand seeped through mine, returning back to the river? A star must spill from it sometimes in order to become a comet—like the one that crossed the sky, twinkling arrow-like and disappearing back into the dark.

I gasped, remembering that you could make a wish if you tied your belt into a knot when you saw one. But my hands were clumsy. I never could do it in time to collect my wish, or else I'd forget to make one altogether.

I lay back in the grass, disappointed; the comet was long gone.

"What were you so excited about?" asked Gu Xiaowu.

"I saw a shooting star."

"Is that so special?"

"If you tie a knot in your belt and make a wish, your wish comes true," I explained. "You Plainsmen wouldn't understand."

He burst out laughing. "What did you wish for?"

I wasn't going to tell him. I could keep secrets too. But after a while, he started to tease.

"*Ooooh*, I know. You were wishing you could get married to the crown prince."

"No!" I shot upright. "I don't want to marry any crown prince!"

He smiled. "I knew it. Of course you were wishing you could marry me."

I turned with a huff and ignored him, lying back across the grass.

The sky was so close, so low, and I yearned to touch it. There must be so many stars in heaven—it must be fun up there. I only had a cricket, who hopped into my hair and got tangled in the strands, chirping impotently. It struggled in my palm when I freed it, odd-looking, and tickled me. I blew softly. It leapt back into the grass and disappeared, but I could hear it singing away in the dark.

Gu Xiaowu lay down too, resting his head on his saddle. He was so quiet I thought he must have fallen asleep, but then he said, lazily, "Hey! Sing me a song."

The wind was as gentle as A'niang's hand against my cheek. Bickering with Xiaowu had become a part of my day, so I turned to him and said, "Why should *I* sing? Why don't you sing *me* something?"

"I don't know how."

"Liar, everyone knows how. Come on, just something your a'niang sang when you were little, please?"

He fell silent. Finally, he said, "I don't have a niang anymore." His voice was casual.

I wasn't sure how to respond to that. One of my brothers lost his mother too, because she'd fallen ill and never recovered. My a'niang treated him better than she treated me, and I pouted, but I knew it was because he'd lost his a'niang so young. Pushing myself up, I looked over at Gu Xiaowu, worried that I'd upset him, but the stars were not bright enough for me to read his face.

"O, there is a fox," I started to sing, sounding a little like the cricket. "He sits upon the dune . . ."

"No, sing another one," Gu Xiaowu said, his brow knit.

"This is the only song I know!"

The sound of a reed flute playing somewhere drifted to us. Delighted, I pushed myself up and looked around for it—it was Heshi, seated on a gentle slope. I hadn't known he could play so well. He couldn't use his injured arm, so he couldn't play all the notes, but it was lovely nevertheless, winding and lilting and resounding in that cold, clear night. The tune was an aching one. The other Jieshuo warriors rose in song to accompany it, their voices low, but strong, colored with a wash of desolation. Like a desert wind, I thought, like the hawk that surged over the grassland, burrowing into the deepest part of you, echoing. Everything between heaven and earth was calm. The insects stopped chirping, the horses stopped nickering, the Plains soldiers quieted to listen to their chorus.

I was struck by it, rooted in place until they finished.

"What song was that?" The question slipped from Gu Xiaowu's lips as though he hadn't intended to ask.

"A war song," I answered. "The song they sing before marching to battle. It's the story of a famously beautiful girl whose lover rides away to join the fighting and doesn't come back—just his horse. So she puts her hand on the saddle, looking at the half-full quiver, and sings this song."

Gu Xiaowu smiled. "Why did he have to go off to war?"

"Because he was a Jieshuo warrior, and Jieshuo warriors have to fight Jieshuo wars, of course. He couldn't help it." I eyed him, miffed at this line of questioning. "You wouldn't understand."

"What's there to understand?" he said. "We have a saying in the Central Plains too: *but pity the bones that line the winding river's shores, alive still in sweet bower dreams.*[5] It's all the same story, isn't it?"

I loved stories, so I asked Gu Xiaowu to tell it to me. He refused at first, but I wore him down until he resigned himself to the task.

"Fine," he said. "I'll tell you a story, but you can't ask me 'why.' If you ask, I'll stop talking."

He was being annoyingly stern, but I wasn't so impulsive that I couldn't control myself at all, so I agreed. He

---

5 From "Journey to Longxi" by Chen Tao.

seemed a little taken aback by this. He hesitated, and then started, "Once upon a time, in a kingdom far, far away, there was a girl."

"Was she beautiful?" I wanted to know. "Was she dazzling? Was she a good horsewoman?"

He smiled indulgently. "She was beautiful, yes, and dazzling, and a fair horsewoman. In this kingdom far away, the girl often went riding, and when she rode, she would cover her beauty with a veiled hat. But one day, as she was making her way through the streets, the wind blew her hat away. It was returned to her by a young man. Though they'd met only the once, they fell instantly in love, and promised each other that they would be married."

I liked how this story started. "Was this boy handsome?" I demanded. "Handsome enough for the beautiful girl?"

"I don't know about that, but he was a general's son, and a brave warrior. Not long after they were betrothed, he received news that he was being sent to battle, so he went to lead his men into war. The girl waited for him like she promised—she waited for years, but the young man didn't return.

"The girl's family told her that she should find someone else to marry—she was getting older, and if she waited any longer, it would be harder to find a good match. But she refused, and she kept waiting, until the day news came from the front that he was dead."

He stopped when he got to this part and was quiet for so long that I worried it might be the end of the story. "And then what?" I pressed. "What did the girl do when she found out?"

"She was devastated. But she was suspicious too, for he

was a strong fighter, a cunning strategist, and had gone to battle so many times. How could he be so easily killed? For ten days, she shut herself up in her bower, and when she opened the doors again, it was with a single purpose: she would uncover the truth of what happened to him.

"Yet—she was a girl, and she had little power of her own. Her family were courtiers, but not influential enough to force an investigation. It was around this time that the ruler of the kingdom announced he was to select another consort. The girl used this as an opportunity to enter the imperial city. She was a gentle girl, and astute, so the king treated her very well. Her rank among the women of the inner palace gradually increased, and she befriended more influcntial officials and used their power to investigate her beloved's death. She found evidence that the young man had not fallen into the hands of the enemy. No—he was plotted against by the very people who were supposed to be his allies. And all the evidence implicated the queen and her family.

"This queen had resented for years the favor the king shewed the beautiful girl. And if he discovered that his queen was involved in this plot, she would have no throne to sit on anymore.

"Right around this time, the girl gave birth to a new prince. The queen had found the opportunity she'd been waiting for. She sent the girl broth under the pretense of looking after her, but she had tainted it with a slow-acting poison, so the more the girl drank the weaker she became, until she fell ill. On her deathbed, her final wish was to bring justice to her beloved, but it was too late. The queen had her confined to her rooms, ordered people to 'look after her' day and night, and took her little prince away—"

"Did the queen have the little prince killed too?" I asked breathlessly.

Gu Xiaowu shook his head. "No. The queen had no children of her own, you see, so she kept him and raised him and taught him all of her smarts and her cunning. So as the little prince grew, he believed her as dear as his own blood-born mother, and he didn't know that she was also the reason he was separated from the very same.

"And then . . . after, the little prince discovered the truth, but he didn't know what to do about it. He was small, and the queen and her family and their allies were so powerful. He didn't have the strength to confront her. Then the king wavered too. The little prince was not his only son—he had many others; they were each of them entitled to be his heir, and all had been itching to be named the lord of the Court of Spring, for it was common knowledge that the little prince was not born to the queen and was not a trueborn son. And the queen herself guarded against him because of all she had done.

"At long last, the king decided to make the little prince his heir. But in this kingdom . . . in this kingdom, crown princes rarely live past thirty. If they aren't assassinated by their brothers, then they are deposed by their fathers and live the rest of their lives under house arrest. Some crown princes would rather raise a rebellion against their fathers than live in peril any longer. The successful ones become king, and then they die. The unsuccessful ones don't become king, and they also die. The Court of Spring . . . it's a manor steeped in blood."

Xiaowu stopped here, abruptly, staring absently into the distance. I stared absently at him too. I didn't like the way his story was going; it wasn't like any of the ones I'd been told. But I couldn't bring myself to interrupt him.

Then he came back to himself and returned to his usual pleasant tone to finish the tale. "Though he was the heir, the little prince's life did not get easier. The queen raised her guard against him, and the king—the king presented the little prince with a difficult dilemma. He said that, as heir, the little prince should set a good example for the citizens of the kingdom. He sent the little prince to a faraway land and gave him an impossible task."

"Poor little prince," I said. "What task did the king give him?"

"Nothing," said Gu Xiaowu. He patted his saddle and rested his head back upon it. "Never mind. Go to bed."

"But I didn't ask why!" I protested. Was I supposed to go to bed without knowing how his stupid, sad story ended? "Why did you stop?"

"I stopped because I stopped—should I keep talking when there's nothing more to say?" He turned, facing away from me. I could see only the curve of his shoulder blades as he huddled under his sheepskin. Perhaps he was already sleeping.

I pulled my blanket all the way up to my chin until I was nice and cozy, thinking that Gu Xiaowu was a stupid boy who was a terrible storyteller to boot, but as I stared at his back, pity washed over me. The little prince in the story had lost his a'niang, and Gu Xiaowu had too. It must have been so sad not to have an a'niang—the thought of losing mine was enough to sting my eyes.

My sleep was fitful. I dreamed of the little prince.

He was young, very young—three or four years old, curled up into himself and crying. The last time it snowed, I'd found a fox pup who'd gotten caught in a hunter's trap—it had looked like that too, huddled into a ball, looking up at me with wet, dark eyes, timid and wary, its sharp little snout hidden beneath its claws. The snow had fallen in sheets, and I felt so sorry for it, reaching out a hand to free it from its snares. But then it lifted its snout sharply, and the fox transformed into Gu Xiaowu.

I startled awake.

It was nearing dawn. The moon slanted westward beneath the horizon; the stars were beginning to dim against the sky. Campfires were burning out. Only patrolling sentries broke the silence. The grass was laden with dew, which dripped onto my cheek and rolled down my face. I darted a tongue out to taste it—it was sweet. I turned over and fell back asleep.

In the morning, we packed up and continued east until we spotted the riders Jieshuo had dispatched. Heshi, hearing that the chanyu's royal camp was nearby, was ecstatic. I was thrilled too, because I could see my a'weng at last. But because the Plains cavalry could not stay in Jieshuo territory, they bade their farewells and turned back toward the Anxi Protectorate.

Heshi liked these soldiers a lot. They were disciplined and

decisive, brave and bold, so he saw them off, riding west with them a long way. I rode with him. The noon sun was strong and hot. Gu Xiaowu's lids were lowered, like he was taking a lazy nap upon the saddle.

"Hey!" I called. "When you go back to Xiliang, can you let my lord father know I've arrived safely?"

"I can if I go back to the royal city," he said.

"Where else would you go?"

He smiled but didn't answer. The Plains soldiers were a distant shadow on the horizon. He waved at me and then nudged his horse to catch up with them.

I raised a hand to shield my eyes against the sun. You could see a great distance on the flat of the grasslands, so when he rejoined the troops, I could see him turning to wave again.

Slowly, they receded into the distance, like a blur of dust caught between the greater expanses of sky and land until they disappeared altogether. I watched him retreat, thinking of the story he'd told me, feeling strangely bereft.

Behind me, someone laughed. I turned to see Heshi.

"What are you laughing at?" I sniped, embarrassed to have been caught looking.

He nodded his head—and then shook it, smiling. "Little princess, let's go home."

I was so happy to see my a'weng, I forgot all my worries.

After a year apart, A'weng spoiled me more than ever and let me do anything I wanted. Though, because Heshi's arm was not fully healed and because I had a knack for getting into scrapes, A'weng had Heshi's little sister look after me. We were the same age, but she'd been in training since she was little and was good with a dagger. I loved to call her name, "A'du, A'du!" like I was mimicking the call of a little bird to get it to come toward you, for she was like a little bird too, hovering near and flitting around.

What I didn't expect was that the king of Mohu had sent a diplomat to Jieshuo about the matter of my marriage. A'weng refused to let him into the tent. He sent a messenger to tell the envoy, "The little princess may not be a princess of Jieshuo, but her mother is the chanyu's daughter. The chanyu wishes to marry her off to a true hero. If your king wants to marry our little princess, then he must come to the chanyu himself and compete against our warriors. If he can kill the White-Eyed Wolf King of Tiangen Mountain, the chanyu will betroth our little princess to him. That is the chanyu's edict, and all, including the princess's own father, must obey."

The diplomat, angered, left pretty quickly after that.

The Tie'ergeda Chanyu spread his edict wide across the grasslands. Soon enough, everyone had heard that if they wanted to marry the youngest princess of Xiliang, they had to kill the white-eyed wolf that ruled Tiangen Mountain.

Thousands of packs roamed the mountain's crags, but the legend was that they bowed to a single wolf—one with white fur around its eyes—for wolves were like humans in that way, yielding power to the strong.

The White-Eyed Wolf King, it was said, had obsidian fur, with a patch of pure white surrounding its left eye like someone had dipped a brush in mare's milk and drawn it on.

People said it wasn't a wolf at all, but something closer to a sprite. Wolf packs were deadly enough, but the White-Eyed Wolf King was terrifying. Small troops of cavalry and shepherds were perpetually threatened by its specter, for it could command hundreds—if not thousands—to attack and leave nothing behind but bone. I'd thought it no more than a scary story told by a'ma to their babies, for no one had actually seen it in real life, but everyone else swore up and down that the wolf king *did* live on Tiangen Mountain and that it *did* lead all the wolves.

Apparently, the king of Mohu had led thousands of troops in search of the wolf king, and when we heard the news, it occurred to me that he really might be the one to kill it. What would happen then? I didn't want to marry an old man.

But everyone rushed to assure me that no one could kill the wolf king—it was what Jieshuo people thought, what everyone thought, and despite bringing heavy troops, the king of Mohu never caught sight of it. No one had. It lived only in stories.

That was the thing that eased my worries. The king of Mohu was getting up in years and declining in health, and Tiangen Mountain was hundreds of miles wide. There were plenty of ravenous animals that lived there. Probably, he would fall off his horse. Probably, he would be confined to bed, and then I wouldn't have to marry him.

I lived better in Jieshuo than I did in Xiliang, because I was with A'du all day. If we weren't hunting, we were birding, and because Jieshuo girls married young and A'du was nearing a courting age, there were always people outside our tent, singing to her all night long. No one sang to me though, because even the bravest warriors knew that killing the wolf king was beyond them.

Anyway, I was too pretty for my looks to be the reason they didn't want to marry me.

One evening, a clamor startled me awake. I scrambled to my feet, calling for A'du. When she rushed in, I asked, "What is it? What's happened?"

A'du was as confused as me. Just then, one of A'weng's servants came. He bowed.

"The chanyu is asking for you."

"Is it a war?" I asked anxiously. The diplomat had been sent crawling away last time, but I doubted the king of Mohu would give up so easily. He'd gone in search of the wolf king, but that was so obviously a trick A'weng played, for the wolf king wasn't real. What if the king was angry, and had decided to attack us instead?

I didn't want to think about what would happen if Jieshuo and Mohu decided to fight. Jieshuo may have been the strongest country in the west and ruled over the entire northern desert all the way to the easternmost seas, but Mohu was not weaker by much. And our ten years of peace, though not long, was enough for the merchant caravans to make all the kingdoms rich. If the wars started again, there would be no more merchants—and no more prosperity, either.

A'du and I rushed to the royal tent. The chanyu's tent was grander than the others, made of sheets of white cowhide stitched seamlessly together and decorated with beautiful floral patterns and lines of benediction. It was dusted with powdered gold and was radiant beneath the late autumn sun, so bright it was difficult to look straight at. Prayer banners danced in the wind, asking for Heaven's blessing.

If I squinted, I could make out a shadow—he wore Xiliang robes, but he didn't carry himself like a Xiliang man.

When he turned to smile at me, my breath caught.

It was a Plains boy.

It was Gu Xiaowu.

"What are you doing here?" I asked before I could think better of it.

"I'm here to marry you."

I stared at him, heart racing, and burst into laughter. "No, tell the truth. Did you come to sell more tea?"

He nudged the thing at his feet.

My jaw nearly fell off my face.

It was a massive black wolf, nearly twice the size of a normal one, as large as a colt. Rigid in death, its eyes were wide open like it was ready to pounce. A ring of pure white fur circled its left eye, like someone had dipped a brush in mare's milk and drawn it on. I rubbed my eyes, stunned, and squatted next to it to pluck some of its fur—white to the root.

Jieshuo nobility packed the tent. They all stared down at the corpse until one brave child rushed forward and copied me, plucking out some fur and raising it to the setting sun, crying, "It's white! It's white!"

I startled from my daze as A'weng's voice cut through the crowd.

"A brave warrior is worthy whether he is from my Jieshuo or not."

The crowd stepped back to let the chanyu through. A'weng

sauntered forward to appraise the wolf. He nodded at it and then nodded at Gu Xiaowu.

"Excellent!"

Getting praise from the chanyu was harder than melting the snow from the summit of Tiangen Mountain—but Gu Xiaowu had killed the White-Eyed Wolf King, and the chanyu had promised to marry me to whoever could.

I hadn't dared to dream it might be him. I followed after, asking how he'd done it.

"My caravan came across a pack of wolves when we were traveling," he said, like it was nothing at all. "So I killed it."

The king of Mohu had brought *three thousand men* to look for it, and Gu Xiaowu . . . chanced upon its path? And killed it?

Who would believe that?

But the chanyu kept his promises. The nobles chattered among themselves in anticipation—a Plains tea merchant, married to the princess of Xiliang? Gu Xiaowu was hailed as a hero. At night, Heshi got drunk and started clamoring that he wanted to have a friendly competition with the new boy.

Since it was dark, the two of them rode out into the desert to shoot bats. It was a senseless game, but a difficult one.

It was obvious that Heshi was going to win the contest, but people made their bets anyway. His right arm had not fully healed, but Heshi could shoot as well with his left, and there was no better archer in all of Jieshuo.

It was hasty and last minute, but within no time at all it seemed like everyone in the camp had heard it was happening. People started whispering that Heshi wanted to marry me—he was the best of the chanyu's soldiers, and someday he might be the best of the chanyu's generals—and though I was a Xiliang princess, everyone knew how much A'weng loved me, so a marriage to me would bring them closer together.

I didn't think Heshi had such ideas. A'du probably told him I didn't want to marry Gu Xiaowu—not because he was a tea merchant, for it was clear he was no ordinary one, but because I was too young.

The priest sang a prayer song, spilling fresh sheep blood into a winecup and handing it to Heshi and Gu Xiaowu. They gulped it down with the whole camp watching, everyone eager to see who would gain the upper hand. I watched them, uncertain what I wanted the outcome to be.

Would I have to marry Gu Xiaowu if he won?

And what about Heshi? What would happen if he did?

But Heshi was only teaching Gu Xiaowu a lesson, telling him not to be so arrogant, the same way he would whenever he came by to torment the boys that crowded outside A'du's tent and sang to her—when they were being too loud, he could find a way to quiet them. A lot of people had been annoyed when Gu Xiaowu came with the body of the wolf king, acting like what he'd done wasn't at all impressive and telling A'weng he wanted to marry me.

Which was why they wanted to remind him of his place.

A'weng had caught wind of this. He was in high spirits as he came to watch. I followed anxiously after him and the crowd of merry people who surrounded him until we came to the riverside, where A'weng ordered the arrows his soldiers had brought to be split evenly between the competitors. Heshi had his own bow but, seeing that Gu Xiaowu was empty-handed, offered it to him.

Gu Xiaowu nodded his thanks, but the chanyu smiled. "Is there no spare bow in all of Jieshuo?"

The chanyu bestowed him an iron bow.

I started to fret. An iron bow was heavier than the others, and he didn't look strong enough to draw it. Heshi probably thought so too, and he wanted to win fair and square, so he turned to A'weng.

"Chanyu, why don't I give him my bow to use, and I'll take the iron one?"

But the chanyu shook his head. "If he can't draw a bow, what right does he have to marry my granddaughter?"

Laughter rolled through the crowd. There were plenty of people who didn't quite believe that he'd been the one to kill the wolf king, and they disdained him for it. Gu Xiaowu raised the bow like he was raising a qin, plucking it with a finger the way you would if you were playing a tune. The bowstring twanged, and people laughed harder. He was a slender, bookish kind of boy—like the musicians that Jieshuo nobility often hired from the Plains, the kind that no one thought much of.

Night fell in earnest, and the sky filled with bats.

The chanyu said, "Let's begin."

They had been given a hundred arrows each—the first to empty the quiver into a hundred bats was the winner. Heshi drew first. Though he was using his left hand, every one of his arrows found its mark. He moved so quickly, he was a blur, and in the space of a few seconds, bats began to drop from the sky.

Gu Xiaowu, on the other hand, did not seem rushed at all.

He carefully selected five arrows and nocked them all at once onto the bowstring.

"Gu Xiaowu!" I couldn't help calling. "You're supposed to shoot them one at a time!" I didn't know how much he knew about archery, but at the very least he ought to have realized that. He turned to beam at me, and then he drew his bow.

He drew it easily—more easily than I could have imagined. Not only did he draw it, he shot his arrows one after the other, and they arced through the sky like shooting stars.

Surprise rumbled through the crowd.

The nobles chattered among themselves, and the chanyu grunted his approval. There had been a Plains general once who was famous for continuous arrows like this. He'd killed a Jieshuo prince with it. But that was a legend from many years ago, and no one had seen anything like it again.

They were seeing it now.

Gu Xiaowu kept shooting, five arrows every time. Bats scattered through the air, but there was no escape. Like rain, they dropped to his feet. As fast as Heshi was, he couldn't outpace Gu Xiaowu, and in no time at all, the latter had used up his arrows.

Bondmen were sent out to gather the bats, and they laid them in a pile. One hundred bats, a hundred odd-looking flowers, a small black hill on the riverbank.

Heshi finished shooting too, but he'd been slower. "I've lost," he conceded.

"I used a stronger bow," Gu Xiaowu said. "If I'd tried using the continuous arrow with yours, you would have been the victor—and your right arm is injured. If I won, it's because it wasn't a fair fight. Neither of us has lost, Heshi."

His archery had startled everyone, but it was Gu Xiaowu's humility that impressed them. The crowd cheered at his words. The chanyu grinned and strode forward.

"Exactly right. Our Jieshuo warriors have not lost." He turned to Gu Xiaowu. "Plainsman, tell me—what would you like as a reward?"

"You've already given me the most precious reward, Chanyu." Gu Xiaowu smiled. "What could be more valuable than your little princess?"

The chanyu burst into laughter. The nobles were excited too, which was how the matter of my marriage was decided.

The priest selected a date on the spot, saying that we should wed ere the crisp autumn turned into a cold one. I hesitated, turning to A'du. "Do you think I should marry him?" I whispered.

She turned her shining dark eyes to me, but I could read no answers in them. Finally, I mustered up my courage and arranged to meet Gu Xiaowu by the river.

I didn't know what I wanted to say to him, but if I married him, just like that, with no fuss at all—that didn't feel right, either.

Autumn nights were brisk, so I wrapped myself tightly in a leather robe, pacing on the riverbank and listening to the water rush by. Wild geese were crying in the distance. Above me, a bright star rose from the west, and the sky deepened into a rich purple like a ripe grape.

Reeds whispered in the wind, and then Gu Xiaowu walked toward me.

I panicked.

He wore Jieshuo robes and a saber at his waist. A'weng had warmed up to him these last few days, for he wasn't just a skilled archer; he also spoke Jieshuo well and had earned A'weng's trust—enough that he was bequeathed the chanyu's personal iron bow. And after the contest, Gu Xiaowu and Heshi were never apart—Gu Xiaowu taught Heshi his archery, and Heshi taught Gu Xiaowu about the grasslands. The chanyu always looked happy to see them together. They wore each other's sabers, which meant that they'd become sworn brothers, closer than brothers in blood, who would look after one another on the battlefield, so the blade on Gu Xiaowu's belt belonged to Heshi. It looked familiar, and then I remembered why—it had been the one Heshi had pressed into my palm.

Gu Xiaowu smiled at me.

I smiled back, suddenly very calm. Neither of us spoke, but I was sure he understood why I'd asked him to come.

"I have something for you," he said.

My heart pounded. It couldn't be a waistband, could it? What should I do if he gave me a waistband? It was a custom Xiliang shared with Jieshuo—after singing, boys were supposed to express their intentions with a waistband—but he hadn't even sung to me—it wasn't proper—my poor heart was racing, but as I fretted over what to do, what I heard was, "You didn't eat enough at dinner, did you? I brought you roast mutton ribs."

My eyes widened as the warmth of bashfulness gave way to the flush of embarrassed anger. I puffed out my cheeks, saying, "You're the one who didn't eat enough!"

He looked confused. "Of course I did! I was eating the whole time. You barely had anything—that's why I brought you meat."

I pouted and crossed my arms. Birds sang in the distance, the river flowed at our feet, and fish flopped around, splashing water everywhere. Gu Xiaowu put the lamb in front of me.

It smelled delicious, and he was right—I hadn't eaten much dinner, because I was too busy thinking about my appointment with him to work up an appetite. Looking at it, though, smelling it—my stomach rumbled.

He grinned, offering me his knife. "Eat up."

Maddeningly, it was delicious. I ate in big bites, lips glossy with fat. "How did you know I liked lamb?"

Gu Xiaowu said something in Plains, and when I couldn't understand, he said it again in Jieshuo: "There's nothing on earth a persistent man can't do."

He hadn't said anything like that before. I didn't know why, but my heart gave a stutter. What kind of man could be considered persistent? We'd met not so very long ago, but it felt like we'd known each other forever, because though he often annoyed me, we'd been through so much together. We sat in silence, listening to the sound of singing on the wind. It was a love song, the kind a courting warrior sang outside the tent of a beautiful maid.

Music had never moved me so much. The voice was so far

away you could mistake it for one coming from celestial palaces. Fireflies floated up from the grass like hazy little stars, or a scatter of golden sand, and I had the thought that they seemed almost like Heaven's messengers, carrying sparkling little lanterns that twinkled in the brisk air.

On the other bank, the campsite was dotted with fires. The laughter and noise were as distant as though we were separated by the sky itself. I wondered if the gods felt as I did when they descended through the clouds to look upon us mortals—like nothing was real, like everything lingered just out of reach.

"Do you really want to marry me?" I asked.

Gu Xiaowu seemed taken aback by the question. He searched my face. "Of course I do."

"But—I have a terrible temper. And I'm from the grasslands, while you're from the Plains. You eat millet and I eat lamb, and I can't understand your language and I don't know anything about where you live, and if I asked you to stay here, you would miss home, but if I went back with you then I'd miss home too. And—and you killed the wolf king but it wasn't because you wanted to marry me. And I'm not very old and I'm not very mature, but I do know that these things can't be forced because other people want it so."

It all came pouring out—all of my worries, all of my questions—all of it until my mouth went dry. He didn't once interrupt. He didn't speak at all until I stopped for a sip of water.

"All of these are peripheral concerns. The only thing I want to know is: Do you want to marry me?"

I nearly spat the water back out. My cheeks burned. "I—I—"

"Well?" he urged. "Do you or don't you?"

I felt so muddled. I couldn't clear my thoughts. It was like I'd been living in a dream. It was all happening so quickly. It wasn't my intention to marry anyone so soon, but Gu Xiaowu—I didn't hate the idea of Gu Xiaowu. Staring up at the twinkling lights dancing through the autumn air, I resolved myself to an answer.

"If you catch me a hundred fireflies, I'll marry you."

He rose to his feet. I watched as he leapt into the air, hand outstretched. He looked like a child then, or like a shooting star—except there was no shooting star like him, his hems soaked through as he landed at the edge of the muddy water, displaying his hands to show me the dozen or more fireflies clasped within, their soft light seeping through his fingers.

Lifting the hem of my leather skirt and making a pouch of the fabric, I called, "Hurry!"

Carefully, he deposited them into it and resumed his chase. He was a painting, a poem, a feeling more than a faithful depiction of a boy. Like a dancer, but there was no dance as dynamic as his, and as he tumbled through the air, chasing after diaphanous lights, I called, "Left! No, farther left!"

Our laughter echoed across the river. More and more fireflies were gathered into the fabric of my clothing. They radiated, a little moon caught in my lap. There were hardly any left flickering in the air, for he'd brought them all to me.

"Are there enough?" He leaned in, his face close to mine as he extended a slender hand to peel back a corner of the pouch I'd made. "Do you want to count?"

We started, but I was soon distracted by the cold, delicate fragrance that clung to him. It wasn't a scent I'd ever smelled, and it was disorienting. My cheeks burned, so hot they were nearly feverish, and I was aware of how close he was standing. Wind ruffled gently at his hair, blowing it against my cheek. The strands were silk against my face, and the hem of my skirt slipped free.

The fireflies scattered. That round moon broke apart, turning into a million comets arcing through the air, surrounding us with soft light. Gu Xiaowu gazed at me the same way the boys who crowded A'du's tent looked at her, but his eyes were much gentler than theirs, and I could see myself reflected back in their darkness. Some secret place in my heart softened. And in a strange way I could not understand, it hurt.

He became bashful, turning away from me to look up into the sky. "They've escaped."

"Like shooting stars," I said.

He laughed softly. "Like shooting stars."

They floated off into the air above us, these stars we could touch. I thought then that I would never forget that night, with its thousands of fireflies, the way they circled us, fluttering into the distance to break up the dark. I remembered an old song about Heaven and the lover he longed for, standing in their river of light.

The chanyu sent a messenger to my lord father to say that he had found a boy for me to marry. Caught between Mohu and the Central Plains, my lord father was all too happy to dispatch a letter back, telling A'weng to please make this decision on my behalf, and to host the wedding. By the time that letter came, the ceremony had already half begun.

Weddings in Jieshuo were simple affairs, but that didn't make them any less grand. All the tents within ten miles of us slaughtered sheep for the feast, and the sweet smell of wine lingered in the air.

Gu Xiaowu had become fast friends with many of the young noblemen. They appreciated a brave, strong warrior, and he had more than proven himself. The priest sang a merry hymn, and the two of us walked slowly down a red carpet to approach the altar that had been erected to Heaven.

But then a flurry of horse hooves bore down toward us, and someone came stumbling in, collapsing at the chanyu's feet. The furrow of his brow was visible from across the crowd. Over the wail of the priest's song, I turned to run back to the chanyu.

"A'weng!"

He smoothed back my hair, smiling. "It's nothing. The king of Mohu is throwing a tantrum, and I'm sending some men to get rid of him, that's all."

I don't know when Gu Xiaowu came up behind me, but he bowed and said, "Chanyu, let me go."

"You?" A'weng appraised him. "They've sent fifty thousand men."

The king of Mohu was no novice on the battlefield. No matter how good Gu Xiaowu was at archery, he wasn't a match against thousands of enemy soldiers.

"Then we should bide our time and send thirty thousand troops against him," Gu Xiaowu said. "If you aren't sure of me, send a general out with me, and I can strategize with him, or try to scatter their formation with my bow and arrow."

The chanyu hesitated, but Heshi spoke up. "Plainsmen are good at strategy—they were the ones who drove the Mohu away when we were coming back to Jieshuo."

At last the chanyu acquiesced. "Go, then, and bring back the head of the Mohu general as an offering for your wedding."

Gu Xiaowu paid his respects in the Plains fashion, by kneeling at the chanyu's feet and saying, "Long live!" Then he rose and turned to me. "I'll be back soon," he promised, despite my worry and my fear.

As he turned to leave, I mustered the nerve to run after him, loosening my waistband and tying it around him. Once the exchange was done, we'd be married for real. I opened my mouth to tell him to give me his, but I didn't have the chance to say anything, for a bondman brought over his horse and the opportunity passed. He swung onto the horse, saying all the while, "Don't worry, I'll be back."

But I didn't want him to be back, I wanted him not to leave. There was so much I still had to say—about the days I waited on the dunes for him to arrive, about the time he rescued me when I fell from my horse, the night he told me stories, the wolf king he killed, the way he'd bested Heshi— and that evening, down by the riverbanks, when he'd caught me a hundred fireflies. I wanted to tell him I'd made up my mind that we shouldn't ever be parted, but now he was going off to battle, and I clung to his sleeve, willing him to stay.

He must have seen something in my eyes, because he

smiled faintly and leaned over to caress my face. Gu Xiaowu didn't have hands like my lord father's, nor were they like A'weng's—they were more like my a'niang's, I thought, though it struck me as odd that he wouldn't have any calluses.

Before I could think too deeply about it, he'd straightened. Thirty thousand troops had assembled. Yimoyan, my eldest cousin, had been chosen to lead them.

"Don't worry, little sister." He smiled. "I'll look after your lad."

He was my favorite cousin because, when we were little, he used to take me out hunting, and he'd always treated me like his own sister.

"Who asked you to look after him?" I laughed. "Look after yourself! I'm waiting for your toast."

The gathered crowd guffawed, saying, "Don't worry, little princess! We'll be back with the Mohu general's head faster than the mutton can be roasted."

Gu Xiaowu rode with Yimoyan's banner. He was wearing leather armor, his face half covered by a helmet, and when he saw that I was scanning the soldiers for him, he waved, smiling. My waistband was around his waist, and worry flashed through me—there had only been time to tie it on quickly, and I didn't want it to fall off—it was such bad luck for the knot to come undone—

And then the army rose, their hoofbeats like thunder, raising great clouds of dust. Like a tide, they surged from the camp and out into the desert. Between one breath and the next they'd galloped straight to the edge of the sky to become a strip of black shadow that, when it passed behind a hill, disappeared into nothing at all.

A'du turned to see me pouting after them.

They'll be back soon, she signed.

I nodded. Mohu may have brought fifty thousand people, but they were weary from their long journey, and Jieshuo's warriors were each worth ten of theirs—thirty thousand was more than enough. Not to mention that the royal tent was defended by ten thousand more cavalry, ready to relieve them if necessary.

Mutton roasted over the pit as bondmen brought us more mare's milk and fragrant wine. Laughter and chatter filled the encampment while we waited for the news that the Jieshuo boys were returning. My face burned every time I thought about the way I'd sniveled as I'd said goodbye, because I was sure that Yimoyan was going to make fun of me for not wanting Gu Xiaowu to go. And if he laughed at me, all the other boys would too. There was going to be a singing competition at night, and I reminded myself to catch Gu Xiaowu first and stop him from being embarrassed, because they were sure to mock him for not knowing how to sing.

Of course, I didn't know then that none of them were ever coming back.

Many, many years later, I read about it in a record by a court historian. A few sentences, and almost ordinary in its description: *In the seventh month, the crown prince Chengyin entered the west, allied with Mohu, and led an army of forty thousand Plainsmen in an ambush on Jieshuo. The Tie'ergeda Chanyu, being fierce and willful, refused to sub-*

mit and died in the ensuing battle. Jieshuo, population two hundred thousand, exterminated.

I remembered nothing about that day. Only that, as he lay dying, Heshi cradled his bow, his broad chest bubbling with hot blood. With the last of his strength he had found me and A'du a horse and lifted us onto it. His last words had been "Protect the princess."

Volleys of black-feathered arrows darkened the sky, falling like rain, like comets. *If Heaven opened his hands, the stars that scattered from his palms would look something like this*, I remembered thinking. A'du urged the horse desperately on, and she and I crashed through the camp. There was fire everywhere, and blood, and terrible screaming.

They had come from the ground, the Plains troops and the Mohu ones, and though Jieshuo fought as hard as it could, there was no way to overcome their combined forces. People collapsed all around us, staining my skirts with splattered blood. If it weren't for Heshi, we wouldn't have escaped. But then Heshi was dead, and A'du and I galloped for six days across the grassland before we lost the soldiers pursuing us.

My leg was injured, and A'du was scraped up too, but she had her dagger in her hand, keeping me behind her, protecting me, but she couldn't protect me from the hate that burned my heart raw.

They killed my a'weng, I kept thinking, *and they killed my Xiaowu.*

They'd killed everyone. I was a princess of Xiliang, but Jieshuo blood ran through my veins. A'du and I were the only ones left who carried it. I swore to myself I wouldn't disappoint A'weng, nor would I let Jieshuo down.

A squadron of cavalry had found us again. One of the Plains riders separated from them and rode toward us. A'du unsheathed her dagger and rushed to meet him, but with a flick of a finger he had disarmed and immobilized her. I was struck dumb.

A'du was frozen stiff, but she still had use of her eyes. She glared. A'du was rarely angry, but today she was furious. Picking up her dagger from where it had clattered across the floor, I stabbed toward her attacker, aiming to kill.

But once again they tapped smartly against a pressure point. I collapsed. The world blackened around me, and then I knew nothing else.

By the time I woke, I'd been slung across the back of a saddle like a sack of millet. Mud splattered across my face, and I couldn't move. I was surrounded by horses, their legs rising and falling as they ran, elegant blades of grass blown by a billow of wind. I closed my eyes against the dazzle of motion. After an indeterminate time, the horse came to a stop and I was brought down from its back and set on my feet. But my legs had gone numb, and I collapsed to the ground.

Thick carpet covered the earth. A general's tent? No—the magistrate's? But when I raised my head—

It was Gu Xiaowu.

Thirty thousand men had ridden out to war.

None had returned.

Except Gu Xiaowu, who was standing in front of me, unharmed.

Instead of Jieshuo armor, he wore Plains clothing, looking as gentle and as refined as a scholar. But no tent of this grandeur would have been reserved for a mere scholar. He was surrounded by soldiers. Bowed to by generals. They knelt at his feet, armor plates chiming as they pressed their foreheads to their hands, the highest of Plains honors for the highest-ranking of their men.

I understood with sudden clarity who he must be—a spy.

He'd spied for them; he'd drawn our enemy straight to our door.

"Traitor!" I don't know where I found the strength to howl it.

The soldiers in the tent berated me—I recognized the tone of voice, even if I didn't recognize the words. Someone kicked my leg, and I fell back to the ground. The magistrate entered. He was bowing too, saying something in that indecipherable Plains. Gu Xiaowu didn't look at me at all as he spoke, but his face darkened.

At long last, after everyone else left, he drew out a dagger and stalked toward me.

I braced myself for the blow, but he only cut through my restraints.

"It's been hard on you," he muttered.

I tilted my head up to look at him, forcing my voice into calm. "I'm going to kill you someday, Gu Xiaowu. I will avenge my a'weng."

And then: "You traitor. Impostor." I couldn't think of anything worse to call him, so I cycled between the few insults that came to mind. None of it seemed to anger him.

"If it makes you feel better, you can keep yelling," he told me, smiling gently.

I was looking at a boy I could not recognize.

He had left our wedding to lead thirty thousand of A'weng's countrymen to their deaths. Then he'd come back and killed A'weng too, and with him, all of Jieshuo—two hundred thousand people slaughtered. The grassland was flooded with their blood, and the person responsible was standing here, not a single speck of it muddying that beautiful face.

What kind of iron was his heart made of that it could be so hard? I curled up there on the carpet, looking up at him. "Why don't you just end it? Why don't you kill me? You've spent so long lying already."

Gu Xiaowu looked at me for a long time and he did not speak. Then he turned away to look at the sun seeping in through the tent flaps, white cloth stained gray with dust. Autumn sun blazed down, lighting everything gold, including my shadow. He grabbed my wrist. The dagger I'd drawn clattered uselessly to the ground.

It hit me with sad irony that this had been his dagger, the same one he'd given to Heshi when they became oath-sworn brothers, one that Heshi had pressed into my hand, at the end. I'd kept it hidden, thinking that I could at least end things for myself if things got too bad, but once we arrived, I changed my mind. *Better to kill the person in front of me.* But he found me out.

"Don't do anything stupid," he said. His eyes were heavy.

Stupid? I could have laughed. Was there anyone more stupid than me? I'd believed him. I'd loved him. I'd nearly married him, and he betrayed me—betrayed us. I'd thought he died defending us. I'd been stupid enough to think him worthy of avenging.

Someone stepped inside the tent to speak to Gu Xiaowu. They spoke in Plains. I didn't know what they were saying, but Gu Xiaowu's face darkened and he scooped up the dagger and stormed from the tent. I sat there for a long time, too weary to move.

"*Xiaofeng!*" someone hissed. There was a tug at my sleeve. I turned to see shifu.

I leapt up, catching his hands in my own. "Why are you here?" I gasped.

"This isn't a good place to talk. Let's get out of here first."

He drew his sword, cutting a long gash through the fabric of the tent. We slipped out. There were fine horses stabled out back, and he was ushering me toward them when I remembered. "A'du!"

"What A'du?"

"Heshi's sister," I told him. "I can't leave her behind."

Shifu had no choice but to turn back and help me—but the guards had discovered me gone by the time we found her. Shifu was a skilled fighter, but he was penned in by the tents. There wasn't another way out.

The whole camp had been roused, and more soldiers drew near. Realizing he was outnumbered, shifu pushed us behind him and retreated, fighting them all the way to the stable, where he knocked a lit torch into bales of dry hay, and spirited us away in the ensuing chaos.

The neatly stacked straw caught flame quickly and the

stable was choked with smoke. Shouting echoed through the camp. The soldiers abandoned us in order to put out the fire—but the Plainsmen were too disciplined to be distracted for long. As the rest of the camp rushed to fetch water, a band of riders galloped at full speed after us.

We fought them all the way to the foothills of Tiangen Mountain.

There were more soldiers after us—I saw the almond-yellow flags they carried, which were emblazoned with unfamiliar sigils.

"Are these the Anxi soldiers?" I asked. It didn't seem like it. I'd seen the soldiers stationed at Anxi, and they were nowhere near as ferocious as these troops.

A trickle of blood inched down shifu's face. He wiped it away and laughed contemptuously. "No. Anxi doesn't have cavalry like this. These are the Yulin Guard, from the Court of Spring. Every one of the men behind us is of noble blood, young lordlings come west in search of fame and fortune."

"Fame and fortune?"

"For capturing you alive, of course."

But I wasn't *that* important.

The Yulin Guard were unrelenting. They jeered in halting, mocking Xiliang, saying that all we ever did was retreat with our tails between our legs. Once, I would have turned and fought them myself for slandering Xiliang, but now . . . now I knew what it was to be a grain of millet floating in a vast ocean, a leaf buffeted by a gale of wind.

No one could turn back the tide of the cavalry behind me—not A'weng, not Heshi, not shifu.

Night covered our steps as we escaped into the mountain. The terrain was too treacherous for armies, so they camped as we huddled in the rocks above, peering down at their fires. Hundreds of fires, which wound like a great serpentine dragon across the grasslands—auxiliary troops.

Finally, I turned to shifu.

"Who is Gu Xiaowu?"

"He's not a Gu," shifu said. He was calm. "He is Li Chengyin, fifth son of the emperor of the Plains, crown prince of the Court of Spring, heir presumptive to the throne."

I'd guessed as far as him not being an ordinary merchant. I'd thought he could have been a general, though sixteen was young to be serving in anybody's court, and as often as I combed through the names of famous Plains generals, there hadn't been anyone named Gu. But he wasn't merely lying about his identity. He'd lied about his name, his title. Everything.

Sobs and hysterical laughter both bubbled to my tongue, but I had the capacity for neither. "Why did he call himself a Gu, then?"

"Because his mother was one."

Something stirred as I looked at shifu. Something was clicking into place.

His voice was soft and slow as he abandoned all his pretense. "Yes, that's right. You're remembering. I told you once that my name was also Gu. His mother, the Lady Shu, was my father's sister. And when the emperor commanded him to come west and subdue Jieshuo, he asked me to go undercover to Xiliang and be his spy."

I sat there. For a long time. Digging through the recesses of my memory to pull out a name: *Gu Jian*. That was what he'd said his name was, the first time we met.

"When will you kill me?" I asked. "Or is the plan to bring me to the crown prince so you can complete your mission?"

Gu Jian didn't answer. Under the cloak of darkness I could see the bitter smile on his lips. "You know perfectly well I won't do that," he said.

Rage seared my heart. It swallowed me whole. My fist tightened around a rock, and I savored the flare of pain that shot through my palm as it dug into the soft flesh there.

"What won't you Plainsmen do?" I asked, cold. "You've been lying to me—you've *all* been lying to me. This was your goal from the start, wasn't it? Gu Xiaowu is a liar, but you lied for longer, again and again and again. My father *trusted* you—*I* trusted you! I called you my shifu!"

I could hardly tell what I was saying anymore. I was cursing him as terribly as I knew how, cursing all Plainsmen for being liars, but as I did it cracked me in two to realize that the one person I truly hated was Gu Xiaowu. I didn't know how he could treat me like this. I didn't know how a human heart could withstand this much pain. If he'd killed me, if shifu hadn't rescued me, I could already be dead.

"Why did you bring me from that camp?" I bit out. "To better claim your reward when you see the king?"

Shifu gazed at me. For a long time he did not speak.

"Xiaofeng." He sighed. "I admit, I did befriend you with ulterior motives. I did lie. But every time I did I was miserable. You're just a child, and you believed. And the more I lied, the guiltier I was, and when I wrote to him, I hoped he wouldn't come. I waited with you on the dunes, you know. You didn't see me, but I was there, making sure you were safe. And then that night, when the moonlight shone on your face, I thought you looked like the little fox in that song you always sang...." His voice quieted.

"I knew I was a monster. I knew we were taking advantage. I prayed my cousin wouldn't come, imagined that I could take you away from Xiliang and keep you from all this, but then he arrived, and everything was going according to plan, so I avoided you. I didn't know... I had hoped... I had thought that maybe you wouldn't fall in love with him.

"And when he found the wolf king, I realized things were beyond saving. There was no way back. I was the one who finished the job—did you know that? The wolf had bit through his leg, so I killed it, and I asked him why he was going to all this trouble. I hated myself for asking, because I'd gone to this trouble too, even though he only wanted to kill the wolf king so that he could see you again and doing so meant I was pushing you into his arms..."

I didn't know what he was rambling on about. I didn't care. The last thing he said was "Xiaofeng, I've failed you."

I neglected to respond.

No one had failed me.

I was the one who had failed everyone else.

I'd failed A'weng, for I had led a wolf into a flock of sheep.

I'd failed Heshi, for he would be alive if it were not for me.

I'd failed A'du, for she would not be hurt if I were not here.

I'd failed all of Jieshuo. They were my family, but all I'd done was bring them death.

No one on earth had failed me except for Gu Xiaowu.

But that was no matter. I could bide my time. I would find my chance. And then I would kill him. I swore to the stars in heaven that I would.

At around dawn I dozed off but was roused by the sound of drumming. Next to me, A'du was pushing herself to her feet. Gu Jian's face darkened.

"Take the princess and go," he ordered.

"I'm not going," I said, setting my chin. "If we must die, the three of us will die together."

"Listen to me. I'll distract them, and A'du will take you away." He drew his sword. "Li Chengyin is obstinate and unyielding. Do you think you'd be worth more than a chip he used to bargain for the subjugation of Xiliang if he finds you again?"

Xiliang!

My heart leapt to my throat. "He wants war with Xiliang?"

Gu Jian smiled, but there was no warmth in his eyes. "To those that would rule, what limits do borders impose?"

Below us, the drums pounded thrice. Plainsmen surged up the mountain.

"Go!" Gu Jian shouted.

A'du pulled at me. She'd sustained light injuries but was agile enough to tug me down over the mountain rock. I whipped my head back to see Gu Jian standing atop a boulder, morning sun illuminating his white robes, stained purple with old blood. He looked like a god in the dawn, a sword in his hand and the wind in his sleeves.

I thought back to what he'd said yesterday. It felt like a dream, the things he'd told me. We'd met when he saved a little boy from being thrown off a startled horse. Yellow sand had mixed with the white of his clothing as he tumbled, and though the robes had been dirtied with dust, he had looked every inch the conquering hero. That had been like a dream too, but all of it had soured into nightmare.

We stumbled blindly through the rocks, sheltering during the day and venturing out at night. Plainsmen combed the mountain regularly, but it was easier to hide with just two people, and we did just that, drinking snowmelt and eating what we could dig out from gerbil burrows, where they hid grass and dried fruit, enough to tide us over. I had no idea if Gu Jian was alive or how long we'd been running. Weeks, perhaps—at least until the eighth month, because snow had started to fall.

In the space of a single night, Tiangen was shrouded in a thick veil of it, yellowing the grass and congealing into ice. By this time even antelope had stopped searching for food. The night wind was bitter enough to freeze you to death. We could not hide on the mountain for much longer.

The Plainsmen had retreated, because if soldiers were caught in a storm without a steady supply of rations, they would starve. But A'du and I hid for three days after they left before climbing back down again.

We were lucky.

We met a group of shepherds a day south of the mountain.

They melted snow for us to clean ourselves with and made mutton for us to eat. A'du and I had been on the run for so long, we must have looked like heathens, but in the warmth of the tent, sipping at goat milk, we returned to the land of the living.

The shepherds were Mohu, but they were kind, for we looked like refugees. They told us that the Plains army had gone southward—and that they'd seen thousands of Jieshuo citizens fleeing west.

My anger melted with the warmth of the goat milk, and when the adrenaline faded it became obvious that A'du and I couldn't avenge A'weng alone. I needed to bring her to Xiliang. I missed my lord father, missed my a'niang. If I rode quick, I could warn him about the Plainsmen, tell him what happened to Jieshuo. A'niang would be devastated. I needed to see her, to comfort her. She might not have had A'weng anymore, but she had me.

Fire burned on my heels, and in my heart the whole ride home the terror that I was too late, that Xiliang had fallen to Li Chengyin, gripped me. They may have been slaughtered by now. Wind and rain battered at us, but we kept riding, riding as quickly as we could, until the royal city rose over the horizon.

I let out a breath.

The gates were open.

It had turned cold and the steady stream of merchants had ebbed to a trickle, but there were guards posted at the door, yawning beneath their leathers and furs. A'du and I slipped past them and into the city.

The frost of late autumn made the palace severe. We snuck through a small side door. It was easy to steal inside—Xiliang hadn't made enough enemies to need tight guarding, and the only strangers in the city arrived in caravans and didn't stay long. There were fewer guards posted in the royal city than in the Anxi Protectorate, and I used to love sneaking out.

The whole palace felt like it was slumbering. I brought A'du back to my rooms, which stood still and empty. She shivered, pale in the cold, and I found leathers for her to put on. The soles on our boots had worn out long ago, and there were holes in the toes, so I found two new pairs for us. It was immediately warmer once we'd slipped into them.

And then I rushed through the hall toward A'niang's chambers. I needed to see her as soon as possible.

The lamps were dark and cold, but someone had lit the brazier, and by its light I saw my lord father sitting there, his head lowered.

"A'die!" I called softly.

He gave a violent start and turned haltingly, almost disbelievingly, around. His eyes reddened. "Where have you been, my child?"

My eyes stung too, like the tears I'd bottled up might come spilling out. I'd never seen him like this. Clutching at his sleeve, I begged, "Where's A'niang?"

His voice came out strangled. *"Run."*

A'du leapt up, drawing her dagger, but all I could do was stare.

Lights flared around us as people rushed to fill the empty room. Their leader was the diplomat who'd been sent with the Plainsmen's proposal of marriage. He sauntered in like a rooster who'd won a cockfight.

"My king," he jeered, not bothering to kneel. "Now that the princess is back, the engagement between our two nations must be honored. There is no reason to delay any longer, is there?"

I glared fiercely at him and turned back to A'die. "Where's A'niang?" I tugged again at his sleeve to get his attention.

The tears welling in his eyes spilled over. Ice raced down my spine. A'die drew the saber at his waist.

"These Plainsmen—" he started, his voice low and hoarse. "Take a good look at them, my child. They are the ones who stormed our palace and demanded we hand over the last princess of Jieshuo. They were the ones who all but put the blade in her hand, who pushed her to take her own life. Who defiled her by demanding to see her body as she lay cold on the bower floor. They are her *murderers*."

His voice trailed off, devolving into a stream of curses.

I stumbled back, horrified. My lord father clawed at his face, insensible to the blood that gleamed upon his gaunt cheeks. Then, too quickly for anyone to react, he raised his saber and charged at the diplomat, fierce and ferocious as a mighty lion. The Plainsmen scattered from the wide arc of the blade—but not quickly enough, for the diplomat's head hit the ground with a dull thud.

A'die panted, weapon limp in his hand as the Plains soldiers pressed in around him.

"How dare you! This is mutiny!"

A'niang.

GOODBYE, MY PRINCESS

My a'niang was gone.

It was all I could think about, that I'd gone through so much to come home to her, just to find that I would never see her again.

I was shaking—with rage, with fear, with fury, I couldn't tell. I shoved through the crowd of people, turning on each one as I screamed, half wild, "Where is Li Chengyin? Where is your prince hiding?"

No one answered, but they parted to let someone through—a general, by his clothing.

"Princess," he said, "the king is not well. The diplomat's death was all a terrible mistake—we can all see that, and I will explain to His Highness when I see him. You need not trouble yourself with this matter, lest you say something neither of us can take back."

I recognized him as the man who had stolen A'du's dagger and taken us captive. I was sure I couldn't fight him if I wanted to. Shifu had helped us the last time, but he was gone and there was no one left to rescue me.

"I want to see Li Chengyin."

"The king has agreed to the marriage. The crown prince is on his way and will arrive forthwith to escort you back to the Plains. You will of course have the opportunity to see him face-to-face eventually. There is no need to rush."

And so I had to watch as the soldiers surged forward. A'die waved his saber wildly, trying to cut them back, but they subdued him in the end. A whole palace of guards and no one came to check in on the commotion—they were all gone, or else long since bought and paid for.

A'die shrieked as they pressed him to the ground. A searing pain enveloped my chest, like I'd dropped it into a vat of hot oil, and I wanted to run up and pull the soldiers away. But they had their swords pressed to A'die's neck and I didn't dare. They called us barbaric, these Plainsmen, but when it came to killing they were more savage than we.

"Princess," said the general as I wept, "you might reason with the king. We would not want him to injure himself."

Regardless of whether it was possible, my voice had lodged itself behind the knot in my throat. Then someone wrapped a hand around my arm—A'du. Her skin was cool and dry, and she held me up, her bright black eyes full of concern. She would fight for me, I realized. As soon as I gave the word. She would die for me.

But what was the use in that? Why had I dragged her into this? Jieshuo had fallen. Xiliang had succumbed.

"As long as my a'die is safe," I told him, "I will come."

Afterward, I heard that A'die had been delirious since A'niang's death. That he had bouts of clearheadedness, but more often, he was muddled. When he was sensible, he spoke of killing the Plainsmen, but when he wasn't, it was like nothing bad had happened. Like calamity had not descended upon the royal house of Xiliang.

It may have been kinder if he didn't have moments of clarity. I wished it, in fact, for his heart had died along with my lady mother's, and my brothers had all been confined to their rooms. The other women tiptoed around the Plains soldiers, but I—I kept my calm.

I wasn't going to die without my revenge.

The Central Plains had just quelled Jieshuo, which meant they needed to throw their weight behind someone else quickly before Mohu consolidated power, for despite Jieshuo's destruction, the grasslands were in chaos. The emperor had named my father the Great Khan of Pacifying the West, a title that Mohu had objected to, for they'd allied with the Plains armies in order to annex Jieshuo's lands. But since it was a Xiliang princess marrying into the imperial family, it was Xiliang who stepped into the emptiness Jieshuo left behind.

As for me, I changed into brilliant red wedding robes and made my way east, escorted by a legion of guards.

We'd reached the foothills of Tiangen Mountain by the time I saw Li Chengyin again. Plains custom dictated that grooms were supposed to see their brides only on the day of the ceremony, but we'd already met, and rules were less strictly enforced in a military procession. So after days and days of asking for him, he finally arrived at my tent.

The servants had long since retreated. We were alone.

I sat on the carpet. I didn't speak, not for a long time. Not until he turned to leave.

"I'll marry you," I said. "Without complaint, if you can promise me one thing."

"What is it?" he asked.

"I want you to catch me a hundred fireflies."

He stiffened. At last he turned, slowly, to look at me.

I looked back, smiling sadly. "Gu Xiaowu, will you agree?"

His eyes looked like they had that night by the river, but there was no warmth in them anymore. I'd been warming myself in the light of a reflected fire; I should have known that then. And him? He must have been so tired of pretending.

"It's winter," he said. His voice was steady, like nothing had changed. "And there are no more fireflies." He paused, and then continued. "The Plains are lovely too. You will like it there, I'm sure."

He looked away then, avoiding my gaze.

"Did you ever love me?" I asked. "If only a little?"

He didn't answer. He lifted the tent flap and strode into the dark.

Snowflakes danced in on icy curls of wind. There had been a brazier, but the dim embers were scattered. They fought valiantly against the snow, but sooner or later they were all smothered. It was so cold, a winter like this.

A'du and I escaped by night, followed closely after by the three thousand cavalry under Li Chengyin's personal command. We slipped into the mountains again, hoping to lose them, but the riders did not relent.

The mountain had been overrun with wolves when we'd sheltered in it last—had been overrun since the death of the White-Eyed Wolf King. Wolves fought each other up and down its slopes, paying no mind to the humans who stumbled across their path.

What was this but the Plains' strategy against us? Jieshuo was a wolf king, and keeping the other kingdoms jostling for power—killing each other—crumbling into war—ensured that none of us would set our sights on the Plains. Fighting each other like wolves to be on top, never noticing the humans who'd caused this.

We came to the top of the cliff at dawn.

The wind was fierce up here, so sharp I could scarcely open my eyes. I stood at the edge, thinking that my troubles could disappear forever if I was brave enough.

Li Chengyin caught up to me, rushing to the cliffside. I took a step back.

The general—the one who'd spoken to me earlier—called out, "Your Highness, let me reason with the princess." With grim satisfaction, I realized he must have been scared I was really going to jump.

I'd picked up enough Plains to know that this general was named Pei, that he was well trusted by Li Chengyin—but not convincing enough, it seemed, for Li Chengyin threw his reins aside and dismounted, rushing forward to climb up to me.

I did not stop him. I watched him ascend.

The world up here was throttled with wind, the world below choked by cloud. I couldn't tell how deep the valley extended. He stood atop the cliff, panting slightly from the exertion.

"Do you know what's down there?" I asked.

Maybe the snow was too bitter, for his face was white and bloodless. Another swirl of frost stung our faces. I raised a sleeve to wipe it away. He probably hadn't heard me, for he didn't respond, but I continued anyway. "It's the River Oblivion, which washes everything away.

"Here in the west, we have a legend: If you can jump into the River Oblivion, you will forget your troubles. The waters will take your every woe, and it will be as though you were reborn. That is Heaven's power. That is His love. But that love is not always kind, for no one has survived the fall. You used my family to force me into marriage." I could not help smiling at him, even now. "But you cannot force me to stay alive."

His eyes were fixed on my face, but what he said was, "Do it and I will bury all of Xiliang with you."

"You won't, Your Highness." I was at peace. It was the first time I'd called him by his title instead of his name—and possibly the last, too. "Subduing the Western Regions, building your empire—those were your aims. Jieshuo has only just been dealt with. But one day Mohu will rise, and then you will need Xiliang.

"You may have used brutality to secure Jieshuo, but Xiliang was won by kindness, by taking a savage princess from a conquered kingdom for your exalted bride. The other kingdoms will remember you fondly, Your Highness." My lips twisted as I spat the words. "You've saved them from Jieshuo, after all. If you slaughtered Xiliang too, you wouldn't be losing a kingdom too small for anyone's notice, but everything you've worked so hard these many months to achieve. And there is nothing more important than your eternal empire, is there?"

For the first time, the indifference slipped from his face. He took a step toward me. But I took an equal step back, heel hanging over the edge of the cliff. The wind made me unsteady, a reminder that I could fall anytime. Sharp as a blade, it cut through my clothes to slice at the back of my hands. He didn't move. He didn't dare.

"My family is dead," I told him. "And my kingdom is fallen. All my suffering—that's the price I pay for trusting you. That's Heaven's punishment." My voice came out in fits and starts. "I will forget you, Li Chengyin. In this life and every life. The River Oblivion will wash all my love away."

His eyes widened. He ran forward to grab me, but he was too late to catch more than the hem of my sleeve. I raised my left hand. A'du's dagger had been hidden there, and it tore through the fabric.

I was falling when I jerked to a stop again—he'd ripped the belt from his waist and whipped it out to catch me around the wrist. I dangled from it. *My* belt, the one I'd given him at our wedding, densely embroidered with coral and gemstones. The one I had wrapped around him as he left because I wanted to grow old with him, to spend forever by his side. Because I thought he'd been bequeathed to me by Heaven, because I had adored him. I had loved him. I had prayed for his safe return, so that he could tie his belt around my waist in turn and make me his wife.

The knife was sharp. Glittering jewels scattered into the clouds. The look on his face when the mask slipped, I realized, was anguish—

I leaned back. I fell. People screamed, and General Pei's voice was horrified as he bellowed, "Your Highness—!"

But the cliff was gone. There was just the blue from above. The wind that carried the clouds. I hurtled downward through them, twisting as I fell, and the sky disappeared and

I could see nothing at all, for the rush of air forced my eyes shut. A'du had told me that the River Oblivion was beneath us, but what did it look like? A pool of clear blue water or a dark abyss that swallowed you whole?

Despair welled bitter in my throat. I missed my a'niang. I was coming to see her, and perhaps it was a good thing, for my hopes had turned to ash, and she was the person who loved me best in all the world.

Someone caught my hand. He pulled me close and held me as we fell, grabbing at the rocky cliffside in a vain attempt to slow our descent, but it was no use. The stones fell with us, like stars falling to earth, like that night by the river when the fireflies had flown from our sleeves, the sky lit up like a meteor shower, casting light on his face and mine. There was nothing between heaven and earth but those eyes, which had looked into mine—

Those eyes, which were full of me.

I hadn't dreamed he would jump too.

I hadn't thought he loved me.

"*Xiaofeng*," he said, but the wind robbed him of his voice. I must have misheard; I must have been imagining things. He wouldn't have jumped, because he was Li Chengyin. Gu Xiaowu had died the night he rode out to battle.

He said something in Plains, but I didn't understand.

Those were the last words he said, and he'd come after me to say them. No matter how much I tried to recall, they would not come back to me. I only remembered I was comforted by the fact that, in my last moments, I would not be alone.

Our heavy bodies crashed into the water. We were surrounded by a dark made of purest blue. The cold was like a knife that cleaved the flesh from my bones, but I didn't struggle against it. I fell. The way an infant longed to return to its mother's womb, the way a flower floated down to earth. This, I knew, was the most tranquil kind of return.

PART FOUR:

渊水
Abyss

The River Oblivion will wash all my love away.

O, there is a fox, he sits upon the dune. Sits upon the dune, watching the moon.

No, not watching the moon—he's waiting for the shepherd girl to come back.

"No, sing another one!"

"But this is the only song I know!"

FEI WO SI CUN

I will forget you. In this life and every life.

A fog has been lifted, revealing the world to be a mirage. I open my bleary eyes, and everything sharpens around me. A'du is guarding me. So is Yongniang, her eyes red and puffy.

Dainty flowers pattern the drapes that curtain my bed, and slowly, I begin to understand that we are once more in my chambers in the Court of Spring.

I let out a long, shaky breath, feeling like I've woken from a nightmare. I'd been abducted by an assassin, and the assassin had been Gu Jian. I'd been beneath Chengtian Gate, watching Li Chengyin standing high above me, and Li Chengyin had been Gu Xiaowu, the boy who wiped Jieshuo from the earth, who killed my a'weng, and drove A'niang to her death. My lord father had gone mad and I—I'd jumped into the River Oblivion. The dream had been a terrifying one, one I'm too scared to relive.

But in the end, it's just a dream.

Smiling, I reach for Yongniang. *I'm hungry*, I want to say, but I can make no sound. Pain pierces my throat, and I grab for it with both hands. Yongniang pulls them away. Tears well in her eyes.

"You have a fever," she says, "but the physicians say it will pass soon if you can rest."

I look to A'du, then Yongniang. The attendants bring forward a cup of clear water, and Yongniang holds it to my lips. It moistens my throat, sweet and cool, easing the burning. I relax against her, all but inhaling it.

"Slower." Yongniang soothes me. "Slower, or you might choke. You haven't had anything to eat or drink in days. Do you know how worried I've been?"

Days?

I've been asleep for *days*?

I gesture for some paper and a brush, so Yongniang orders someone to fetch them. Someone brings me an inkstone and I wet my brush but hesitate before it can touch the paper.

What do I say?

What should I ask?

Is it true Jieshuo is gone? Is it true my lord father is mad? He hasn't sent anyone to visit me, not in all the years I've been living in the Central Plains. Xiliang seems to have forgotten all about me, and I'd not once found it strange. I'd blamed A'die for his heartlessness. But Xiliang ... the Xiliang I remember exists only in my dreams.

I don't dare ask A'du, and I certainly don't have the nerve to ask Yongniang.

So I ask nothing at all.

Ink pools at the tip of the brush and plops onto the paper, a dark flower blooming against all that white. It reminds me of the doors Li Chengyin painted that night at Mingyu Lane, the step-song we fumbled through together, the flash of blades—and the arrow he broke, swearing to trade his life for my safety.

And the blood, the dunes, the fireflies—

The freezing wind blowing atop the cliff, the anguish in his eyes when I cut through the belt.

I throw down the brush and pull the blankets over my head, burying myself in them. Terrified of remembering any more.

Yongniang rubs my back the way someone does when they

are trying to get a baby to sleep. She pats me gently, soothingly. A'du pads away. She's quiet, but I hear her anyway.

A surge of sorrow threatens to overtake me. I'm too scared to ask her about Jieshuo, about my dream, for if it's real, then she's lost more than I, been hurt more than I. A Jieshuo girl, coming all the way to the Plains and living among her enemy, all for my sake. I have never considered myself a coward, but I don't have the courage to know.

I drift in and out of sleep. Yongniang wakes me at night to choke down bitter medicine. She asks if I want anything to eat, but I shake my head. I'm not hungry. There's nothing I can stomach.

Still, she has someone fix up something light, saying, "This flatbread is nice and soft, and you can soak it in soup if that makes it easier to swallow. It'll be good to give your stomach something to tide you over."

But I don't have the appetite for it. After prodding at it with my chopsticks, I push it away.

It reminds me too much of Li Chengyin.

Though in truth, everything here reminds me of him.

I don't want to see him. I'm repulsed by the very thought of him.

Yet I can't avoid him forever.

He arrives when Yongniang brings the food away, a gentle smile on his face as he approaches, looking as he always has. Nothing has changed for anyone but me. We share such a wretched past, and I'd forgotten. He'd forgotten too, and in mutual forgetfulness we found ourselves married. Three muddled years I've spent by his side.

I can't follow this train of thought any longer, for he's drawn near, and is reaching out to caress my forehead. I flinch away from his hand.

He's not angry at all. "You're awake," he says. "I've been so worried."

He looks like a stranger.

"When you were taken," he starts, when he finally catches on, "it was Shangyuan. We weren't allowed to close the city gates. Tradition forbade it." What use is it to say any of these things? Does he think he can use honeyed words to explain it all away? Already I've forgotten how he looked atop the gate, but I will always remember how I looked at the edge of the cliff. I remember, I remember it all.

" . . . I looked for you for days," he's saying, "and I thought—" His voice quiets. "I thought I wouldn't see you again."

He smooths a hand over my shoulder, but all I can see are my lord father's cloudy tears, my a'niang's blood. I hear A'weng's last breaths and feel Heshi's crimson hands push me onto the horse.

With as much force as I can muster, I plunge a hairpin at his chest.

He doesn't see it coming.

Stunned, he stares at me and raises a hand to his chest at the very last moment. But the pin is sharp and pierces straight through his palm. He doesn't move. He doesn't scream. He just stares. The emotions that flicker through his eyes are unreadable, but most of it, I think, is disbelief.

I can't quite believe it either. I shrink back, pressing a hand to my own chest. I'm shaking.

There is a long silence. Then he lifts his other hand to grab the head of the hairpin and tears it out. There's nothing to indicate his pain—no gasp or hitch of breath. A mere knitting of the brows, like he doesn't realize he's made of the same flesh we all are, the same blood, not even when it seeps from the gash, down his long fingers and slender wrist into his sleeve. Bright red tracks like a winding snake, creeping into the fabric.

He clutches the pin and turns his eyes on me. I'm frozen in horror.

Purple crystals scatter across the floor as the pin clatters to the ground. His voice is soft, like he's afraid of startling a wild creature. *"Why?"*

What can I say? How can I tell? I have loved him and I have hated him, and we're separated by an ocean of blood. Forgetting isn't an affliction. It's a blessing. How I long to be like him and escape my own memory.

I turn away. I can lie to him, at least, if I can't lie to myself.

"I understand," he says. A chill has crept into his voice.

I don't.

"I didn't want to bring it up because you've been sick," he continues, "but it seems I must. How did you escape the assassin? A'du wouldn't tell us where you'd gone or how she found you, and I can hardly force it out of her, but you—*you* will tell me."

This boy had jumped after me into the River Oblivion. The one who killed my a'weng and destroyed my family. He's the reason I can't return. I open my mouth, but there's nothing to say. Mockery is the only thing on my tongue. Am I to believe that a soak in the River Oblivion made him forget his own cousin?

For a long time we stare at each other, and then he draws a pair of pendants from his lapels and throws them at my feet.

A matched set. A lover's promise. Mutton fat jade, carved in the shape of yuanyang.

One of them had been mine, and I'd held it through three days and three nights of waiting. He'd been Gu Xiaowu then, and I'd been delighted, though I didn't want to show it, for I had thought I'd met the boy of my dreams. He'd held the other, smiling teasingly at me. In the desert outside the royal city, the sky had been clear and beautiful, and he and I had ridden back together.

Neither of us had been as hideously savage as we are today, glaring fiercely at one another. I'd been the carefree ninth princess of Xiliang, and he'd been a tea merchant's fifth son.

Li Chengyin grabs my arm so tightly the bones grind against each other, forcing my chin up so he can stare into my eyes and ask a second time: "Why?"

I too want to know why. Why fate is so intent on punishing us, forcing us again and again past the point of forgiveness. I am lost in his anguish—and in his hope, too, the last glimmers of it as he wills me to say something, anything to make him understand.

But I am silent. His blood trickles down my face, cooling as it rolls down my cheek.

"Why did the assassin let you go unscathed? Why won't A'du tell me where he is? Why are *you* carrying a set of lovers' pendants? Did I take you from him? Is that what this is?"

I deflate. Why had he jumped after me? Just to say what he said to me, what I didn't understand then and can't remember now?

His eyes are so dark I can see myself reflected in them. Who is he, really? The boy who caught fireflies for me or the husband who left me on our wedding day? The pain in his eyes when he watched me fall—had that been real? He's lied to me so many times, who knows if he's lying still? He'd sworn to trade my safety for his life, but he'd been atop Chengtian Gate with Lady Zhao the very next day.

Li Chengyin isn't Gu Xiaowu. Gu Xiaowu is dead.

My voice is like ground glass. "You did. You stole Gu Xiaowu from me."

"Gu Xiaowu?" He's taken aback.

I'd thought my heart utterly dead above the River Oblivion, but true death is not having the strength to struggle anymore. I'm so tired of fighting.

"You killed him," I say, for he had—the only boy I've ever loved—in Jieshuo, on the day of our unfinished wedding, and again at Xiliang.

"Good!" he says, smiling wrathfully. *"Excellent."*

And then he turns and storms from the room without a backward glance.

Yongniang is astonished when she returns. "Why did His Highness not stay longer?" And then, "Goodness, why is there so much blood?"

Attendants are ordered in to clean the mess while she asks me what happened. She plies and wheedles, and I let her, but I am lost in thought. What should I do? Can I go back to Xiliang? And whether or not I can, I can never bring Gu Xiaowu back.

Yongniang must think I'm tired, for she stops her interrogation and brings A'du in to sleep with me. A'du tucks herself into the thick blanket at the foot of my bed.

But I can't rest. I push myself up and A'du follows suit. Thinking that I'm thirsty, she brings me a cup of tea. I take her hand instead and start writing on it.

Do you want to go home?

She nods.

I feel better knowing that she'll be by my side. She's suffered so much, more than I can imagine, and yet she's come all this way with me. I fold my hand around hers. A tear drops onto our entwined fingers. A'du looks up, startled to see me cry. She wipes my face with her sleeve, and in her other palm, I write, *Don't worry.*

A'du looks pained. She pulls me into an embrace, stroking my hair like a child. Finally, I close my eyes.

There is no escape. I know this in my heart. I loved him once, as Gu Xiaowu. I loved him again as Li Chengyin. After the lies, the countless lies, I still love him.

The River Oblivion is supposed to wash everything away—love, woe, all that hurt. Our paths never should have crossed again. We never should have met again. I never should have fallen in love with him again. He has never been good to me. How many times in the course of three years have we pushed each other away, only to retrace our steps back to the start?

Heaven had granted my prayers, had allowed me to forget.

Why punish me and make me remember just as I have begun to love him again?

Li Chengyin never returns.

For a long time after that I am ill, and it isn't until the magnolias beyond the eaves are blooming in a frost of tiny pink flowers that I regain the strength to speak.

Cherries flower earlier than peaches or plums, so their open buds are a harbinger of spring. The ones in my yard have straight trunks and full canopies that bloom in clusters, patches of pale clouds caught in time, veils of fine gauze tumbling from the eaves to drape long sweeps of fabric in the window.

Much has happened while I've been sick. Yongniang tells me the gossip every day—the senior-most grand secretariat has been impeached for selling official posts. It has implicated a great number of people, so all the ministers are on edge.

General Pei Kuang—Pei Zhao's father, who had been sent to war against Gaoli—returned home victorious, and the emperor was so pleased that the general has been rewarded handsomely.

Lastly, the emperor has selected a new consort, someone young and beautiful and adored. Even Lady Gao, the highest-ranking consort since the empress's departure, is threatened by her. Everyone, apparently, has been speculating that the emperor is going to make her his new queen.

I listen to it all when Yongniang relates it to me, and then I forget it immediately after. I don't have the patience to hear these things anymore, for I've decided that there's nothing trustworthy about the favors of men.

What are women worth compared to their thrones? Gu Jian said once that emperors have to be hard of heart and cold of blood, and if I didn't believe him then, I believe him now.

Noontime brings a sudden storm. Yongniang sighs at the flowers in the yard, saying, "What a shame the buds won't have a chance to blossom."

I'm feeling better, but I've come down with a lingering cough. Physicians prescribe tonic after tonic for me to drink, but none of it is much use. Yongniang rushes inside to bring me a heavy cape and bundles me up tightly within when she hears this, but mostly, I hope it will disappear, because once I'm well, me and A'du can start the journey back to Xiliang.

Whatever it's become, I have to go home.

Soft petals droop beneath the incessant beating of the rain. I sit at the window to watch. Yongniang has had people erect brocade tents in the trees to protect the flowers from the storm—it's a custom here, so that the blooms won't be destroyed. Golden bells have been hung from the tent corners to scare away the birds, for the wind rustles them into a chorus of sound when it passes.

Yongniang must think I'm a changed person, for I'm often quiet. She used to complain that I was too rowdy, but since I've stopped, she looks at me with concern.

A'du is worried too. More than once she tries to convince me to go out into the city like we used to, but I can't muster up the interest. I haven't told her yet that I remember—there are some things, I think, that are better to bear alone.

When the season for cherries has passed, the weather begins to warm. Everyone changes into lighter clothes for spring, and when that too passes, early summer is upon us. Yongniang has someone construct a swing in the yard. I used to love swinging back and forth, flying higher and higher, but Li Chengyin finds it frivolous. I might have a new one to swing on, but I don't care to anymore.

Pei Zhao comes by when the workers are building it. I haven't seen him since he told me to stop meeting with Yueniang. I'm reminded of the first time I saw him, when he took A'du's dagger from her, when he screamed after Li Chengyin. I can't imagine that he knows I remember.

Which is how I intend to keep it, for if he knew, he would certainly be on his guard against me. Plainsmen are good liars. I must learn to keep my own secrets if I want to find an opportunity for escape.

He's brought something for me. All the bequests that his father brought back from his successful campaign have been split up among the ministers. His Majesty had given something to everyone.

But I hadn't any interest in jewels or antiquities, so Yongniang had put them away.

Pei Zhao holds up a basket.

I don't take it. Yongniang lifts the cover instead. A kitten peeks its head out, the size of a fist. Its whole body is covered in downy white fur, like a little rabbit. It has one blue eye and one green eye and climbs up against the edge of the basket, mewling at me.

"Is this from His Majesty?" I ask.

"I—it's a tribute gift from Xianluo, which my father brought back from Gaoli. My siblings are too young to be responsible for it, so I thought I would bring it to keep Your Highness company."

I scoop it from the basket. The kitten basks in my palm, making its presence loudly known as it sticks out a pink tongue to lap at my fingertips. It's scratchy and ticklish, and I smile up at Pei Zhao. "Thank the general for me, then."

He lets out a breath like he's relieved. I stare at him, perhaps brazenly, thinking about how he'd gone west with Li Chengyin, how he knows everything. He had watched me jump from the cliff, and he hadn't once said anything. His loyalty is unshakable.

Would he change if he knew? Would he raise his defenses? I should learn from him, if I want to hurt them the way they've hurt me.

I tease the little cat, saying, "Kitty, kitty, would you like some fish?"

It mewls again and returns to licking my finger. Despite myself, I smile and bring him to A'du. "Look! Its eyes are so pretty."

A'du nods. I ask Yongniang to bring a bowl of milk, and as it eats, A'du and I discuss what to name it.

"What about Spotty?" I ask.

A'du shakes her head.

She's right; its fur is pure white.

"Then . . . Xiaoxue?" There are so many things to figure out—where to put its bed, for one—that I don't notice when Pei Zhao leaves.

Admittedly, it *is* less lonely with Xiaoxue around. It's a

playful little beast and delights in chasing after its own tail. The plum flowers have opened, a mess of red that swirls through the air like snow. The kitten jumps up to try to catch them with its little paws, paying no mind to the ones that have already fallen. When the occasional butterfly flutters by, it dashes all over the yard to try and catch it.

"That can't be a real cat," Yongniang tells me. "It's naughtier than a spirit fox, I say."

And so the days pass. Xiaoxue zooms around the yard. The flowers bloom, dangling heavy from the branches like bunches of pearls until they fall again. Peach and plum trees start to bear fruit the size of soybeans, sheltered beneath wide green leaves.

Time snakes by like the palace rivers—soundless, imperceptible, but it does flow. At night I sit at the top of the stairs, watching the moon rise from behind the trees, the same silent way it's done for thousands of years. It feels no joy, no sorrow. It has no heart, no mind. It just shines out over the dew-laden tiles that shimmer like a field of frost. Above us, the river of stars is silent and unmoving.

Xiaoxue leans against me, crying out for pets. I scratch it behind its fluffy neck and lift it onto my lap. I'm waiting. Waiting for an opportunity to escape this gilded prison.

But as I begin to recover, Miss Xu falls ill.

She's frightfully unwell and doesn't respond to any treatment, but no one in the manor seems to care much at all. If Yongniang hadn't let it slip, I wouldn't know she is at death's door.

I don't know why I decide to see her. Pity, possibly. Or maybe I don't want Li Chengyin to know that anything's changed; maybe I want him to believe I am a naive, carefree princess who is too stupid to think much about anything.

Though Miss Xu still lives in her remote little courtyard, her loyal attendants have been switched out for new girls. The matter of the talisman had been all but dropped, but Lady Zhao uses it as an excuse to treat Miss Xu worse than ever, and I've been in no state to look after her. Regret sits heavy on my shoulders. If I'd found out sooner, it wouldn't have come to this.

She's so thin, there's nothing but bones left of her. The tips of her once-silky locks are as dry and yellow as withered glass. I recall the first time I saw her—she'd been wan and pallid from the loss of her child, but in the way flowers are after being battered by heavy rain, beautiful despite her sorrow. This time, she looks like a chrysanthemum spoiled by the westerly wind, drained of the last of her color.

It takes a long time to rouse her. Her gaze is glassy and unfocused. She doesn't recognize me and is conscious for mere seconds before slipping back into dreams.

In her delicate, tactful way, Yongniang says that the imperial physicians have given her just days more to live.

She's only eighteen. Gone is her youth, it seems, disappeared between one breath and the next. The loneliness inside these walls is a beast that devours everything good, and kind, and beautiful. A girl at her brightest bloom can wilt so quickly.

I wander listlessly out.

"Where's Li Chengyin?" I ask.

Yongniang doesn't know. When she sends someone to inquire, the answer is that he and the Prince of Wu have gone to play polo together.

I walk to his rooms in the main hall and wait. At sunset, eight or so riders trot to the front gate, escorted by a squadron of Yulin Guards. All but one of them dismount. That single silhouette enters the square, heading toward me.

My heart beats at double speed. I'm not ready. I'm not prepared. I don't know what to do. We haven't seen each other in months. Ages ago, we would go days without seeing each other, but then he would always find some excuse to come to my rooms to pick a fight over nothing. These days we don't meet, and so we don't argue either.

I've been avoiding him.

The rational thing to have done the instant I regained my memories was to kill him. To avenge everyone. But . . .

The visit to Miss Xu may be an excuse I am giving myself to come see him. His horse draws close, but the image in my mind is of his brilliant, careless smile as he gallops across the desert to me.

Has Li Chengyin smiled like that? He's not Gu Xiaowu, after all.

An attendant walks to him with a stool and helps him dismount. He tosses his crop over to a page boy as he swings from the horse, as though he doesn't see me sitting on the threshold.

I stand and call out. "I went to see Miss Xu."

Finally, he turns to me.

"She's on her deathbed."

He ignores this and walks into the hall.

The humid summer breeze is a reminder that spring is gone. Once, I would have fought him over this. I would have forced him to see her if I had to tie him up myself to do it. But now?

Now I know you can't force someone to love you. So what if she dies tonight? He's probably forgotten her—her bright eyes, her gentle smile—forgotten that once upon a time, he liked her enough to bed her, forgotten how many nights she must have spent hoping he would arrive at her door.

Just like he's forgotten me. Forgotten how much I've loved him, and hated him. Forgotten that he once caught fireflies by the river to please me, that when I cut through the belt that should have tied us together, I was telling him I'd rather be apart. I'm looking for humanity where there is none. I shouldn't be surprised.

Each day passes warmer than the last, and Miss Xu is weaker by the day. She slips deeper into unconsciousness. At the very end, she's too feeble to swallow the drops of water we wet her lips with. I go to see her every day, though Yongniang reminds me that I've just recovered myself.

I look after her because, inside, I'm dying too.

I sit, waiting with her. The attendants are scared enough of me to avoid speaking ill of her, which is better at least than the carelessness they've customarily shown. But she's so sick that tending to her feels superfluous.

Sunset is hot, and dragonflies flit around the yard. There is no whisper of wind to shake the banana leaves, and when the sky deepens into purple, a surge of dark clouds to the west hints at a storm.

Miss Xu is feeling better today. She opens her eyes, glancing blearily around at the people in the room.

"Do you want anything to drink?" I ask, slipping my hand around hers.

At last, she recognizes me, and smiles.

She doesn't drink. After an hour, she falls back asleep, her breathing growing steadily weaker. I summon a physician, who takes her pulse and says, "Miss Xu has Heaven looking after her."

I don't know much, but I do know that when a physician brings up Heaven, it's because things are past the ability of humans to salvage.

Yongniang tries to wheedle me away, but I'm stubborn. All she can do is start preparing for a funeral. As the sky deepens to black, the temperature in the room rises until it's as hot as the inside of a steamer. Despite this, Miss Xu's attendants tiptoe around the room lighting candles. Illuminated by their flame, Miss Xu's face is stark and white. Her lips are trembling.

I scoot closer, lowering my ear to her face to catch two words, so faint I can scarcely hear them: *"His Highness—"*

I bite my lips to choke back the sob that nearly breaks free. Her one wish is to see him one last time ere she goes, and I can't convince him to come.

He is the one who disturbed her peace. He's the one who has abandoned her, left her to die alone in the manor, and still she can't forget him. Even if he's faithless. Even if he's false. Even if he's indifferent.

How little she desires—a kind word or a look back when he leaves, yet even so little as that is asking too much.

I fold my hands around hers, hoping to give what little warmth I can offer, but her fingers cool in mine.

Yongniang says we should go. Her body needs to be dressed, and there are many things to attend to for the burial. The best thing I can do, she tells me, is pen a letter to the Ministry of Rites and ask if she can be posthumously promoted to lady, or if her family can be given some minor office.

Attendants drape a kerchief over Miss Xu's face. She makes no sound. No movement. Joy and sorrow, anguish and pleasure—all of that is beyond her, disappeared into her lost years.

Thunder, low and heavy, rolls in from the distant horizon. Yongniang stays behind to manage Miss Xu's washing and dressing while A'du accompanies me back. As we wind through the open hallways, I hear the distant sound of music drifting from the main hall, and I'm brought back to the night we sat on the riverbank listening to Jieshuo warriors singing their love songs so far away you could mistake it for music from the heavens.

Music has never moved me quite so much. The voices then were so distant you could mistake it for coming from celestial palaces. Fireflies had floated up from the grass like hazy little stars, or a scatter of golden sand, and I had the thought that they were almost like Heaven's messengers, carrying sparkling little lanterns that twinkled in the brisk air.

The camp on the opposite bank had been dotted with

firelight, the laughter and noise as remote as though we were separated by the sky itself.

I'd watched him catch handfuls of those little stars, their light seeping through his fingers. He'd been a painting, a poem, a dance. He'd captured a hundred fireflies. And then they had scattered, surrounding me and him, illuminating our faces as I looked into his dark eyes and found them looking back.

Anger surges in my blood. Lightning cracks the inky sky, the purple light a sword that cleaves the night in two.

"Go on back without me," I say to A'du.

But she won't and follows me until I take the dagger and its hilt from her waist.

"Go and pack our bags," I say. "We're leaving as soon as I get back."

A'du looks confused, but I shoo her away.

Today is as good a time as any to settle things.

I had assumed the music was coming from a banquet or a feast, but there's nary an attendant around when I approach. Just Li Chengyin, sitting in a window, playing a xiao.

Clothed in plain robes with his brows knit in concentration, he looks almost peaceful. Gu Xiaowu had been this tranquil too when I first met him, but unlike the boy in front of me, he'd been high-spirited and carefree, and smiled the brightest of smiles.

I hadn't known Li Chengyin could play.

I don't know the song, but it's faint and bitter and sad, as though in mourning. He stops when he hears footsteps and sets the instrument down. When he turns to see me, his face settles back into indifference.

He doesn't see the attack coming, and I unsheathe A'du's dagger, lunging at him as soon as I enter. Instinct takes over and he ducks.

The blade rings as it slashes through the air. I'm not well trained, I don't know how to fight, but I have a knife and he doesn't. No matter how agile Li Chengyin is, all he can do is dance away from me. But I put all of my rage, my anger, my resentment into attacking him, and he is beginning to tire. More than once, my blows are inches away from landing—yet he doesn't call for aid.

Anger can only fuel me for so long, though, until I too begin to fail. It's harder and harder to find an advantage, much less press it. We fight in silence until he pins my arm down and wrenches the blade from me, throwing it across the room while I watch, panting for breath.

I bite, hard, on the flesh that connects his thumb and pointer finger. Blood gushes, salty and rank, seeping between my teeth. He pushes at my shoulder. I bring him down with me, and we both go tumbling to the ground. I fumble for one of the lichen-covered copper lions that stands guard in his study and slam it down. The intricate engraving catches on his pants, ripping a long tear down the cloth.

His brow wrinkles in pain and he presses a hand to his leg, but not fast enough to hide the old scar, big and ugly and deep, shaped like the jaw of some massive animal. The scar is horrible. Gu Jian told me once that Li Chengyin had been bitten by the White-Eyed Wolf King. But he hadn't been hurt trying to marry me—he'd gone to deceive A'weng, to connive with Mohu.

Hatred aches in my chest. In the space of that moment, he pushes me back against the carpet and twists my arms behind my back.

I kick until he's forced to press the weight of his body against mine to keep me down. My collar is soaked with sweat. Muslin clings to my skin. His forehead is beaded with sweat, and one droplet slips down his face to hang from his chin. I jerk to avoid it.

Li Chengyin thinks I'm struggling to grab the other copper lion. He seizes my shoulder as I turn, and the sleeve of my robe separates from the seam with a loud tearing sound. His nail catches on my skin, leaving behind a long red mark.

Hissing in pain, I go to kick him again, but he ducks away. Thunder claps outside. Purple lightning pierces through the curtains to turn night into day, bright enough to see how red his face is, and how bloodshot his eyes.

Unsteady, he lunges at me.

I dodge away, but he grabs a handful of my skirt and doesn't let go when I kick his arm. He reaches for my waistband. The knot my attendants use looks intricate and complicated, but it falls away with a tug. I leap for the band, trying to snatch it back, worried he'll use it to restrain my hands again.

The thunder sounds like it's boiling over. Lightning continues to flash. The long, heavy curtains dance in the wind. Abruptly, he lets go and I fall backward, carried by my own momentum, slamming my head against the copper lion that lay where it fell. Pain cracks through me and I am immobilized.

He is furious, and is all I see. For half a second, I think he means to hit me, but as the storm continues to rage, he lowers his head and presses his mouth to mine.

Blood fills my mouth; he's bitten my lip. I clamp my teeth down on his tongue, but he doesn't falter though he's bleeding too. His voice is murderous when he asks, "Who is Gu Xiaowu? Is it the assassin? Tell me!"

I hit him and he lets me, focusing his attention instead on my clothes.

Finally, I cry, "Gu Xiaowu is Gu Xiaowu, and he's a thousand times better than you!"

I'm telling the truth, at least to myself. He can't compare to Gu Xiaowu. He's not the boy who killed the White-Eyed Wolf King to marry me, who caught me a hundred fireflies, the boy I should have married. That boy is dead. He died the day of our wedding. I dissolve into sobs that echo in the hall.

Li Chengyin looks so angry he could rip me to pieces, and for the first time, I'm truly scared of him. I scream and cry for Gu Xiaowu, but Gu Xiaowu isn't coming back. This boy is like the lone wolves I used to see out in the desert, fiercer and more savage for their desolation.

His mouth is on mine again. Salty tears make their way down my cheeks, and he kisses them away, kisses me like I'm another country he means to conquer.

Rain comes down in sheets, drumming against the roof. The thunder picks back up too, like a cavalry of ten thousand horses who have ridden in on the wind, and the last thing between heaven and earth is the sound of the deluge. My eyes are swollen.

It stops storming near dawn. The last signs it had rained at all are the trickles of water that stream through the gutters, the bronze bells rustling in the breeze.

Inside, it is as quiet as a tomb. I am curled up on the bed, spent from crying. The only sound is my shuddering breath.

Li Chengyin draws me to his chest, encircling me in his arms, but I don't want to see him. The pillow is wet with my tears, freezing against my face. Carefully, he brushes the damp hair from my neck and presses his lips against it.

I wish I could kill him.

"Please," he whispers. "Could you try to forget him? I'll do anything. I'll be better, I promise. The truth is that I—I really do—" But for all his efforts, he can't finish the sentence. He's not the sort of boy to beg.

I turn on him furiously. Li Chengyin shrinks back like my rage is a burning thing.

"I will *never* forget him."

I won't forget the way Li Chengyin looks, either. His already pale skin is nearly bloodless, sickly and green in the predawn light. He stills, staring at me, and I laugh to see him hurting.

"You will *never* compare to Gu Xiaowu. Do you think you can bully me into liking you? That your kisses mean *anything* to me? I was bitten by a dog, nothing more."

I triumph in how his face crumbles, but I can't revel in it for long before the bottom falls out of my joy, because it feels hollow. His eyes are empty, and his face is blank. I'd expected him to argue with me or throw me out of his rooms and refuse to see me again. But he does neither. He is silent.

Everyone knows what happened last night, all the more because my wrists and ankles are bruised, and Li Chengyin has scratches on his face and bite marks all over. The Court of Spring is gossiping, and it's left Yongniang in an awkward position.

"You ought to be gentler with His Highness, my lady," she says as she soothes ointment over the blotches.

He's breathing, so all things considered, I'm treating him well enough. If I were better at the martial arts, he'd be long dead. I'd thought about waiting for him to fall asleep and slitting his throat, but he was awake till dawn. Yongniang massages my hands.

We're interrupted by a frantic-looking attendant.

Xiaoxue is very naughty, often slipping out from the courtyard when we aren't looking, so Yongniang has someone looking after it. She's the one who bursts in to tell us that Xiaoxue has disappeared. Yongniang has a dozen people go looking, but no one can find it anywhere.

The next day is Duanwu, when the calamus must be picked. An attendant spots a lump of white fur floating in a pond, and when they scoop it from the water, they realize that it's Xiaoxue.

Drowned.

Nothing can survive this place. Not even a cat.

Somehow, Li Chengyin finds out, for the day after, he sends someone over with another cat. It's identical, right down to the mismatched eyes. I hear that he went to the ambassador from Xianluo to find another, but I can't bear to look at it. I sit there, bitter and dejected, not yet knowing what waves the death of a tiny kitten can raise.

For someone had witnessed one of Lady Zhao's attendants tossing Xiaoxue into the pond.

Li Chengyin is furious when he hears and orders the girl responsible be caned forty times. Forty times—who could survive it? Yongniang rushes back to tell me and says I should leave well enough alone, but since there's a human life at stake, I decide to intervene anyway.

The atmosphere inside the main hall is murderous. Li Chengyin has changed into fresh clothes and is looking down at a row of attendants kneeling at his feet, weeping softly into their sleeves. I've just stepped inside when a page boy follows on my heel to announce the arrival of Lady Zhao.

She looks less put together than usual and falls to her knees as soon as she's here, wailing, "Your Highness, my girls have been framed! They know their place, they would not *dream* of doing anything so wretched, I swear—!" Tears spill prettily from her eyes as soon as she's done.

I sigh, turning to Li Chengyin.

"Never mind," I say. "This doesn't have anything to do with her."

I'm heartbroken that Xiaoxue is gone, but the death of a cat is no reason to take the life of a human.

"If they have the nerve to kill a cat today, they'll have the nerve to hurt a person tomorrow," Li Chengyin retorts.

Lady Zhao jerks her head up, her eyes shining with angry tears. "Do you suspect *me*?"

I've come to plead her case, but Lady Zhao doesn't seem particularly grateful. She looks at me. "It's *you*! You are a *vicious* woman. This is a setup; I know it is—you have killed Miss Xu, and you want to get rid of me, too!"

I don't get a chance to protest, for Li Chengyin cuts her off. "Bullshit."

She wipes her face and straightens her back. "I have said nothing wrong. She was the one who framed Miss Xu with the talisman—she was the one who chose all of Miss Xu's attendants, so who else could it have been? We asked her to investigate and she refused, you see? It's easier to get rid of us both if we were divided, and now Miss Xu is dead. *She* is behind this, I am sure of it!"

"Liar!" I shout, so angry I can hardly form words.

Tears are streaming down Lady Zhao's face, but her voice is utterly calm. "If you had not tried to frame me today, I would have been happy to keep your secrets. But you killed Miss Xu, and I have the proof."

"Why don't you show it to me then, since you've got it?" I snap.

"Of course I have it," she says. She summons an attendant, who sends for her people. When they enter, they're dragging two girls in behind them—Miss Xu's old maids.

They confess to having hidden the peach-wood talisman in Miss Xu's rooms at my behest. "Her Highness said that she wanted to get rid of Lady Zhao, and that if she did die from the curse, she would convince Your Highness to elevate our lady—"

"And she said that it didn't matter if someone did find the talisman, for she would make sure Miss Xu wouldn't get in trouble."

My heart freezes over as I look at them.

How long has Lady Zhao been planning this? How wide of a circle has she drawn around me? When did she first start luring me into her trap? I haven't been so naive that I thought she liked me—I'd stolen her title, after all, and I'd been the one person standing between her and Li Chengyin, but I did not know how deeply she's loathed me.

"This whole time I have said nothing," Lady Zhao says. "My prince, you can attest—I have only ever spoken in the princess's favor. I have only ever tried to persuade you to be more generous with your affections. I have *never* doubted her—not until Miss Xu was murdered, and still I kept silent for her sake. And—and she tries to frame me over some *cat*? It is preposterous! She is trying to turn you against me, Your Highness, can you not see?"

Li Chengyin eyes the two kneeling maids. "Have someone bring the remnants of Miss Xu's medicine."

And then he summons a physician to come take a look at the sealed-up remains of Miss Xu's tonic. The physician says there are traces of huamei bean in it. Huamei bean isn't itself poisonous, but Miss Xu's prescriptions included ginseng—and when combined with ginseng, the bean does release a mild toxin. And if, as Miss Xu had done, the combination is drunk day after day, the toxin will accumulate to dangerous levels.

The maid in charge of brewing Miss Xu's tonics says that I've always been particular about brewing it personally. She says she doesn't know anything about medicine. She says she doesn't know what herbs were in the formulae I brought from the apothecary, that all she did was brew the stuff and help Miss Xu drink it.

And what is there left for me to say? No matter how I try to defend myself, I have the nauseous feeling that I will be damning myself more. There's nothing I can say to prove my innocence.

"Why should I kill Miss Xu?" I laugh. It's so absurd. "Do you think I'm so stupid I'd try to kill you with a piece of wood?"

Lady Zhao turns to Li Chengyin. "Your Highness . . ."

Unexpectedly, he smiles. "A most poisonous heart."

I stare at him, at a loss for words. "You believe her?"

"Why should I not?" he says, his tone light.

I slacken, suddenly feeling more at ease than I have in a long time. "Very well then. Depose me if you like; I don't care. I'm tired of being your consort anyway."

If he deposes me, I can go home.

But his voice is placid. "Wouldn't you like to be let off that easily."

He summons a minister to the manor to come read me my crimes, one by one by one, and I have to sit there and listen to how frivolous I am, how many palace rules I've broken, how I am nothing like the model of virtue I'm supposed to be. When the man is finished with his recitation, I have to admit that he hadn't said anything that was untrue. The only lies I'm accused of are attempting to curse Lady Zhao and killing Miss Xu, for which I am confined to Kangxue Hall.

It's the farthest flung of the manor's courtyards, where no one comes. I imagine it's not too far from those lonely courts where the king banishes his consorts after they've fallen out of favor.

It was when the emperor deposed the empress that I realized how difficult it would be for Li Chengyin to do the same to me. The emperor had had to issue an edict to the Office of Imperial Decrees, and then he had to get the Chancellery to agree—but those old men are as stubborn as mules, and when the queen had been deposed, some of the chancellors threatened to kill themselves in protest. One of them really tried it, too. He'd rammed his head against the stairs outside the main hall, but he hadn't succeeded. The emperor had been furious, but in the end, he got his way. The empress was deposed.

The thing that I'm thinking about, more than anything, is that the guards here are less vigilant. Perhaps it will be easier for A'du and I to escape if we do it from here.

I'm planting flowers when Yueniang comes to visit.

She walks in, smiling to see my hands covered in mud, and then knitting her brow after. "His Majesty bade me to come see you," she says. "How has it come to this?"

And I realize that the new consort Yongniang had spoken of, the one the emperor adores—is Yueniang.

I look her up and down. She's beautiful in her new clothes, her expensive powders. I muster up a smile. "Thank heavens Li Chengyin doesn't want me anymore or else I might have to call you *mother*."

Yueniang looks at me in disbelief. "How can you make jokes at a time like this? How can you be in the mood to plant flowers?"

She relates to me everything that's happened beyond the walls of my lonely little courtyard.

Lady Zhao's family have influence at court, and since she's produced evidence of my supposed crimes, they've been railing at the emperor to put me to death. Li Chengyin was ordered in to see his father, but no one knew what was said because His Majesty dismissed everyone. What they do know is that the emperor was in a flying rage and Li Chengyin stormed out, equally furious. They aren't speaking to each other, and Yueniang can't do more than try to soothe His Majesty's temper.

"I know you didn't do any of what they're saying," says Yueniang. "But the emperor is in a difficult situation, and I had to beg to come see you. Don't you have anything you *want to say*? Isn't there anyone you *want to see*?"

I don't understand what she's trying to say. "No, no one."

At my confusion, Yueniang explains—she wants me to ask for Li Chengyin and make nice with him. As long as he doesn't want to press the issue, it doesn't matter how much dust Lady Zhao kicks up. The emperor can find a way to make the whole matter disappear. Miss Xu was no one of consequence and the talisman was as big a deal as one made it.

"I once heard that something similar happened years ago, during the reign of emperor Zhongzong, but it had implicated his favorite consort. The whole ordeal was swept under the rug with the execution of a few attendants, and no one investigated any further. People may have talked their mouths off about it, but what could they do?"

But I would rather die than lower my head to Li Chengyin.

"I didn't do any of the things they accuse me of doing," I say frostily. "And if they want to put me to death, then so be it. But I won't beg forgiveness for something I didn't do, not to please anybody."

Yueniang implores me to listen, but I don't. She's so worried, she starts to weep, but I focus on my flowers. I've been planting roses all over Kangxue Hall. The guards posted here are kind enough to A'du and me, buying me sprouts when I ask for them, carting over fertilizer when I bring it up. These kinds of roses only bloom here in the Plains—Yueniang used to pin them in her hair when she worked at Mingyu Lane.

"When these roses bloom," I tell her, "I'll send some to you."

"You aren't worried at all?"

I ladle water over the roses. "Look at these flowers. They were so happy growing in the dirt, and then we had to go and uproot them, trading them for a handful of coins. But they still bloom so beautifully. Do you think they worry about their own survival? What does it matter how much I do? I'll do what I ought, when I ought. Either I'll make it through or I won't—why spend every day wondering if the sky will fall?"

Li Chengyin wouldn't believe me anyway. At least he doesn't remember any of what happened. I'll bide my time. I'll find an opportunity. I'll end all of this and escape, and then I'll never have to think of him again.

Yueniang looks caught between laughing and crying and, not finding a better way to coax me into submitting, she returns to the palace.

It's blessedly quiet in Kangxue Hall, though the food isn't as good. I used to love noise, before.

One night, at midnight, A'du shakes me awake. I push myself up, rubbing at my eyes. "What is it?"

A'du looks nervous, and she pulls me to an east-facing window to point at the courtyard wall.

Smoke, heavy and dark, rises from a bright sea of light. Shock sears me. A fire? How?

But there's no time to think. It's spreading fast, and it's almost upon us. A'du kicks open one of the westward windows and we crawl through it to run to the soaring wall that surrounds Kangxue Hall. She rushes me up it, but I don't get a chance to steady myself before a sharp surge of air whizzes toward us. A'du shoves me back. I catch a glimpse of her drawing her dagger as I fall, and something clatters to the ground with a hollow ring—an arrow.

A'du is reaching down for me when a second arrow shoots past, then a third. She knocks them from the air, but they come quicker than a plague of locusts, and soon the tiles beneath her have all been shattered to dust. An arrow pierces her shoulder. Blood bursts from the wound and I scream her name, but her first instinct is to plunge after me.

The wind rushes past my ear. I'm reminded of the last time we tried to scale a wall and were met with a volley of arrows. A'du had not been able to catch me in time. It had been Pei Zhao who saved me, but Pei Zhao isn't here, and she knows that as well as me.

I jerk to a stop. A'du has grabbed my arm. Her dagger carves a line of sparks against the stone as it seeks purchase, shaking ceramic dust from the roof tiles, but I'm slipping out of her grasp. Her right arm is too injured to exert any effort, and the second volley of arrows is thicker than the first.

"Let go!" I scream. "A'du, let go!"

If she doesn't, we'll fall to our deaths together. The wall is high, and the ground is solid stone.

The blood from her shoulder drips onto my face. I try to tear her hand from mine, but she heaves me upward. I am soaring—and then I crash against the tiles. I scrabble for something to cling to, pulling myself on top of the wall, but when I turn, it's to see A'du, struck by more arrows. The dagger has found purchase on the smooth manor walls. She hangs from it, limp, until her hand loosens around it and she falls, heavy, to the ground.

I scream.

In the pitch of night, the arrows clatter all around me and break the ceramic tiles into pieces. The shattering shards scrape painfully against my face as I wail A'du's name. Arrows fall like a heavy rain, and I am closed within. I've never felt so helpless nor so alone.

Someone steps in front of me. He needs only to wave a sleeve for the arrows to come clattering down. Through bleary eyes I can see long white robes, clean and radiant as moonlight.

Gu Jian.

He folds me to his side and leaps to the roof of Kangxue Hall, but I shout, "And A'du—you have to save A'du!"

Once he pushes me to safety, he darts back to where A'du is lying, crumpled in a heap at the foot of the wall. His robes flutter in the breeze, a massive white bird alighting upon the ground.

A flaming arrow breaks up the long dark of night, arcing through the black like a shooting star—then another, and another, like a shower of meteors until they dim again. They thud against the wall, the sound of moths throwing themselves against summer lanterns. Gu Jian is fast, though, and in moments he has A'du in his arms.

But the flaming arrows come again. The air is sharp with the acrid smell of burning. The arrows whistle as they pierce through the air. They come from every direction, but they are all pointed toward one man. I peer out from behind the soaring edge of the roof to see line after line of black armor pressing closer. I can't count how many thousands of soldiers have been lying in wait.

Gu Jian has one arm around A'du and the other around his sword, knocking arrows from the air. A heavy layer of them lie at his feet, burning, their flame refracting off the white of his robes and turning everything hazy. He moves like a specter, and the arrows keep falling, but the soldiers keep shooting too, and he can't make a clean escape.

Blood stains the white of his clothes. I can't tell if it's his or A'du's—though he has her in his arms, she's limp and unmoving. From my distance, there's no way to tell how badly she's injured. If this goes on any longer, I'm sure they will die.

Who are these soldiers? To be able to congregate in such numbers in the Court of Spring, wearing such heavy armor, making such a ruckus—they can't possibly be assassins.

I rise to my feet, craning for a better look at them, but someone presses down lightly on my shoulder. "You'd better duck, Your Highness."

Pei Zhao.

On the ceramic tiles behind him there is an army of Yulin Guard, dressed for battle in their light armor. They've been waiting here in silence, their bows half drawn and pointed down. From such a height—Gu Jian might escape the others, but these will force him back.

"Tell them to stop," I beg.

"Forgive me, my lady, but His Highness has ordered us to kill the assassin. I cannot disobey."

I grab his arm. "That's not an assassin, and look—he's holding A'du! She's no assassin, either—you *must* tell them to stop—you *must*—"

For all that Pei Zhao looks aggrieved and apologetic, he still draws his arm from my grasp.

I'm furious. "Gu Jian might have tried to abduct the emperor, but he didn't hurt him. And if you want to, capture him, but none of this has anything to do with A'du! Please, you have to tell them to stop!"

"I have orders," he murmurs. "When the assassin shows himself we are to deal with him at once. He must not be allowed to escape again. I'm sorry, Your Highness, but the command is not mine to give."

"What if that was me down there?" I demand. "If Gu Jian had taken me with him—am I to be killed as well?"

Pei Zhao raises his eyes to look at me. They're shadowed, but the fiery arrows reflect in them like pinprick-sized fireworks.

"Tell them to stop or else I'll jump down and die with them."

But I don't get the chance to, for Pei Zhao stretches forward, saying, "Forgive me, Your Highness."

There is a numbness at my pressure points, and suddenly I'm too heavy for my legs to carry. I collapse onto the tiles, immobilized. He's paralyzed me. I scream at him, curse at him, but he ignores me, turning to yell, "Rise!"

The Yulin Guard rise to their knees. They string their bows and draw, pointing directly at the two figures encircled below.

My tears are hot and desperate and angry. "I'll kill you!" I scream. "If you *dare* tell them to shoot, I'll *kill* you!"

"Release!"

The arrows sing.

They arc over my head, hurtling toward their target. Gu Jian leaps into the air, intending to break through the soldiers on the ground by force, but he's pushed back by the hailing arrows above. I can't see anything through my tears, just that deadly rain, and then the figure of Gu Jian laying A'du carefully on the ground.

I think he means to leave her behind, but then they both disappear beneath another volley. I howl for Pei Zhao to stop, but he acts like he doesn't hear me. I beg, but he is unmoved.

I don't know how long it is before he gives the order to stop. There is a mountain of arrows on the ground, and I can see no trace of anyone beneath it. The first row of soldiers steps back to reveal another line of guardsmen, these armed with spears, who dig through to reveal Gu Jian, his white robes scarlet with blood.

I open my mouth, but there is no voice left to scream with, just tears, big and fat, that slip down my cheeks and onto my tongue. They taste bitter. Biting.

A'du, my A'du.

Three years she's spent by my side. Three years without being able to avenge her family, her people. Three years so far from home, to keep me company. Three years of risking her own life to save mine, yet I can't do the same for her. I can't tell when Pei Zhao brings me to the ground again; I'm only aware when he releases me from my paralysis.

He stares down at me. "Your Highness, you may dispose of me however you like, but I have my commands, and I cannot disobey them."

I stumble toward the soldiers. At first they refuse to let me through. I glare back at Pei Zhao, and he waves a hand. The Yulin Guard parts easily for him.

A'du's face and clothing are covered with blood. I wail when I see her, tears landing heavily against her face. She's still warm, and I reach for her, trying to see where she's hurt, if she can be saved. Miraculously, her leg and shoulder are the sole injuries. And as I sob for her, I swear her lids flicker.

I gasp and call her name again. Finally, her eyes crack open, but she can't speak. With the last of her energy she points to Gu Jian, but I don't understand what she wants. She gazes and gazes at him, her hand viselike around my lapel.

"You want me to go see him?" I guess.

She nods.

I'm not sure why she would want me to, but I'm not going to disobey her now. Whatever she wants, I will do it.

When I walk over, I'm surprised to find him alive.

His gaze flickers when he recognizes me. I can't count the number of arrows that have pierced his skin. No inch of him has been left intact. I kneel by his side and, despite everything, I find that I'm sorry. He's saved me time and time again—it had been him at Tiangen Mountain, too. I call his name.

This was a trap Li Chengyin set. I dragged him into it. This is my fault.

His mouth trembles slightly. When I bend closer to hear, Pei Zhao comes up to stop me. "Careful, Your Highness."

"What's there to be careful of when he's already half dead?" I snap, and scoot closer to catch the softest of whispers.

"A'du . . . how is . . . A'du . . . ?"

"Don't worry," I tell him. "She's okay. Just hurt, that's all."

The corners of his mouth twitch into the faintest smile.

A thought strikes me when I see the state of his injuries compared to hers. "Did you—use your own body to protect her?"

He says nothing, just looks at me dazedly—looks, and looks, and looks.

My heart softens. He could have escaped by himself, this I know. He could have left her there on the ground, and he might have been able to carve a bloody path toward freedom. But he hadn't. He'd laid his life down to save A'du. But why?

I think perhaps I know the answer this time, but I ask him anyway.

"If she . . ." His voice is thin and faint, like it could be blown away by the night wind. I have to press closer to hear him. "If she . . . you'll . . . be so sad . . ."

The pain nearly cripples me, but he's smiling. "I—I can't . . . break your heart . . . again . . ."

"I never even loved you," I weep. "Why should you be so silly?"

"Because I . . . let you . . . down . . ."

His eyes are full of regret. My own fill with tears. "Shifu—"

His gaze roves to the sky above us and he sucks in unsteady breaths. "The stars . . . that night . . . as bright . . . as tonight. And you were . . . sitting on the dune, singing . . . about a fox . . ."

"I understand," I tell him. My voice is soft. "I'll sing—I'll sing it for you."

Cradling his head in my arms, I feel a heavy sort of grief. That song, the only song I know how to sing—

> *O, there is a fox,*
> *He sits upon the dune.*
> *Sits upon the dune,*
> *Watching the moon.*
>
> *No, not watching the moon—*
> *He's waiting for the shepherd girl*
> *To come back.*

I sing it in fits and starts. This song is one I know better than the back of my own palm, but every line is out of tune today. I've started crying again, but he's looking at me, smiling softly until he cools, until he's frozen through, until his hand falls to the ground. The luminous white robes have long since been reduced to rags, but something in his lapels catches my eye.

Hairpins. The same ones he'd bought for me the night of Shangyuan, soaked through with blood. I'd thrown them angrily at his feet, and he'd kept them tucked away so carefully. The things I'd discarded, folded safely against his heart.

Half kneeling on the ground, voice ragged and wavering, I continue:

> *O, there is a fox,*
> *He sits upon the dune.*
> *Sits upon the dune,*
> *Soaking in the sun.*
>
> *No, not soaking in the sun—*
> *He's waiting for the horseback girl*
> *To ride past.*

Pei Zhao walks forward to guide me to my feet. "Your Highness..."

I slap him.

He freezes, taken aback, but collects himself and pulls me up regardless. "Let me take you to the prince, Your Highness."

"I won't see him," I snarl. "I won't see anybody. The two of you—" But I can't summon the words to yell at him. He was following orders, that's all. Li Chengyin's orders.

Gu Jian is dead. A'du is hanging to life by a thread.

My fault.

My fault.

Gu Jian wouldn't have fallen into their trap if it wasn't for me. Gu Jian wouldn't have died if it wasn't for me. I'd begged him to save A'du, and so he'd fought to do just that.

Again and again, the people around me have lost their lives, and it's all my fault.

They killed A'weng. They killed A'niang. They killed Heshi, and they've killed Gu Jian, too.

Everyone around me, everyone who's loved me—they've killed them all off, one by one.

"Miss A'du needs a physician, Your Highness," Pei Zhao says. "I've sent for someone."

I glare up at him. He doesn't look away. He doesn't offer up any defense of his actions. And I—I have nothing more to say to him.

It's for A'du's sake that I tolerate any of them at all, but I won't let them touch her. I pick her up myself. She had always been the one to carry me, and I'm surprised by how light she is. Gu Jian had been the one to bring her back from the brink of death last time. Now that he's gone . . .

A'du's right collarbone is broken, as is one of her ribs. The physician extracts the arrow shaft, sets the bone, and spreads a poultice over her wounds. She slips into sleep.

I sit at her bedside, ignoring everyone. I hug my arms around myself and think that, as soon as A'du is well enough to travel, I'm taking her back to Xiliang.

Li Chengyin comes to see me.

My clothes are stained with dried blood, and my hair is a tangled mess. He furrows his brow. "Help her into something clean," he says.

Poor Yongniang approaches me hesitantly. I draw A'du's dagger and glare.

Li Chengyin dismisses everyone with a wave of his hand.

He walks toward me. Through the curtain of my hair, I count his steps, meaning to take the blade and plunge it into his chest. But then he slowly seats himself and looks into my eyes. I stare sullenly back.

"Xiaofeng, I couldn't let him live—you understand that, don't you?" His voice is soft. "He could kidnap a king with impunity. I couldn't *not* kill him."

I don't have the strength left for anger. I just look at him.

"I shouldn't have used you as a lure, I know that, but I—I couldn't think of a better way. Lady Zhao's family is so powerful; her father and brother are both influential at court—I couldn't get rid of her without a good enough reason. The Zhao collude with Gao Yuming, and His Majesty is constrained by the power of their faction. That's why I had to get the Chen case overturned, don't you see? And once that was overturned, we could take down Gao Yuming—but then Lady Zhao was always conniving, always conspiring against you—I could only keep you safe by besting her at her own game, but—you needn't worry about any of that anymore, because it's all over—"

I don't understand a thing he's saying.

Every word, every explanation starts and ends with the court, and the court, and the court.

He tells me that he used the wrongful death of Yueniang's family to find proof of Gao Yuming's corruption, that his crimes have been exposed, his assets seized, the clan all executed. The Zhao, too, have been put to death. Lady Zhao was thrown from the manor for her role in killing Miss Xu and framing me for it. She'd killed herself, he tells me, out of shame.

Once, the Gao had enjoyed the protection of the empress, but when she was deposed, they tried to get Lady Gao in a position to be the next queen, and the Zhao grew more daring by association, but these people, he tells me, are all the same people who conspired with the empress to kill his mother.

The inner palace, I'm beginning to realize, is nothing more than the same vicious play staged over and over again. He's avenged his mother's death; he's punished everyone who was involved in this twenty-year plot, and I imagine this is the most satisfied he's been with anything in his life.

The Gao, the Zhao, the Gu, the Chen.

There's nothing about it that I understand.

Especially not the way he talks about Lady Zhao, like her death weighs on him no more than the death of an ant.

I could have sworn he loved her. At least, he'd treated her like he did.

And all of it, the entire time—he's been pretending? He hasn't loved her—not for a moment?

I'd hated Lady Zhao. I'd resented her. But now, mostly, I pity her.

Li Chengyin's heart must be carved from stone. How could you bear killing someone you spent three years with? A dog, a cat, should have enjoyed the luxury of clemency, much less a person.

The world has changed in the last three years. The only thing that hasn't is him. He may have jumped into the River Oblivion. He may have forgotten me and everything we shared. But he will never forget his power, his treachery. He will never hesitate to use the people around him, nor flinch at using our feelings to advance his own goals.

He reaches out a hand to caress my cheek.

I push him away. "Leave!"

"They wouldn't have hurt you," he says. "The soldiers, they're the best archers in the Yulin Guard. Did you notice how none of the arrows landed near you? But I shouldn't have—I oughtn't to have put you in danger. I miscalculated, I know that, it's my fault—"

"And A'du?" I ask. "If A'du had died with Gu Jian?"

He seems startled by the question. "Xiaofeng, A'du's just a servant."

The crack of my palm against his cheek is loud and sharp, but he doesn't duck away. I'm so angry, I'm shaking. "A'du has protected me with her life. She's come with me all the way from Xiliang. She may be nothing more than a servant to you, but she's my sister." Even Gu Jian had known how much A'du means to me.

Li Chengyin pulls me to him. "Please, Xiaofeng. *I love you*. Can't you feel it? Couldn't you tell? Do you remember that day when I was sick, and you sat there with me and I wouldn't let go of your hand? I was wondering then how anyone could be so silly. But I didn't realize I would love you for it.

"You don't know how delirious I was after you'd been abducted—I couldn't think straight—I didn't know what I'd do if I couldn't find you. I hadn't been scared of anything until then. But then you came back, and you said you loved Gu Xiaowu, and you don't know how jealous I was. I was nearly mad with it. I didn't just want him dead because he was the assassin, I—I wanted him dead because he was Gu Xiaowu. You can blame me for it because it's my fault and I shouldn't have done it, but—but you have to understand—for all my life, none of my choices have been my own. There's never been another way. But it's over, I swear it. No one can hurt you anymore. Will you trust me, just this once?"

Tears plop softly against the back of my palm. Why am I such a crybaby?

All I'd wanted three years ago was to forget this boy. And I had, for a time.

All I'd wanted when I married Li Chengyin was for him to love me, or at the very least smile at me every once in a while. He'd been so beautiful, the most beautiful boy I've ever known, genteel and bright-eyed and well-bred. Today he's folded me into his arms and is talking to me of his heart.

But I hadn't wanted any of it like this.

I shake my head and push him away.

"He wasn't Gu Xiaowu," I say. "Gu Xiaowu is long dead."

Li Chengyin pulls back, staring at me in surprise. "But I've admitted I was wrong," he says dumbly. "What more could I do?"

I don't want him to do anything more. I'm so tired, so weary. I lean my head back against a column. "You used to love Lady Zhao so much. You used to fight with me about her all the time, and now you say it was a lie. You used to be so close with Prime Minister Gao—you used to be his protégé, and now you tell me he's a monster deserving of execution. You used to hate me, tell me every day how you wanted to depose me, and now you say you love me. Tell me, how am I supposed to trust you?"

He freezes. "Xiaofeng," he says, "I'm the crown prince. There are so many things I want to do but can't, and so many things I don't want to do but must."

"That's right." I smile. "You must harden your heart and freeze your blood over if you mean to be king."

I hadn't taken Gu Jian seriously when he said it, but I understand now.

The closer a person is to power, the further he moves from warmth, from humanity. Li Chengyin can't understand the love between me and A'du because he hasn't felt it. He doesn't know what it's like to trust someone, to rely on them.

"Someday, if I become a threat to your throne, would you kill me too?"

He avoids the question. "Xiaofeng, the only place more dangerous than the palace is the Court of Spring. The only thing harder to be than a king is his heir. You don't know how difficult it's been—"

"Would you?" I cut him off.

He looks at me. Finally, he says, "I won't."

"You would," I tell him, smiling. "Do you know of a river called Oblivion?"

He doesn't answer.

"The River Oblivion washes all love away." I turn away from him, humming that song, that same old song. "O, there is a fox..."

The Gu Xiaowu who lives in my heart is well and truly dead.

Li Chengyin had known Lady Zhao would send people to poison Miss Xu, but he didn't intervene. A girl who had spent a night with him, her life worth less than the grass beneath his feet.

Li Chengyin had been using Lady Zhao, but he still pretended to all the love in the world. A girl who had sworn the rest of her life to him, her love worth less than weeds.

Li Chengyin had known Lady Zhao was plotting against me, but he hadn't defended me, hadn't interceded. He watched as I fell deeper and deeper into danger and didn't once think of pulling me back to safety. And then he'd used that danger to lure his own cousin into death.

He won't jump after me a second time.

For days, I don't leave A'du's side. When the infection flares into fever, I think again of Gu Jian. He'd been around last time to save her. This time, he isn't.

When she is at her worst, I take ill.

It's storming again that day, and I am bringing a pan of ice up from the cellar when I slip on the slick wood of the corridor, slamming hard to the ground. At first I think it's nothing worse than a scrape, but at night I begin to run a temperature.

And because A'du has a fever too, Li Chengyin blames my illness on her. He orders someone to take A'du from my rooms. He says that I'm recovering from a long illness, so I can't risk catching what she's got.

Whose fault is it that she's as sick as she is?

I grab the dagger and step in front of her, forcing them all back.

But Li Chengyin has no patience for it. He has a guard pull me away from her.

I don't know where they bring her, for I'm locked inside my rooms all day, but I don't have the energy to make a fuss. I want my A'du, but she's gone too. I can't eat, I can't drink, and when Yongniang brings my tonic, I use the last of my strength to knock it to the ground. I can't stay another day in this manor. I want A'du. I want to go home.

All day I'm plagued by nightmares. I dream of A'niang and A'die, who smooths his rough hands over the top of my head and whispers, *It's been hard on you, my child.*

It hasn't, not really. It's only been tiring, and I don't want to fight anymore. Like a fish sucking in its last breath, or a flower the instant before it loses its bloom. Li Chengyin and his Court of Spring are the heaviest chains in the world, and I'm not strong enough to wear them anymore.

Yongniang rouses me gently. "A'du is back."

And so she is. I don't know why Li Chengyin has changed his mind.

I brush a hand over hers, which burn to the touch. The fever isn't broken yet, but as long as she's here and I can stay by her side, everything will be okay.

Yongniang doesn't say much, just, "A'du is back, my lady, so you'd best take your medicine."

Taking the bowl from her, I swallow the bitter liquid down in large gulps. I make a face, wishing that I'd had the foresight to suck on a candied apricot to sweeten the acrid film that coats my tongue. I smile at Yongniang, but she's crying.

"What is it?"

She doesn't answer me. "Your hair is tangled, my lady. Let me dress it."

The pull of the ivory comb through my hair is soothing. Yongniang's hands are gentle and warm like A'niang's were. As she brushes, she begins to natter. "I remember when you first came to the manor. You were so sick then. The physicians didn't dare prescribe anything, lest they get it wrong. And I sat by your side, watching you. You didn't know how to speak Plains very well then, and you used to cry out in your dreams for *shanzi, shanzi*. I didn't know until later that *shanzi* meant *a'niang* in Xiliang."

I'd forgotten all that. Of my illness, all I can remember is that it had been right after I arrived in Shangjing, and that A'du and Yongniang had looked after me.

"You were fifteen then." Yongniang coils my hair. "Three years have passed so quickly."

I turn to look at her. She's smiling.

"Your birthday," she says. "The palace forgot, the prince forgot, but you turn eighteen today."

Truthfully, I'd also forgotten. I've been too occupied with A'du to think much about it. The Ministry of the Inner Court ought to have remembered, but I heard something big happened up at the palace, so no one has any mind to pay to anything so small as that.

Only Yongniang remembered.

She switches to a fine-toothed comb and carefully smooths back my hair. "After today you will be an adult. You mustn't be so willful anymore, my lady."

Willful?

The word doesn't fit quite right anymore.

The willful girl, the headstrong one—she doesn't exist.

Three years ago, she died in the waters of the River Oblivion and I—I have been borrowing her body for the last three years, living with her enemy.

He won't remember her.

But that might be for the best.

By the time A'du recovers, summer is drawing to a close.

She signs to me while she convalesces, telling me things I hadn't known. Like the fact that Gu Jian had rescued her last time by sacrificing a great deal of his own internal energy—and that if he hadn't, he likely wouldn't have died amid the arrows.

I find that A'du is as silly as I am.

"Did you love him?" I sign back at her.

She doesn't say anything, but a cloud passes over her eyes, and she turns to look at the lotus that blooms in the pond outside. Then she turns back and beams at me.

It's obvious she'd been crying.

We're cut from the same cloth, she and I. We even have the same bad habit of trying to smile when we're weeping.

I learn a lot from A'du. I learn, for example, that the empress didn't send the assassin who made an attempt on Li Chengyin's life.

"It was His Highness's men," she writes. "Under Sun Er."

Sun Er?

I stare at the name in shock.

If Sun Er is one of Li Chengyin's men, then had the empress been framed? She hadn't sent anyone against him; he'd hired someone to assassinate him to get the emperor to move against the empress. And then, at Mingyu Lane, when Sun Er raised a ruckus and distracted us—all of that had been planned by Li Chengyin?

What has he done?

Li Chengyin, what have you *done*?

In careful, deliberate strokes, A'du continues:

That night at Mingyu Lane, she'd sensed something was wrong and had gone to tail Sun Er. But she was found out. And she'd been one against many skilled fighters, but they didn't kill her. They didn't hurt her. They just locked her away in secret until Gu Jian rescued her and brought her to the dilapidated temple to meet me.

She'd asked him why I was there, and he revealed that both he and Sun Er had been under orders from Li Chengyin— that Li Chengyin wanted Gu Jian to force the emperor's hand because he wanted the emperor to believe someone didn't want the Chen family's case to be overturned. And I'd burst in, demanding to be taken hostage instead, and Gu Jian hadn't known what else to do but abduct me instead.

I don't want to think about it anymore. I can't. Every time I do, my heart goes cold.

Li Chengyin is a stranger to me—a fearsome, terrifying stranger. Three years ago he'd been ruthless. Three years later he's grown even more so. When he killed Gu Jian—did he mean to silence a witness? But Gu Jian had been his own cousin, his uncle's child. How many contemptible things did Gu Jian do on his behalf? By not trying to spare A'du—had he intended to keep this from me forever by silencing her as well?

What has he done?

For the first time I truly understand how abject a thing the human heart is, how wretched a place the Court of Spring is, how cruel a person my husband is.

I shiver.

A'du and I are confined to my rooms, but that means little to me anymore. In a place as lonely as this, we are each other's sole comfort.

Yueniang comes to see me a few times. I warn her, "You must take care of yourself in that place."

A king's love never lasts very long. The emperor brought her in to use her as a lead in the old Chen family case, that's all. She's not the only beautiful woman in the palace, and I'm afraid it is more dangerous than the Court of Spring.

Lady Gao died recently after a sudden illness, but the rumor is that she killed herself by swallowing gold after her family fell out of favor. Palace gossip spreads like wildfire.

I know too that Yueniang is in a peculiar position—the emperor seems as fond of her as ever, but she is not nobility, and she has been an entertainer besides. A new faction's formed at court, and the emperor has taken another consort at their recommendation. The ministers are still persuading him to install another empress; he just hasn't made his mind up about who.

And if there is a new empress, then Yueniang might be the target of her jealousy. Yongniang told me once about a Lady Lan from a former kingdom—she hadn't come from a good family, so when she died at the hands of the queen, it had been of little consequence. I don't want Yueniang to suffer such a fate.

But she smiles. "I can handle myself."

And then she plays a song for me. Her voice is exquisite, as soft as mist and supple as dew, like a light breeze that soars over the walls, past the swing, beyond the blue sky, above the clean white clouds. I imagine a little bird soaring through that endless blue, flying, flying west, flying straight to Xiliang. Xiliang doesn't have the kind of lovely garden ponds she sings about, nor lovely girls who pluck lotuses from the gardens, but it is my home.

When I went to Mingyu Lane, I'd been such a happy girl. Carefree, without woe.

"I don't know when I'll hear you sing again," I sigh.

"I'll come see you soon," Yueniang promises.

I don't tell her I've decided to leave as quickly as I can. Since A'du's healed, there's no reason for us to stay any longer.

Li Chengyin has Pei Zhao select new guards for my quarters. He claims it's for my protection, but it's closer to supervision, I think. The men they choose are stern, and if we try to force our way out there's no way we'll succeed. So I bide my time.

The seventh day of the seventh month is Qixi, as well as the emperor's birthday, which means it'll be another celebration. For nearly half a month, the palace has been decorated with strings of brilliant lanterns. New parks have been built and a new boat constructed, for the banquet will be on Qiongshan Island in the southern parklands. Towers and pavilions dot the water, and the breeze off the lake will dissipate the last of the summer heat.

Li Chengyin is summoned early, so I follow some time after. I board the boat behind Ganlu Hall, and above the sound of the water, I can hear music from an orchestra that the new consort, the Lady Xian, has arranged beneath the shade of some large lakeside trees. Carried out over the water like this, the music floats to us as if from a long distance away.

The banquet begins at sundown.

White lotus fills the southern parklands, their blooms full and unblemished, a fragrance lilting through the air. The Lady Xian has had people float lanterns on the water with perfume cakes held above open flame on a copper stand inside. When burned, the perfume is so strong you can smell it across the water, and the incense that girls smoke their clothes with smells faint by comparison. Across the lake, a dance group performs in a pavilion, their green robes making them look like flower sprites, rippling in movement. Candlelight reflects on the surface of the water, shimmering on the waves like fragmented stars.

His Majesty is delighted with the feast. He compliments the Lady Xian on her attention to detail—especially the perfumed lanterns. She giggles.

"How could I have thought of that myself?" she demurs. "I'm always complaining that it's a shame that such a beautiful flower carries no scent. It was one of my attendants who thought of the perfumed lanterns. Your compliments, my lord, are better directed toward A'man. Shall I summon her?"

A'man is a year or two younger than me. She walks gracefully from the retinue to dip into a polite curtsy for the emperor. When she lifts her face, more than one person has to stifle a gasp of pleasure, for A'man is prettier even than Yueniang. Her features are exquisite—limpid like the white lotus she'd used to such great effect.

His Majesty seems startled by her beauty and takes a moment to compose himself before having someone present her with a pair of jade vases and a box of precious agarwood. At first, I imagine he will want to take her as his own consort, but he turns to Li Chengyin instead.

"Yin'er, what do you think of the girl?"

Li Chengyin sits opposite me. He must be tired, for he hasn't spoken all night, but now that the emperor has called on him, he raises his eyes to glance over and says, dispassionately, "A beauty, indeed."

"You're in need of attendants," the emperor says. "Why don't I send A'man over to the Court of Spring? I'm sure the Lady Xian can spare her."

"Thank you, Your Majesty, but I've no shortage of handmaidens," says Li Chengyin.

I shift in my seat.

The emperor turns his gaze to me. "And you, my dear? What say you?"

"Your Majesty, the prince is only shy. A'man is so pretty; if he won't take her, I will."

The emperor smiles and allows it.

I can feel Li Chengyin's glare boring a hole in my skull, but I choose not to notice it. The Lady Xian looks pleased and sends A'man to my side at once. When the banquet is over and we're all preparing to leave the palace, she has someone prepare a carriage to take A'man back to the manor with me.

Banquets are tiring, especially when you're wearing a head of heavy gold. The carriage sways, and I can just about feel my neck cracking under the weight of it, so I pull the pins from my hair, letting out a slow breath. Hopefully, this will be the last banquet I have to attend.

The carriage pulls to a stop. The page boy ties the curtain back. He carries a lantern in one hand and is setting out a stool for me with the other when Li Chengyin leaps from his horse and storms over in a huff. He kicks the stool to one side, frightening the poor page boy enough that he scampers back and collapses onto his knees.

"What are you doing?" I ask.

He takes me by the arm and tugs me from the carriage. A'du rushes forward, but Pei Zhao steps between her and us. Li Chengyin heaves me over his shoulder as I protest, kicking at him and pinching his waist until one of the pieces of white jade inlaid in his belt clatters to the ground, but he pays me no mind and carries me all the way to his rooms, leaving A'du and Pei Zhao to exchange blows behind us.

And then he tosses me onto his bed like I'm a sack of rice. My head slams against the cool ceramic of a pillow, and the pain stuns me. I push myself up only to be shoved back down. It's been months since we've had a proper argument and I'm out of practice, but not so much so that the two of us don't all but tear the whole place asunder.

One of his attendants sticks a head in to see what the matter is, but Li Chengyin hurls a vase at him, and he ducks back before it cracks against his head, thoughtfully closing the door behind him. When we're done, I have to stop and catch my breath, sprawling back against the sheets, completely spent. I don't fight him anymore, and he cools down too.

Li Chengyin pulls me to him from behind. He seems to like hugging people this way, but his arm digs uncomfortably into me. He must be thoroughly worn out; his breath is warm and ticklish against my neck as he mutters something I can't hear—more lies, probably, or promises he can't keep.

I wait for his words to fall into silence and then turn, slowly, to face him. His eyes are closed. I brush a finger against his lids, but he doesn't stir. He's sound asleep.

I crawl from the bed, shrugging on my short jacket and skirts, and push open the windows. A'du enters, silent, and passes me a pair of scissors. She lights a lamp, and I sit beneath its light, clipping my nails fastidiously, taking care not to breathe in any of the white powder hidden beneath.

The strength of the sedative surprises me. It took the tiniest scratch on his arm to knock him thoroughly out. I wash my hands, scraping under each nail to make sure it's gone before changing into a darker set of robes.

A'du passes me her dagger. I glance over at Li Chengyin.

All I have to do is pass it across his throat, and my hatred will dissipate into smoke.

Despite the heavy sedation, his sleep is not calm. His brows are knit, and beneath his lids those clear eyes are moving like he's dreaming of something. Cold metal meets the warm skin of his neck, but he's insensible to it.

Haltingly, I increase the pressure against his neck. A bright line of red blood seeps out from under the edge of the blade. I need only to press a little harder—

He must feel the pain, for his lips tremble and his fingers start to twitch, like he's trying to grab for something. He's muttering, so softly I can hardly hear him, but it sounds like he's calling for someone to *come back*.

My hand shakes. The blade slips to the ground.

A'du rushes forward, worried he's awake, but I sink down, pressing my hands to my face.

I remember.

Three years ago, he'd jumped after me. Had grabbed me and pulled me to him. We'd fallen together into the abyss. He'd tried to stop our descent, but we were falling too fast, and I remember the loose pebbles looking like falling stars, like the night he caught me a hundred fireflies. How his eyes had been so full of me.

The dream I dreamed again and again, but hadn't known it was him until I remembered. And then I hadn't known what his last words to me were. I'd thought them lost to the wind.

I've found them again.

"If you want to forget, I will not force you to remember."

Icy water had swallowed us. I'd fought to breathe, swallowing down lungfuls of river. He'd jumped after me, he'd wanted to grab me, and at the very end, what he'd said was that, since I wanted to forget, he wouldn't try to remember.

He too had known how much he owed me.

Atop the cliff that overlooked the river, he'd followed me without hesitation, not knowing what was beneath, because he also wanted absolution.

He knows as well as I do that Gu Xiaowu is dead. That, like me, he'd drowned in the depths of the river.

We're both such lonely ghosts. Neither of us truly woke up after the fall. I've spent the last three years of forgetfulness eking out a pathetic existence. He has spent the last three years of forgetfulness obliterating all traces of the past.

Could I say my pain is worse than his? Who in this world isn't suffering? Forgetting may be a more contented state of existence than remembering.

A'du puts the dagger back into my hands.

But I don't have the courage to take his life.

Instead, I watch him. How sad he is, even in his dreams. The little prince he once spoke of had suffered so much, and the young man he's grown up to be suffers still. There is no one left on earth who can love him without condition, and he lives all alone in this great big manor, walking toward that loneliest of thrones, giving up all of his love and devotion, his compassion and his tenderness. Perhaps forgetting is his best punishment, for he won't know how ardently I've loved him.

I grab A'du's hand and walk away.

Even if I hadn't been planning this for weeks, sneaking out of the manor has become second nature. I've long since memorized the Yulin Guards' routes, and had taken the precaution of leaving a side door open. Tonight's massive row in Li Chengyin's rooms has been more than enough to keep the guards in hiding, which is how A'du and I slip from the hall. We duck and crouch the entire way to the side door. It's within sight when A'du pulls me to a stop.

Yongniang. She has a lantern in her hands. It swings in the wind as she looks about, as though expecting someone. A'du and I duck behind a grove of bamboo. But though we wait for a long time, Yongniang does not move.

She sighs then and sits heavily down.

A'du sneaks up behind her, using the hilt of her blade to seal Yongniang's pressure points. She freezes there, unable to move.

I slip out from the grove to hug her stiff body.

"I'm going now, Yongniang," I murmur. "But I will miss you."

In the Court of Spring, she's the only person who's treated us well.

She struggles to open her mouth but can make no sound. I hug her again, tightly, which is how I discover something hard in her lapels. A bag of gold leaves. Yongniang looks up at me, eyes filling with tears as she blinks meaningfully. My nose stings, and I understand that she's been waiting for me.

She wants me to have this money ere I go.

I don't know what to say. She has always made me learn my books, made me learn the rules, made me do this and do that and try to win over Li Chengyin—

Which is why I tried to keep my plans from her.

But she'd found me out, and she hadn't told. If she had, I'd never be able to leave.

There's someone here who cares for me after all.

A'du tugs my sleeve. We have to leave before someone raises an alarm. My eyes well with tears, and I fling my arms around Yongniang again and pull A'du out the door.

It's left unlocked for the footmen and scullery maids, but we're the ones who use it to reach the small alley outside today. We pass through the many residential streets and city blocks of the east market until, as the sky lightens in a hazy mass, we make it to Miluo's tavern.

Miluo is waiting for us. In a low voice, she says, "Security is sure to be tighter around the west gate, but there's a caravan of Gaoli merchants leaving Shangjing today, headed northeast. I slipped their leader a little cash, and he's agreed to sneak you out. They weren't very tall, so you'll fit right in once you have your disguises on."

She's prepared two sets of Gaoli-style robes in addition to hats and false beards. Once we get everything fastened and pasted, two merchants stare back at us from the mirror.

By then, the sky has begun to brighten and the marketplace wakes with motion. The inn starts to bustle and the storefront next to it opens its doors as its proprietress brushes her teeth with a bit of poplar bark. Her husband, a round man, chats idly with Miluo. Then the merchants come downstairs, speaking to each other in their native tongue.

The last battle between Gaoli and the Plains ended brutally, but strangely enough, their caravans come more often now, because merchants chase profit, and the Plains are filled with valuable goods—goods that Gaoli citizens cannot live without.

After splitting a breakfast of flatbread with the merchants, we pack and prepare to leave. There must be a hundred horses or more in their train, coming all the way from Gaoli with ginseng and medicinal herbs, and returning with silks and tea leaves. The caravan waits in the yard for its wares to be packed and loaded. Cases and cases of goods are secured to the horses' backs. Bells ring from their saddles between chatter we don't understand, and everything chimes with life.

A'du and I share a single horse, buried in the depths of the convoy. The city gates are tightly guarded. Someone tells me that there's a rumor there are escaped convicts about, which is why the nine gates are all under heavy surveillance, but the tightest-guarded by far is the west gate. Everyone leaving through there is searched, and anyone suspicious is immediately brought back to the magistry. A'du and I shift uneasily in our seats, the likely convicts in question.

Because everyone is being interrogated, the line is long—and behind us, it's lengthening. My heart is a frantic drum in my chest. When finally, finally, it's our turn, a guard takes the merchants' travel papers and scrutinizes them. Then he scans us, frowning.

"Why are there two extra?"

The convoy leader isn't fluent in Plains, but aided by some vivid gesticulation, he manages to convey that we are fellow countrymen they met in the city, who were stuck in Shangjing during the war. Now that it's over, our weary hearts longed to go home.

"Not good enough," says the guard. "If there are fourteen people on the papers, then fourteen people may leave."

In my panic, I strike on a clever idea. I point to A'du and myself and, mimicking the merchant's accent, say, "We stay. These"—I point at two of the merchants—"out."

The guard eyes us, considering. Then he returns the papers to the convoy leader, pointing at the merchants I'd indicated. "Those two must stay behind. The rest can go."

The head of the convoy is agitated. He pleads with the guard, saying that if they go, they go together, and I join in the commotion. Muddled by our accents, the guard snaps, "Take it or leave it, or you can all stay behind!"

We press close, circling the guard. Behind us the line grows longer and people start chattering impatiently. It's not long before everyone is yelling. The two kingdoms have been fighting for years, so the Plainsmen don't have many kind things to say about Gaoli and they make that known.

The merchants' ears are red. They start tying back their sleeves, as though preparing for a fight. The guard, fearing a bigger commotion than the teeming crowds, bellows to his soldiers, "The two that I pointed at—they stay behind. Throw the others out of the city!"

So we—and all of our horses—are forced from the gate, while the two unfortunate merchants are made to stay behind. I'm still feeling guilty when the convoy leader tugs at my sleeve and shows me his palm.

I don't understand what he wants until he says, in his halting Plains, "Money!"

"But didn't Miluo pay you?" I ask, astonished.

He grins fiercely. "Two people stay. Add money."

And as it is our fault, I gesture for A'du to give him a gold leaf. A generosity I come to regret.

The convoy leader's eyes sparkle when he sees it, and for the next few days, he finds all sorts of creative ways to get us to pay—for their lodgings, for their meals—and the expenses are piling up. I don't know everything, but I know enough about how much things are worth. The gold leaf I gave them was enough to buy an entire house, and the merchants are demanding one for every meal.

But then, the money is Li Chengyin's anyway, so I don't mind spending it. It is my fault that their companions got left behind, and it costs me little to let them press their advantage. Merchants might be greedy, but the work they do is hard. Every morning we wake before dawn and do not rest until well after twilight. We travel for eighteen hours a day. I haven't ridden this much in over three years, so every night when we get to an inn, I'm asleep as soon as my head hits the pillow.

One night, though, I'm shaken awake by A'du. She holds her dagger in one hand, and in the dark, all I can see is the brightness of her eyes. I clamber up, whispering, "Is it Li Chengyin's men?"

She shakes her head, but I can't tell if it means *no* or if it means *I don't know*.

We wait in the dark.

There's a soft popping sound; if we hadn't been listening for it I don't think we would have heard. A bamboo straw is stuck through a hole torn into the papered windows. Me and A'du exchange a look.

Powdery white smoke puffs out from the end of the bamboo. My limbs go numb the second I smell it. I sway on my feet. *A sedative*, I realize, much too late.

A'du's one step ahead of me. She rushes forward, using her thumb to stop the straw, pinching it shut. She holds it there, then shoves it back through the window screen.

There's a soft thump, like something heavy has fallen. I'm dazed from the smoke. A'du pushes the windows open so the crisp night wind can clear my mind. She passes me some water. I gulp it thirstily down, feeling the effects of the sedative receding.

A'du opens the door. There's a person collapsed in the hallway outside—the head of the merchant convoy, who had been immobilized by the bamboo straw when A'du used it to seal his pressure points. He sits there, mouth frozen in surprise. A'du presses her dagger to his neck and looks to me.

Worried there might be some bigger conspiracy, I have her bring him into the room for questioning and close the door securely behind us.

I kick the man. "Who are you?"

But he doesn't answer. "Kill me if you want; a man is only as good as his deeds, and since you've caught me, you can do what you please."

"Ambushing people in the dead of night is being as good as your deeds, is it?"

But the man does not look ashamed of himself in the slightest. "Anything to win," he shrugs.

"You've lost big then," I tell him.

But his mouth remains sealed, so A'du draws her dagger

lightly across his leg. Blood wells from the cut, and he starts howling like a stuck pig, crying that he'll tell us everything.

It's because we've been so generous with our money that he started thinking about doing away with us and taking all of our money for himself. He just didn't think we'd be able to fight back.

"So you're a thief then, pretending to be a merchant." I kick him again. "Tell me! How many people have you killed!"

He snivels, begging for our forgiveness as he insists that he is a merchant, he had his head turned by gold, he's never hurt anyone, and he has an old mother and three young children at home who depend on him—

Are all people so ravenously greedy? The merchant wants more money, the ministers want more power, and the emperor, who already has everything, wants to expand his borders, sending out troops year after year to fight his endless wars.

No one is satisfied with what they have.

I think of Li Chengyin again. Of the little prince he used to be, of every step he's ever taken and how each one has led him to today. Of his father, and how he's used the lure of the throne to lead Li Chengyin onto a path paved with blood.

And me, all I've wanted—the only thing I've dreamed of having—is to have someone by my side. Someone to stay with me in Xiliang, where we would raise horses and herd sheep. Such a simple dream, and an impossible one.

A'du knocks the merchant out with a light tap of her blade. We tie him up and stuff fabric into his mouth to keep him from calling out when he wakes. A'du asks me if I want to kill him, but I shake my head.

"He won't report us," I say, "or he'll have to explain that he tried to kill us first. Leave him here. We wouldn't have been able to travel with them much longer anyway, so we may as well head west now."

We leave the inn early. We ride for hours, until the sun crests the horizon, and in the afternoon, we trade our horses for an oxcart. A'du and I disguise ourselves as a farmer and his wife and slowly make our way toward the sunset.

Troops have been dispatched to find us—dozens and dozens of them gallop up the path—but they pay no mind to our sorry little cart and storm past in a whirlwind of dust.

All the cities on the road to the Yumen Pass are under strict guard, so we try not to enter if we can help it, taking small country roads instead. It's not the most comfortable journey, but at long last, we make it.

Seeing the massive gates rising up between the mountains, I come alive again.

As long as we can make it through, we will be in the territory of the allied kingdoms of the west. Even if he was king, Li Chengyin couldn't send troops through these gates without stirring up a war, which is why portraits of our faces have been posted all over the pass—our faces, in men's clothes, though the names are not our own.

The portraits are startlingly true to life. Li Chengyin's only seen me disguised as a man once, so I'm amazed he was able to find someone to capture such a likeness.

But me and A'du have traded our oxcart for horses and

are both dressed like girls again while the posters are of two men, so we decide to join the line of people looking to cross the border. The problem is that we don't have travel papers, and whether or not we can leave without incident . . . that's a question for later.

I'm not worried, though. There's plenty of coin in my pouch, and A'du is a better fighter than most. If we do find ourselves in hot water, all we need to do is fight our way out of it—and if we can't win a fight, then we have money enough for a bribe.

Then I see the general who's doing the inspections, and I realize that no amount of money in the world can buy our way over the border.

It's Pei Zhao.

Li Chengyin is so cunning.

No matter what path I take, no matter how many circles I run around him, Yumen Pass is the only way to get to Xiliang from the Plains. There's no hope of slipping past Pei Zhao. We couldn't do it if we grew wings, not when he has an army of men under his command.

I smile at Pei Zhao, and he smiles back.

"What are you doing here, General?"

"His Highness has sent me here to capture an escaped convict," he says.

I'm amazed I still have a sense of humor. "General Pei is the Jinwu General, the commander of three thousand Yulin Guards. What kind of convict could bring you to Yumen Pass?"

"One that's wanted by the crown, of course." His voice is light.

I laugh. "Wanted by the crown..."

A'du shifts. Above us, behind the battlements, the lines of soldiers have drawn their bows, pointing their arrows straight at us. I sigh.

"I'm going through those gates, General. You can shoot me dead if you'd like to stop me. It won't be the first time."

"You mistake the crown prince, Your Highness," Pei Zhao says patiently. "He loves you truly."

"It doesn't matter if he loves me or not; there's nothing between us anymore."

"The fire at Chengtian Gate wasn't an accident," he blurts.

I freeze.

"We weren't permitted to close the gates. It was Shangyuan; the enjoyment of the people of Shangjing *had* to come first, but His Highness was terrified that he wouldn't find you again once the assassin brought you out of the city. So he set fire to the gate." Pei Zhao's voice is calm as he delivers this news. "His Highness is willing to go to such extremes for you, my lady; why aren't you willing to forgive him?"

For a long moment, I forget how to speak.

Chengtian Gate is the symbol of royal power—since it burned, the ministers haven't been able to stop gossiping about what it means, and the emperor himself has issued an edict accepting all blame, citing a lack of virtue. Even in my dreams I wouldn't have imagined Li Chengyin was the one who set the fire.

"His Highness is the heir," Pei Zhao continues. "So often is he forced to act against his will. So often he's forced to make choices that are not his own. That night, when we killed the assassin—I was the one who made the decision to continue, Your Highness. I was the one who hurt Miss A'du. If that's what you're angry about, I am the one to blame."

I'm not smart, but I'm not stupid, either. "Don't think you can lie to me."

"I wouldn't dare."

"What wouldn't you dare, as long as your lord commanded it?" I ask him. My voice is cold. "If you weren't under his orders, how would you have been able to move the Yulin Guard? If you weren't under his orders, how could you tell them to shoot? You're claiming it's all your own idea, but I won't be lied to so easily. Pei Zhao, *I remember*. I'm sure you didn't think I could. I won't forgive Li Chengyin for what he's done, not *ever*. And if you don't let me through these gates today, then I will force my way through if it kills me."

Pei Zhao looks at me, shaken. He stares as though he can see right through me. He is silent for a long time, so long that I lose my nerve. He's so loyal to his cousin; could I really expect him to let me go?

"I wouldn't."

"What?"

He raises his eyes. "That night, you asked if I would order the archers to kill you if you were the one the assassin had taken. I can answer you that I wouldn't."

I understand his meaning. I sign to A'du. She walks her horse to mine, unsheathes her blade, and holds it to my neck.

"Open the gate," I say.

"An assassin has the princess consort," Pei Zhao calls. "Hold your fire; open the gate!"

The heavy wood creaks, inching open as a dozen people throw the full weight of their strength against it. Blazing sun streams in, burning on the skin. The sun is so hot outside the pass, and I have to keep myself from grinning. I dig my heels into the sides of my horse, urging it forward toward freedom.

There is a rush of hoofbeats behind me.

A battalion of soldiers, holding a flag emblazoned with dragons, is gaining on us, and once they are closer, I realize that the person leading them is Li Chengyin.

My heart sinks.

Our horses are already galloping toward freedom.

I hear a faraway shout: "Close the gate! By the crown prince's orders, close the gate!"

The hands that had been pushing forward quickly reverse course, pulling the doors closed. We're close, but that broad band of sun is narrowing, and soon there's only a horse-sized sliver of light. I've run out of time.

A'du's horse is in front of mine. She turns, hand extended, to pull me onto her steed, but it's too late. I bring my crop down on her horse's flank. It shrills out a pained whinny and thunders through the last of the fading light.

Through the closing doors I see A'du turn, panicked, to look at me. She bounds toward me, and then her dagger is embedded in the heavy wood, but it changes nothing. They close with a heavy grunt. The bolt is lowered. She hacks furiously at the iron, and though her blows land heavy, I can't imagine that they do more than raise a few sparks.

The Yulin Guard has caught up, so I swing off my horse

and run up the battlements, up and up and up until I'm standing atop the gate tower. I lean over the parapet to see A'du swinging her blade, alone, at the gate. But how can one person topple an entire fortress? I see her scream, see her tears, though they make no sound, and I'm reminded of Heshi. He'd left me to her. If it wasn't for me, she might have lost the will to live long ago, just as I would not have made it so far without her.

Jieshuo is gone. I have Xiliang, but two hundred thousand of A'du's countrymen have been killed by Plains soldiers. She's lonelier than me by a thousand times—ten thousand times—yet she swallowed her hatred, swallowed her anger, to stay by my side for three whole years.

She's the one person I owe anything—everything—to.

On the opposite side of the fortress, the Yulin Guard has reached the gate. From the clamor behind me, I assume they're ascending the stairs.

I'm not scared. I stand there, waiting for him.

There's white gauze wrapped about his neck. Had my blade gone a hair deeper, he mightn't be standing here today.

I was expecting a crowd, but he's the only one who starts toward me. For every forward step he takes, I take an equal one back. I retreat until there's nowhere to retreat to, until I am standing at the very top of the battlements. The westerly wind billows through my robes, whipping them sharply, as it had above the River Oblivion, where I'd stood at the edge of the cliff with a cloudy abyss beneath my feet.

His eyes are as unreadable as ever. "Do you hate being married to me so much?"

I smile, but say nothing.

"What's so good about Gu Xiaowu?"

My heel is hanging in midair. Only my toes are on the battlements. The Yulin Guard is far away, looking silently on. There's a strange, complicated sort of anguish clouding Li Chengyin's eyes—half the weight of hiding his pain, half the pain itself.

It's like I'm dreaming. Three years of wasted time, and we're back where we started.

"I'll never say," I tell him.

His smile is a cruel, mocking thing. "A pity he's dead, then."

Yes, a pity.

"Come back with me. I can forget this happened. I don't care if you still love him, if you still think of him—as long as you come back, I shan't bring it up again, I swear."

It's my turn to smile again. "If you promise me one thing, I'll come back with you."

"What is it?" he asks. There doesn't seem to be any expression on his face at all.

"I want you to catch me a hundred fireflies."

He hesitates, knitting his brows as though puzzled. Tears blur my vision, but I'm able to maintain my smile. "The waters of the River Oblivion wash all love away. They allowed me to have three years, but they couldn't allow me a lifetime."

A hot tear slips down my cheek. "Wouldn't it be nice to be like you, to forget and keep on forgetting?"

He stares at me, lost for words, as though he doesn't understand a thing I am saying. What a state I must look. I'm smiling, so why do I weep?

"This time, it'll be for good," I tell him.

And I turn. I jump. Like a bird flinging itself from the nest, like a butterfly dashing toward a flower. I know this isn't the River Oblivion. I know there is only the sharp of mountain rock waiting for me, that once I fall, there is no returning.

People scream. And then I jolt to a stop—Li Chengyin's waistband—again. Everything like it was before. I dangle from his arm, swinging in midair as he, pulled downward by my momentum, hangs from the parapet. He clutches the stone with one hand and me with the other, straining until the veins in his smooth skin tense up. The cut on his neck has opened and is weeping scarlet blood, but he's calling for someone to come help us.

Once the Yulin Guard comes, I'll have lost all chance for freedom. I know this, so I wave my hand, cold steel flashing, and he bellows, "NO!"

The light silk of his waistband flutters in the air as I force out one last smile. "I'm going to forget you now, Gu Xiaowu."

The last things I see are the shock in his eyes and the red that trails down his neck. He draws back like he's been hit—his blood drips onto my face—and then he dives for me, grabbing at my fingers, but he misses by a whisper and catches wind in his palms. His voice, disconsolate, echoes in my ear: "I—?"

And I know he remembers, and I know it's the best revenge I could have taken.

Three years ago, he forfeited our love to a field of blood. Three years later I'm forfeiting it too, and ending it entirely.

He means to leap after me. He tries to, anyway, but this is not that cliff. Death waits on the other end of this fall, and Pei

Zhao heaves him back. Li Chengyin shoves Pei Zhao away—and must have done so with great force, for there is blood trickling from the general's mouth—but Pei Zhao doesn't let go. Soon they're surrounded by an army of men who drag Li Chengyin away.

The sky is so blue. When the wind whistles past my ear, everything is lost in a dazzle of sun.

I see myself sitting on the dune, watching the sun dip behind the horizon, taking my heart with it, until it's lost forever behind the rolling desert. The heavens and earth are entwined by night, and there isn't a spot of light anywhere.

I see a crowd of people laughing and smiling, people who can't believe Gu Xiaowu killed the White-Eyed Wolf King, who don't take him seriously because he doesn't have the look of a warrior. And then he raises the bow, plucking it like a musician would, and as it twangs they laugh harder, jeering until he shoots a hundred bats from the sky.

I see fireflies swirling in the air around us like comets that pass through our fingers. This must be what it's like when Heaven sends out his shooting stars. Little lights bob around us, floating gently by, and I remember an old song about Heaven and his lover standing amid a river of stars.

I see myself on the cliff above the River Oblivion, the wind so strong I can't keep steady, my heels in midair. The cold air cuts through my clothes to slice at the backs of my hands. He doesn't move. He doesn't dare.

"My family is dead," I tell him. "And my kingdom is fallen. All my suffering—that's the price I pay for trusting you. That's Heaven's punishment." And I say, "I will forget you, Li

Chengyin. In this life and every life. The River Oblivion will wash all my love away."

I see the night we were wed, when he lifted the veil. One moment I am suffocating under the heavy cloth, and the next the world bursts into a radiance of candlelight, illuminating the planes of his face. He's dressed in richly embroidered black robes, wearing the crown he'd worn at the ceremony, with its nine strings of white pearl tassel, fixed beneath his chin with black silk cord and secured into his hair with a rhinoceros horn pin. His face is as smooth and lovely as whitest jade, a prince in look and manner.

I'd thought then that was the first time I had met him. I didn't know we'd met under the boundless moon of Xiliang.

The last thing I remember is the tears that sparkled in his eyes when I tore through the waistband.

But he's too late. It's too late now. Three years we've fought against fate only for it to sweep us up into its currents again. We were meant to stay away from each other after the waters washed us clean. We weren't meant to know anything about each other again. But we fell in love, and that, I suppose, is our punishment.

I close my eyes, waiting for the end.

My falling comes to a halt, but the pain I expect does not come. I open my eyes. It's A'du, her cool arms firm around me. She'd leapt upward to meet me. But no amount of force is strong enough to overcome the momentum of my descent, and I hear the horrid crunch of bone as she throws herself bodily beneath me. I see the blood that gushes from her ears, her nose, her eyes.

I scream.

My legs must be broken, for I cannot push myself to my feet. I try to crawl toward her, to hold her, but every little bump is agony.

Her eyes, too, are welling in pain, but she fixes me with that crow-dark stare, and there is nothing in it but calm, nothing but peace. No blame, no resentment. She looks at me as if I've done something naughty again and she's humoring me. Finally, I manage to maneuver her into my arms, sobbing out her name.

I knew we wouldn't go back to Xiliang. I wanted her to go on without me, but I knew she wouldn't abandon me, for I wouldn't abandon her, either. A'du closes her eyes, and no matter how much I shout, no matter how many tears I cry, soon she is beyond knowing.

The gates creak open. Hoofbeats pound toward me. Those people, the ones who ride the horses, they will force me to stay in this wretched world, drag me back to that freezing manor. But I don't want to hurt anymore.

"Let's go home," I say to A'du.

I palm her dagger. There are nicks in it from where she'd been hacking at the gates, but it's sharp enough to serve its purpose. I bury it in my chest.

It doesn't hurt like I'd imagined—but what is the pain of death compared to all I've suffered?

Blood seeps out. I cradle A'du's hands in my own as I sink to the ground beside her. *We are going home at last.* And the warmth leaves me. And the light leaves me. And I see Gu Xiaowu, and he is galloping toward me. He's not dead at all;

he's gone to catch me a hundred fireflies. I am making him tie his waistband around me so he'll never, never leave me again.

With a smile, I suck in my last breath.

Across the boundless reaches of the earth, someone is singing that old song:

> *O, there is a fox,*
> *He sits upon the dune.*
> *Sits upon the dune,*
> *Watching the moon.*
> *No, not watching the moon—*
> *He's waiting for the shepherd girl*
> *To come back.*
>
> *O, there is a fox,*
> *He sits upon the dune.*
> *Sits upon the dune,*
> *Soaking in the sun.*
>
> *No, not soaking in the sun—*
> *He's waiting for the horseback girl*
> *To ride past.*

Once there was a fox.
He waited for a girl.
But the girl, she never returned.

Stories from the Court of Spring

太液芙蓉未央柳
The Blooms of Taiye Garden, the Willows of Weiyang Palace[1]

"A'mu!" I pulled on his sleeve and then remembered myself. "Your Highness—"

A'mu raised his head, looking confusedly at me. He was wearing everyday clothes, the undyed fabric making his hair and eyes look darker by contrast, but the moment he caught my eye, he looked like a child still.

I shouldn't have called him by name. The rules were rigid about things like that. But I was just seven the year I entered the palace, and A'mu five, so we'd grown up like brothers. As the elder, I'd often had to look out for him. When he fell behind on his studies, I did his work for him, and when he was disciplined I could mimic his handwriting and copy out the assigned books on his behalf. We'd run through gardens with our slingshots, we'd catch crickets, annoy stuffy attendants...

And then slowly, we grew up, though our friendship never changed. He shared with me his woes, and for them I could give any number of remedies.

There were plenty of troubles, for he was the emperor's

---

[1] From "Song of Everlasting Regret" by Bai Juyi.

only son, and everyone expected great things of him. His Majesty was a wise ruler and a good king—by comparison, anyone would seem merely ordinary.

"How can I be more like my father?" A'mu asked me once.

I didn't know how to answer.

The emperor wasn't just a capable politician. He was adept on a battlefield, too. He'd fought the allied kingdoms of the west, pacified the ones to our south, was the conqueror of so many cities that our empire was larger than it had ever been, and it seemed like a crowd of millions would come to pay their respects during the annual tribute.

Once, I went up to Chengtian Gate with him and A'mu to watch the people of Shangjing wish him a long life. Their shouts had echoed off the mountains. I was so moved, heart thundering in my chest, but the emperor himself only smiled faintly in acknowledgment.

He never stayed long. He would pause atop the tower gate before having the curtains drawn and returning to the imperial city, as though in his eyes, all the beauty in the world was as ephemeral as smoke, or clouds.

With a father like that, I sometimes pitied A'mu.

Our empire had been built on horseback, so all the highborn boys were expected to ride well and shoot well and fight well. Father trained me himself, so I fancied myself a fine soldier until the first time I had reason to compare myself to His Majesty.

We had been walking with him through a garden. A pair of birds was chirping in a nearby tree, so loud it drove us to distraction. He'd palmed A'mu's sling, fixed a pellet to it, and took them both down with a single shot. I'd looked at him, startled.

But then, His Majesty never did like things that came in pairs.

Double-headed lotuses bloomed rarely enough that the sight of them was a good omen, but in the second year of the Qinhe Era, when a double-headed lotus appeared in Taiye Park, no one dared tell the emperor. It had taken a brave servant, under orders from a royal attendant, to destroy the flower.

Because of this odd aversion, the workers who constructed the new garden had to attend to giving each building an odd number of rooms. Zhang Lian, the normally meticulous man who ran the Ministry of Public Works, had allowed this, and the Ministry of Rites, though disapproving of this departure from convention, looked the other way on account of the fact that a garden home was at least not an official residence.

They'd given up this fight mostly because the emperor's temper worsened year after year.

He was no tyrant—he attended court fastidiously and appointed good men to office, but there was no one of whom he was particularly fond, and he rarely attended to his consorts. Occasionally, he went hunting, but didn't seem to take any pleasure from that, either. Faced with a king who had neither desire nor want, the ministers could find very few opportunities to rein him in.

They fretted too over the matter of his heir, because for a royal line to have only one boy to carry it forward was a dangerous thing. Admonishments flew like a blizzard from the court to the emperor's study, all but accusing him of dereliction of duty if he didn't have another dozen sons or more, but His Majesty ignored them all.

The Lady Xian became pregnant in the fourth year of the Qinhe Era. The court held its breath for another boy, another potential heir, but after a difficult labor, she gave birth to a princess and closed her eyes forever.

That princess was Chaoyang.

She was granted that title after the main hall of the palace, Chaoyang Court, and from that alone it was obvious how fiercely she was loved.

Princess Chaoyang was a frightfully charming girl. Perhaps because he felt sorry that her mother had died, the emperor took her with him everywhere, even to court, where he bounced her on his knee as though it were more important than matters of state.

The ministers had taken offense at first, until they discovered that having her around had its benefits. Like when the emperor was angry, and they were too cowed to defend themselves, all they needed to do was have a nurse bring the princess in, and the typhoon would scatter into a spring breeze.

She was a smiley girl. When His Majesty extended a hand, she would throw herself into his lap, and when he folded her into his arms, his face was always gentle.

By the time she turned four, the princess had enough riches to sustain a village of thousands and too many servants to count. Her father ordered a new manor to be built near Lishan, for she had a persistent cough, and the physicians said she should visit the hot springs there.

She was the one person His Majesty truly adored.

"Zhong'an," A'mu often mused, "I wonder who will be lucky enough to marry my sister."

I knew what he meant. Whoever the groom was, he would have everything under heaven that he should desire.

Chaoyang grew, day after day and year after year, becoming prettier, livelier. In the whole of the palace, she alone had no worries at all.

I heard her laughter often. It was as crisp and clear as a silver bell, like the loveliest birdsong—but then, wasn't she like a little bird, spirited and free?

When she was older, she liked to chase after A'mu and me, for he was her only sibling and we were the only children in that colossal manor. She would dress in men's clothes to sneak out with us—not that it mattered if she was caught, for no one could stop her from doing what she wanted. We would sit in teahouses to drink tea, to watch performers put on skits, to listen to the storymasters spin their tales.

Our lives were simple then, blissful and bright. It was the happiest time of my life. Just the three of us—A'mu, Chaoyang, and I.

When she died, we were heartbroken.

But His Majesty was devastated. In the space of a single night, his dark hair went white with grief. He sat alone in Chaoyang Court, refusing to see anyone. A'mu knelt for hours, begging to be let in, but he was turned away.

She was to be interred at Yuling.

Yuling was the mausoleum the emperor had prepared for himself, so it had been prepared with the funeral of a king in mind—and because of the extraordinary labor required as such, it wasn't yet completed by the time he ordered it to be used to bury his beloved daughter.

The ministers were in an uproar. It wasn't advisable, they argued, and it was hardly appropriate. His Majesty was forced to compromise. He agreed to take away some of the tomb guardians and shorten the spirit path to her grave, but court was dismissed for ten days and a period of public mourning was imposed for another ninety after that. But the reality was that court never really reconvened, because after her death the emperor didn't much attend.

Memoranda piled up outside His Majesty's study. Our tutors sighed about it, and A'mu tried again and again to visit his father to no avail. He was worried; I could do little more than comfort him. "It'll be better after he's had time to grieve, you'll see."

But it was clear there would be no after, for he would never stop grieving. He became a different person entirely. He didn't look at anyone, or anything, with interest again. If he'd once been a reserved, but principled, ruler, he was now a father who had no hope of coming out of his despair.

His health declined sharply. There was a period when he was gravely ill and called for the diplomat of Xiliang to be summoned to see him.

Xiliang was the strangest little country. A tributary, and not a very powerful one, but entitled to privileges beyond what other larger nations were afforded. Flagrantly so. Everyone else's princes were sent to Shangjing—ostensibly to study our ways but kept here in truth to keep their fathers from revolting—but Xiliang sent none. Some years, they didn't even send tribute.

Yet His Majesty was careful with them. He may send armies against all the other kingdoms to the west, but he wouldn't send them against Xiliang.

Once, I heard from an older attendant that this was all because of the Mingde empress.

A'mu and I knew better than to bring her up—the Mingde empress had been His Majesty's wife when he was still the heir presumptive, but she'd died of illness ere he'd been crowned.

From what I could tell, he didn't care much for her. He hadn't given her a title until nine years into his own reign, when the Ministry of Rites had all but forced him to name her the Bright and Virtuous. And he didn't visit her grave, not before or after she was posthumously made queen.

Palace rumor was that he'd hated her. She'd been a treaty princess he was forced to wed, and he'd never stopped seeing the imposition of a foreign princess as an insult to the royal family. The historians hadn't bothered to write more than a dozen words to describe her short tenure on earth.

Once, Princess Chaoyang put on a set of robes much like the ones empress Mingde would have worn and went delightedly to see her father. It was the first and last time he was angry at her. His rage had been like a thunderclap. He'd ordered all of her servants executed, and it had taken Chaoyang screaming and weeping and finally passing out to bring him back to his senses.

Lady Chen had been deposed over this, because she'd

been the one who gave Princess Chaoyang the clothes.

When I went to see her with A'mu, one of her old nursemaids murmured to us that His Majesty hated for anyone to resemble the empress Mingde. It had been sabotage to urge Chaoyang to wear Xiliang clothes.

A'mu was braver than me. He asked, "Then does she look anything like the empress?"

The nurse shook her head, stone-faced. "Nothing at all. The empress was nowhere near as beautiful."

I didn't think it was likely either. How could a foreign girl look half as pretty as one of our own? But the nursemaid continued.

"The empress Mingde was very fair, very dainty, and spirited, but she wasn't as captivating as our Plains girls." And then she sighed. "It's been thirty years. . . . I hadn't imagined . . ."

She didn't continue. I looked over at A'mu, but he was lost in thought.

A'mu once said that the only person His Majesty loved in all the world was Chaoyang. Deep in my heart, I agreed, though I did not say so.

But Chaoyang was dead.

Since then, the emperor had grown frailer and more weary of court. It was like he'd grown as sick of living as he had of politics—he didn't hunt anymore, and hosted no banquets. He stayed in his own rooms, not losing himself in alcohol or the companionship of his consorts, just losing . . . himself. Her death took all the life out of him.

I had never seen anyone as heartbroken as this. A'mu and

I had cried too, and we missed Chaoyang desperately, but our grief was nothing to the king's.

Father went to the palace personally to talk some sense into him. Father's health was declining too—a result of all the old war injuries he'd suffered—but he forced himself out of bed, insistent.

No one at home was more obstinate than he, so all that was left to do was find a suitable carriage. Every servant, attendant, and palace official had long since been ordered away from the emperor's quarters, so I alone was left to ease Father to his knees. I could feel him shaking, and I couldn't let go, for if I did he would not be able to hold himself upright. I ought to have given them privacy, perhaps, though it was impossible to leave Father in his current state.

His relationship with the emperor was different from other people's. I could tell, because the emperor agreed to see him, and extended a hand to help him to his feet.

Father panted slightly. He grabbed His Majesty's hand the way I would A'mu's and said, "A'yin, she's dead."

His voice wavered, so quiet I could barely catch the words. But His Majesty froze, staring vacantly into the distance. The white in his hair, the watery eyes, the shake in those fingers that were clasped around Father's—when had the emperor grown so old?

"She's been dead thirty years." I thought I saw tears swimming in Father's eyes when he continued. "Cousin, you must be sensible. She's been gone for so long."

His Majesty had never looked like he did now. He was always gentle with Father, for they were old friends, but his face twisted into something fierce and malevolent. He grabbed Father's lapels, pulling him close. Green veins protruded from beneath the papery skin of his hands. His voice was low and ferocious.

"A pack of lies!"

Father shook so much, he could scarcely breathe. I didn't dare make any sudden move. The only sound in the whole of the room was my father's labored gasps, one after another like an old, worn-out pair of bellows.

The emperor's voice softened. "A'zhao, you know as well as I that she's only gone back to Xiliang. She has everyone fooled—including you. And you call yourself smart."

Father coughed. His voice was low when he spoke again. "Your Majesty . . ." He looked pityingly at his king. "Princess Chaoyang was not her daughter. They looked nothing alike. You know in your heart that she's the Lady Xian's daughter, that the crown princess is thirty years dead. I went to see her ten years ago, and the grass had grown long over her grave."

It was the first time I saw His Majesty weep. A single tear slipped silently down his face, landing on the front of his lapels. It clung there above the richly embroidered head of a dragon. Father folded the emperor into his arms, perhaps in comfort, perhaps in consolation, perhaps most of all in pity, as His Majesty, like a child, dissolved into heartbroken wailing.

不信人间有白头
I Would Not Have Known Hair Could Whiten with the Heart[1]

The sky was a swath of greenish gray, the earth was broad and vast, and stars blurred into the western horizon. Condensation frosted the tips of the grass as a chorus of bugs rose from within the shrub. Dawn was arriving. A wisp of white light surfaced in the east.

Gu Jian reined his horse and stood quietly upon the hill, waiting.

Dark retreated as the white expanded, like clear water flowing into an inky sea—it wasn't noticeable at first, but slowly, the sky became as clear as glass, rich peacock threaded through with lavender. Night was leaving more quickly now, until even the edges of heaven purpled. Soon, the horizon brightened—the red sun about to erupt from the earth, shooting out the first golden ray.

A field of dewdrops scintillated beneath the light, as though someone had scattered glistening crystal beads across the verdant wilds. The horse whickered. Lowering its head to nip at the pasture, it startled away a clutch of grasshoppers. It was the most beautiful season in this foreign land, when

---

1 From "To the Tune of Partridge Skies: Written for a Friend" by Xin Qiji.

slopes were lush with life and dawn wind brushed over a sea of green speckled with wildflowers. In the distance, snowy mountains stood like a screen of ice, peaks gilded by sun.

Still, Gu Jian waited. Distantly, there came a sound—like rain, or like the rustle of greenery caressed by a passing breeze.

It came again, closer, and heavier, too. At first it resembled the low, rumbling thunder of a summer storm, but soon revealed itself to be the beat of horses' hooves.

Gu Jian narrowed his eyes. It drew nearer, became clearer, as a troop of riders galloped toward him, toward the morning. Eventually, he recognized the riders' livery and the resolute face beneath the helmet of the man leading the charge.

He swung onto his own horse, urging it forward to greet the riders. Having rested for the better part of an hour, its step was light, and it closed the distance quickly. The leader of the cavalry was Pei Zhao, who Gu Jian knew but did not like. "Where's Wulang[2]?"

This intimate address was reserved for those closest to the aforementioned, and Pei Zhao was a scrupulous person—it was this that Gu Jian found most tiresome about him. As expected, he replied, very attentively, "His Highness has gone to the city."

This surprised Gu Jian, who asked, "Alone?"

Pei Zhao nodded. He was Li Chengyin's closest confidant, highborn, and would not normally have associated with the likes of a wandering errant like Gu Jian. So while

---

[2] Wu, used in reference to Li Chengyin, refers to his role as the fifth son of the Li family; lang is a term of endearment for a young man.

the two were familiar, they had little conversation to share.

Gu Jian furrowed his brow. "Why didn't you stop him?"

To this, Pei Zhao had no answer. Li Chengyin was usually careful—anyone who lived in the Court of Spring had to be—but when he was out with the troops, he became willful and reckless, even impertinent. Since the establishment of the kingdom, tradition had been that the crown prince led the army and was conferred the title of commander in chief at the emperor's discretion. Li Chengyin had been something of an exception. Before he was named heir, he'd been given orders to join the Changzhou Army under an assumed name and serve as a junior field officer under its regional commander, Wushu. It so happened that during this time, a group of western raiders crossed into Plains territory and launched an ambush as Li Chengyin was patrolling the border with a group of scouts. Despite their panic, they did not scatter—instead, they waited and ambushed back as their attackers forded a river, fighting a brave and bloody battle, buying enough time to sound the alarm and bring in the regional commander with his auxiliary troops. The hundred or more riders under Li Chengyin's command were either dead or about to give out, and he himself had been wounded by two arrows. At this, Wushu had broken into a cold sweat and immediately composed a secret missive to be sent by fast horse to the capital to shoulder the blame—after all, if anything were to happen to a son of the emperor, who could ameliorate?

But Li Chengyin behaved as though nothing had happened. He had a physician pull the arrows out and arrived bandaged at the commander's tent to stop the messenger Wushu was dispatching and then, while he was at it, fling the self-censuring letter into a brazier. The white silk, dense with black ink, caught quickly and turned to ash.

"I'm not so badly hurt," he said, "and my lord father is so far away. Why worry him?"

Wushu was born into a family from the western kingdoms, and he was furthermore a man with a rough and frank nature for which he was often privately mocked by the civil officials at court as oafish. But how could an oaf rise to the position of regional commander? The arrows had come from behind. It was lucky they hadn't pierced any vitals, but that didn't mean the danger had passed. Wushu was bright as the snow. He knew battle might be chaotic, but Li Chengyin had led an ambush, catching the raiders off guard as they crossed the river. And because they'd attacked at close quarters, all the fighting had been hand-to-hand, and there simply wouldn't have been the opportunity to organize any archers. There was something *not right* about those arrows.

Wushu sighed to himself.

Li Chengyin did battle under Wushu for two years. He was brave and eager, successful in every endeavor. Gradually he built a reputation for himself among the men. They didn't know exactly who he was, just that he came from an illustrious Shangjing family. But he didn't carry himself with the airs of a lordling, for in battle he was on the front lines, and in peace he never shirked camp duties, not even the unpleasant ones—shoveling horse dung, hauling in sacks of provisions, repairing the irrigation canals.

At first, Wushu thought of the emperor's son as nothing more than an inconvenience, a hot potato to be passed from hand to hand, but the boy had proved himself a pleasant surprise. It was a shame, really. He taught the child as much as he could about military strategy and dispensed attentive guidance—if it wasn't for the fact of his identity, Wushu would happily have taken him under his wing, for they had become fast friends in their mutual admiration despite the years between them.

In the time Li Chengyin dallied at Changzhou, he collected a record of meritorious service—and his talent slowly revealed itself. At long last, someone in Shangjing took notice and talked the emperor into summoning him back.

Wushu personally escorted Li Chengyin to Winding River, accompanied by a handful of light cavalry. By then the suggestion of autumn had deepened into fact. Reed catkins filled the shore, looking like fresh-powdered snow. Wushu did not dismount, but he threw Li Chengyin a wineskin. "If the capital is too stuffy, come back and drink with us."

Li Chengyin caught the wineskin and tipped it back. Then he tightened the silver cap back onto the leather pouch, fastened it behind his saddlebags, waved to Wushu, and urged his horse across the river. He turned when he reached the other bank. Wushu sat on his horse among the reeds, their fluffy white flowers billowing in the breeze, catching in his beard.

He watched, astonished, as Li Chengyin crossed back again, but by then the boy was there, plucking catkins from his beard. Only then did he understand. He grinned, spreading his arms wide, and, in the tradition of the western kingdoms, folded Li Chengyin within them, giving him a few gentle pats on the back. There were thousands of words that wanted expressing, but no more need for them to be said.

This time when Li Chengyin crossed the river, he did not look back. Wushu waited until he was far, too far to see. Then he turned his horse for home.

Li Chengyin couldn't bring himself to drink the liquor the whole way back to the capital. It had been fermented from Changzhou broomcorn mixed with mare's milk, stronger than any wine in Shangjing. Accustomed now to spirits, Li Chengyin found alcohol from the capital tasted too mild, too delicate.

Who could know then that this parting would be forever? Within a month of Li Chengyin's departure, Wushu was dead—murdered by his godson, Qiqiya, who assumed military command and amassed an army for himself before submitting a self-satisfied missive to the emperor, requesting to be named the new regional commander of Changzhou, as well as governor of the Yanran Protectorate.

This caused uproar at court. Li Chengyin pleaded to be allowed troops to put down this revolt, but as there were more urgent battles to be fought in the prefectures by the Bohai Sea, the emperor decided, after much deliberation, to grant Qiqiya the commandership. Governorship of the Yanran Protectorate, however, fell to the Prince of Jin, Li Chengyin, to take on from afar.

In the ninth year of the Yuanqing Era, the Prince of Jin was named heir to the throne. With the Bohai matter quelled and with an awareness that the new presumptive had long borne him a grudge, Qiqiya's situation became precarious. He gritted his teeth and made a decision: to raise a flag and revolt. He named himself khan, broke Changzhou and Yingzhou away for his own khanate, and stirred the Shiwei and Mohe tribes into unrest. Li Chengyin personally led expeditionary forces into war, with Pei Zhao following as his second-in-command.

That was when Pei Zhao first saw Li Chengyin wild and unrestrained. He was the one who jumped naked into rivers with the infantrymen when he wanted to bathe, who, as the general abroad, sometimes disregarded his sovereign's orders.[3] He who, when the supply lines stuttered and could not provide consistent rations, marched them through a blizzard against all advice, so they were cold and hungry, with little to eat but the shells of grains and beans. And he too who gave his own horse to the transfer of wounded soldiers.

Yet despite this willful leadership, the army managed victory after victory. Qiqiya, seeing at last that the die had been cast, turned tail and fled. The army blocked him in at Guanquan Mountain, their tens of thousands surrounding his remaining one thousand men. At first, he relinquished his weapon and attempted surrender, but all Li Chengyin said was "I don't accept."

Three little words, but they fell from his lips so easily as to be entirely merciless. The generals sucked in sharp breaths when they heard this. Even Pei Zhao was moved to intervene.

---

3 From *Master Sun's Art of War* by Sunzi.

"Commander, it is inauspicious to kill prisoners of war...."

"We haven't taken them prisoner," he said. "They may yet fight."

Qiqiya had the reckless bravery of a rebel. He really did rally his men and his horses. But they were surrounded by a much larger force. There could be no other outcome. In the end, he took a horse, as though to charge the line himself. He fell half an arrow's length away.

The vanguard was careful and ordered its men to use their long spears to impale his corpse, throwing it heavily upon the ground to ensure he was well and truly dead. Under the protection of his guard, Li Chengyin rode over. Cold stung his face—it had begun to snow.

The snow fell silently and without rest, turning the world into a borderless expanse. Occasionally, a horse would whinny. Li Chengyin stared down at the flakes that drifted soft and downy, one by one, like the catkin fluff by the Winding River, onto Qiqiya's bloody face. He untied the leather pouch from behind his saddle, twisted the silver cap open, and spilled its liquor onto the vast white plain. It seeped into the ground and disappeared, just as the warm embrace of the man who once held him like a father had done.

When he finished, he tossed the pouch aside and galloped away. Pei Zhao looked back to where it lay in the snowdrift, shabby and worn. He recognized the object, for in the last few years Li Chengyin had rarely been without it. Pei Zhao found himself at a loss. He had the feeling that the brash field commander was gone, that this was once more the crown prince he'd known in Shangjing—steady and reserved, reticent and unreadable. Despite being surrounded by soldiers, he looked utterly alone.

On the journey back, before they crossed the Wei River, Li Chengyin fell suddenly and violently ill. First, it was vomiting and the runs, and soon after he developed a high fever. In another three days, he was coughing up blood. The army physicians were confounded. All they could offer was that it may have been the miasma.

Pei Zhao ran to dispatch a fast horse back to Shangjing to report this to the emperor and scrambled, too, to open the embroidered pouch his father had given him ere he left. It was something his father said he should not touch unless the situation was desperate, but since they'd won the war, Pei Zhao had thought he wouldn't have cause to anymore.

There was nothing in it, only a jet-black pellet wrapped in oiled paper. He couldn't even tell what it was.

He stared for a second, then drew his sword and shaved a powdered sliver from the outside of the pill. Hesitant, he brought it to his lips, but swallowed it down resolutely. It was fiery beyond belief, drenching him in sweat.

He waited another half day, until he could be sure nothing adverse would happen. In the interim, Li Chengyin spat up another lungful of blood and fell into a deep slumber. Every four hours the physicians came to administer medicine, but it had yet to have any effect. Pei Zhao glanced into the tent and, finding it empty, crept inside, ladled some water into his waterskin, and heaved Li Chengyin upright to feed him the pill.

By then Li Chengyin was delirious. He struggled to open his eyes, peering at Pei Zhao, and swallowed without question or complaint.

In days he was on the mend. But still Pei Zhao could not allay his fears—using the excuse of negligence on the part of the attendants, he had them all reassigned to the stables and replaced with guards he'd brought from home. Even then he had the food tasted first.

Once they were alone, Li Chengyin said, "A'zhao, you've saved me again."

"It was my oversight," Pei Zhao said. "I should have known there were people in the capital who did not wish to see you return."

Li Chengyin laughed. "It's not as if this was the first time. I'm neither firstborn nor trueborn, and yet I presume to be crown prince—for that crime I must bear the envy."

Pei Zhao stopped himself from saying what he wanted to say—that when this war had first broken out, he'd begged Li Chengyin not to take the commandership precisely because it would have been bad if he lost and terrible if he won.

He was already heir. All he should worry about now was not making any missteps. What need was there to put his own body on the line?

As if sensing this, Li Chengyin said, quite placidly, "You don't understand. I had to take Qiqiya's life." Had someone else been in charge, they would have made a captive of him to present to the emperor. The emperor would have pardoned Qiqiya, kept him in confinement in Shangjing, and made an example of him to the rebel Shiwei and Mohe.

It was true—Pei Zhao did not understand why an otherwise shrewd and decisive person would have been so bullheaded on this matter.

Like this insistence on infiltrating the western kingdoms. Pei Zhao had wanted to send someone to Xiliang to gather intelligence—how could he have expected Li Chengyin to give them the slip and sneak in himself?

He'd tried to intercede, but Li Chengyin had said, "I'm the one who's getting married off anyhow; I can't go and see her first?"

This had silenced him. Older and wiser he may have been, but he was no match for the brazen tenacity of youth.

So all Pei Zhao could do was lead the Yulin Guard to rendezvous with Gu Jian first. As they did, Li Chengyin crept into the royal city.

Xiliang was the place all merchants had to pass through on their way west to the caliphates, but it was far less opulent than the Central Plains, with a palace encircled by dirt walls that were packed with Spiranthes and smoothed white with a layer of clay. Most of its rooms were empty, with nary a bed to lie in—just woven mats and sheepskin felt.

Li Chengyin had not imagined that a royal city could be so crude. It was his first time as a thief in the rafters, so he held his breath, creeping through room by room until the sun rose.

Futile though this effort may have been, he wasn't all too discouraged by it. He was just planning to retreat when noise startled him behind a wall—only a few maidservants, carrying a sloshing bucket of water between them, laughing and giggling as they went. He heard their chatter, catching the words "ninth princess," and hurried to catch up.

But the maids brought their water into a suite of rooms with nary a roof beam between them, so he had to make a wide circle around and double back through a rear entrance instead. Seeing no one about, he crept in through a window. Reed screens draped to the floor, and he was using the hilt of his sword to nudge one aside when a red cloud came hurtling toward him from the other side. Thinking he'd been discovered, Li Chengyin drew his blade. His was a fine weapon, sharp, and in a flash it had sliced through the red cloud, which split clean in two and dropped soundlessly to the floor. A girl stood in Li Chengyin's line of sight, her bare back bright and smooth like jade. Morning light passed through the woven reeds, coating her tallow skin.

The girl sat by the bathing pool, humming a little tune as she unlaced her skirts and tossed the fabric behind her. As her skirt flew toward him, Li Chengyin realized he hadn't been found out after all.

She rose, and the sun shone off her frame until she glowed. Li Chengyin was too shy to keep looking. He whipped back around, heart pounding, and withdrew behind the window screen. But it was not entirely opaque. When he turned at the sound of splashing, he could see through the weave that the girl had jumped into her bath.

Her long hair scattered on the surface like seaweed. Dense steam made her dark eyes as dewy as ripe, sweet grapes. She sang as she washed, raising her arm to scrub herself and dispelling the water around her pale bosom to reveal a lovely curve.

Li Chengyin stood, unbreathing, listening to her tune—something about a fox, a dune, merry and mirthful.

The Central Plains was strict in its etiquette. In his entire life Li Chengyin had only known girls from noble families, the kind who were fastidious in following every convention and every rule, or else court ladies who were modest and careful, virtuous and proper. He'd never met anyone so brilliantly carefree. She seemed to him like one of the birds who flew blithely through the heavens, unburdened by worry or woe.

For a time she sang to herself. A handmaiden came to add hot water to the bath and curtsied. "Ninth Princess."

She chirped happily back as the handmaiden collected her clothes, saying, "Ninth Princess, you mustn't fling your clothing about like this; if the queen finds out, she will scold me again...."

Then she picked up half a red cloud—it had once been a tunic—and exclaimed in surprise.

"What is it?"

"How did this shirt get ripped in two?"

And it was torn so neatly—like someone had taken a sharp pair of shears to it. Suspicion rose in the maid's heart and she pulled the screen back, but the long window behind it was empty—there was just the golden sun, scattered upon the ground.

Pei Zhao had brought a band of cavalrymen to the foot of the snowy mountains and set up camp there, in a hidden spot that faced the river and protected them from the wind. For this sojourn west, Li Chengyin had been placed in command of the three thousand Yulin Guards from the Court of Spring, every one the son of a courtier or an aristocrat. It was the first time any of them had garrisoned a border so far from the capital. They'd brought falcons and hounds and were in high spirits, as though this were nothing more than a hunting expedition. At least Pei Zhao could quell them now. All along the journey he had trained them as they marched, and by the time they made it to the western kingdoms, they'd been whipped into some kind of shape—the camp they built was secure, orderly, almost professional.

Once it had been built, they sent some men out to scout while the rest got to preparing provisions. Food was eaten in shifts. As an officer, Pei Zhao had the last, but as he lifted his bowl of barley meal, a scout's warning flared—and then, just as quickly, it was rescinded. A horse was trotting toward the encampment: Li Chengyin, returned.

Seeing him none the worse for wear, Pei Zhao let go of the breath he'd been holding and walked up to meet him. Someone took his reins, and Li Chengyin leapt easily from the saddle, saying, "Where's Gu Jian?"

"Your Highness was away for so long, he went back to the city." And then, "Did you see the princess?"

Li Chengyin nodded. "I did. A face full of immaturity, not a hint of conniving on it—she's nothing more than a half-grown child." But then he remembered the flash of skin he'd seen beneath the ripples and his ears reddened like he'd been caught in a lie, so he ducked into the tent and muttered, "I'm starving. Bring me a bowl too."

Pei Zhao didn't notice anything amiss. They had been

burdened with a great undertaking on this long road westward—all the better if the Xiliang princess was without guile.

After days of travel, the troops were covered in dust and grime. But the men were hardly discerning. They jumped into any water they encountered to wash. The camp had been built on the bank of a river, and that river was fed by snowmelt from the nearby mountain, so though it was the height of summer, the water was cold enough to chill the bone.

They bathed in the evening. A flock of Yulin Guards splashed in, all yelps and chattering teeth. Pei Zhao and Li Chengyin were trying to see who could swim the fastest. They rose and sank in the waves, farther and farther downstream, but neither could get the better of the other. The Yulin boys liked this kind of playfighting, hollering and whooping from shore as they beat a pace on a narrow-waisted drum, and running alongside, called out words of encouragement. But then there was an onslaught of rapids, and the two were swept along too quickly for those on shore to keep up. Gradually, day dimmed into evening.

Pei Zhao won, in the end. Exhausted, Li Chengyin choked on two lungfuls of water and had to be dragged along with one hand. They found a stretch of sandbar, working together to wade back to the bank. Lights twinkled in the distance—Yulin Guards with torches, most likely, coming to look for them.

They collapsed onto the grass. A river of stars shone above them. Here the sky felt lower than the one that hung above Shangjing, so low you could touch it.

Lying there as bedraggled as drowned rats, they burst into loud fits of laughter.

"A'zhao, have you ever thought about what kind of person you're going to marry?" Li Chengyin asked lazily.

"I want to marry someone I love, someone who could respect me as much as I respect her. But . . ." He didn't continue.

Given Pei Zhao's family, he would more likely than not be chosen for a prince consort. But in this matter he could at least make some small intervention, so Li Chengyin smiled, saying, "Well, if there's a princess you particularly like, I could put in a good word."

"Then I'll thank you in advance, Your Highness," was Pei Zhao's easy answer.

A clamor drew near. The Yulin Guard had found them and were overjoyed to have done so, bringing along horses and coverings and blankets and cloaks. Li Chengyin dried himself with a cloth and donned a clean set of robes. He bumped into a freshly changed Pei Zhao as they were both mounting their horses.

"Do you want to make another wager? See who can make it back to camp the fastest?" Li Chengyin asked.

Pei Zhao replied, "Your Highness has lost once today—are you sure you want to taste defeat a second time?"

Li Chengyin raised his riding crop. "I wouldn't count on it!"

The torches lit the pride in his eyes, and the high-spirited youths bounded away. Under the glow of the escorting fires, the stars lost their shine. Back then, they both thought that, though the road ahead would be a difficult one, a world of endless options sprawled out before them, ripe for the picking.

The first time Pei Zhao saw the ninth princess was after Li Chengyin became Gu Xiaowu and was living in the royal city. Disguised as a tea merchant, he bumped into her on the threshold—he had been wearing Xiliang clothes and had affixed a false beard to his face, so she took him for one of Gu Xiaowu's friends and smiled at him. She was holding a cage with two gerbils aside. "Look, look!" she called delightedly to Li Chengyin. "These are A'ba and A'xia!"

The gerbils were spirited. Their fur was soft and shiny, and they were round and plump, like two fat balls of dough. The princess stuffed a broad bean into Li Chengyin's palm, saying, "You try!"

He extended his hand. One of the gerbils dashed forward to snatch the bean into its mouth. The other crammed forward to try and steal the food, but because it was too chubby, it rebounded onto its back instead, tiny paws in the air, revealing a pink tummy. It squeaked, grasping at the air, but could not climb back onto its feet again.

The princess was so tickled by this that she threw back her head and guffawed. Li Chengyin couldn't hold back a smile either. They leaned close to the cage, head pressed against head, as Li Chengyin flipped the gerbil rightways with a finger. He accidentally jabbed the poor thing in its soft tummy, which set off more peals of laughter. Pei Zhao didn't know why, but he felt his heart sink. They were clearly so happy. So why did it feel like this boded ill?

Li Chengyin hadn't noticed. Once he finished feeding

the gerbils, he left to go riding with the princess.

Sunset dazzled the sky. They'd first let their horses wander, then spent some time galloping, and now they were seated on a sand dune watching the sun sink beneath the horizon.

Needlegrass swayed in the slanting light. Faraway camel bells signaled the passing of a merchant caravan. The princess rested her chin in one hand and pointed to the scarlet clouds with the other as she said, "There's a kind of tree by the desert lakes whose leaves are as red as that, and when they reflect in the water it is the prettiest thing you'll ever see. When I was born, my a'niang said, 'Ah, it's a girl!' She was so pleased because she'd had only boys, and she thought that if she had a daughter, she would be bound to wear bridal red someday, as red as the leaves of the ma'erqima tree and as lovely too. That's why she named me Ma'erqima, after the tree."

The last twilit rays shone on her face. It wasn't rouge that flushed her cheeks, but the sun. She hugged her knees, her skirts painted scarlet by evening. She loved to wear red, Li Chengyin realized. Every time he'd seen her, she'd been wearing that color. Even that first time, when he'd accidentally come across her—but then he remembered the clouds of fabric that had drifted down and revealed her back, and blushed hotly. Thankfully the sunset was at its most splendid and the princess was not a discerning sort, so she did not attend this diffidence. He raised his eyes toward the brilliant clouds and said, "In the Plains, we also have a kind of tree whose leaves turn as red as this in autumn. We call it feng."[4]

The princess clapped, delighted. "Oh! That means if I had a Plains name, it would be Feng."

"Plains girls often carry the word *niang* in their names. Why don't you call yourself Fengniang?"

"I don't like that at all, it's too ugly." The princess pouted. "I want to be called Xiaofeng. You're called Xiaowu, I'm called Xiaofeng—that way we'll match."

Her eyes glistened like gemstones beneath the glow of the heavens. Absently, he nodded. "Xiaofeng is a nice name."

"Then that's settled." The princess rose to her feet and shouted into the sunset: "I have a Plains name! I'm called Xiaofeng! I'm called Xiaofeng!"

Her voice reverberated in the great wide empty, and when wind rustled the loose sand, it sounded like harmony.

Observing her as she gesticulated, Li Chengyin's face eased unwittingly into a smile.

It was routine for Pei Zhao, who camped with the Yulin Guard at the foot of the snowy mountains, to enter the royal city a few times a week, but one day Li Chengyin rushed from the city into camp. Seeing him so upset, Pei Zhao feared that something had happened, but the other boy only dug a gerbil out from his lapels. It lay in his hand, unmoving.

Surprised, Pei Zhao said, "Your Highness."

"I was distracted for *one second* and let A'ba slip out. He climbed into the feed jar, gorged himself on too many broad

---

4 maple

beans, and now he's choked to death," said Li Chengyin. "And then I remembered that when we were making camp we'd seen hundreds of gerbil tunnels, so if we catch one that looks the same, she won't know the difference."

As it was such a trivial matter, Pei Zhao relaxed and sent some men out to trap gerbils. The guards were in the habit of making trouble when not given adequate diversions, so they treated this, too, as nothing more than a game, raising a ruckus all the while. The poor gerbils at the foot of the snowy mountain—in the space of a single afternoon an endless number had been dug out of their hidey-holes. They were separated by color and by size and put in cages for Li Chengyin to pick from.

He took forever to choose. Finally, he found one that looked exactly like A'ba and, pleased, said, "This is the one." He shut the cage door. "You mustn't let the cat out of the bag—if Xiaofeng calls you, remember you are A'ba."

The gerbil squeaked and squeaked. Of course it did not take any notice. He brought it back with him, but Pei Zhao could not, ultimately, settle his heart and went into the city the next day to find Li Chengyin, only to run into the ninth princess as she was storming out. She'd found out after all. Shoving the portiere aside, she stamped her foot and screamed, "That's not my A'ba, liar! Gu Xiaowu, you are a big fat liar! I am *never* talking to you again!"

The portiere slapped the earth with a loud *bang* as the princess whipped her horse and galloped furiously away. She didn't even acknowledge Pei Zhao. He lifted the curtain and entered the room, where Li Chengyin sat at a table scrutinizing the little gerbil, saying glumly, "How do you think she figured it out? They look exactly the same."

"She raised it herself," Pei Zhao replied. "Of course she would know the difference."

Li Chengyin sighed. "This is the first time since we met that I've seen her so angry. What's to be done?"

For days the princess avoided him. But Li Chengyin wasn't overly worried, for there were Yulin sentries stationed all around Tiangen Mountain, and they had reported seeing a troupe of acrobats traveling with a Xianluo caravan that would be passing Xiliang soon, and said they were planning to put on a show in the royal city. With such a to-do, the princess was bound to come out and see the fuss.

When the day came, the city bustled. Of every ten caravans, nine stopped here to rest, to organize themselves and their wares, or to trade for cloth and silk from the east to sell farther west. Crowds teemed inside and outside the city walls, and when the acrobats started their performance, they clanged their gongs and banged their drums until the streets filled with curious onlookers.

The warehouse Li Chengyin had rented under the name of Gu Xiaowu was on the main thoroughfare. Tea from the Central Plains sold well, so people were constantly coming and going—some were Yulin Guards disguised as merchants, while others were true customers. With people packed in so tightly on the streets that water would not have found a way through, Li Chengyin closed his doors and went up to the roof to watch instead.

Roofs in Xiliang were flat because it rarely rained, and

consequently, there were racks of tea drying atop the warehouse. He stood on a corner, looking out. There was the princess, buried among the crowd, clapping and shouting encouragement to the Xianluo man who was walking a tightrope. Though the rope was no thicker than a thumb, he swayed upon it, balancing two buckets of water without spilling a drop. Below, the crowd, already moved to thunderous applause, roared in approval. The Xianluo man teetered to one end and drew a small white cat from his lapels, placing it onto his pole.

The cat was the size of a human palm. It mewed and mewed, too terrified of heights to jump down, so it hunched there, trembling.

The Xianluo man spoke as someone translated into Xiliang from the sidelines: this time, he would be walking the rope while swinging the buckets, and he would not lose a single drop.

The crowd sucked in a breath. But he was as good as his word—his buckets were filled almost to the brim as he started to sway them lightly—and then he continued, saying that on his last rotation, he would be swinging the cat in a bucket.

At this, this princess leapt up. "But there's so much water in there, the kitten will drown!"

But it was just this that he was proudest of. The man put down his buckets and grabbed it to show everyone that this was a real live cat, with one bright green eye and one deep blue one. This kind of cat was a specialty from Xianluo, which was famous for them.

He asked if anyone was willing to come up on this rope

to compete with him. If they could get to the kitten first, he would give them one hundred pieces of gold, but if he got there and drowned the kitten, then he would win one piece of gold.

This stirred the crowd. *One hundred pieces of gold*—even merchants who often traveled through the region could not make this much money at the end of their journeys.

There was always a brave man when a heavy prize was to be won, to say nothing of when there was so much to be won and so little to be lost. It sounded like a good deal. A whole host of volunteers leapt up to give it a try, but the tightrope was far from the ground, and it was both high and thin, so many lost their nerve. The princess was growing agitated. She didn't care much for the hundred gold pieces, but she was afraid he would really drown the little cat.

"Don't use the cat for your bet!" she cried. "I'll give you ten gold to use something else."

The cat may have been a rare and precious thing, but it wasn't worth all *that*. The Xianluo man, seeing how upset she was, dug in his heels. He said he wouldn't, that it was the prize for his show, meaning to coax more money out of her. He held it, letting her see it struggle in his hand as he shook his head to indicate he would only gamble, he would not sell.

The princess was so flustered she was stamping her foot and was about to yank off her shoes to get up on the wire herself when the flash of a figure scrambled onto the tightrope. It was the tea merchant, Gu Xiaowu.

Her eyes widened. Gu Xiaowu stood, wobbling like he couldn't find his balance, as the onlookers held their breaths.

He tottered two steps forward and pitched toward the ground. The princess screamed. But before the sounds of shock dissipated, he had hooked a foot around the rope and was hanging from it as he stretched a hand out to snag two buckets of water. With a twist of his body, he pulled himself back upright again.

Knowing he'd met a formidable match, the Xianluo acrobat put the kitten back onto the pole, grabbing two buckets of his own to stand in front of Gu Xiaowu and block his path.

They stayed like that, one advancing while the other retreated, and in that back-and-forth, both found it within themselves to give serious thought to simply kicking the other off. The buckets in the acrobat's hands whizzed as they spun, nearly smashing into Li Chengyin more than once. The crowd cried out in alarm, and the ninth princess's heart nearly leapt out of her throat.

Tightrope walking was the acrobat's stock-in-trade, but though they tangled for a long while, he could not spot any weakness—Li Chengyin was steady as a boulder. The tricks he kept up his sleeve weren't enough to knock the boy off, and he began to worry for his gold. In his anxiety, he brought out one final trick.

He stopped swinging and sank down, using the rope's elasticity to vault into a backflip. Thunderous cheering sounded. His jump caused the tightrope to rebound high into the air. The buckets began to spin again, and bore down toward the kitten on the wooden pole—all the acrobat needed to do was scoop it up to drown it in the water.

No sooner had he jumped than Gu Xiaowu, borrowing

the same recoil, bounded after. But his was a leap. The acrobat was midflip when Gu Xiaowu hurtled overhead, landing sooner than him and knocking the water out of the man's hand. He grabbed the kitten, which mewed weakly, and stuffed it into his lapels so he could extend an arm to catch the falling bucket. It swung, but not a drop sloshed out.

The crowd was stunned into silence before bursting into hearty applause. Some folks even climbed onto their roofs and blew their horns. The ninth princess jumped with glee as she shouted his name: "Gu Xiaowu! Gu Xiaowu! Gu Xiaowu!"

The acrobat, in his dismay, loosened his grip. His remaining bucket fell to the ground. There was no time to avoid it. Water splattered all over the onlookers, and they yelped, laughingly, causing a ruckus.

Li Chengyin climbed down. The audience had recognized him as the Plainsman tea merchant and they rushed up to circle him, chattering noisily as they offered their congratulations for winning a hundred gold. But he looked behind him to where the ninth princess stood.

She had been beaming when he rescued the kitten, but now, having recalled the A'ba incident, she snapped her head away and pretended not to see him.

Li Chengyin dug the cat out from his lapels. It was the size of his palm, with snow-white fur and heterochromous eyes, looking unspeakably adorable. She couldn't resist a longing stare, and he couldn't suppress a smile. He held the kitten out. "Here."

The ninth princess gave a shout of excitement. She took it gingerly from him. It gave a thin meow and stuck out a tiny pink tongue to lap at her finger. She giggled. "It's licking me—oh, I can't believe it's licking me! That tickles!"

"Then you can't be angry with me anymore," he said. "If you are, I won't give it to you."

The princess pouted. "You won *a hundred gold*! I can't believe you're being so stingy."

Li Chengyin laughed. The acrobat had long since disappeared into the crowd—he was unlikely to see one coin, much less a hundred of them.

But the ninth princess was cuddling the cat; what care had she for whether there was gold or not? She skipped happily with Li Chengyin all the way back to his warehouse. It had been days since she'd last visited, and the gerbils she'd left were rounder and plumper than ever. She hugged the cage. "A'ba, A'xia, look—you have a new friend."

The two gerbils shook in their enclosure, looking like they might faint. The princess grumbled. "Why are you such a scaredy-cat, A'xia? And you, A'ba . . . hmm, you look like A'ba, so you may as well be named like him too. . . ." Her voice grew sorrowful. She rested her cheek in one hand and used the other to poke at the new A'ba's fat little tummy.

Seeing her sulk—and knowing why she was sulking—Li Chengyin changed the subject. "Why don't you name the cat?"

She gave it some thought. "It's so white. Why don't we call it Snowflake? No, wait—you're called Xiaowu, I'm called Xiaofeng, so it should be called Xiaoxue!"

Xiaoxue was naughty. It spent every day terrorizing the gerbils. Though they were fed plenty of broad beans, they slimmed, for they were being chased around all day. But Xiaoxue was so small, and wanted nothing more than to play, so eventually the gerbils learned to stop fearing it. Sometimes, they even stuck tiny paws teasingly out from between the bars of their cage.

The little princess loved Xiaoxue dearly. She brought it with her everywhere, while the gerbils, used to the warehouse, remained there. More experienced now, Gu Xiaowu took scrupulous care of A'ba, and the gerbils grew shiny and smooth, healthy and well. The princess came by to amuse herself daily, and the two of them would go out to go riding, or drinking with the merchant caravans, or racing camels....

What a wild and happy dream.

Li Chengyin was raised deep in the palace. From infancy he had lived on thin ice—for every one step he took, he had ten more to think about. Never had he been this carefree, this boisterous; never had he spent all day just playing around. With her, he seemed easy, relaxed, as any child might be. There was no need to bustle and scheme. He longed for the days to be longer, then longer still, so he could fling the Plains, the empire, the Court of Spring to the back of his mind.

Then, Mohu sent an envoy to Xiliang with a proposal of marriage. The ninth princess, displeased, snuck out that same night to see A'ba and A'xia.

Li Chengyin had grown used to her visits. When he saw her sitting alone at the table, he crept in, intending to cover her eyes and give her a good scare, but she stopped him with a faint sigh.

The princess slumped despondently. "What should I do?" she asked the gerbils. "I don't want to marry the king of Mohu. He's such an old man, older than my a'die even." She pouted. "But I don't want to marry that crown prince either. I heard that Plainsmen can't even draw a bow, and all they know is how to read and write all day long. I'd be at such a disadvantage if my husband couldn't shoot."

As she sat there grumbling, a voice sounded from behind her.

"What, so eager to get married off?"

She grew annoyed when she saw it was Gu Xiaowu. "That's right," she snapped. "I can't wait!"

"Well, if that's the case, you'd better give Xiaoxue back," Li Chengyin teased. "That's my cat, not your dowry."

Anger mixed with her irritation. "Even if I marry, I'm not leaving Xiaoxue behind. Xiaofeng and Xiaoxue are never going to be apart."

Then she stormed out, feeling exceptionally sorry for herself.

By the time she peered over her shoulder, she was a long distance away. The market was empty—there was only her own long shadow. The warehouse was a patch of darkness, for Gu Xiaowu must have closed his doors, blown out the lights, and, minding his own business, gone to sleep.

Her heart pinched. Hugging Xiaoxue, she walked away without a backward glance.

She couldn't pin down why she should feel so slighted. Possibly it was because Gu Xiaowu was so stubborn, because every time they bickered, he would refuse to cede to her, and he made no effort to sweet-talk her after, either. If he'd just come after her now, she might even have married him. He was a better option than either the king of Mohu or the crown prince of the Central Plains, at any rate.

She stomped a little, vexed that she would think up such nonsense. It wasn't like she wanted to wed Gu Xiaowu anyhow.

In her hurt she decided to flee—flee to Jieshuo, for her a'weng loved her best.

So she packed her things and ran, taking Xiaoxue with her.

The men under Pei Zhao were in charge of keeping an eye on the princess, so they were aware of her every little move—much less something as significant as running from the royal city to flee an arranged marriage. They split into two, one half to tail the princess and the other to report the news. Pei Zhao was silent for a long time when he heard. Then he dismissed his troops.

He went alone to see Li Chengyin, but found him in no rush. He said, "There's someone trailing her, no? I'll catch up shortly."

Pei Zhao could not resist prodding. "But the princess didn't bring anything. Just some provisions, some water, and a cat."

Li Chengyin laughed. "It's one thing to flee a marriage, but to bring Xiaoxue along?"

Then he startled, remembering the previous evening. He'd teased her about marrying the king of Mohu, and she'd gotten very upset, snapping that *Xiaofeng and Xiaoxue are never going to be apart* and storming out.

She often threw such tantrums, so he hadn't given it much thought, taking it for nothing more than a spoiled princess and her temper. But those words . . . they sounded like she'd truly been angry.

Pei Zhao had long since had an inkling of where all this was headed, and seeing the prince look so ill at ease, called to him. "Your Highness."

"So childish," Li Chengyin said. He rose and took his sword. "Get me a horse, then, I'll go after her. In another moment she'll be too far, and it might be impossible to catch up."

Pei Zhao grabbed the sword and pressed it back onto the table. "Your Highness, have you thought this through?"

He paused between nearly every word. The flame of the oil lamp flickered and danced, and in the dim light, Li Chengyin's expression was obscure. He didn't say anything, but Pei Zhao knew he understood what was being asked. He slowed his voice and repeated, "Have you thought this through?"

Li Chengyin did not speak. He picked his sword up and walked through the door.

Pei Zhao heard the clatter of hooves disappear into the distance of the night, and he let out a frustrated sigh.

He and Li Chengyin were lord and vassal, but more than that, they were friends. They had grown up together and shared a greater degree of understanding than others could claim. It was fair to say he could guess seventy, eighty percent of the young Highness's thoughts. Tonight, for him to have twice risked insubordination to question his master—this was a mark of his affection.

But in a house of kings, what room was there for such a thing?

They had come west with a plan. Plainsmen excelled in strategy, always seeking the surest solution. In deploying soldiers, they were still less disinclined toward craftiness, and in every aspect they had made their considerations.

Pei Zhao was a cautious person, but this time—though he couldn't give a reason for it—he didn't report back to his father in the capital, nor did he mention it to anyone.

He couldn't explain it to himself.

It could have been because a few days earlier, when he had come to see Li Chengyin, he arrived to an empty room—just the gerbils eating broad beans in their cage. The ladder had been let down, and knowing therefore that someone must have been on the roof, he ascended. Racks of tea had been drying in cakes on the roof, but the ninth princess, perhaps having worn herself out with cavorting, leaned against a rack with her cat in her arms, asleep. Li Chengyin sat by her side, using his sleeve to block the sun. Girl and cat dozed sweetly as he hid a smile, his face turned toward the slumberer.

The strong sun had shortened their shadows so that they shrunk into little balls, like those of two children nestled together.

Pei Zhao did not disturb them. Instead, he retreated back to the cool seclusion of the warehouse, through which the delicate fragrance of tea emanated. He steeped himself a cup, but the roof above remained silent after he'd finished, as though nobody was there. Light shifted lazily through the latticed window. In his heart, Pei Zhao understood how short this time was—and yet how long. What need was there to disturb this fleeting reverie?

Especially one so fragile.

Did the dreaming Li Chengyin ever wish he really were the tea merchant Gu Xiaowu?

He might not have been able to say.

On the riverbank, next to the campground of the royal tent of Jieshuo, when Gu Xiaowu caught one hundred fireflies, the princess's eyes reflected back ripples of starlight.

They stood among the floating lights, and it was as if they stood in the heavenly river, numberless meteors flitting past.

A wish must be made, you know, when shooting stars are seen.

Li Chengyin remembered what she'd once said, with that naive, earnest look of hers—that if you knotted your waistband, then your wishes would come true.

He tried to do just that, but he knotted it all wrong, and it wouldn't take. Beside him, she reached over, laughing and saying, "Stupid!" as she tied it for him.

By then he'd forgotten what wish he wanted to make. Gleaming fireflies illuminated her face. One stopped in her hair, flickering, flickering, like she had adorned herself with the brightest nightglow pearl.

From somewhere he found the courage to lean in and press a kiss to her cheek. Maybe he scared her, for she did not move for a long while. Then she stamped her foot and ran.

"You already agreed to marry me!" he called after her.

She was too bashful to look back, scampering off with her hands over her ears for half an arrow's length, and then doubling back to fish a sleeping Xiaoxue from his lapels. The little cat meowed in protest, batting drowsy eyed at her finger with not a clue of what had passed. Li Chengyin took this opportunity to catch her hand. "The cat belongs to me, why are you taking it?"

"Nonsense!" A guilty conscience, possibly, but it made her more brazen. "Xiaoxue is mine. You gave it to me. And anyway, this is my dowry."

Having said this, she turned tail and dashed away.

Soft heat lingered in the heart of his palm—it could have been Xiaoxue's, or it could have been hers.

Without understanding why, he brought it to his cheek.

She hadn't kissed him yet, but she had agreed to marry him.

And he knew it for an answer sincere.

An answer for Gu Xiaowu.

The tea merchant from the Central Plains, Gu Xiaowu.

He stood in the night wind, turning back to see the scattering fireflies. It was all like a misty dream, dissipating. A lingering song wafted from a long distance away—a Jieshuo man singing before the tent of the girl he loved.

Water rushed past. Beneath the glittering sky it looked like a bolt of gauzy silver muslin. He sat there until dew condensed, until the moon westward sank, until the fireflies sputtered out one by one, and were not seen again.

The day of the wedding, when Pei Zhao and his troops lay in ambush, there was a thread of apprehension that lay at the bottom of his heart.

Behind him were tens of thousands of soldiers—strong horses and fierce men. They roused themselves in preparation for the coming battle.

But he was thinking: *What if the prince reneged, and did not come?*

The idea flashed through his mind like lightning and left like lightning too, for if that came to pass, then His Highness could really only stay in Xiliang and become a tea monger. It was clearly a terrible thought—so why did he feel a sliver of yearning?

Yet it would have been catastrophe to raise such a ruckus. The fury of an emperor could make corpses of a million men, could turn blood into a river that ran a thousand miles, and if His Highness did abscond, His Majesty was more likely than not to send armored cavalry to raze every last one of the western kingdoms from the earth.

When Li Chengyin lured the best warriors of Jieshuo into the ambush at the appointed hour, Pei Zhao couldn't tell whether what he let out was a breath of relief or a sigh.

It was a bloodbath. It was the bitterest battle Pei Zhao had experienced. The men of Jieshuo were fierce and would rather die than submit. Forty thousand men surrounded the clans of Jieshuo, and the war waged for days until the chanyu died in the heat of battle and the Jieshuo vanguard fell apart. But still they were valiant. The warriors fought until their last to provide cover for the women, children, and elderly to escape.

In the chaos, the ninth princess also disappeared. Some Yulin guardsman sent word back that he'd seen her killed in the fray, and when Pei Zhao heard this, he felt, surprisingly, that it may be for the best. But there were so many corpses on the ground, layers and layers of the mangled and bloody, that there was no way to tell whether this news was true or false, nor any way to tell which of the bodies was the ninth princess of Xiliang.

It was total victory. When night fell and the Mohu set up their camp, Pei Zhao took the more careful path of settling upstream from them.

By the time the sky darkened completely, fireflies dotted the riverbank.

There Li Chengyin sat, watching them rise, the little shooting stars.

Pei Zhao neared slowly and called, "Your Highness."

Li Chengyin made no sound. He caught one. In his palm it brightened and darkened like a faltering lantern—or like a dying heart.

"Your Highness hasn't eaten, and there is a long march ahead of us tomorrow. . . ."

Li Chengyin opened his hand. The firefly struggled to take to the air, bobbing and swaying until it climbed high enough to drift to the shoreline and rejoin its friends. All the heavens were reflected in those waters, whose waves shattered the light until star and bug were indistinguishable.

"A'zhao . . ." When he spoke, his voice was as amorphous as the fireflies—like if the wind blew past, he too would scatter. "Am I very much a coward that, even when she is dead, I am afraid to go see?"

Pei Zhao was at a loss for how to answer. He had been holding a sesame flatcake, for Li Chengyin hadn't eaten all day, and he had wanted to come and coax him into some food, but he found he could not open his mouth.

Li Chengyin's voice grew fainter yet. "*Xiaofeng and Xiaoxue are never going to be apart.* It was clearly Xiaofeng and Xiaowu she'd meant, but I was too afraid, so I pretended not to understand. A'zhao, did you know I was so timid?"

"Your Highness," Pei Zhao started, meaning to offer some consolation, but he was interrupted by a burst of noise. A Yulin Guard came galloping toward them, shouting, "General!" He scrambled off the saddle as soon as he stopped. "The Xiliang princess escaped. We followed her thirty miles or more, and have almost caught up—I was dispatched back to bring the news."

Alarm shot through Pei Zhao and his head jolted toward Li Chengyin, but the prince did not look like he'd heard. Only when the guardsman repeated himself did he say, "If it is so, you'd better keep following." He smiled a little. "Bring my horse. I'll go myself."

"Your Highness!" Pei Zhao stopped him. "Your Highness, you have gone several days without rest. Why don't you let me bring some men to go after her?"

Li Chengyin fixed a long gaze on Pei Zhao, staring at him as though he were unrecognizable. He nodded. "Then that's settled."

Pei Zhao clasped his hands in deference and turned quickly away, but not before catching Li Chengyin's voice, soft and unhurried, saying, "Don't kill her."

Pei Zhao had been planning to do just that, but now that the order had been given, there was nothing to do but obey.

He and his men chased the princess for six days and six nights. They split into four contingents to surround her and head her off. One caught the ninth princess when she ran out of road at last and brought her back to the central encampment, alive.

She had been fleeing for a week on end. There was blood all over her, her hair was in unbound disarray, but she had the sharp intellect of cornered prey, two eyes glowering wide, two hands bound and raised in front of her chest like she was protecting something. The cat, Pei Zhao realized. A snow-white lump, so hungry it couldn't summon up the strength to yowl.

In the panic and the fluster of escape, how had she managed to bring it along?

Blood crusted on the cat's ears. It was impossible to tell whether the blood belonged to the princess or to someone else, but she hugged the kitten closer to herself and glared viciously up at Pei Zhao.

She spoke Xiliang. The cadence of it was soft and unhurried, rather the way Li Chengyin's had been by the riverside. It wasn't until long after that Pei Zhao realized this was the sound of utter despair.

She said, "You blackguards—when my husband returns, he will kill you all to avenge me."

As she spoke, she gathered the cat tightly in her arms. She was trembling so, yet her words were adamant, as though she truly believed there was such a man who would descend from the heavens to rescue her.

Until she saw Li Chengyin. She was struck silent by the sight of him, and her hands unwittingly unclenched. She didn't notice when the cat crawled away.

Gently, Li Chengyin scooped the cat up. Xiaoxue recognized him, lapping weakly at his fingers.

Understanding dawned, and she used the last of her strength to howl, "Traitor!"

Naturally, this meeting was disagreeable, and not entirely civilized. The ninth princess cursed Li Chengyin in endless waves of Xiliang. There were other matters Pei Zhao needed to attend to—not to mention how awkward it was to stay—so he retreated quickly. Once he was outside, he turned back around but could see only Li Chengyin standing there, holding the cat.

Pei Zhao was at sixes and sevens. It wasn't until after Gu Jian extricated the princess that he set his resolve and made a request of his lord. "The Mohu are a suspicious sort, and victory fears the unforeseen. Please, Your Highness, you must stay here to secure the larger aim. Let me go after the princess."

This time, Li Chengyin did not acquiesce. "No," he said. He was exceptionally calm. "I will take some men myself, and you will come with me."

How well Pei Zhao knew that the prince saw through his furtive plans, but despite that, he pressed forward, saying, "Decisions must be met with decisiveness, Your Highness, else you will suffer their consequence."

But Li Chengyin was unmoved. He smiled. "To kill her like that . . . how would it differ from killing myself? A'zhao, I can't do it a second time."

This shook Pei Zhao to the core. He retreated a step—and then strode forward again, calling, "Your Highness."

"You needn't try to stop me," said Li Chengyin. "This is my decision, and if it carries consequence, then on my head be it."

He said it so blandly. Especially those words, *on my head be it*, like they were hardly worth speaking. But Pei Zhao's heart thundered in his chest.

Li Chengyin bundled the cat in his arms; when the ninth princess ran away, she had left it behind, and it was being cared for in Li Chengyin's tent. He petted it softly, saying, "Look, she doesn't want Xiaoxue anymore. Or maybe it's life she doesn't want."

He and three thousand Yulin Guards chased her all the way to Tiangen Mountain.

Snow found them faster, and when it snowed in the mountains, Tiangen gave up all its secrets. More than once they almost recaptured her, missing her by seconds.

Pei Zhao tried to persuade him. "Your Highness, it's time to let it go. If we continue on like this, the Yulin Guard will freeze to death."

The guardsmen all hailed from Shangjing; they had never endured such a painful freeze as this. *In foreign skies the eighth month brings flights of snow*[5]—the wind here was so bitter it pierced the bone, and any moment of inattention could mean frostbite.

If they in their furs with their abundant grain could feel so cold, it was hard to imagine how the ninth princess, whose shoes had been tattered when she'd left, was enduring.

---
5 From "A Song of White Snow in Farewell to Field Clerk Wu Going Home" by Cen Shen.

But Li Chengyin refused to call the soldiers off. Through the thick flurries, he looked to the misty world around him, the hazy peaks, and he said, "I've already taken everything from her. If I don't leave her hatred, she might not survive."

The troops combed the mountains, but the princess escaped their grasp. There were a few times when they came close, but she and the girl called A'du were like gerbils, nimble enough to wriggle out of a bind.

Pei Zhao began to allow himself hope. *Let it be like this.* Let her escape, and quickly, someplace far, far away. Let her go with the Jieshuo refugees, farther west, more distant, let her be reachless to the empire, and knot that loose end forevermore.

But fate refused him this.

Ultimately, the princess of Xiliang snuck back into the royal city. She was taken by the soldiers they'd left in the palace and was, once again, brought to Li Chengyin.

This time, she was noticeably more docile. She'd even accepted the marriage decree.

Pei Zhao could not think of a worse idea, because once, he'd spotted Li Chengyin slip away to go see her, and when the prince placed the cat in front of her, she did not look at it—just as she did not look at him.

Li Chengyin carried the cat with him as he left. The weather had cooled, and errant flakes of snow danced in the night. He walked by himself over the frost-covered earth, his countenance vacant and forlorn. It wasn't clear where he was headed. Nothing more than a stroll around the encampment, it turned out, but Pei Zhao followed behind, unspeaking. Long moments passed until he spoke. "A'zhao, I heard

Gu Jian say that the people of Xiliang believe there is a river called Oblivion in the Tiangen Mountains, that if you drink its waters you can forget all that troubles you."

Pei Zhao answered, "The Master[6] spoke not of the strange, the violent, unrest, or the supernatural.[7] I do not believe in such a thing, my lord."

"I don't believe it either," said Li Chengyin. "Nothing comes so cheaply as that, much less the ability to forget."

He lowered his head and toyed with Xiaoxue's downy fur. The cat mewed and snuggled its head into one of his sleeves, curling into a ball within.

Li Chengyin became the one who brought Xiaoxue everywhere he went, hiding it in sleeves and lapels.

He treasured it like he treasured his own eyes until the princess of Xiliang escaped that final time, climbing up the high cliffside, though he did not forget to hand Xiaoxue over to Pei Zhao before climbing after her.

It was a narrow ledge, not wide enough to hold many people. Pei Zhao was standing a ways away.

So when the princess leapt toward the River Oblivion, when Li Chengyin grabbed her sleeve and followed after, he was unable to stop them. He could only watch as they plunged into the endless abyss, the world crumbling around him in the space of an instant.

A long time later, he led his men downstream along the bank, hoping against hope—hoping Oblivion really was water, was a deep, deep river.

---

6 Confucius
7 From *The Analects*.

They searched day after day, night after night.

They searched until no hope remained, until the Yulin Guards sank into themselves with grief. No one spoke, for they feared ill omens outnumbered the kind.

Pei Zhao alone refused to give up, and he brought a contingent of men back upstream. The valley was deep and crags towered overhead. Here the river raged—many an inattentive horse slipped into the water and was washed bodily away by its current.

He could not say what kind of faith drove him then. He clung stubbornly to the thought that if they were alive, he wanted to see their persons, and if they were dead, he wanted to see their corpses.

Thousands of men trawled that valley until all but half were dead. When at long last they found Li Chengyin, Pei Zhao was almost afraid to believe his luck.

They had washed up on a massive sheet of limestone, submerged to the midriff by water, but Li Chengyin had used his waistband to bind his arm tightly to that of the princess—a dead knot, impossible to untangle. Pei Zhao had no option but to grab his sword and cut through the cloth.

Their wrists were bruised from the abrasion, but Pei Zhao could not separate them after he got the waistband off either, for Li Chengyin was holding tightly to the princess's hand. His fingers had gone stiff with cold, and there was no way to peel them away. Perhaps in the midst of their long fall, the thought that there was no surviving this had compelled him to cling on so fiercely to her, to not let go again.

There was little other recourse than to have them lifted carefully onto horseback together, and to split the added burden by switching steeds regularly.

It took more than half a month to transport them out of the valley.

In this time, neither Li Chengyin nor the ninth princess woke. They had sunk deep into an oblivion, their breath weak, and every day Pei Zhao worried it would be their last.

But they did live. The army marched slowly, retreating several hundred miles eastward before making a sharp turn south, for Pei Zhao wanted to enter the pass as quickly as possible to find better physicians.

Li Chengyin first woke at dusk. When Pei Zhao rushed back to the tent upon hearing the news, he was being fed rice porridge by attendants. He'd gone so long without eating and looked terrible for it. But he smiled wanly and called, "A'zhao."

"Your Highness!" Pei Zhao nearly wept. He rushed forward and clasped Li Chengyin's hands. "Oh, you've woken."

Li Chengyin considered him thoughtfully, then dismissed his attendants with a wave of the hand. Everyone else retreated, leaving Pei Zhao behind.

The prince looked as pensive as he ever had. He glimpsed the ninth princess sleeping on a mat in the corner of the tent and asked, "Who is that girl?"

Pei Zhao opened his mouth but found he could not speak.

"Why is there so much sand flying about?" Li Chengyin asked. "Weren't we on our way back to Shangjing?"

Pei Zhao hid his alarm. "Your Highness, don't you remember?"

Li Chengyin looked askance at him, saying, "We're returning to court, aren't we? We killed Qiqiya." He paused. "I know I was ill for a long time; did it muddle me so much?"

Pei Zhao didn't know where to start, and upon some reflection told it to Li Chengyin bit by bit from the very beginning—how Qiqiya had been executed, that this time they had come west on behalf of a marriage treaty decreed by the emperor, that he had led the Yulin Guard outside the pass to personally escort the ninth princess of Xiliang.

He did not know why, but when he came to this part, he paused.

Li Chengyin glanced at the slumbering princess. The sky was darkening, and though a fire did burn inside the tent, its light flickered gently. She slept on, oblivious to it all, curled up like an infant.

Li Chengyin rose to approach her. Pei Zhao wasn't sure whether to stop him or not. The prince extended a finger, then snatched it away, as though afraid to startle her. He reached out again, tentative, and turned the princess's face gingerly toward himself.

Beneath the dancing blaze, she looked to be dreaming, peaceful. Long lashes covered her cheeks, casting a shadowy crescent onto her fair face, but her breath was shallow and she was still deeply insensate.

Li Chengyin startled back half a step, furrowing his brow.

Pei Zhao thought, *has he remembered?* How should he be advised? Once, he had fought with his life to save her. He had not hesitated to fall from that soaring cliffside. What was the best way to convince him to give her up?

After a long silence, Li Chengyin said, "Why did my lord father want me to take *her* for my bride? She's so ugly."

Pei Zhao was astonished.

Li Chengyin wiped his finger disdainfully on a cloth as he said, "You'd better find her a tent and move her into it; every time I see her it feels repulsive."

At a loss for anything better to say, Pei Zhao gave a hum of assent and had attendants bring the princess elsewhere.

From then on, Li Chengyin looked scornful whenever the subject of the princess was brought up, though Pei Zhao didn't know why.

He retreated from the commander's tent, mulling upon one thing over and over: How could he tell the crown prince, how should he say it, how much to say?

This situation with the ninth princess had been an affair of the heart, and no one in the Yulin Guard had been privy to it. Knowledge was restricted to himself and Gu Jian, but Gu Jian had disappeared. So he alone was left.

He spent a sleepless night pondering, anxious and ill at ease, until the day brightened around him. The cat named Xiaoxue lay on his pillow, meowing. He extended it a finger. It clung to him and was quickly snoring away—it was to this that Pei Zhao slipped into sleep at last.

He'd been resting for about as long as it took to brew a pot of tea when he felt someone's presence inside his tent and startled awake. It was Li Chengyin, who had lifted the flap and ducked inside. He hurried to his feet and made his courtesies. "Your Highness..."

But Li Chengyin was looking at the cat on his pillow. He scooped it up, smiling, "A'zhao, I can't believe you'd be raising a cat." He cradled Xiaoxue in his palms to play with, and, recognizing him, it began to groom his hand. "Look"—Li Chengyin laughed—"it's licking me." As he said this, two tears slipped from his eyes and pattered onto Xiaoxue's fur. Pei Zhao froze. Li Chengyin also looked aghast, raising a hand to his eyes and staring dazedly at the wetness on his fingertips, as though he could not believe the tears had been his.

Silence filled the tent. Only Xiaoxue's faint and plaintive meow broke it.

Li Chengyin put the cat down and said, forcefully, "It must have been quite the illness if the wind can sting my eyes so badly now."

Pei Zhao was more shaken by this than he, and could not stop himself from calling, "Your Highness...!"

"What is it?"

Yet Pei Zhao could not bring himself to go on. Li Chengyin was such a strong-willed person; he never cried. The burst of tears was not something he could find any reason to justify, because he had long since forgotten.

But these two drops of water were worth a thousand catties of gold, for they sealed everything away—sealed away all the words Pei Zhao had ever thought about saying.

Let it be, Pei Zhao told himself. *Let them be strangers.* For him, for her—who could say that it would not be a good thing?

He would become the keeper of this terrible secret.

Li Chengyin recovered quickly and was once again lord of the Court of Spring, that prince who planned for the good of the realm. As for the princess, he did not seem to regard her at all.

"She's nothing more than a Xiliang chit," he said to Pei Zhao one day. "Don't think I don't know the empress is clacking her abacus ere the sale's gone through."

For the princess had woken, and she too had forgotten all. She only remembered her own identity, that she had been ordered to Shangjing for a treaty marriage.

And yet she was as lively and as joyous as ever. She might not have been well-liked by Li Chengyin, but she was carefree again, as though there was nothing beneath the heavens to trouble her.

Pei Zhao could not discern if this was a good thing.

He raised Xiaoxue fastidiously, taking care to keep it out of the ninth princess's sight. He raised it for a long, long time, until Xiaoxue had its own kittens, but the passing years did little to soften the enmity between the prince and his princess, who butted heads as they'd always done.

By now the princess was the princess consort, though she was not beloved. Indeed, the prince seemed to take an active dislike to her. More than once, he would complain to Pei Zhao. "That Xiliang barbarian," he'd spit contemptuously.

He was not to be won over by any convincing.

On Qixi, the two of them had yet another row—possibly she had said something to irk him again—and Li Chengyin summoned Pei Zhao into the manor to take wine together. The palace bustled with festivities, but as it was a holiday only the women celebrated, it had bequeathed nothing more than some fruits and melons for the ladies in the crown prince's court.

Bringing her up was enough to send Li Chengyin into a fit of pique. "That Xiliang barbarian. She's been in the Plains for years, but she can't even thread a needle for Qixi? All she knows how to do all day is make trouble and inconvenience people. This is no kind of life, and I don't want to live another day like it!"

Feigning innocence, Pei Zhao asked, "Why do you dislike the princess so, Your Highness?"

Possibly because he'd imbibed, Li Chengyin looked rather dejected by this line of questioning. "I'm not sure. It's just . . . when I look at her, there's this aggravation in my heart." He paused. "Or not an aggravation. I don't know, I can't describe it. I don't want to see her, that's all."

"As you don't want to see my family cat," Pei Zhao said.

This caught Li Chengyin off guard, but then he nodded thoughtfully. "That's right, as I don't want to see your family cat."

For everyone in the Pei household knew that when His Highness bestowed his company upon them, they shouldn't let him catch sight of it, for it brought him great displeasure.

Pei Zhao drank a few more rounds before making his excuses and withdrew. For some reason, Li Chengyin felt sulky—it must have been because Pei Zhao had brought up that cat. He always thought of that incident with intense shame, for why should he have cried when he'd been perfectly well? Not merely that, but that he felt so *wretched*, like someone had taken a sharp blade and gouged out his heart. It had been many days since, but he was still scared to look upon the beast.

The mighty Lord of Spring, afraid of a cat!

Bitterness settled in his heart. He tossed back another cup and rose to leave his rooms. He wouldn't let anyone follow him, telling them that he was going to walk off his inebriation.

The moon had just risen; the night wind was chill. In the courtyard, flowers and trees bloomed in luxuriance. He walked along the covered bridge to a chorus of chirping bugs. Crystalline lake water reflected back the moon in the sky, shimmering with radiant light. He lingered there, awash with a sudden regret, so he strode across, past a row of buildings that lined the corridor, to arrive back at his own main court.

Servants' quarters, but their inhabitants had gone out to thread needles and pray, so the rooms, though brightly lit with candles, were empty.

Li Chengyin was passing beneath the windows when a red cloud came hurtling toward the screen. He reflexively twisted his head toward it. A palace maid, tidying away some clothes within. Summer clothes were light, and she'd been hanging them up on the rack without a second glance, but she was moving quickly, and a robe had slipped like a gossamer cloud to waft to the floor.

Li Chengyin stopped. The maid did not seem to have noticed anything amiss and was humming a ditty, tidying as she sang. Something about this was so familiar, as though he'd seen it somewhere. Like a shadow, impossible to grasp. Like it had happened in a previous life.

The maid startled back when she turned and saw him. She sank to her knees, stammering, "Y-Your Highness."

Candlelight illuminated her slender figure, filling him with a tenderness he had never known. Unconscious of the fact that he was doing it, he raised a hand to hold hers. Her fingers were cold as ice; she was trembling.

And he thought, *Don't be afraid, it's me—it's me.*

The girl, he felt certain, would recognize him. She would give him one of her beaming smiles like she'd done a thousand, ten thousand times.

If she smiled, the snow atop Tiangen Mountain would melt.

The name was practically upon his lips, but he could not recall it. Despite himself, he felt somewhat dejected. "Who are you?" he asked eventually.

"I am A'xu, my lord."

But he thought, no, this wasn't a good name, it wasn't this name, it was wrong, wrong. Then what *should* she be called? He couldn't remember—nothing like this had happened ere now. Then he was too lazy to try to recall any further, for she spoke her own mind well enough to know it, and she would remember what she was called.

He must have been drunk, madly so, for why else would there be a corner of his heart that was so miserable, and yet so sweet?

He was frightened, though he didn't know what of—the occasional snatch of something that came together only to dissipate like mist. He clutched her hands, bringing them unhurriedly to press upon his breast, where it ached. She shivered so, but he was delighted. "Come back with me."

He'd been searching for so long, for what, he no longer knew, but it was a loss, a massive one, one that terrified him. It had startled him awake, shaking and dazed with fear, on many countless midnights. It was the listless, acrid remorse he could not explain, the corrosive wound in the bottom of his heart, so deep it reached bone.

Thank heavens he'd found it.

And he was perfectly content, the way he had been a long, long time ago.

He took her by the hand and led her past beautiful towers, glorious halls.

Tonight, it was Qixi, when the weaving girl met her cowherd atop a bridge of magpies, a good day for autumn wind and dewdrop to meet.[8]

The stars reflected in the pond water seemed to be a sea of endless fireflies, like an intoxicating dream.

He didn't know that when he awoke on the morrow, he would be as bereft as he ever was.

He took her by the hand and led her into his own court.

The new poem written in wine on the silver screen would fade, obliviating all traces of the words, as the fireflies too would scatter.

Had I not seen what sorrow it is to part, I would not have known hair could whiten with the heart.[9]

---

8   From "Qixi in the Year 851" by Li Shangyin.
9   From "To the Tune of *Partridge Skies*: Written for a Friend" by Xin Qiji.

鸳鸯瓦冷霜华重
Heavy the Frost on the Paired Roof Tiles[1]

At dusk, the lamps had not been lit. The sky was a gloomy dark. Dragonflies flitted hither and thither through the court, and beneath the steps, plantain lilies blossomed. A few of the dragonflies stopped upon the sprays, but their leaves did not tremble. The air was so dense and humid that it felt like thunderstorm.

Sitting in the covered walkway was enough to drench me in perspiration.

A'wu worried that I might take things too hard, so she perched silently by my side and fanned me.

I thought back to the year I was seven or eight, still a child without worry or care, and A'wu had been then as she was now—at my side, fanning me—watching as I read and practiced my penmanship.

Summer days were long, and because I had seen the white silk fan in her hands, I copied out some lines of poetry onto the thin fabric.

> *Cut into a fan of happy days, round and*
> *full as the moon*

---

1 From "Song of Everlasting Regret" by Bai Juyi.

Coming and going from my beloved's
breast, stirring gentle breeze.[2]

I had only written it because I had been moved to do so by the object, but A'wu blanched when she saw it. Sternly, she told me, "Little girls should not write poems like these."

I was perplexed.

"It bodes ill," she said.

Of course, I remembered the second half of that poem:

But how often I fear the coming fall, when
chill replaces flaming heat
Forsaken in a bamboo box, love expired
too soon.

It—"Song of Resentment"—had been composed in the former kingdom of Han by the Lady Ban, who was a noted talent of her time. She was also famous for her virtue, but her life had not come to a happy end. While she had the emperor's favor, she fastidiously declined to share his royal carriage, though it frightened her to refuse, and when she had lost it, she whiled her days away deep in Changxin Court, leaving nothing behind but a few lines in some books to give any indication that such a woman had lived, that she had ever written anything at all.

But I did not really attend to A'wu's words, for I was to be empress someday.

---

[2] From "Song of Resentment," a poem from the Western Han Dynasty of contested authorship that is traditionally attributed to Lady Ban.

And an empress was hardly the same as any mere concubine.

For a consort, to lose the emperor's favor was to lose everything and to live life on tenterhooks. But an empress was a *wife*. She stood at the shoulder of the one who was honored above all.

It was not just I—my father, his lordship, expected this too. We were the Zhao, highborn Guanlong aristocrats,[3] so of course we had the right to marry into the palace.

I was thirteen the first time I met the Prince of Jin, Li Chengyin.

Among the emperor's many sons, he was singular. His birth mother had died young, so he had been adopted into the queen's court. My father, his lordship, had once privately sighed, "What a shame he isn't trueborn. There *is* a difference, at the end of the day."

The emperor had other exceptional children, after all, and the Prince of Jin was not highly beloved.

His birth mother, the Lady Shu, existed only as a furtive rumor. People often whispered about her in secret, for she had once been only a step away from queenship. The empress had borne no child and the lady was a shrewd woman—everyone who had met her in life praised her intellect, and she always knew what the emperor was thinking. It was said that once, he had given her a blank sheet of paper from which she, whether through writing or by drawing,

---

[3] A group of allied aristocrats who settled in Guanzhong (Shaanxi) and the Longxi Commandery (Gansu) who exercised great power from the Southern and Northern Dynasties into the Sui and Tang Dynasties.

reproduced the original letter he had written, sealed it, and sent it back with the envoy who had brought it to her. None could say the emperor was not pleased.

In those days, she had been like the moon. Her brilliance radiated over the whole of the inner palace, and though her light was not as fierce as that of the sun, she outshone the numberless stars she had shared a sky with.

In another few years she would surely have replaced the sitting empress.

But then she died.

No one smart lived very long in the inner courts.

Especially not the ambitious.

Sometimes, concealment was therefore the truest form of cunning, and the Prince of Jin was just so cunning a man.

He did not stand out. The emperor had no hopes for him. In a crowd of brothers, he was nothing short of ordinary.

But *I* knew that this was a true mark of his acuity.

When my father, his lordship, wavered between him and the other princes, I said that he was the one I wanted to wed.

My father, his lordship, asked if I was certain.

I nodded.

Father did not know then that I had already met the Prince of Jin.

It was not on purpose. I had gone out with my older brother to watch people shoot the willow,[4] and someone pointed him out, saying, "That one is Prince Jin," so I turned on my steed to see.

---

[4] Archery game that involves shooting at clay containers tied to willow branches.

He was riding his horse, holding his bow, beaming as he spoke to the person next to him.

I recognized his companion—it was the boy from the Pei family, A'zhao.

Pei Zhao was referred to endearingly as a boy made of jade, for he was more elegant than most, and the girls often spoke of his entanglements in our bowers.

I had not expected the prince to be his equal in looks. When they cantered abreast, they looked like two tender buds on a summer lotus, each reflecting back the other's splendor.

Then I thought, distractedly, that the emperor had such a noble mien and the Lady Shu was said to have been a great beauty. It was only natural for their son to be so becoming.

A round of drumbeats signaled his turn at the pigeons, and I stopped, wanting to see how he would do.

The Prince of Jin urged his mount forward as he drew his bow and, almost like he had not meant to do it, let loose an arrow.

It was not the best shooting I had seen, but the arrow did not stray. It hit the bottle gourd tied onto the willow branches, and it dropped to the ground with a splat so that the black-headed goldfinch within burst into flight. Behind him, onlookers cheered. The prince lifted a hand to his forehead to shade his eyes, tipping up his chin to watch the finch fly higher and higher. Bright sun hit his cheek. In its light, the sweat that slid down his face glittered like dew trickling down translucent jade.

I watched him gaze into the horizon, feeling a strange,

cavernous distance between us. Like he was a dream just out of my grasp. But he was mere yards away. I didn't like the feeling, and I was defiant of it, for in the whole of my life there had not been anything I wanted that I could not have.

Why should I have been so set upon it? Perhaps it was the sun that beat fiercely overhead, or the prideful expression that dissipated easily into indifference. I could remember the green barbarian robes he had been wearing, the shining threadwork on its collar, how he had seemed utterly radiant.

And I thought, *Him, then.*

The court historians often described Taizong's[5] sun-and-moon countenance, his dragon-and-phoenix bearing. I did not know how that should look until I saw the Prince of Jin.

So I decided to marry him.

Father hesitated, but I explained it very rationally. If the Prince of Jin was named crown prince, then I would be crown princess.

My family was of two minds. But he was already closest to the title by virtue of having been adopted by the empress—what I needed was nothing more taxing than for the people at home to nudge him onto the seat when opportunity arose.

Father still dithered. But the prince turned out to be smarter than I had given him credit for, because he did not wait for my family to act. He became crown prince all on his own, without moving a muscle.

It happened because the Prince of Wei blundered.

He never could keep a cool head. Though the emperor was

---

[5] A temple name used often, but not exclusively, to denote the second or third king of a dynasty.

still healthy and well, he could not help trying to push things along by reaching—overreaching—and attempting to eliminate his brothers. How could the emperor let a waking dog rise?

When waterbirds do battle with mollusks, it is the fisherman who benefits. And Li Chengyin benefited very soundly.

This had everyone raising their brows.

I was quietly congratulating myself for my foresight. Father had hinted at his intentions to the Prince of Jin—no, *His Highness, the crown prince*—and the prince had hinted back that he was willing to take a daughter of the Zhao for his bride.

The person who complicated things was the empress.

Because she was loath to see me be princess consort, she incited the ministers at court to give the task of quelling the western kingdoms to the crown prince, and negotiated a treaty marriage for him besides.

This I would not take sitting down, and bade someone to arrange a private rendezvous.

I trusted that he would come, and indeed, he kept the appointed hour.

It was, in truth, our first real meeting. To prevent any gossip, I veiled myself. Through the thin gauze that hid my features, I could see him standing at the railing in front of the courtyard well, smiling lightly at me.

He was beautiful when he smiled—like that day, when the sun had shone on his face, as clear as it was bright.

And suddenly I could not find the words. An apricot tree burst with blossoms in the corner of the courtyard. A black-headed goldfinch perched on its branches, pecking at its blooms. Wind chimes, which had been hung to keep pests away from the flowers, tinkled in the breeze, and the bird startled up before settling back down to resume its work.

I thought of that goldfinch from the day of the willow shooting. I wondered where it had gone, whether it was this one.

I had always been brave, and there were many things I wished to say, but seeing him now—there felt like no more need for them.

And he did understand why I had come.

He broke off a sprig of blossoms and gave it to me. "Worry not, miss."

I received it, an elegant and fragrant thing. Apricot flowers were a good omen. "I wish only for my lord's victory and early return," I said.

I had embroidered a pair of bracers for him. On this skill I had expended some small effort, and I had a reputation for it among the girls—after all, even the empress had to make personal sacrifices to silkworm and mulberry.

Stitched inside was my bower name, Sese.

The crown prince was a man of refinement and a man of perception, for the next day, he gifted me fifty liters of my namesake agate bead. I loved their green clarity and ordered them strung into a curtain. Even Father, who had seen many riches in his life, was stunned. These were more precious than pearls, a tribute gift from a faraway kingdom.

For the crown prince to have done this meant, naturally, that he viewed *me* as treasure, which pleased Father immensely.

Someone at court had a clear bone to pick with the crown prince, for they insisted that it be the Yulin Guard he took on his mission. The sons of the wealthy and influential—what did they know about waging war? But he only furrowed his brow, and with Pei Zhao at his side, led them west from Shangjing.

All that was left for me to do was to wait endlessly for news.

Their destination lay thousands of miles away. Getting there took months of travel, and as for the expedition back . . . pine as I might, all I could do was watch for wild geese at the very edge of the sky.

It was said that the ancients used to tie their letters onto the feet of those geese to send missives home.

But I could not write him any.

I had no word of whether he was well, or if he had been successful in his undertaking.

Not until Pei Zhao sent a fast horse back to the capital.

Only then did I hear that he had met with disaster. That he had lost his footing and fallen from a cliff, that they did not know if he was dead or alive.

Oddly enough, I was not worried. No one I set my sights on should be abandoned by heaven, nor should his fortune be so lacking.

What was more, he had the protection of thousands of guards; how could he have simply slipped and fallen? I had no faith in Pei Zhao's vague, shrouded words. Someone must have been scheming against him and must have been trying to take his life.

He had lived so long in the deep palace courts without yet coming to harm, so I did not believe he would fall victim to conspiracy.

And as I had expected, he made a safe return.

But he brought a woman with him. A princess of Xiliang, they said.

Each courtier made their own calculations, but the crown prince had accrued great merit in pacifying the west, so they advised the emperor not to make that foreign girl consort. Some suggested she be married to the Prince of Huainan instead. Father was exerting himself discreetly as well, for no one *really* wanted the title to be conferred onto an outsider.

I feared it would be difficult to find consensus on this matter, for the emperor's inclinations were difficult to read. Sure enough, he issued a decree ordering that the Xiliang girl be married to the crown prince and become his crown princess.

Father was extremely disappointed. "My daughter," he asked me, "should you wish still to marry him?"

With a word, someone would rid me of that girl. She was living between relay stations where there was no one around. She could not speak Plains and had no one attending her but a maid she brought who was a mute besides. Whichever the method, it would be the simplest thing in the world to dispose of her.

I hesitated, not because I cared much to preserve the Xiliang princess's life, but because I feared the emperor would feel the Zhao had overextended.

If he would not tolerate such methods from a son, he would tolerate it less from a vassal.

Forget it, I told Father. As for whether I would marry the crown prince, I would decide that after we had a chance to speak.

He had changed tremendously in the year since we had seen each other; he had not changed at all. Paler and thinner, for he had been badly injured, and though he had recovered, traces of weariness lingered on his face.

But in some subtle way, he felt even further from me now. I could not say what it was, just a sort of womanly intuition, I suppose. He treated me as dearly as ever he had, yet I had the sense that there was no *me* in his eyes—that his gaze passed right through me, that he was always looking elsewhere.

He gifted me another fifty liters of agate.

"You gave me some already," I smiled.

"These are for you to string into a rabbit and amuse yourself with," he told me.

I did not know beads could be made into such a thing. His spirits rose and he ordered someone to fetch a needle and thread, insisting on stringing one together for me to see.

He was unexpectedly attentive to these girlish crafts. The rabbit he wove was exceptionally lifelike, with black carnelian for eyes, looking like it was ready to hop about.

Knotting off the thread, he presented me a tiny, translucent bunny. "Look, it's finished," he said, smiling.

I had not heard him use such a gentle voice before, as if he were a different person entirely. My heart leapt, for he no longer seemed so distant, so alien—he was close and he was near, especially those eyes, which were fixed affectionately upon me. "Isn't it nice?" he asked. "Tomorrow I'll send you a real one and you can compare them, see if they're alike."

I placed it in front of the portiere, where candlelight could catch on both sets of beads to make them glow green, and leaned on my sleeping mat, gazing at it. In the fire, its shadow shrank into a ball, like a tiny mouse. Another flicker and the shadow lengthened, growing out the ears until it looked like a rabbit again. I thought of the way he had bent his head to string it together, so earnest, so exacting, slipping bead after bead onto the thread with care. My heart softened, and I finally determined to marry him.

For though I might be nothing more than a Noble Lady, the princess consort would be his wife in name alone.

And thus it was.

The crown prince disdained that Xiliang girl; he barely looked at her.

It was I who would coax him to make some effort, for appearance's sake, and do enough to get by. But since the crown prince truly did not like to, I let him be.

As I lived longer in the manor, I began to hear rumors of the princess doing the oddest things. She was younger than I, and childish, but more than that, she was born to savage and uncivilized lands. She spent all day on nonsense, turning herself into a laughingstock.

So the crown prince's antipathy intensified.

While my days in the Court of Spring were happy ones indeed.

For my lord respected me, he loved me, and apart from that title, I had everything.

The Xiliang girl would not be empress. Sooner or later he

would depose her, and what should have been mine by rights would be returned to me. I would be his real consort and then, someday, his queen.

Of this I was certain.

Yet the princess did not treat anyone with malice. She even, for a time, tried to befriend me.

The first time she visited my courtyard, she fell as soon as she stepped from the stairs. It had been a hard spill and an ungainly one, all arms and legs like a clumsy toddler, and I almost burst out laughing. I rushed up to help her, for she *was* the crown princess, if only nominally.

She spoke in apishly lofty tones, so I answered courteously back.

But I found her stupid, dumb as a puppy dog.

In a few sentences I had taken her measure. I knew exactly what she was: simple as a cup of water, someone you could see straight through, clear to the bottom.

Truthfully, she was not a bad sort. There had even been a period when we played cards together daily. I gave her some offhanded compliment, which was enough to make her so happy that she gaily promised me a pair of boots.

Increasingly, I humored her, for the more the crown prince detested her, the more important it was for me to seem high-minded. I was untouchable, so why should I not be more generous?

Once, she caught a glance of my beaded rabbit and said, "Ah! I've got one exactly like it, but it was made from grass seeds. When I was in Xiliang, someone . . ."

She cut herself off dazedly and stared blankly for a long

breath before admitting, shamefacedly, "I must be remembering it wrong. We don't have such clever craftsmanship in Xiliang."

I laughed it off. How was she to know that it had not been made by any mere craftsman, but by the crown prince himself?

That evening, she fell mysteriously ill. She was racked first by nightmares and then by fever. Because she had not yet acclimated to the capital, she often suffered from this affliction. When she first entered the Court of Spring, she was sick for a long time—long enough that I worried she might actually die and the emperor would shift the blame onto the Zhao, so I sent people to guard her, lest anything untoward happened.

Thankfully, she pulled through.

This time, she took ill quickly and recovered quickly too. In a few days she was hopping about as usual and came to find me for some diversion. She had found, heaven knows where, a set of utensils for eating crabs and bounded up ecstatically to show them to me.

I laughed as I watched her take the implements from her embroidered bag. "What are you doing, Your Highness?"

She looked so much like a puppy—all she was missing was a wagging tail. "I don't know how to eat crabs, and Chongjiu is coming soon. There's going to be a banquet up at the palace, and if I make a fool of myself, it will make the entire Court of Spring look bad. You have to teach me!"

This had me at a loss for words, and I had little other option than to order the kitchens to steam us a basket.

Maids brought us basins of water, and the princess and I each washed our hands, wiping the excess off on soft cloth and seating ourselves at the table.

Worried that she might feel embarrassed with all the servants watching, I sent them away.

Sure enough, when she saw how large the crabs were, she turned them about in circles, unsure where to start.

One by one I laid out the utensils and picked one up to demonstrate.

First, I snipped off the pincers and legs. "Look, lift up from here. These are the gills; they are inedible, so you must remove them." Then I used a pair of silver nippers to cut them away. Because it was such detailed work, she scooched her whole body over for a clearer look, leaning against me as her large, dark eyes took in every motion, gaze worshipful.

Patiently, I went over it all, bit by bit, until I had disassembled the whole crab.

I took the discarded shells and arranged them into the shape of a white cat.

Her eyes were bright, first on the shell-cat and then turning to me. "You're so talented!"

I demurred with a smile.

I loved cats. I used to keep quite a few, but ere I married into the Court of Spring, my family had bribed one of the crown prince's personal guards to learn his likes and dislikes, and they had found that he hated cats. I thought it was owing to the fact that the empress loved cleanliness and hated their mess that he was raised with her disinclination, so I left mine at home, and when I entered the Court of Spring, I kept a small lapdog instead.

But nice as a dog was, it was no cat.

"Li Chengyin is good at eating crabs too," the princess said. "I saw him eat one once and when he was done, he pieced the whole thing back together. But it wasn't as cute as yours."

She called the crown prince by his full name, which was tremendously rude, but I rather pitied her for it, for there was no one in the Court of Spring to teach her any manners, and because the crown prince did not like her, the servants did not respect her either. Not that this affected her at all—she spent all day gadding giddily about.

How did someone as stupid as she manage to live so long?

Perhaps all people from Xiliang were so dim-witted.

As the crown princess spoke, she took another crab from the steamer, trying to copy the way I had cracked it open. But she was so bumbling. She had just lifted the shell when she pricked herself with a silver utensil and flung her hand reflexively out. The crab flew through the air and smacked into my bosom.

It was boiling hot. I cried out in surprise. The princess was scared to her feet and, spotting a basin of water with chrysanthemum leaves soaking within, grabbed it with quick fingers and upended it over me.

It soaked me through, but the heat did dissipate.

She looked timidly at me. "Ah! It's blistering."

I looked down at my chest, which had developed a large watery blister. Chrysanthemum leaves caught in my dress, and my silk shawl dripped with water. I cut such a sorry figure.

"No matter," I said, "nothing a change of clothes cannot fix." I did not call my servants, opening the trunk myself and going inside to change.

The crown princess could not sit still and came to help me.

These robes were intricate, and without anyone to wait upon me, they were hard to don, so I did not stop her.

She worked carefully around the blister and arranged the cloth, asking, "Does it hurt?"

It did, a little, but I shook my head.

Remorsefully, she said, "I'm sorry, it's all because I'm so stupid."

A peculiar feeling came over me then. On my last birthday she had a bowl of longevity noodles sent over. I had not taken a single bite, but I did use the opportunity to raise a ruckus. His Highness believed me, of course, and gave her a great rebuke.

Seeing her, so confused and unknowing—it struck me that whether or not she was deposed, she was unlikely to live to become queen.

Because in truth, the Court of Spring was a more dangerous place than the palace.

And whichever the household, the women within were not to be made friends of.

She would have died a dozen times over if people did not fear the consequences the emperor might wreak.

But she did not seem to have noticed this at all. She

pouted, sighing, "Now Li Chengyin won't let me come spend time with you again."

He did often tell me not to fraternize.

I said, very graciously, "I shall not speak one word of this to His Highness."

For I was surrounded by the crown prince's people—I might not say, but he would still hear.

"But it's such a big blister," she said. "When Li Chengyin comes back he'll see it straightaway."

The crown prince spent most of his time with me. Yet there was no resentment in her voice, almost as though he were not her husband at all.

"Worry not," I told her.

From my vanity I plucked a papered ornament and raised it to my lips, warming the adhesive with my breath and affixing it to my breast, where it was just large enough to cover the blemish.

"See?" I smiled. "No one will notice."

The crown princess tottered away, uneasy, but with all this fuss she never did learn how to eat crab.

Toward midnight, when the maids went out to extinguish the lanterns and I was sitting alone in my room, preparing for bed, a box appeared on my windowsill.

No one was about, nor could I tell where it had come from. I picked it up and opened it. There was some kind of medicinal balm within, along with a letter, written on silk. The handwriting was crooked and ugly, like its author had just begun her schooling, and unbearable to look at.

I got this from outside. It's the best medicine for burns. I'm having A'du bring it for you to try. It was signed *Xiaofeng.*

That was the princess's bower name, though it was a strange one. I had heard this was her first word in Plains, *Xiaofeng,* like someone had once taught it to her.

Why would I use any medicine *she* sent me? I tossed it into a box beneath my dressing case.

The fact that I had been burned had made its way to the crown prince's ear—of course it had. Though I had stuck an ornament upon the wound and had sent everyone away when the princess consort and I dined on crabs in the afternoon, there was nothing in the Court of Spring, large or small, that escaped the notice of its lord. I said I had burned myself by accident, but he gave a laugh and said, "You're protecting that Xiliang woman."

I was peevish and told him that, unseemly as she was, she was at least the rightful princess consort, the wife he *ought* to be intimate with, unlike *certain* shameless trollops who knew nothing save how to bewitch their masters.

He was aware I referred to that Xu girl. It was one of his sore spots, and he was wordless to defend himself whenever I brought the topic out for a stroll.

And I was aware he treated her differently, but did not understand what he saw in her. She was no great beauty. All she seemed to do was cringe and cower, and the crown prince had kept invariably clean of improprieties his whole life. He was not in the habit of plucking flowers or sowing oats. It was once the thing I had been proudest of—that though he had a wife, he had ever been loyal to me.

How could I imagine there would come a Miss Xu? Why

should *she* of all people have won his favor? There was something in the way he looked at her, like he was at a loss, like she perplexed him.

It might be true that it had not been love, but he *was* attracted by her. Once, I saw him staring absently after her retreating figure, and in his eyes there had been a certain inexpressible devotion, a longing, like he was looking at treasure he had thought long lost.

As if this was something I could put up with. I did not quarrel with him, but I made no effort to attend my tone when she was brought up either.

I ought to have been more gracious, truly. As I would be empress someday, I should learn to be high-minded enough to tolerate all the women who were to live in the palace with me. And I was with the princess.

But Miss Xu was an annoyance I could not swallow.

I did not know why, either.

Maybe because he would not look at me like that.

The thought was a viper; every so often it would lash out to bite me.

Sometimes I thought it might be better to live as the princess consort did. She had no trouble or woe, and spent all day finding amusement for herself. She did not seem to mind how the crown prince treated her or when people were unkind, and she only cried when she missed home.

But it was too far away, and in any case, a princess consort could hardly return to her maiden home. She was not going back to Xiliang—not in life, nor even in death.

It was sad, really, if you thought about it.

And then, unexpectedly, news came that Miss Xu was with child. How could I have seen it coming? Li Chengyin had once made a solemn vow that he would never be disloyal.

In no time at all, he had tossed that to the back of his mind.

Moved by rage, I locked him out of my courtyard, refusing him entrance through my gate.

This might have been an embarrassment, but I had set my heart on teaching him a lesson.

Then the girl was sent into the palace to nurse her pregnancy. And with the empress about, I could be secure in the knowledge that her child would not be born.

So I calmed myself. A man was like a wild stallion, for you could not point a dagger at it to make it move, you had to get a bridle over its head and lead it where you wanted it to go.

The empress took advantage of the Xu girl's miscarriage to demote me and have me confined deep within the manor. And though Li Chengyin made every effort to shield me from his mother, he was prevented from seeing me.

I was not worried, for I was certain to return soon.

And sure enough, all the empress's dirty little secrets came quickly to light after the attempted assassination. The emperor even ordered an investigation into the Lady Shu's death almost twenty years ago.

Ultimately, the empress was deposed, and the shockwaves it sent out reordered the entire court. This, I knew, was the day the crown prince had waited years for.

But I very carefully concealed my glee.

Restrained, patient—this was what an heir ought to be.

Yet something shifted. I do not know when it began, but the crown prince's attitude toward the crown princess . . . changed.

Once, while passing through a corridor, I caught the two of them talking, and as they did he darted out a hand to pat her upon the head. She pouted angrily, shielding it as she disappeared like a wisp of smoke.

He smiled. His eyes were full of laughter, like he had done something so amusing. But it had just been a pat on the head.

I had arranged for some of my people to be among her retinue. They had seemed useless at first, but now that every bow looked like a snake to me, I could not resist ordering them to keep a sharper eye out for the princess's movements.

She might have been nothing more than a half-grown child, but compared to Miss Xu, she was the bigger threat.

Yet despite this, she ignored the crown prince—it was he who found every excuse to see her.

This I could suffer to pass.

She was his wife, after all, the woman who had more right than I to stand at his side, whether they had kissed in the three years they had been married or not.

Then there came a day when one of my spies crept by with a report that the princess had gone to the crown prince's court for her noontime rest, that His Highness had rushed back and dismissed everyone, including that maid the princess had brought from Xiliang.

She thought this was big news, so she had come to inform me specially.

This too I could suffer. I smiled. "What could possibly

happen? His Highness is going to scare the princess awake, that's all."

When night fell, was it not my courtyard to which he returned? He would often come by when he was free to eat supper with me. That night, I sat at my dressing table, readying myself for the evening. He had picked up a book to read, but after a time, I noticed that he had not turned a single page. I peeked at his reflection in the mirror. Very innocently, I asked, "Is something troubling you today, Your Highness?"

He looked startled and stared blankly at me. Then he smiled. "Why do you say that?"

"You have been reading that book for quite a while," I said carelessly.

He lowered his gaze to the volume and then threw it aside with a placating laugh. "I'd arranged to play cuju with the Prince of Wu tomorrow; I was thinking how best to win."

This made me unexpectedly sad.

There had been no wind today at noon; all the curtain screens hung straight to the ground. Through their heavy drape, I watched the crown prince from afar.

He had not been doing anything, just sitting at the foot of the bed. The princess consort was deep in slumber, oblivious as an infant. Then he glanced furtively around and extended a hand to gather up some of the long hair that spilled across his pillow, splitting it into several sections and wrapping the strands around the wooden poles from which the bedcurtain hung, knotting them in place with hair ribbon.

He snickered as he worked; his smile was exuberant.

He looked like a naughty little boy.

Should the princess be careless when she rose, her scalp would surely be tugged sore. This was not behavior I would have thought possible from the steady, serious crown prince, but the princess had been willful and spoiled for too long. It may be good should she suffer a little.

I was about to turn and slip away when the princess consort opened her eyes.

The first thing she saw was the crown prince, and this clearly startled her, for she gave a big yell and shot straight up.

She had used too much force. Even I was frightened she might pull out half the hair on her head. It happened all in a flash—the crown prince did not seem to have guarded against the possibility that she would wake so abruptly, for he stopped her from sitting forward, using his hands to press her back onto the bed.

Her head bumped heavily against the wooden pillow. Furious, she yelled, "Li Chengyin, what do you think you're doing!"

She was flopping about the bed like a fish and the crown prince almost lost his grip on her. In a fit of irritation, he said, "If you keep squirming around I'll kiss you."

This did scare her. In an instant, she had stopped resisting, hands pressed over her mouth and bright eyes staring wide at him. Her eyes were so dewy, like a cat's, clear enough to see your own reflection in.

The room stilled. It was only the two of them, gazing at each other. The crown prince leaned over, hands on her shoulders, while she stared unblinkingly up at him. I had ducked behind an artificial mountain and saw him in profile, so I could not discern his expression.

It was like someone had cast a charm over them, for neither moved, not for long minutes.

Worry hiked in my heart.

As I was growing uneasy, the crown prince rose wordlessly to untie her from the bedposts.

Her hair, released from its bindings, scattered like airy black clouds upon the pillow.

He turned and retreated.

For a long time she sat there and did not speak. "Who does he think he is," she finally muttered angrily, "going around and being so mean all day?"

She rose and tidied her clothing, moving to sit at the mirror and comb out her hair.

It was all tangled and mussed and extremely hard to straighten back out, but as she brushed and brushed, she stopped, resting a cheek in her hand and staring vacantly into her own reflection. I could not tell what she was thinking.

I crept away.

Because I was afraid of being seen, I took the narrow alleys, circumventing the main hall to return to my own quarters. I had just squeezed through the tiny side door when I saw the crown prince standing alone by a covered bridge. I could not tell what he was thinking, either. He just stood there, looking up at the sky.

I followed his gaze, but there was nothing there. A few wispy, white clouds.

He looked at the heavens and I looked at him. He did not move, and neither did I.

I thought of the princess, staring blankly into the mirror, and the thing that entered into my heart had no name I was willing to give.

It felt worse than if he had killed me.

And I regretted my initial disregard of the princess, for it turned out that she was the true malady.

Very calmly, very carefully, I tucked this thought away.

Until the princess consort was abducted, and my chance came.

I hoped she would die out there, wanted her never to return to the Court of Spring.

Father sent out his most trusted errants and valiants. The moment they found the opportunity, they would kill her outside the manor to end this once and for all.

In any case, her chances of survival were already slim.

I thought, *That stupid, annoying woman will not appear before me again.*

On Shangyuan night, for the very first time, the crown prince had me accompany him to Chengtian Gate to enjoy the lanterns and celebrate with the people.

It startled me, but it pleased me too.

This should have been the sole privilege of the princess consort.

Though the crown prince shewed me much favor, he had not brought me here—the royal family's reputation had to be protected, and rules had to be followed.

But he had not brought her to Chengtian Gate either.

I was so excited.

I readied myself early and waited all day for him.

The princess's abduction was a great secret, though the crown prince did not seem much worried by it. It was instead the emperor who begged off, for he had caught cold and could not attend, and he gave the crown prince special use of his carriage and retinue for the evening. People would not be able to tell the difference. All they could see was the magnificent convoy swaying to and fro, and they shouted out, "long live."

I disembarked at the foot of Chengtian Gate. The crown prince had already arrived, and one of his attendants stepped forward to greet me with a careful lantern to light the path underfoot. I climbed, step after step, upward. Though I wore the ceremonial blue robes of a Noble Lady, my heart could not help skipping a beat. Because the crown prince had used the emperor's carriage, the tower was flooded with the imperial troops of the city guard.

He stood by himself, cutting a lonely figure as he surveyed the sea of lanterns, his face inscrutable.

He was often like this of late, so much so that the man I had shared a pillow with for three years, whom I ought to have been closest to, felt like he was moving further and further from me.

An attendant stood to one side, a gold platter in his hands. Folded upon it was an overcoat, which I took in hand, and with it I walked to the front of the gate. The light cast my silhouette onto the curtains—my swaying ornaments, my golden hairpins, my elaborately coiffed hair, my face like a flower. I circled behind and draped it upon him.

He turned his head and looked at me, but said nothing.

The streets below us were laid out like a chessboard. The easterly night wind[6] opened the flowers on a thousand trees, blowing down a rain of stars.[7] I heard the noisy sounds of percussion—a troupe of dragon dancers performed in the distance, spewing forth billows of fire. Lanterns hung from the top of every tree, like ten thousand celestial bodies had fallen to earth and sunk to this mortal realm.

Basket upon basket of gold was brought to the front of the tower gate. Maids and attendants grabbed handfuls of coin and scattered them downward, where people jostled over them. Thinking that their emperor was above, they shouted out their worship and prostrated themselves on their knees.

I thought that, though this was the first, in the coming years there would be many nights like tonight, where I would accompany him above all this splendor to survey this dreamlike city, this beautiful land.

Everything beneath heaven was his, and I would be the one at his side.

The crown prince paused there, then said, "I'm going to the palace to see my lord father. Stay here and look after things, won't you?"

"Worry not," I told him.

There was no real ceremony to this. It was nothing more than waving through the curtain and occasionally having the servants empty some baskets of money to add some merriment to the flourish and bustle.

The prince and his people left, taking a portion of the

---

6 the spring wind
7 From "To the Tune of *The Green Jade Bowl*: Lantern Festival" by Xin Qiji.

Jinwu soldiers with them. In moments the tower gate had emptied by half.

I had a maid go fetch some coins.

Things became quiet once he departed—too quiet. From faraway, the sound of the crowds still reached me. From nearby, hundreds of citizens still cheered. Gold was still being scattered from atop the tower gate, the sound of it clanging like the pelting of rain.

But how much loneliness lay in all this sound.

I suddenly wanted for a draught to drink.

A'wu ordered an attendant to bring me a crystal cup. He carried a pot of grape wine and filled it to the brim. I took a sip but, remembering that it was a tribute gift from the western kingdoms, lost interest.

I was giving instructions to switch it out for a native wine instead when we heard a maid's shrill shriek. I turned to see. I did not know when it happened—someone might have spilled some lamp oil—but a fire had begun to rage. It spread along the curtain, and in seconds the whole thing was alight.

I managed to remain calm. I ordered one person to alert the Jinwu soldiers and told another to send a fast horse back to the palace to report this, but in the space of a few words the fire burned higher. No amount of water seemed able to quench it. Everything turned to flames.

A'wu supported me, meaning to hurry us down, but the stairs were choked with fumes so dense and heavy it stung the eye. Someone beside me was so frightened he burst into tears—a little eunuch, just old enough to tie up his hair.

"What are you panicking for?" I snapped. But no sooner

had my words landed than did a surge of roiling fire flare up, blocking our egress.

Smoke thickened into a black dragon that ambushed us from all sides. Fire broke out everywhere we looked, and there was no escape. People screamed, running about. I could not have dreamed that anything could change so drastically, so quickly, and I could do nothing but watch as the flames rose. As I hesitated, someone grabbed me. I was about to scream when I felt a lightness—I had been lifted off my feet. He had me in one arm and A'wu in the other, and he pulled us from the tower, out of the conflagration.

I do not know how we got through the thick smoke or the fierce flames. I only felt the scorching heat singeing my fringe as I tried my hardest to hold my breath, using a bundled shawl to cover my nose and mouth. Nor do I know how long it was until I realized I was at the foot of the tower, and that the entirety of Chengtian Gate was aflame.

I was set back down, in shock, while the person who had rescued me said, apprehensively, "Miss."

Chengtian Gate had become an inferno. Its savage flame illuminated half the sky, and by that borrowed light I recognized that my savior was an attendant that Father had arranged at my side. I remembered that his family was Lu, and that he was the second born, so everyone called him Erlang. He was not one who liked to talk.

A stream of people flowed without end from Chengtian Gate. Attendants and maids ran from the blaze, their faces blackened by smoke. A few wept upon seeing me, especially those who served in my court. Distraught, they clung tightly to A'wu and me like a flock of frightened birds.

Thunder sounded behind me. The streets devolved into chaos. Every year during lantern season, the capital made preparations for such a disaster, and there were water pumps in every neighborhood, but this fire was so strong, so intense, that the tower gate might have been beyond saving.

Orders came quickly from the imperial city that the Longwu General was to take personal command of his troops to contain the situation—half to close the city gates, and the other half to fight the fire and rescue those inside.

The curfews would soon be reinstated, and I was sent back to the Court of Spring.

Though it was all somewhat mortifying, at the very least I had not come to harm, so as I sat in the carriage, I quickly calmed.

Lu Erlang, on the other hand, murmured something to A'wu through the carriage window and she in turn whispered to me that I ought to be careful, for there was something not quite right about the way the fire had started.

I nodded.

Now that I had regained my senses, I also felt it odd. It had come too quickly and too fiercely—but it was Chengtian Gate. Who would dare set such a blaze beneath the gaze of the emperor himself?

It was tantamount to treason.

At first I thought the fire had been targeting the crown prince, for though not *many* people knew the emperor had taken ill, it was more than *none*. Everyone in the imperial city would have known the emperor did not leave that night, as everyone would have known it was the crown prince who had been there on his behalf.

My heart tightened when I thought of him. Thank the heavens he left when he did, or else . . . or else what a terror it would have been.

Much, much later, when I thought back on this night, I would feel that I had been stupid, and utterly ridiculous.

Who else had the wherewithal to set fire to Chengtian Gate? Who else could move the Longwu General so quickly, could order the gates closed? There was only one person capable.

He had done such a thing, with His Majesty's tacit approval, all to rescue the princess.

And me . . . I would ultimately understand that he had meant to burn me atop the tower gate too. Why else should it have started right in front of me?

But it was not until I saw the cat that I realized he was so cruel a person.

It was a cat General Pei had given the princess consort.

She had been ill for a long time after she returned to the Court of Spring, and he had brought it into the manor—specially to please her, perhaps. She named it Xiaoxue and doted upon it all the time.

But for all I loved cats, I would not have liked this one, for it was *hers*.

I had not considered there might be someone who hated it more than I.

Xiaoxue died, drowned in the pond.

The princess was heartbroken.

She had lost so much weight from her illness, but after that, she looked ever more like a candle flickering in the wind, like the whole of her might scatter in the next breeze.

The crown prince went searching for another cat that looked exactly like Xiaoxue; I did not know from where. I stood in the narrow alley, watching him cradle it carefully in both hands like he was cradling a treasure, watching as he walked to her courtyard before changing his mind and ordering someone else to bring it in while he waited at her door.

And I remembered when, a long time ago, he stood beside the covered bridge, lost in thought.

In truth, I had known then he was thinking of her.

To yearn for, to gaze at, but never love to conjugate[8]—it was because he loved that he would stand there, so silent, so alone.

And I—I was nothing more than a joke.

So when things did begin to happen, I was not shocked.

I knew there would come such a day, and that he must have been long in planning it, for the crown prince was someone who must consider a hundred steps ere he committed to one. For all my little smarts, I was not his match.

It was annihilation.

I knelt there, listening to myself say, "Do you suspect *me*?"

What a farce it was, performed so laughably.

Poor, loyal Lu Erlang, killed on a busy street—silenced.

My father, his lordship, was led to panic. He expended

---

[8] From "To the Tune of *Spring in a Painted Hall*" by Nalan Xingde, referencing "Free Verses Upon Missing a Friend on a Cold Night" by Wang Bo.

the effort of bulls and tigers in making contact with me. He deluded himself thinking that it was still possible to kill the princess consort, but I told him, coldly, "As for those things that would displease the prince, my lord had better not try them again."

For the crown prince had grown more and more like the emperor. Neither reacted, but both saw everything.

He was the man who would someday be king, after all—how could he not resemble his lord father?

But Father could not resign himself to this loss. He made one final bid to keep us in play, but he miscalculated, and so the whole game was lost.

I was expelled from the Court of Spring and kept in secluded confinement.

It was all too easy to imagine what happened at home.

For the great crime of treason, Father had been executed. All the men over twelve years of age were put to death, while those under were sent into exile thousands of miles away. And the women . . . well. Under an upturned nest there is seldom an egg intact.

It began to rain at last.

I caught it with my fan. When water splattered onto its white silken face, it blotched as if with tearstains.

"Do not fret, miss," A'wu said. "His Highness may only be angry for a time. We have his lordship's efforts to rely on, and it won't come to such a bad state that they can push you around. Sometimes in life we meet with misfortune, but it could turn into a blessing in disguise."

I was too lazy to dignify this with a reply.

A'wu had no idea what things were like outside. She didn't know that there was nothing, no one, to rely on anymore.

What blessings were left to disguise? The best days of my life were behind me.

At least there was not much time left in that life, and its remaining days would not be so difficult to bear.

Rain fell harder. Scattered drops blew beneath the eaves and onto my collar, soaking my clothes so they stuck to my skin.

I looked down at the red mark on my chest, the scar from the day I'd eaten crabs with the princess. When the blister healed, it left behind a red splotch, like a petal.

What had I been thinking then? That the princess consort was so pitiable.

But I was the more pitiful one, in the end.

The rain grew louder and louder, pitter-pattering on the banana leaves. I sat at the window, watching the sky dim.

Night fell.

Li Chengyin followed. I'd thought that I would not see him again.

But he came, bringing with him the cool draft of the storm.

I stared a little sadly at him.

His face was easy as he sat. "I heard you wanted to see me."

I said, "Thank you, Your Highness."

My words were what they were, but I couldn't be bothered to make the effort of curtsying. All that etiquette, all those hierarchies—what care had I for them now?

A'wu looked to me, uneasy. I waved her away.

She kept glancing back, apprehensive, but I hardened my heart and refused to return her gaze. I smiled fixedly at Li Chengyin. A'wu may have thought his arrival was a stroke of luck, that I would have the opportunity to beg for forgiveness and return to the Court of Spring.

Oh, the Court of Spring. It was such a strange and distant place.

Servants came to light the candles. In no time at all they'd all been kindled. I'd been held in confinement for so long; this place had never seemed so bright.

Under the glow of the lamps, Li Chengyin's face was pure and luminous.

I thought of his birth mother, the Lady Shu, a girl who had been a radiant moon deep in the imperial city—what had she been thinking, prior to her death? Did she think of the gurgling infant who hadn't yet been fed, or all the kingly favor she had endured, the jealousy of the six inner courts?

Or that terrible secret, the one that had cost her her life?

Attendants set the table, and it was like any of the countless nights we'd spent together, he and I sitting face-to-face, dining together.

Tonight, they'd brought all my favorite dishes.

Good of him to remember.

I raised my chopsticks, picked at my food, and then put them down again.

"Won't you eat some more?" he asked.

I shook my head.

The attendants retreated, leaving us behind in the candlelight.

Our shadows intertwined, as intimate as they'd once been.

During that time, many, many days ago, he would read at dinner while I curled into his side, watching the night deepen and the moon rise beyond the window. It would shine softly upon the two of us, and I would lie quietly upon his knee. It was always quiet then.

When spring came and the apricots blossomed, he would snap a sprig and slip it into my hair. In the summer, I would use a lotus leaf to cover his face, and he would push it laughingly aside and turn it into incense for me. Autumn brought chrysanthemum viewings and crabs, and when it snowed in the winter, we'd lean against the brazier and listen to the rustle of falling flakes.

I had believed wholeheartedly that he was my beloved, in heaven as on earth, who would not break faith with me, who would not forget me, who would love me in this and every life.

What delusion was this! What madness?

It was like I had woken from a long dream and found myself bereft.

I gave an abrupt laugh. "I fear it's only the matter of the Lady Shu's death that could move Your Highness into agreeing to meet. Am I right?"

After all, I knew a little of what the Zhao had done.

Placidly, he said, "That's not important anymore."

Yes, that's true. *Not important anymore.* He'd had his vengeance. No matter what the deposed empress had done, no matter what the Zhao had done, none of it was *important anymore.*

That old matter had been a convenient excuse, that's all. What he wanted was to kill those he needed to kill and eliminate those he needed to eliminate in order to sit steady in his position and someday hold all beneath heaven in his palm.

"Your Highness is a decisive person indeed," I said. "I would have thought you'd have long since severed yourself from emotion. If I hadn't seen you hold that cat underwater with my own eyes, I couldn't have imagined you capable of anything so straightforward as hatred."

He was unmoved. What did it matter that he was the one who drowned Xiaoxue? The princess consort would never find out.

Though I knew, I wouldn't tell it to her.

Let the stupid lass live in her stupidity.

I said, "Did Your Highness think that killing the cat would stop her from liking General Pei? Love is not something that the loss of a thing or two can change."

The crown prince remained silent.

I smiled, vanquished at last.

"Your Highness fed me three years of abortifacients to keep me from child. Could it be that even you, so aloof, so coldhearted, could love someone as warm and spirited as the princess?"

Once, I'd thought that his reason for having me dosed was to shield me from the empress, to spare my feelings if he could not protect a fetus to term.

But that was wishful thinking.

He kept his peace. For all that I brought up the princess,

he was not inclined to so much as look at me.

And whatever the things I wanted to say, there was no use for words anymore.

"Is there wine?"

There was a pot on the table, but I insisted on asking anyway.

For a breath, he did not answer. Then he raised his hands and gave a sharp clap.

The crown prince did not like having people around. Every time he came to visit, he would order the servants away, and it had made me so giddy then, for it was the two of us together, and it was lovely.

Sometimes in the middle of the night, I would grow thirsty and want for a cup of water. He would clap just so for the attendants waiting in the courtyard to hear and come hurrying over for orders.

How silly that I should think of these trivial things at a time like this.

The sound traveled far in the darkness. Rainwater whispered beyond the curtains. But this was a summer rain—why should it be so lingering, so melancholy, soft and murmuring like an autumn drizzle?

Distant footsteps drew closer.

Someone brought us a lacquered tray, atop which sat wine in a celadon bottle, wafting a pleasant fragrance. The attendant put it politely onto the table before bowing and taking his leave. The man did not look once at me.

I poured myself a cup.

My fingers trembled slightly, but thankfully it did not spill.

I peered into the vessel—good liquor, amber in color. *Lanling fine wine like tulip smells, jade cups flowing over with amber light.*[9] I raised the shallow cup and drained it without hesitation.

It burned going down.

Once, when I'd just entered the Court of Spring, the crown prince had me temporarily accommodated at Congyu Tower, which was not far from his courtyard and suited me immensely.

It had originally been a place for people to gather and admire the rain. In summer a canal would be built and a wheel installed nearby so that, on the hottest days, water could be taken up from the canal and poured onto the roof tiles, bringing a refreshing coolness as it cascaded down.

What I liked most, though, were the tiles that covered the tower. Every shingle was carved with mandarin ducks, ever in pairs, swimming side by side. Washed clean by the constant trickle brought by the water wheel until not a speck of dust remained, they resembled black jade, each slate clear and distinct.

What had I been thinking then?

That my love was the moon in the sky, and I a flower in the water.[10]

We reflected each other, like shadows, forever intertwined.

But the reality was that the frost was heavy on the paired

---
9 From "In a Foreign Land" by Li Bai.
10 From the song "Step Song," words by Wang Jian.

roof tiles, and the emerald quilt cold without someone to share.[11]

Poison from the zhen bird's feather took hold, and though my eyes looked, they could no longer make out the shape of him. Blearily, I recognized that he had risen, that he had turned, that he had left me.

I would not see him again.

This separation had come so painfully, so slowly.

I leaned against the table as blood poured from my nose and mouth, and the death that was so close at hand no longer upset me. Instead, it was a release.

There were three things I'd wanted to say to the crown prince.

The first: that I knew it was he who killed the cat and used it as a pretext to force mine and my family's hands, expelling me from the Court of Spring.

The second: that I knew he had dosed me for three years in order to keep me from conceiving, which was why I had been riled into misstep by the matter of Miss Xu. That despite everything, I could not but love him as I'd done so very, very long ago.

As for the last . . . it would remain unsaid.

So be it.

Blood gushed faster, soiling my clothes. My vision darkened until I could see nothing at all and I lost control, crumpling into the table and overturning the food.

I thought of the princess consort.

---

[11] Paraphrased from "Song of Everlasting Regret" by Bai Juyi.

Had she ever learned to eat crab?

Why should I have thought of her? Perhaps it was because when she'd heard of the Lady Xu's death, she'd mourned for a long time. Would she mourn me?

In the whole of the Court of Spring, she might be the one person who would.

Rain roared outside, but in my ears it grew softer and softer until the world, at last, quieted.

月照离亭花似雪
The Moon like Snow upon Pavilion Flowers[1]

It was only the ninth month, but there had been several bouts of snow, falling thick and without interruption in the evening, and again in fits and starts through the night.

A fire had been lit in the tent, so it was warm within.

I lifted the tent flap to find that the princess had disappeared.

The cow's milk in her bowl had been left untouched. I brushed it with a hand: still warm, so she could not have gone far.

The junior field officer in charge of guarding her worried. "Should we order the camp searched?"

I shook my head and replied, "Fret not."

I walked alone from the campgrounds and discovered her in a sheltered area on the backside of the mountain. She was skulking about and shoving beef jerky into the hands of someone wrapped in a lamb's pelt, whose scattered, overgrown hair made them look savage.

They unsheathed their weapon as I neared.

It was a gleaming gold-inlay dagger, a fierce blade wielded by the wasp-women of Jieshuo. Such a thing was rare even

---

1 From "To the Tune of *Springtime in the Jade Pavilion*" by Cai Shen.

among the western kingdoms, for it was bequeathed upon the maids most trusted by the chanyu who, once they'd been hand selected from infancy for the role, had their tongues cut out so they could not reveal their secrets. The wasp-women were brought up under the royal tent, trusted deeply by their sovereign, and raised in luxury for the sole purpose of training daily in the art of assassination. They were able to disappear into the night and kill without revealing themselves. The aristocrats of Jieshuo were said to be most terrified of these golden daggers, for if any dared shew disloyalty to their lord, their heads would be quietly removed from their necks in the darkest hours of evening.

I stopped, raising the wooden bowl in my hands to demonstrate that it was cow's milk I carried. Slowly, the wasp-woman put away her blade. I set the bowl on the ground before retreating back, and the princess gave me a careful glance, creeping over to carry the milk away.

The wasp-woman ate quickly, like she hadn't been full in a long time, polishing off the last drop of milk in mere moments.

I was about to leave when the princess called after me. Her Plains was not very good, but she said, stutteringly, "Tha . . . nk you, General."

I did not turn, just stopped a minute to say, "There is no need to stand on courtesy, princess."

I hadn't really expected her to not stand on courtesy, but the next day I saw the wasp-woman again, this time in the princess's tent. She had washed herself clean, shaved away the hair that had been so matted it resembled lambswool, and was now dressed in the rough-spun clothes of a servant. She looked young, like a child who had not yet tied up their hair.

The princess looked embarrassed and explained in her halting speech, "A'du . . . she . . . doesn't want to . . . leave me . . . behind."

I looked around at the Plains handmaidens who had been sent by the Anxi Protectorate to serve the princess. They knelt, shaking, too frightened to rise. I said, "The army cannot take in persons of unknown origin, much less a foreigner. Princess, please do not put me in so difficult a position."

She looked at me with her reflective, crow-dark eyes and managed a rare sentence. "But I am a foreigner too."

I did not bat an eye. "Your Highness is a daughter of the king of Xiliang, a treaty princess escorted by the crown prince himself. You are not of unknown origin."

Little by little, the princess hung her head. It was flurrying again, large flakes rustling against the fabric of the tent.

We journeyed south for days against it, but the wasp-woman did not give up. She trailed after the army, neither too close behind nor too far away, making little effort to conceal her tracks.

One of my aides could not resist the question: "General, ought we to kill her?"

I wavered.

Because the princess had fallen ill.

Since I'd sent the wasp-woman away, the princess had been ill.

It was a serious illness, with a high fever that would not

break, and every day she lay dozing in her carriage. Life in a military convoy was difficult, and with no outstanding physicians among the troops I had begun to worry she might not recover.

One night as we made camp, a handmaiden came to me in a panic, saying that the princess would not wake, that she feared the worst. Her fever had raged for days, but she had been conscious. My first thought was to rush to the tent to see for myself, but on further consideration, I decided to visit the prince instead. He had grown stronger and more alert by the day, and when I arrived, he was practicing his swordplay. The sword was his favored weapon, though he did not reveal this to others. He was in good spirits, his longsword dancing like a dragon startled into flight, its flashes of white light enveloping his body. Then it flared and darted forward, piercing toward me.

I was not stirred.

The edge of the sword passed my ear with a rush of frosty air. The tip of the blade cut through a tieback that had been holding the tent flaps closed. Gusts of snow surged in, a confusion of flakes that landed on my clothes.

I didn't move to dust them off. It was warm in the tent, and they would melt soon into tiny rivulets and disappear.

The crown prince drew back with a smile. "A'zhao, you've come at exactly the right time. It's snowing again, so I've told them to roast some lamb, and tonight, we will drink to keep the cold away."

I said, "The princess is very sick. Will Your Highness not see her?"

His smile disappeared as quickly as it had come. "That ugly thing? Why should I?"

"If Your Highness is dissatisfied with this union, then it may be better to settle things now instead of returning to the capital with this hot potato binding our hands and feet."

The crown prince's eyes flashed, fixed upon me. "And how do you propose to settle it?"

"She has been weak," I said, "and ill. It would be no great matter for her to have perished on the journey. We can go back to the king of Xiliang and request another daughter. If he has none suitable, we can find a match from Qiuci or some such—a princess from any of the western kingdoms would resolve the matter."

For a while, he was silent. Then he shook his head. "You've finally brought the Yulin Guards under your authority, but that's no guarantee His Majesty doesn't still have eyes among them. If we killed the princess, my lord father would be unhappy."

"That's nothing for you to worry about, Your Highness. The princess has been sick this entire journey—everyone in the Yulin Guard knows this. No one would suspect you."

When he heard me say this, the crown prince fell silent again. He sighed. "Never mind," he said. "That barbarian girl may be detestable, but it wasn't her idea to marry me. Neither of us had a choice in the matter, so why take her life for it?"

"If you are of such a mind," I said, "why don't you go and sit with her? She is alone in the world, Your Highness, and for the rest of her life she will be tied to you. If you can't harden your heart to kill her, then why not play along?"

The crown prince considered this, convinced at last.

I walked with him to the princess's camp. She was burning up, unconscious. Her handmaidens hovered, trembling, by her sickbed, and upon seeing our arrival dropped hurriedly into their courtesies.

He waved them distractedly off. The maids retreated hastily and I was about to follow them when he called out to me.

"A'zhao, don't go." Then, complaining, "What are you thinking, leaving me alone with an invalid?"

So I had no choice but to return to his side.

The princess was in a very bad way, her mouth so burned that white skin flaked from her lips. A bowl of temperate lamb's milk had been placed on a small side table, but though her maids tried again and again, they could not get so much as half a spoonful down, and without a drop of water passing her lips, it seemed the end might be near.

She'd started to babble feverishly. I knew a few of the western languages, but could only discern that she was speaking Xiliang, though what she said I could not hear.

The crown prince hardly had the patience to look after an invalid. He did nothing more than sit a while until he rose, preparing to go.

There wasn't much I could say to stop him, so I lifted the tent flap for him to step through. The princess continued to natter. She gave a sudden, bleary shout. "Gu Xiaowu—!"

I panicked, whirling around to face her, but she lay there, still in a haze of sleep.

Those words seemed to hold some strange power, for the crown prince missed a step, staggering, and he turned too.

487

She called out again, softer this time, but the words were very discernably Plains—Gu Xiaowu.

The expression that crossed the crown prince's face was illegible to me. He covered his heart with a hand, looking like he'd had some revelation, which sent my own to stutter as a thousand possibilities flashed through my mind.

If he were to remember, how could I put this to rights?

He walked from the tent, half hunched, while I followed silently behind. The snow had stopped falling, and a crescent of cold moon shone down on the great desert wastes. Rows of army tents sprawled out endlessly. It was time for the changing of the watch. We could hear the guards' distant calls.

He dropped his hand, saying, "I must have strained a muscle earlier when I was training. It felt like I'd been stabbed. My whole chest was aching."

"Shall I order a physician to come take a look?" I asked.

He shook his head. "No matter." And then, abruptly, "I hadn't expected the princess of Xiliang would have a Plains lover she cared for so."

It wasn't for me to say anything.

He sighed again. "Poor girl."

I escorted the prince back to his tent, but could not settle my worries and doubled back to see the princess. Upon my arrival I discovered two handmaidens collapsed on the ground, having clearly been knocked out. My heart sank. I slipped my sword silently from its scabbard, stepping farther in.

Beneath the dancing oil lamps, the wasp-woman cradled the princess, feeding her lamb's milk by the spoonful. The princess could not swallow; with every spoonful more than half seeped from her mouth, but the wasp-woman was fastidious, using a silver spoon to gently pry her lips apart, ladling the milk into her mouth with another, then using a cloth to wipe away the spilled portion, and waiting a breath to continue.

She was more vigilant than most. I had not drawn close, but she seemed to sense something and whipped her dagger out, leaping to her feet. I dropped the tip of my sword. Seeing that it was I, she lowered her blade as well.

I stayed almost an hour, watching her feed the princess. Finally, the lamb's milk was depleted, and though the princess hadn't woken, she breathed more easily than she had. The wasp-woman looked pleased at this and dug a handful of medicinal herbs from her lapels, chewing them up in her own mouth to administer it, bit by bit, to the princess. In all this to-do, another hour passed.

The moon had by then risen to its zenith. I stood on a gentle slope and watched as the wasp-woman crept from the tent. Before I had the chance to approach her, she drew her weapon again.

I blocked it with my sword, and we skirmished many passes beneath the watching moon, its radiance coaxing forth the sparks that burst from our clashing blades.

At long last I halted my sword, for I wasn't able to kill this wasp-woman.

She stopped too, watching me warily.

"You can stay," I told her, "but from this day forward you

must treat the princess as your master and keep your tongue to yourself. Do not tell her anything about Jieshuo, and especially not anything about what happened between the two of them. Should you reveal anything, I will take your life first, then the princess's."

Cool light illuminated her face. She gave me a wan smile, and I remembered then that she had no tongue to loose or to keep.

Of course she would not reveal anything.

She saw that I understood, but nodded anyway.

People from Jieshuo honored their promises, and the wasp-women were especially loyal. If she had agreed the princess would be her mistress, she would not betray her.

I didn't know where she found medicine, but under her watchful care, the princess's illness abated. She gradually recovered consciousness and could recognize the people around her again.

She was so grateful I'd let the wasp-woman stay. When she recovered the strength to leave her bed again, she came to thank me specially.

"It was His Highness who commanded me to look after you," I said. "If you're looking for someone to thank, Princess, you'd better thank him."

She took my courteous words for serious ones and did go to offer gratitude, but he shut his doors and refused her entrance.

He only seemed to detest her more.

"A barbarian girl from Xiliang," he said. "Someone so ugly, and yet she already has a lover. A'zhao . . ."

I didn't know where this was going, so I smiled, waiting for him to continue.

He was unable to get the words out. "Anyway, I have Miss Zhao."

The twelfth young miss of the family Zhao was another private worry of mine, but in the here and now I said, mildly, "The Xiliang princess is young, and she may not understand a good deal about love and affection. There's no need to be troubled by that matter, Your Highness."

But the crown prince did not look like he cared very much.

To everyone else, anyway, this princess was nothing more than a pretense.

When she was officially conferred the title of princess consort, the twelfth miss of the family Zhao was also brought into the Court of Spring and made a Noble Lady.

Spring passed, autumn came, and the days slipped by, one after another.

The crown prince was cool toward his consort, and it could not be said he treated her with great fondness, for occasionally, they would fight about the Lady Zhao.

And because there was discord in the crown prince's court, the empress found endless excuses to stick her hand into the crown prince's affairs.

This, the crown prince knew well, but the Court of Spring leaked like a sieve. His previous life with the princess was something that no one left on earth had knowledge of, for he—and she—had wiped it clean from their memory. I alone fretted.

Fortunately, he had bigger things to worry about, and she was a carefree sort. In a place as solemn and forbidding as this, she spent every day frolicking with the flowers and feeding the fish, living just as she liked.

The River Oblivion washed everything away.

This, too, could be good.

She was as childish as ever. Sometimes when she saw me, she would call me with a smile, saying, "General Pei!"

And abruptly I would be reminded of that time long, long ago.

After they'd leapt into the River Oblivion, I rushed my troops from the mountains, detouring dozens of miles to find an entrance to the valley, holding fast to the hope of maybe, possibly, finding them.

The army spent days searching that deep and narrow gorge.

Cliffs soared above us, stacked with precipitous outcroppings of rock. When the rains came, they came like white water, drenching us in dust and silt—and after, raindrops turned into flakes of snow.

They fell in thick flurries, drifting to the ground.

A horse lost its footing and slipped. Men rushed forward, pulling desperately at its bridle to haul it back onto solid ground, but though the bridle dug so deeply into the horse's nose it drew blood, their strength failed them. The reins slipped from their grasp. The warhorse gave a shrill cry as it plummeted into vicious currents. Torrential green waves churned in surges, swallowing the beast quickly, until there was nothing left of it but a swirl of white foam.

"What kind of hell is this place?" someone murmured.

It was no strange thing for snow to come so early in these

parts, but this gorge was pressed between two massive peaks such that we could only see a sliver of the heavens when the weather was clear. The first few days after we'd entered, windblown sand had blotted out the sun. Following that, it stormed.

There was no road through. We were forced to tread carefully, arduously upstream along the banks of the surging river that had carved out this valley—a valley in name, though it was a precipice in truth, for above us the rocks fell without pause and below us were the rushing rapids, with waters so fierce and fast that anything that tumbled in was beyond rescue.

The camps we made could be pitched only on the mountain slopes. Any wrong turn could send you plummeting into the river. One night, we were met with a landslide—the craggy cliffs came crumbling down, burying hundreds in mere seconds. After that, we slept in shifts, wrapped in our blankets and pressed against the cliff face, ready to run at any sign of disturbance.

Man and beast grew weary, and in the course of the long journey, some of the transport horses fell into the water.

Our food was almost entirely depleted.

Not since becoming a commander had I been in such dire straits.

The junior field officer who walked in front of my horse could stand it no longer. He grabbed my reins. "General Pei, if we keep going, none of us will make it out alive."

I did not respond, just raised my voice in encouragement. "Once we find a more open area, we shall light a fire and eat!"

The snow came down thicker. Few had the energy to hum an assent.

Morale had dipped so far that it could go no lower. These Yulin Guards were the sons of wellborn Shangjing clans. Many had come west under the belief that meritorious service would be easy to earn, and had left home as excitedly as if they'd been departing on a hunt.

Their participation in previous battles had been under the auspices of the standing army of the Anxi Protectorate. All they'd done was stand, scattered along the back of the battalion, and once the enemy line broke at the tail of the fighting, they would go charging aimlessly forward and tell themselves that this was tantamount to whetting their blades with blood.

Only when they walked into this desolate gorge did they know what true loss looked like.

But I could not retreat.

For we had not found the crown prince.

He was the lord I'd served since youth, and someday, he would be master of all beneath heaven. From the time I was six I knew that, even if it came at the cost of my own life, I would keep him safe.

The green waves stopped churning. In the near distance, we could see a slope where the land was flatter. I brought my horse to a halt and had my orders disseminated: the army would rest on the slope for the rest of the day and through the night, and we would take lunch there too.

Wind and snow filled the sky; the men were too miserable to respond.

I dismounted and stood in front of that gentle slope,

watching the last stragglers pass. This time, we set up scouts to watch for rockfall.

Campfires rose and men huddled around them, shivering.

Of the rations we'd brought, only hardened flatbread remained.

Many of the horses had injured their hooves, and where they stepped, they left blossoms of red seeping into the white, like ill-boding flowers.

I hardened my heart. Removing the rations from their backs, I ordered the injured horses slain. Soon, the savory scent of grilled meat drifted through the air. After days of cold and hunger, the men's stomachs rumbled loudly.

I looked at the thousand or more men who remained. Of the three thousand Yulin Guard we'd brought, more than half had lost their lives. And yet—the crown prince was still missing. If we kept pushing, we would be beset by peril. If we retreated, it was possible we would lose more men before we made it out anyway.

There was no room for advancement, no room for retreat.

And above us, snow kept falling.

Once the meat had finished grilling, every man received a portion. I accepted some as well, and had just taken a zealous bite when we heard scouts screaming. "Rockfall! Rockfall!"

Alarm ripped through me. Rockfall was often accompanied by landslide. Everyone leapt up at once, and I yelled, "Flatten yourselves against the rock face! Find higher ground!"

We ducked between the plummeting stones, but my heart sank when I heard a dull rumbling from the high crags overhead. I'd heard that sound during that frightful night when the mountain collapsed upon us. The rocks came, denser and denser. Some of my men were hit, falling into the turbulent water. Others, faces bloodied, crawled across the earth, sobbing in despair. More dodged the debris, shielding their heads as they tried to get to higher ground.

And then I noticed, not far in the distance, a wide beam of stone jutting forward into the air like an eave. If there really was a landslide, it might collapse too and crush everyone beneath it into mincemeat. But as rubble kept raining down, there was no room for hesitation.

"The overhang!" I bellowed. "Under the overhang!"

I ducked one stone and pushed an officer away from another. The men had all seen the massive slab that spanned the air and were now climbing toward it.

I hauled an injured soldier up with one hand and yanked a junior officer, who had almost lost his footing, up with the other. Each man pulled his fellows onward until, though I don't know how long it took, we all ducked beneath the beam.

Rubble fell like rain. We pressed silently against the rock face, watching.

Many of the men had sustained injuries, but they gritted their teeth, biting back groans.

In the days past, they had all suffered losses, and though no one was brave enough to say anything to my face, there were private murmurings that this was a sacred mountain to the Jieshuo, that trespassers disturbed the gods who resided here, that the landslide must have been the mountain god's rage.

No one knew what other kinds of rage the mountain god

had in store, and as the rockfall came in greater quantities, as the debris grew denser, faces grew ashen and wan. If, like last time, half the ridge came down, the beam above us could not stop it.

The low rumble grew louder—and closer—as the rocks became boulders.

Was this it?

A tremor shook through the stone beam. It made a frightful sound. Perhaps because too many rocks had landed upon it, the overhang was about to crumble.

We looked up, hopeless in the knowledge of our impending doom.

I did not fear death. I was only sorry.

That I had not found the crown prince was disloyalty. That I led everyone to this place of death was unrighteous. That I would lay my life down here, force my mother and father to bury a child, was unfilial.

How shameful it was to be all those things.

I guarded a wounded soldier, plunging my sword into the earth next to him. It might not be strong enough to hold up the stone beam, but it could at least help someone suffer less when it came crashing down.

"Fear not," I said.

The wounded soldier nodded. His eyes were full of tears, and he said, "General."

At the very end of the rope, to cling on for any additional moment was an additional moment to live.

The stone beam swayed again, emitting another horrifying rumble, but it held on.

Outside, the rockfall gradually slowed. I did not know how much time passed until we stopped hearing it altogether.

The landslide was over.

We climbed, trembling, out from beneath our shelter. Only then did we discover, atop the beam, several massive boulders threatening to fall.

The wind and snow had long since stopped. A sliver of new moon hung low in the sky.

Suddenly, someone exclaimed, "Lake! A divine lake!"

I stepped around a rock—and was also stunned.

In the space of an instant, the fierce and winding river disappeared from the valley, revealing a rocky riverbed. And not too far past that was a calm and tranquil lake.

Set off by the gleaming crescent in the sky, the deep blue water looked like a smooth crystal plate.

No one dared speak for fear of enraging the mountain god again.

The stone beam did not look long for the world, and as such was no place to linger, so I organized the men and the horses and led them onward along the lakeshore.

After the landslide, the path was more treacherous than it had been, and we lost more horses as a result. Many of those who remained had suffered light injuries. They all looked dispirited.

We walked wordlessly through the valley for most of the night until we found a patch of slope level enough to set up camp on. The men were so tired and worn that I stood watch personally, waiting until dawn to switch out with another. No sooner had my head hit the lambswool mat than I fell asleep.

After the sun rose, we ate some hasty rations and broke camp.

We traveled for four hours or more. By noon, sunlight finally filtered into the valley, but it brought no suggestion of warmth.

I could no longer think of any way to urge the men on.

Much of our food had been lost in the landslide, and what did remain was not enough to last more than a few days. If we didn't retreat soon, this would be a death sentence.

Was this stubborn obsession right or wrong? I wasn't sure.

Then a scout at the front of the line shouted, "People! General, there are people in the lake!"

I raised my eyes to see what he was talking about. By the side of the lake there were some jagged rocks—and a massive sheet of limestone that sank into the blue like a folding screen—and something seemed to be floating indistinctly upon it. But the sun glared off a thousand crystalline waves, and I could not see clearly against it.

Shaking off my reins, I dismounted, rushing in without much heed for anything else.

In steps, the water was up to my waist.

It was people, truly—it was *them*.

The crown prince and the ninth princess had been swept onto the limestone. They were half submerged in the lake, the princess's waistband tangling them tightly together.

What had I thought then?

That heaven had taken pity on us.

That I had found them at last.

I extended a hand, trembling. Under the watchful gaze of

my men, I prayed, deep in my heart, though for what I could not say.

They lived, though their breath was weak—and I let out the one I was holding, too. I swayed on my feet, nearly falling into the water.

It wasn't until a long time after that I remembered—when I checked for their breathing, it had been the princess I reached for first.

Why had I done so?

It could have been because I thought that if the princess died, the crown prince would not survive it.

It was something close to a miracle.

The River Oblivion washes all love away.

I'd not truly believed they would so totally forget their past.

After the princess became the princess consort, she would babble on about returning to Xiliang every time she was upset. She didn't know there was no return.

It wasn't that she was unhappy—it was that sometimes, there was something in her eyes that worried me.

The crown prince arranged to drink with me one day and told me about all the princesses who were of a marriageable age, asking me which was most to my liking.

"Anyone will do," I said immediately. I was to be consort. What difference did it make whom it would be for?

His Highness glanced at me. Abruptly, he said, "It's marriage. It's the rest of your life. Don't you want a choice?"

I smiled into my wine cup. "It's always been Their Highnesses who selected their consorts—who would dare be choosy about princesses? You oughtn't put me in such a difficult position, Your Highness."

"What, is there someone you like?" he asked.

I gave him a look and he burst out laughing. "See? I know exactly what you're thinking."

He continued to tease, but seeing that I would not rise to it, he gave it up.

After, I returned to my own manor. It was twilight, and a fuzzy drizzle had started up. The parasol trees in the courtyard were verdant with leaves, casting the rooms in a haze of shadow.

Xiaoxue came mewing up to greet me. I bent to scratch its chin. The golden bell tied onto its neck gave a few thin chimes. And I remembered the first time I'd seen this cat.

The princess consort had been the ninth princess then, and she had shown it to me blithely, saying, "Look! Gu Xiaowu won it for me! It's called Xiaoxue!"

Xiaoxue had been as big as a fist then. She had held it, and both girl and cat had looked like balls of fluff.

The princess had been wearing a chain about her ankle, with a string of golden bells strung onto it so that when she moved they emitted clear peals of sound. One of the little bells had fallen, rolling to a stop by my boot.

I had picked it up for her.

She had taken it back, grinning, and said, "What luck! I won't have to get a goldsmith to solder it back on for me." As she spoke, she unwound her hair ribbon and strung the gold bell upon it, tying it to Xiaoxue.

Xiaoxue hadn't been used to it and had scratched at it

nonstop. The princess grabbed it to stop it from clawing itself, asking, "Where's Gu Xiaowu?"

"Probably upstairs," I told her.

She kept a hold on Xiaoxue's paw, taking it back into her arms as she climbed the ladder to the roof in search of His Highness.

The bells on her anklet chimed, and I heard her singing.

It wasn't the song she usually sang. This one went: "A'gua is at the riverside hunting wild wolves. The wolf didn't come but the cat came by, the cat came by and broke his heart. . . . A'gua broke his heart. . . ."

People in Xiliang called their older brothers *a'gua*, but it could also mean lover. She'd sung a line or two when His Highness's voice sounded. "Who's making all that awful racket, is it Xiaofeng?"

"It is!" She stood smiling upon the ladder and raised the cat up high in excitement. "Look, Xiaoxue's wearing a bell."

The upper half of her body was leaning out onto the rooftop. I couldn't see her face, but I knew it must be bursting with joy.

I never heard her sing that song again.

Not for the rest of my days.

满架蔷薇一院香
A Rack Full of Roses, a Courtyard Perfumed[1]

When A'mu comes back from hunting, he gifts me a sprig of rose.

It's a fragile flower—even a gentle brush is enough to cast its petals endlessly to the ground. I have people put it into a crystal vase right away, for though it's a wildflower, it is sweetly fragrant, with a natural grace that is entirely its own.

Near evening, Yaoniang comes to speak with me. When she sees the wildflower blooming in its vase, she asks after its origins and, upon learning, cannot help her smile. "His Majesty is making jest with you, my lady."

I pretend not to know what she means.

I am the only girl at home and have ten brothers ahead of me. Father didn't have me until he was forty, so I have been spoiled out of shape by everyone, and when I was younger and mucking about with a pile of boys, I'd loved roughhousing and making trouble every bit as much as they did—until my adolescence, when I had thrashed the prince of Qi for harassing commoner girls. He was a shameless letch, and when he heard that I was Pei Yu's[2] daughter, he mockingly

---
[1] From "Summer Day in a Mountain Pavilion" by Gao Pian.
[2] Pei Zhao. Pei Yu is likely a courtesy name

named me Wildrose—which is to say that I was fragrant and fair, but full of thorns.

One thing led to another and the name spread. I hadn't thought it was accurate at all, but it sent Father into a fit, for he thought I'd never find anyone to marry if he didn't cure me of my temper, so he locked me at home and invited ever so many tutors in to guide me, to force me to learn the womanly arts and learn to write, which very nearly suffocated me.

It was His late Majesty who saved me, in the end, for when I was about fourteen he trothed me to the crown prince. I heard that he'd joked for my father not to worry, as he was "groaning and moaning day in and day out that your daughter will be difficult to find a match for—why don't you send her to my house for a bride?"

When Father received the edict, he nearly passed out. Though he did spend all day worrying that I was going to be difficult to marry out, he hadn't once thought of my wedding into the royal family, especially because the late emperor only had the one son. A'mu was crown prince, and someday, he would be king. Any way Father looked at it, he felt I would not make a good princess consort, to say nothing of an empress.

But the decree had been passed. However Father indulged me, there was hardly a means to refuse, and he had no recourse but to invite even more tutors to come in and teach me, with the idea of whipping me into shape before the occasion of my wedding.

To tell the truth, I hadn't thought of marrying A'mu either. I knew him too well. My second brother, Pei Zhong'an, had been his study companion in the Court of Spring, and they had grown up together. The prince had no brothers, just a younger sister, the Chaoyang Princess. The late emperor had adored her, so I was often summoned into the imperial city to be her playmate. I saw the crown prince often when I was young, and had just as often pushed him about, but very quickly stopped being a match for him, for of course he was a boy and had grown stronger than me. We fought endlessly, and more than once I stuffed dead snakes or rats into his bags, while he returned the favor with all manner of strange bugs. Chaoyang always laughed that A'mu and I were natural-born enemies. But Chaoyang and I were true friends. Neither of us had any sisters, but she said that if she had, then her sister would have been like me. She had been delighted that the late emperor decreed I was to be crown princess, for it meant we would be in-laws and could be more intimate still.

But by the time I married A'mu, Chaoyang was dead.

Her death had left the late emperor in a deep depression. He was intermittently sick for years after—he even presided over my wedding to the crown prince in the middle of a relapse. It had been a long illness, one that left the royal physicians on tenterhooks. There had been cruel words among some of the ministers, who said that to hold a royal wedding while the emperor was at death's door was to be like those commoners who hoped to flush joy.[3]

I had been crown princess six years when the late emperor

---

[3] The folk belief that a joyful occasion (such as marriage or birth) will flush away bad fortune and bring a cure for those with chronic or terminal illness.

passed. A'mu had ascended the throne and proclaimed his regnal era Chengping, naming me empress. Now, it is the fourth year of the Chengping Era—to count it all up, my marriage to A'mu was a decade ago.

In that time, A'mu and I have both grown up, and I've come to realize that willfulness is a privilege of the young, for how could I do whatever I desire as queen? I've been ten years at A'mu's side, weathering wind and rain. Added to our childhood comradery, we get along like kinsfolk, so though I cannot say that I've been a very *good* empress, I've also not made any major missteps.

And with my temper, no major missteps is fortune above all.

Yaoniang dines with me, but ere the soup is brought out a messenger enters to report, "His Majesty has arrived."

There is a long-standing rule in the palace that the emperor should visit his empress's court every fifth, fifteenth, and twenty-fifth of the month, but A'mu and I are young, and we don't follow those musty old precedents, so he comes and goes as he pleases.

He walks in before I have a chance to stand. Evening sun shines in through the window, illuminating his tall frame. I don't know why, but there is something ineffably different about him today. Maybe it's because we've been together too long. I've known him since I was four, and we've been married a decade—he's accompanied me longer than anyone else in the world.

I ought to make courtesy, but by the time I hasten to rise, he's pressed my shoulder down and indicated that I should return to my seat. This too is a common occurrence, for when we lived in the Court of Spring, neither of us had stood on ceremony, for which I had once been rebuked by the tutors.

A'mu sits and looks at the sweet soup on the table. "I'd thought to come sup with you," he says, "but it seems you've eaten."

"We've not finished yet." I have servants switch out the old food for new dishes and bring up clean tableware. At night, A'mu sometimes drinks and tells me all about the gossip at court or among the people. Other times, we slip out to Taiye Pool to row boats together when the maids aren't looking. But something is clearly on his mind today. I pour him wine, which he finishes quickly. I pour another. His chopsticks pause as he says, "There's something . . ."

Seeing him hem and haw, I burst into laughter. "What's the matter, my dear? Could it be you'd like to make some beautiful lady a consort?"

A'mu grins. Perhaps because the late emperor had taught him by word and through example, A'mu hasn't much interest in beauty. In the palace someone might occasionally stroke her hair coquettishly to try and catch his eye, but he does not bother to look, which is why I tease him thus. But the smile drops from his face and he says, "Shiliuniang, the Princess of Zhao is returning to the capital."

It takes some reflection for me to understand why he would bring her up to me.

For the Princess of Zhao is Yuanshan.

It's been ten years since I last saw her.

When people are young and ignorant, they often do a handful of preposterous things. When I was young and ignorant I must have done a hundred or more, but A'mu is different. In his entire juvenescence, his one indiscretion had been to love Yuanshan.

A'mu is not like me. High hopes have been placed upon him from the day he was born. Though his birth mother had been lowborn and a commoner, the empress had no sons, so she raised him in her court. When he was young, the empress passed, and a few years later his birth mother took ill and followed. The late emperor had placed very little import on the matter of female beauty, and the inner courts had no favored consort in its halls, so A'mu had no brothers. All the ministers knew he would someday become king. He had been steady and measured since youth, and by the time he entered adolescence, he had gained the praise of the court.

But the late emperor disliked Yuanshan. Once he guessed A'mu's intentions, he had her married to the Prince of Zhao, whose fiefdom was far from here.

We'd been so young then, but I once heard A'mu tell Chaoyang, "This is all my fault."

It is true, generally, that childhood infatuations are the hardest to forget.

So I give it some thought and say, easily, "No matter. I will take good care of Shanniang."

A'mu looks like there are many things he wants to say, but ultimately, he doesn't give air to any of them.

Night has fallen, and the attendants bring candles to ignite the lamps. The bright, full moon has risen, its muted, pale radiance scattering upon the stairs. Sconces leap to life one by one, and the moon grows paler, as though a thin sheet of airy silk has enveloped the front of the palace hall. It is early summer, and the night breeze carries a light perfume. "What incense is that?" A'mu asks. "It's floral."

Smiling, I tell him, "That's the scent of roses."

Then he notices the crystal vase beneath the curtain. In the dim glow, the rose's petals droop low like thin jade, exquisitely carved. He brushes the bloom, and a rush of petals flutter down.

I give a shout. Though these flowers grow in the mountain wilds, they're so tender, so delicate—it's been no more than a day since it was transplanted, but it's already withered.

A'mu looks apologetic. "Tomorrow I'll bring you another sprig."

I smile. "As you say."

A'mu sits with me a while longer, drinking the tea I steeped for him, and then returns to his own quarters.

Teaware is scattered across the low table. I rest my chin on my hand, watching the attendants clear everything away. Yaoniang walks out soundlessly to kneel at my side.

When everyone's retreated, she says, "The Princess of Zhao has been widowed. This return to the capital . . . I fear she's come with the intention of remarrying. My dear lady, you are so muddled. Why offer to make another woman's bridal clothes?"

The night is quiet save for a little bug somewhere that won't stop chirping. Seeing that I'm not paying this any mind, Yaoniang grows more agitated. "My lady, it has been ten years since you entered the palace, do not you know how dangerous people's hearts can be?"

I bend an ear to the insect instead, yawning wide. "Yaoniang, I'm tired."

She looks at me and must see how willing I am to smash the pot of my marriage for a single crack, for she swallows back everything she'd been wanting to say. Much as she dislikes it, she has little recourse but to let me do as I would.

It isn't until bedtime, when the candles beyond my bed curtains have been blown out and I'm lying dazedly on my mat, trying to sleep, that I remember her words. I've lived in the imperial city for ten years, but it's all passed by so quickly. A'die had been worried when I first married in, but A'mu was good to me. His Majesty had been precipitously ill by then, and though he was as stern with A'mu as ever, with me he was indulgent and affectionate, and he often told his son, "Now that you have welcomed a new bride, other matters ought all to be dispensed with. You must do your best to take care of her."

And of course he has. Chaoyang had been of such delicate constitution that he is used to being the older brother, thoughtful and proper in all regards.

Having known each other since childhood, there are many things we do not keep from one another—nor could we, if we tried. Like the fact that Yuanshan was the one person A'mu had loved in his youth, or the fact that, in mine, the person I'd most hoped to marry was actually Han Zhi, the handsomest boy in the capital.

But then, had there been any girls who hadn't? After I

became the princess consort, he was occasionally the crown prince's guest. Once, A'mu summoned him into the manor for a round of hand-talk[4] specifically to show me that the famously romantic youth of yore had become an ordinary old uncle.

I'd been so disappointed to see him. I told A'mu that if someone as dashing as Han Zhi could become so ugly once he grew a beard, he mustn't follow suit. A'mu guffawed and agreed on the spot. I don't know if he meant it, but in the years since, he's always been clean-shaven.

Amid these motley remembrances, I slip into sleep, and I sleep until the dawn bell sounds. Mornings are a tedious routine of washing and primping. As my hair is being dressed, A'mu has someone bring over another sprig of roses, so fresh that dew clings to its petals. I receive it and, as I'd done earlier, place it into the crystal vase. Yesterday's flowers have withered, making today's blossoms look more dazzling by contrast.

"But it's so early! Where did His Majesty find these?"

A'mu's messenger replies, "His Majesty went to Chenghui Hall this morning and gathered them there."

I freeze. Chenghui Hall is a secluded place. When the late emperor was crown prince, I've been told, the princess consort lived there. During the Qinhe Era, the courtyard had caught fire, an inferno that had destroyed many of the manor's residences, some of which were rebuilt, while others had to be torn down and turned into gardens. Yet there

---

4 Playing weiqi, or go.

were others still that, for no reason anyone knew, had been abandoned. When I'd married A'mu, the Court of Spring had already been renovated, and the residence of the crown princess was far from Chenghui Hall.

I can't say why, but I want to see it. Yaoniang is helpless against this impulse; all she can do is suggest that she accompany me.

Chenghui Hall is not far from where I live. In a light carriage traveling leisurely, it takes us about two brews of tea to arrive. The courtyards here have not been damaged so badly—the walls are blackened, but cerulean roof tiles gleam beneath the sun as they must always have done, the spaces between them thick with moss. Birds dart to and fro. Under the bright sun, it all holds a hint of desolation.

Because A'mu had come this morning, the entrance has been given a rough sweeping. I walk along the winding corridors and into the courtyard. Long vines of roses have climbed onto the false mountain rock, blooming, resplendent in their whites and pinks. But on the other side, a rack of flowers has collapsed and weeds have spread everywhere—it's easy to see that no one has lived here in a long time.

I stand in the covered corridor. The morning breeze ruffles my sleeves, bringing a light chill.

"My lady, you have sailed in smooth waters your whole life and have had all that you wished for," Yaoniang says. "You have met with no difficulty, so you approach others with goodness and generosity, but in the palace, people's hearts are dangerous. Take the late emperor's Mingde empress for an example. She was killed by just such conspiracy."

I'd not heard of any Mingde empress, but Yaoniang tells me that she was the late emperor's first crown princess, when he lived in the Court of Spring.

Standing in the corridor, surrounded by the perfume of the flowering roses, I listen as Yaoniang recounts a story of the deep palace that chills my blood.

She had been a foreign girl who married into the Plains court, guileless and unaffected. But there had been another consort who, despite having the favor of the crown prince, conspired to poison the princess in order to usurp her.

Yaoniang gives a long sigh. "After, when His Highness discovered this, he stripped the consort of her titles, demoted her to a commoner, and had her put to death. But the crown princess could never be brought back to life."

"It's not like A'mu has any favored consorts," I argue.

In her pique, Yaoniang's gracefully curving brows nearly stand up straight. "My queen ought not to use His Majesty's pet name so cavalierly. Preparations must be made before the rain, trouble must be forestalled—that is the way things ought to be done."

Back and forth and back and forth and all she wanted to tell me was to guard against Yuanshan.

But if one person loves another, how is that a thing anyone else can stop?

I feed Yaoniang a few perfunctory lines, pluck a few more rosy sprigs, and return home.

Again I put them into the crystal vase. It brims with flowers now, lovelier than ever. Large handfuls of fresh new blossoms conceal yesterday's bloom, and though beneath the curtain the petals continue to fall, their smell lingers, and the effect is one of abundance.

Yaoniang makes every patient effort to persuade me into wariness, but I march stubbornly along my own course and send people outside the city to meet Yuanshan. Because she is a widow, she demurs politely, and it takes my personally writing for her to agree to come.

It's been so long since I last saw her. She is highborn, for her father is the prince consort Liang Zhang and her mother the Princess Royal Yongshou. It had been known in the capital that Yuanshan was highly eligible, and she was my playmate in those olden days, though no one had known how we would get along, for our temperaments had been so wholly different.

I sit in my hall, watching Yuanshan slowly ascend the stairs to the palace. Her figure is elegant, her steps are lithe, and a gentle breeze billows her sleeves, her clothes fluttering like wisps of clouds as she nears.

Her face becomes clearer to me by degrees. Despite the passing years, she hasn't changed, her delicate complexion as gentle and smooth as jade. Because of her widowhood, her dress is austere, and the radiance of her youth has been replaced by a reserved allure that gives her an air of self-assurance. It makes her even lovelier to behold.

Our conversation, distant at first, warms as we talk. I ask after the scenery of Qingzhou, and her answer, though brief, is engaging. I rarely leave the capital, so I hunger to hear of these lands unknown to me. Yuanshan says, easily, "If Your Highness does not disdain it, I have with me some local wares from Qingzhou as a gift to the king."

Yuanshan used to call me as my family did, by Shiliuniang, so hearing the words *Your Highness* fall from her mouth saddens me. She has turned her face, her back straight as she sits, and though her bearing does not come off as reserved, the intimacy and ease of our girlhoods is, it seems, not to return.

We take lunch in Hanbi Tower, so named because it faces the green ripples of Taiye Pool. This time of year, new lotus buds are poking their heads out from the lake. Tender yellow leaves, no larger than a human palm, float across the glassy water, looking like the gold ornaments ladies brush upon their brows. They drift, unfixed, with the wind and the waves, emerging and submerging like dimples.

I cannot help bringing up the past. "Do you remember that time we snuck onto Taiye to go boating with Chaoyang, only to realize that none of us knew how to paddle? And then the boats floated out into the middle of the lake and we kept spinning and spinning, but no one was strong enough to row them until that eunuch saw us and had some servants bring us back. Ah, I was so terrified of catching a scolding."

The sun is strong above us. Curtains have been lowered in the tower, but refracted light shines through the gap beneath them, making Yuanshan's face look more like lustrous white jade. Her eyes reflect the gleaming waters, bright black gemstones until her gaze shifts and her eyes dim again. Her voice is tranquil as she tells me, "That must have been more than a decade ago."

We'd been young and did not yet know how vast the heavens and the earth were, nor that the world could hold many sorrows.

"Let's steal some cherries!" I say.

Yuanshan is startled by my excitement.

"That biggest, purplest cherry tree is still in the imperial garden," I say.

At this she laughs behind a courteous hand.

It used to be that every year in late spring we would sneak in to take cherries. The palace would bequeath us some anyway, but those were never sweeter than the ones we stole. I'm about to have a change of clothes brought over to better climb in when suddenly, from beyond the curtain, a spate of whispers sounds—like Yaoniang is murmuring to someone.

"Who's there?" I ask.

Unable to keep it from me, Yaoniang reports back through the curtain. "His Majesty has sent someone over."

This surprises me. "Let him in."

It's a court eunuch bearing a golden platter, atop which is piled a flourish of freshest cherry. The eunuch says, very politely, "His Majesty happened to see that these had reddened, so he picked some to give to my lady."

Looking at the plump, juicy fruit, I can't swallow back my sigh. Perhaps he sees my dejection, for the eunuch takes a bold step forward and says, in a low voice, "His Majesty said that, as my lady is seeing old friends today, she may find it hard not to be up to her old tricks, and that my lady should please not climb any more trees."

I can't decide whether to laugh or to weep. Yuanshan hears all of this, naturally, but she keeps her gaze fixed forward and pretends not to have noticed. What option do I have but to give up the thought of theft and have sulao[5] brought to the table so Yuanshan and I can eat?

The cherries are very sweet, but a thread of unease snakes its way into my heart. Had I been the intended recipient of A'mu's gift, I wonder, or had Yuanshan?

Ordinarily, I love cherries, but today I cannot swallow more than a few. Maybe the sulao that had been poured over them was too cold, or the lakeside wind had blown into the tower, but by nighttime my stomach mounts a protest. It's such a to-do that I don't take supper and have to call in an imperial physician to prescribe two large bowls of bitter medicine to be able to doze.

I'm not sure how long I sleep before I'm roused by someone gently smoothing the hair away from my face. It must be late, though candles burn beneath the bedcurtain, flames flickering in the dark. A'mu is dressed in his casual robes. He holds me in his arms, asking, "How are you feeling? Do you want some warm water to drink?"

"What time is it?"

A'mu is about to call someone to see, but I stop him. "Why did you come?"

"They said you'd caught cold; I wanted to see how you were."

I lean against him, resting my head against his arm, and feel more at ease. The night is long and the wind rests, and occasionally I hear the ding of the chimes that hang beneath the eaves. I mutter, "Do you still love Shanniang?"

---

5   A custardy pudding resembling yogurt, made from sweet rice wine (jiuniang) and milk.

He's silent for a long moment. "Where's this coming from?"

"Shanniang loves cherries the most."

This was all in the past. Yuanshan has always been steadier than I. Between myself and Chaoyang, we could make trouble where no trouble was to be found, but Yuanshan was the one who dissuaded us from it. The only time she'd gotten into hot water with us was when we'd all gone to steal cherries.

We called it stealing, but it was nothing more than harvesting. It was just that Chaoyang was asthmatic, and everyone in the palace fretted over her illness. The maids and eunuchs treated the possibility of her wearing one less layer of clothing than usual the way they would have an invading army. Chaoyang hadn't liked being fussed over and, one day, managed to lose all her attendants to sneak into the orchard with Yuanshan and me.

The trees had been trimmed carefully back to make their fruit easier to pick, so it was simple enough to climb onto them. The cherries glistened bright red like countless coral beads strung beneath the leaves. I sat among the branches, feasting as I plucked, passing the majority to Shanniang, who stood below. Chaoyang was fearless, and she'd climbed higher than me. Through the thick leaves all I could see of her was the flash of her goose-yellow shawl. She'd tucked the hem of her skirt into her waistband and was on tiptoes for the brightest, plumpest of the yield.

Yuanshan craned to look at her. "Be careful!"

"Come up, Shanniang!" Chaoyang picked a clutch of cherries from the branch and turned, one hand against the tree and the other wagging the fruit about, teasing her.

I'd kept urging her on too, but she refused to climb and picked her hems up instead, laughing. "You two toss them down, and I'll collect them for you!"

Chaoyang and I exchanged a glance and began grabbing cherries as quickly as we could to throw down by the handful.

Yuanshan was dizzy from all the cherries hailing down toward her, and she giggled as she ducked. Ere long, she could not resist tucking in her skirts to climb after us, yelling, "Look at all that nice fruit you've ruined, see if I don't twist you off this tree myself!"

Chaoyang and I had cackled gleefully, ascending higher and higher in an effort to evade her. Then Chaoyang yelped, "Ah!" And then, loudly, "Oh, no, no! The imperial fans, I see the imperial fans—A'ye must be coming!"

I'd been more or less fine, but Yuanshan panicked. She lost her footing and fell head over heels from the tree with a smack. Chaoyang and I cried out at the same time, but there was no time to react. She grabbed a branch, but it snapped under her weight. She seemed certain to slam into the earth when someone rushed forward and caught her by the waist— in the nick of time.

Bowing as I was up in the tree, I could see nothing but Yuanshan's skirts as they fluttered in the breeze, like a petal unfurling from a beautiful flower. Someone had caught that lovely bloom in their arms, folding her within them. Yuanshan's cheeks reddened; she looked bashful. Sun shone through the branches to scatter down limpid light. Her half-lidded eyes, thick lashes haloed, fluttered like startled butterflies. I hadn't noticed how long they were.

When A'mu set her down, I saw the imperial fans. His Majesty had indeed come.

I climbed down in utter humiliation.

Though His Majesty adored Chaoyang, he was solemn with everyone else, so Yuanshan and I were both terrified of him, especially since we'd gotten into such trouble. The two of us curtsied politely. Chaoyang remained among the branches like nothing was the matter and called down, sweetly, "A'ye!"

"Who taught you to climb trees?" His Majesty's voice was cool and calm, but Yuanshan must have heard the same rebuke in it that I had, because from the corner of my eye, I saw the slight tremble in her skirts. The emperor was temperamental, and he was strict with his ministers. There was no one at court who did not fear him.

Chaoyang alone was not intimidated. Gleefully, she told him, "Gege did!"

"That was when you were little. You shouldn't do it now that you're grown up." A'mu gave her a meaningful look. "Why don't you come down?"

Chaoyang wheedled, "I want to jump down and have you catch me too."

"What nonsense," A'mu said. "What if I miss?"

"You're playing favorites!" Chaoyang had pouted. "A'xiong is all grown and he only cares about pretty girls. That's why you're catching Shanniang but won't catch me."

Yuanshan's face grew hotter, and a blush surfaced on

A'mu's face too. I looked between them as they stood beneath the cherries, one tall and slender, the other delicate as a butterfly—they *were* well matched.

From then I'd known that A'mu loved Yuanshan.

The pity was that the late emperor did not consummate their happiness.

"Everyone has regrets, kings included."

A'mu's voice is placid. The candles cast his face in flickers of light and dark as he speaks, but I feel him to be so distant from me, too far to reach. The night is cold as water, and I tug at the brocade blanket.

"That was what my a'ye told me." A'mu does not look at me. He's staring instead at the swaying flames on the candelabra. "Before anointing the crown princess, he summoned me to him and told me many things.

"He said, 'You are the heir. Someday, you will be king. The Six Courts will have its three Consorts, its nine Concubines, its twenty-seven Ministresses of Succession, and its eighty-one Imperial Mistresses. You will have many, many women. But it makes a difference if there is someone you truly love. And if there is, then you must be sure to treat her well, for there is no way to mend a broken heart, and you will lose your own as well as hers.'

"I didn't understand what he was saying then. He'd not had any favored consorts, nor many concubines, and I hadn't been in a position to ask after his past, either. But when a man's heart's been broken—that I could tell. So I asked, 'What ought I do if there is a person I love, but they don't love me back?' And he said that it wasn't something you could force.

That it didn't matter if you were emperor. If she didn't love you, then there was nothing you could do."

A'mu hangs his head slightly. I don't know what it is I'm feeling. That A'mu loves Shanniang is something I'd known, but I hadn't given much thought to how Shanniang feels. If she doesn't love him, then it's true there's not much he can do.

Abruptly, A'mu asks, "What would you do, in that position?"

I don't have to think. "I'd use every trick in the book and every means within my disposal, of course. If I had to lie or cheat or steal, I would make him love me."

This catches him off guard, and he turns his face away, saying, "What childish talk."

This annoys me. A'mu's older than me by a scant few years, and because I'd been close with Chaoyang, he treats me like I'm so immature. We've been married ten years, but often he seems more like an a'xiong than a husband.

But he doesn't know that children have their woes too.

And mine are not ones I'll share with him.

Night breeze stirs the curtains. Candles ripple like reflections in the water. I think back to when I was younger, to those things that seem separated from me by the broad span of Taiye Pool, suffused with the light fragrance of cool dew upon lotus, and the angelica floating on the misty waters. There had been the bright moon shining down, the crystal beads swaying in the rising wind. There had been the cherries that rolled around in the bottom of the cup, the longing that lingered in the twang of a qin. There had been A'mu, bending his fingers to flick me on the brow, teasing me with,

If you can't marry yourself out to anyone, then come and marry me. No one would dare cast aspersions if you were the crown princess.

What had I thought then? I must have retorted with something like, *Who told you no one wants to marry me? I'm going to marry someone handsome, like Han Zhi!*

But I'd been wed to A'mu after all, and no one did laugh at me again—only me, to myself, alone in my heart.

"It's late," he murmurs, smoothing a hand against my back. "Sleep."

I lie back on my pillow and close my eyes.

The truth is that if I loved someone and he didn't love me back, I wouldn't have the courage to make a fool of myself by harassing him into it. People pretend to be so obstinate, so brave, but it's a coward that lives in everyone's heart. There are those who you could neither harass nor hoodwink into being a person who loves you.

I must have a nightmare near dawn. It's A'mu who shakes me awake. I'm crying so hard I can't catch my breath, and he pulls me into his embrace and comforts me, saying, "A'xiong is here, Shiliuniang, A'xiong is here."

"You're not . . ." I say around my sniffles.

My a'xiong had died in the war on Gaoli. For court and common it had been a great triumph, but for my family, it was a world-shattering tragedy.

Though I have many brothers, the one I'd been closest to was my second. Since I was a child, I'd toddled after him, calling him *A'xiong* in a voice that carried the scent of mother's milk. When we were older, he was given the responsibility of entering the Court of Spring to be the crown prince's reading companion. Fortunately, by then I could also enter and leave the palace, and I often saw him there.

When I was younger, there were many things I didn't understand, so I followed Chaoyang's example in calling both my brother and hers *a'xiong*. For her to call my brother that was kind, but for me to call hers that had been presumptuous. No one corrected me, perhaps because they could not bring themselves to rebuke an innocent girl who did not know any better. It wasn't until I grew up and understood more of the world that I stopped calling A'mu my brother.

It ought to have been A'mu who was commander in chief, with my a'xiong as his second-in-command to lead the army as Marshal of the March, but then he died on the battlefield. Since the establishment of the dynasty, there hasn't been a prince of the royal house who did not command an army—the Taizong had been conferred the title of crown prince for his military success, which is why all subsequent crown princes have followed suit.

But A'mu is different. The late emperor only had this one son. He actually *had* intended for A'mu to serve as the regional commander of Liangzhou, to take charge of its troops and march on Gaoli, but this sent the ministers into an uproar, and they wrote in a tide of remonstrations that finally put a stop to this plan. So he settled for the next best thing and appointed A'mu commander from afar.

When A'xiong went off to war, A'mu and I saw him off. No one thought then that this parting would be forever.

Before A'xiong mounted his horse, he'd caressed my hair,

saying, "A'mu may be good to you, but you mustn't be too willful."

The warmth of his palm sometimes feels like it lingers still, yet I won't ever see him again. I am sad whenever I dream of him, but . . . I hadn't tonight, and I am miserable even so.

After dawn I start to run a fever. Despite A'mu's worry, he has court to attend, so he summons a royal physician. I am sick for an unexpectedly long time, and physicians come into the palace day after day, switching out prescription after prescription. The medicine is bitter, and though I force it all down, none of it makes a difference.

Every evening at sunset I start burning up, and when the sun rises the temperature recedes; at night I am dizzy with delirium, and during the day I am sluggish and weak. Yuanshan, hearing of my illness, comes into the imperial city to visit me, and sometimes she bumps into A'mu too. One afternoon, I wake from my midday nap to hear Yuanshan's voice faintly in the front of the hall. I peer out from behind the heavy curtain and make out the corner of her robes. She sits straight-backed, but her voice is clear and agreeable, melodious as a yellow oriole. A'mu wears a smile different from the one he usually does. I can't describe the change really, just that it's courteous, with a measure of restraint and solemnity. He hasn't smiled at *me* like that. When he smiles at me, it's with a kind of tolerance, an exasperation. Sometimes he ruffles my hair, laughing at the silly things I say and laughing at my silly thoughts too.

I didn't see anything untoward about it then, for my brothers had treated me thus, but I know now how terribly inappropriate it is that we should be ten years wed and for him to never have treated me as he does Yuanshan—that he should never have given me such a smile. It *is* different with a person you loved.

The more awful I feel the worse my illness is. A'niang and the aunties come into the palace to see me. I force myself to sit and talk with them, and afterward, A'niang dismisses everyone to tell me, quietly, "You needn't worry about this matter with Shanniang. What young man doesn't like a beautiful face? Anyway, she is a widow now, and inauspicious—who's to say His Majesty still harbors affection for her?"

I have not fully recovered. Bouts of perspiration surface on my back. The layers of robes are drenched through, and I cannot summon the desire to say anything. A'niang natters on and on, but her voice seems sometimes distant, sometimes close. Outside the curtain, there is a peach tree, which has long since erupted into thick green. Beneath the leaves, fuzzy buds emerge. I'm parched and crave a draught of cold water, but though the palace keeps stores of ice in the cellars, I am sick, and A'mu would certainly not allow me anything cold to drink.

Thinking of him sets my heart further to flame, and a dull ache seethes in my insides, painful in the extreme. A'niang notices something amiss. She takes my hand, astonished. "What's happened? Your face is so red, are you feverish again?"

It's only impatience. What does Shanniang have to do with me? Since she's been back, even A'niang is urging me to be more accepting. Everyone agrees that A'mu *must* like her, and no matter if I hate it, all I can do is bear it. My ten

GOODBYE, MY PRINCESS

years are nothing compared to these few short days she's been back.

I hold my temper and see A'niang and the aunties off. It's almost sunset, right around the time my fever returns, so my dinner is very light. Once I polish off my millet porridge, I remember I have a large, bitter bowl of medicine to swallow and feel all the worse for it. Yaoniang walks in, her countenance ugly, and I ask, "What's happened?"

Yaoniang refuses to say, telling me again and again that it's nothing. I think back to A'niang and the aunties' visit and wonder if something has happened at home that they're all keeping from me, so I send Yaoniang away and call A'chan in for questioning. A'chan is not so brave. The second I ask her, she falls heavily to her knees and sobs, "Please, my lady, I truly, truly do not dare tell. Yaoniang says that anyone who tells you anything will be beaten to death."

Yaoniang is a flinty woman. All the eunuchs and maids fear her, but she would hardly threaten to have people beaten to death over nothing. My heart skips a beat, but I pretend to be calm. "Do you think I wouldn't have you beaten to death if you *don't* tell me?"

I haven't ever said anything like this. Next to my bed, the bronze mirror where I dress myself each morning has not yet had its cover let down, so I can see myself in its reflection. I've been ill too long and have lost much of the fat in my face. Now that it looks so solemn, I *am* rather horrific—at least to A'chan, who stammers out the story.

A'mu brought Yuanshan to Wangxian Palace today. It's an imperial residence not far from the city, conveniently located for royal hunting parties, and I've often gone there with him for sport. But it's past curfew and they haven't returned, which can only mean they will spend the night there.

There's no word for how I feel, but I leap to my feet and cry out for A'yu. A'yu does not come. It's Yaoniang who enters instead, hurriedly pushing the curtains open and making her courtesies. "What would you have me do, Your Highness?"

Yaoniang never calls me that. I hear the warning in it—it tells me to *remember my status*—but I have borne more than I can bear. In a loud voice, I say, "Fetch my riding clothes, I am heading out."

She raises her voice. "Your Highness, it is past curfew."

"*I am the empress.*" In my fury, I have not forgotten the things to which I am entitled. "Bring me my insignia, and order General Chen to open Jiade Gate."

Yaoniang looks like she might say something else, so I call again for A'yu. A'yu bursts into the room with my riding clothes, fluttering about like a bird. Yaoniang glares, but A'yu and I grew up making trouble together and she is not intimidated in the slightest, quickly getting me changed. Yaoniang kneels as she tries strenuously to dissuade me, in tears as she does, like it's some horrid breach of conduct for me to leave the city for Wangxian. Through gritted teeth, I order, "Have Yaoniang watched. Don't let her go blathering about."

The maids are already ashen faced, so, hearing this, they lead her immediately away.

I bring the insignia out from my box of powder and rouge. Clutching the cold metal so tightly in my fist that the pattern work imprints onto my palm, I walk from the palace.

A palanquin has been prepared at the foot of the stairs, and by the time I am at the gate, General Chen has arrived. He kneels. I pass the insignia to A'yu, who passes it to him. He inspects it, but hesitates.

"Why are you leaving the imperial city so late in the evening, Your Highness?"

I give him a bright smile. "His Majesty has decided to spend the night at Wangxian Palace, so I am surprising him there."

General Chen is of my a'die's generation. He has been the Longhe General, commander of the imperial guard, since A'mu was a child, and he could be said to have watched A'mu grow up, so he falters. Seeing that I've brought only a few maids, he says, "The night is cold and the road is long. Why don't I have some men escort you, Your Highness?"

He is worried, I know. No one becomes commander of the imperial guard by being careless, and General Chen has held the title for decades and is a man well trusted by the late emperor and the new one both. But I'm going to stop a tryst, not start a rebellion, so what objections could I have? I smile sweetly. "That would be good of you."

General Chen sends Lieutenant General Guo, along with two squadrons, to escort me at a quick clip all the way to the palace. On fast horses, it takes fewer than four hours for its lofty gates to appear in the distance. Because A'mu is within, it is surrounded by guardsmen. Someone yells down a question from atop the gate, and General Guo is about to respond when I look up and ask, "Is that General Wei speaking?"

General Wei is startled at the sound of my voice. He orders his men to bring more light so he can lean out and look down at us from the ramparts. The pine torches that burn beside me are exceedingly bright, enough that he can see me from afar, so he has the doors opened and comes down to greet me personally.

"No need to disturb His Majesty," I say. "I'll go to him myself."

The entire troop of men and horses are left outside as I take a palanquin deep into the endless courts, passing through hall after hall, gate after gate. Slowly, the hubbub grows dimmer, distant. Around me are only the leaves that dance in sweeping winds, the soft of their rustle, and the chirp of unknown insects in the thicket.

I don't descend from the palanquin until it comes to his quarters. I lean against A'yu, feeling like I am being relatively composed, all things considered. This terrace, built over water, is called Qingfeng Pavilion. It has long windows on all four sides; A'mu runs hot, so when he comes to Wangxian Palace, this is where he often stays. Last autumn, I lived here with him when the moon had shone like a sheet of frost and its light upon the reed catkins made them look like an expanse of snow. Nighttime fireflies had flown in, which A'mu caught and placed inside a glass that had been a tribute gift from one of the caliphates to the west. The fireflies had flashed again and again within the bright blue bottle as they bumped into the sides, unable to escape. It had been a sorry sight, so I'd blown out the candle with a *huff* and uncapped the bottle to let them out.

The airy pinpricks of fluorescence had looked like shooting stars. Some landed in the netting, others on A'mu's shoulder. I'd lain my head upon his knees and watched the moon that seeped in from the window. The fireflies paused on my sleeves, but I couldn't bear to catch them. There are none in the imperial city, though no one knows why. Some say it's because no larvae can hatch from Taiye, some say it's because no grass decays in the emperor's quarters,[6] and still others think it's because the late king could not stand them, which is why we don't see them in the palace. I had been curious then, and asked A'mu about it. Now I'm glad it's late spring and the waters have not yet yielded any, or I would not be able to bear it.

I waver once and waver again. When I turn, I see that A'yu has brought some people to intercept the eunuchs who stand at the door. I point to one at random and ask, "Has His Majesty gone to bed?"

He had probably not expected me to come in the middle of the night, so he's more than a little alarmed and sputters out, "His Majesty . . . His Majesty . . ."

I give this one up and point at another. "And Shanniang? Where's she?"

This one drops to his knees and presses his brow to his hands. Realization strikes, and a wave of murderous anger surges through my chest. I am at the top of the pavilion in a few short steps and kick the door open. It slams open with a bang and I storm in, head high, but though the hall is replete with candles, there is no one around.

I go left. The curtains have been lowered, and when two

---

6 Historically, people thought that fireflies were born from decaying grass, similar to the concept of spontaneous generation.

attendants see me stalking toward them in a fit of rage, they let out yelps of horror and fall to their knees. I boil over, shoving the drapery aside as I yell, "Li Mu, you *liar*!"

Everyone at the banquet raises their heads. Some watch me, curious. A'mu sits in the middle, flanked by royal kinsmen who kneel beside him—like his uncle, prince consort Gao Jing; as well as the princess royal, Princess Yong'an; her sister, the Princess Tai'an; the Prince of Qi, Li; the Prince of Qin, Qi; the Prince of Han, Qi; and my own fourth brother, Pei Jichang. Yuanshan is there too, but she sits with the Princess Tai'an's daughter, the Lady of Yuanning, and the two of them are whispering together.

My face flames. A'mu stands, astonished, and asks, "Why've you come?"

Everyone else makes their courtesies. I'd not anticipated there would be so many people present, and I am thrown off guard, unsure of what to do.

It's all too humiliating. I'd thought to muster my forces in order to catch an adulterer in the act. I didn't know it would be *this*.

A'mu walks toward me, drawing closer and closer, closer and closer. My brow erupts into a cold sweat, my thoughts are all a muddle. *How am I to explain myself?* And when he's almost upon me, panic swallows me and I collapse to the ground with a thunk, unconscious.

When I wake, the wind is stirring, billowing the pavilion screens. I don't know where the people have disappeared to, for the hall is silent. Distant candles have been lit, but the room itself is dark. Moon leaks in to land upon the floor-mats, a shallow, silvered light. A'mu kneels beside me, holding my hand in his. I'm so angry and so hurt, and when I think of the fool I've made of myself, all I want is to close my eyes and pretend I haven't woken. But A'mu says, in a low, gentle voice, "Shiliuniang."

I'm so ashamed I don't want to look at him, but he pulls me into his arms. I struggle against it but can't shake him off, so I let him do as he pleases. He rests his chin atop my head, his warm breath fluttering against my brow. Reproach moves in my heart, but he calls me again. "Shiliuniang."

"What?" I yell crossly, opening my eyes wide. This trick is one I used to use when I got into trouble, for when A'die saw how self-righteous I acted, half the time he would think he'd gotten it wrong, and the other half that someone else had wronged his darling daughter. His anger would turn into self-doubt and I would get off scot-free.

But A'mu looks like he doesn't know if he should laugh or cry. "Why are you yelling? I'm not going to eat you."

My conscience is not the clearest, which is why I retort hotly, "Say what you want to say, then!"

He changes the subject instead. "Did General Chen not question you when you left the city today?"

I flush. The Taizu[7] had won the world on horseback, and in those days, his empress had spent years accompanying him to battle. She'd been the foundation upon which our universe was built, which is why our empresses have more power than most and why most of us have come from martial families. In

---

7   Temple name for the founding emperor of a dynasty.

the twenty-seventh year,[8] during an attempted coup at the palace gates, when all else was lost, it had been the Empress Shen who led troops into battle, reclaimed the Xuanwu Gate, and rescued the Shizong.[9] Thereafter, it has always been that when the emperor is not within palace walls, the empress has the right to open its gates with her insignia. But the rule had been established a hundred years ago or more, and the kingdom is peaceful, so though the empress does technically have the right to lead the Kun'an, Qin'an, and Sheng'an divisions of the imperial guard, it is indirect, and she does not interfere with the daily duties of the troops. For me to have left as I did today is profane by any measure.

"I told General Chen I wanted to see you," I say shamefacedly.

"Silly girl." A'mu pokes at my forehead with a finger. "To be so sick and ride so far. You could have sent a messenger and I would have gone back to see you."

I'm too embarrassed to tell him I'd come with the intention of catching him in a tryst, so I hang my head and keep silent.

But A'mu is in a good mood and begins to chatter at me. "There is a matter on Shanniang's heart, did you know?"

When I hear the name *Shanniang*, I feel myself burn up. My temple starts to throb, so I give a few grunts and try to muddle through. But A'mu catches my chin and tips it up so he can look in my eyes and ask, "What do you think this matter is?"

---

[8] Of the sixty-year cycle.
[9] Common temple name for an emperor.

"She's so pretty and clever, how should I know what her troubles are?" I bite out.

A'mu laughs. "That's true, it is hard to guess what's in a woman's heart."

I bow my head and stay quiet. A'mu is good to people—good in the way of tender wind and soft rain, forever considerate on others' behalf. His temper is unlike that of the late emperor's, for his father had been severe and indifferent, and most everyone at court held some fear of him, but A'mu is warm. The ministers call him *virtuous*, though he is meticulous in his management of affairs and they are not emboldened to deceive him for his benevolence.

Sometimes even I find it hard to hide things from him—like now.

I change the subject, hemming about this and hawing about that, when A'mu leans down and kisses me. I go a little stupid, and as his lips press insistently against mine, I am dizzy, like I've run out of air, like I can't breathe. A'mu lets go of me and says, in a low voice, "Inhale!"

Only then do I suck in a breath, for I'd nearly suffocated. A'mu smooths his hand over my back, remarking leisurely, "Shanniang would like to marry again. Tell me, should you like to help her make this match?"

Maybe I haven't caught my breath, because it takes me a minute to understand what he means. My heart gives a sour little pinch as I thrust him away and push myself to my feet, yelling, "You might be the emperor, but that doesn't give you the right to be a bully!"

I'm feeling more and more wretched, and the longer I

think about it, the angrier I become. I kick at him. He doesn't move, so the blow lands soundly on his leg. He furrows his brow, but it's my tears that spill. Seeing me cry, he rushes to say, "The Prince of Zhao was your brother-in-law and so is the Prince of Qi—how could that be bullying you? If the Prince of Qi offended you, hasn't he been punished? Why keep tallying his faults?"

I stare blankly at him. He thinks this is very funny. "Shanniang wants to marry the Prince of Qi. If you don't want to play matchmaker, I can get my aunt to do it."

The Prince of Qi? Come to think of it, he *had* been present. We'd been little the last time we fought, when he'd tried to name me Wildrose, but he has been in Yizhou these many years and I have forgotten all those childhood enmities.

I don't quite know what to say. A'mu rubs his leg, muttering, "A'ye said the young miss would be difficult to marry, for you'd have to wait ten years for her to be more mature and when she is you still won't know what she's thinking—and so it is."

My ears burn. "Who told you to marry me, then?"

But A'mu laughs merrily. "Yes, yes, when A'ye came asking, it was I who said I wanted to wed. He sighed and said that one demon could only be quelled by another, but he didn't stop me, did he?"

I hadn't been prepared for this and am flustered by it. A'mu's voice softens. "Shiliuniang, I've waited ten years. Don't you think you ought to give me an answer?"

My heart flutters, shy and anxious all at once. "What kind of answer?"

"I want to know what you're thinking," he says. "Han Zhi is ugly now that he's grown out his beard. But look at me, nice and clean-shaven. Am I prettier than the Prince of Qi?"

It's rare for A'mu to be so straight-faced, so I give him a good glancing over. I hadn't seen the Prince of Qi in years, and had caught a mere snatch of him earlier—I hadn't seen his face at all, recognizing him vaguely from his clothes and coronet. But I don't know how to answer, so I give a haphazard nod.

This is not good enough for A'mu.

"What does a nod mean? Am I better looking or not?"

Chagrin turns to irritation. "What does this have to do with the Prince of Qi?"

"It has everything to do with him!" A'mu says, astonished. "Didn't he send a matchmaker to your a'die to try and propose marriage after you thrashed him? I went to my father as soon as I heard so that he would issue the decree to make you crown princess."

I hadn't known such a thing had happened, nor that I'd been snatched away by A'mu to be his wife. But then, what had he meant when he said what happened to Shanniang was all his fault? I'm muddled, I'm confused, and A'mu is here, tugging at my sleeve. "Shiliu, if you don't tell me today, I'm not letting you go to bed!"

My heart is such a mess, but I'm struck by a bolt of brilliance. "I'll tell you if you can catch me a firefly."

A'mu grows anxious. "There aren't any fireflies this time of year!"

Cheerfully, I say, "Then you'd better wait until you catch some!" There are months before they will emerge. By that time A'mu might be distracted by other matters and forget all of this entirely.

A'mu is stumped for ideas. But then the breeze stirs. Outside, soft pinpricks of light twinkle and a firefly drifts in through the screen, winking. A'mu is delighted. He catches it in his hands, saying, "Look! Now you have to tell."

I look hurriedly in his palm. Indeed it is a firefly, though I don't know why it's come out so early, fluttering as it flashes brightly, buzzing in circles in his grasp. I puff up my cheeks, blowing hard, and it uses this gust of air to open its wings and fly back out again.

Upset, A'mu leaps to his feet to go after it, but I hold firm to his sleeve and refuse to let him. After some tugging, A'mu turns with a smile and flicks my earlobe. "Dummy!"

I cover my ears, laughing, and escape back into the hall.

Wind gusts through the long corridor. New buds rise from the surface of the lake, frogs chirp in chorus, and the firefly crosses the water as it goes its own way. The pale moon hangs high, its reflection shining in the glistening waves. A'mu catches up to me, snaking an arm around my waist, and though the breeze tosses our robes about us, he holds me tightly to him and I do not feel the cold.

"When summer arrives," he says, "and they come out, you'll have to say it again."

This is baffling, for I'd clearly not said anything. Why should he tell me to say anything again?

A'mu laughs softly. From afar, another firefly twinkles toward us. I fluster, but thankfully A'mu does not reach for it. Something ripples in the lake, shattering the image of the moon, and I, unsettled, long for him to catch another and at the same time for him to never catch one again.

POSTSCRIPT

银烛秋光冷画屏
Autumn Candlelight Cold upon the Painted Screen[1]

All at once, July is half over. The sixth month of the agricultural calendar means entry into the dog days, the hottest and most unbearable time of year.

This summer, there were very many unhappy things. It's said that in life, things are bound to not go your way eight or nine times out of ten, but very few are things you can confide to others.

I often opened my playlists and listened to endless songs, one after another, on repeat.

All that youthful passion shared, without restraint, with tens of millions—but it disperses like clouds beneath the wind. The moon climbs higher in the sky, and from the depths of night, the light of fireflies grows dimmer and farther away.

Like this story.

In the end, the story is false.

But the feelings within the story, they are true.

I hadn't thought that I'd write so much additional content for *Goodbye, My Princess*.

Aside from "The Blooms of Taiye Garden, the Willows

---

[1] From "Autumn Evening" by Du Mu.

of Weiyang Palace," and "A Rack Full of Roses, a Courtyard Perfumed," which I'd already written, I've also produced "I Would Not Have Known Hair Could Whiten with the Heart," "Heavy the Frost on the Paired Roof Tiles," and "The Moon like Snow upon Pavilion Flowers."

Every short story is one I personally feel is indispensable.

"Autumn Candlelight Cold Upon the Painted Screen."

I gave the postscript this title because it was a poem I'd memorized when I was young, and I always used to remember the line *lithe silken fans dart at fireflies*.

For if there was a *stone step, icy like water beneath the moon*, the person who held the fan has long since gone.

As I poke this sore spot, tears patter onto my keyboard.

It's actually something of a surprise, for I've become hard-hearted, so why should I cry?

From the distance of so many years, it seems that these short stories are the most immediate way of telling this story, while the original text of *Goodbye, My Princess* ought to be considered a long, endless bonus episode.

The forgotten memories, that first meeting, that fluttering of the heart, the sentimental vows—all of it found its way to the page.

Looking back now that I've finished, it's been much shorter than I'd imagined—just like Li Chengyin, for he, like me, had imagined that there would be a forever for Gu Xiaowu to enjoy.

But how should he know that miserly fate would never allow so much?

I think that it may be fine like this.

If Heaven were to feel, after all, it too would age.[2]

And Li Chengyin should have been an unfeeling person.

While Xiaofeng is honest and true to herself. This kind of prelapsarian spirit from a tender young woman is among the most unadulterated kinds of dispositions.

Even the most, most heartless cannot help but be attracted to it.

It's impossible to say who loved more than the other, nor is there any way to compare who, in the end, made the better choice.

If this is fate, then to meet again is to be moved again to love.

I can forget everything about you, I can forget the person themself, but the one thing I can't forget is the feeling of loving you.

In the text, Li Chengyin set Xiaofeng aside in the Court of Spring for three years, indifferent to her, but his attitude toward his princess consort changed in some subtle way after they were alone together for the first time.

Such that, in a time of most danger, he pushed her instinctively aside.

This is the reflex of love.

He may have forgotten everything, he may be bound by countless considerations, but instinctually, he has the reflex of love—and the ability *to* love.

I will forget you. In this life and every life.

Xiaofeng had said this, too.

---

[2] From "Song of the Bronze Transcendent Bidding Han Farewell" by Li He.

It was just that she also could not overcome that instinct.

After some years, I've come back to patch in some of the most important parts of the narrative. I've written some of these past events through the eyes of the Lady Zhao and Pei Zhao that, though they had passed again and again through my mind, I found hard to commit to. I sometimes wondered if I had chosen the worst way to write these stories. But I had to get them down somehow, the better to share with everyone.

And yet my heart still feels scattered, because, back when I started writing, the words came easily and confidently, and when I finished the book, it had been done decisively, like the swing of a sharp blade. It is only when the vestiges of passing time are clear that, looking back, I faintly feel the heartbreak and the pain.

In every heart there may be a stubborn, striving youth, holding fast to a truly felt dauntlessness to love another, who fought on without regard for their own well-being until their heart shattered utterly, and then retreated into indifference, tired of it all, hiding their pain and pretending nothing was the matter as they continued to live in this mortal silt.

And it is when they are alone, in the middle of the night, glancing at the moon outside the window or hearing the sounds of the wind and the rain, that they think of the person they used to be.

Stupid, and naive.

But there is tenderness for that silliest self who, though they knew nothing at all, flew mothlike into the flame.

At the very least, they may have seen that light and known

its heat would burn their wings, but they were without fear.

I can't bear to write Li Chengyin again, so I will leave him there, before the dream ends, before the day breaks.

I would not have known hair could whiten with the heart.

And those that do know are not promised white hair.

To say nothing of those that don't.

This stretch of memory is like a sparkling ripple in a clear pond, swallows flitting in a garden of roses, agarwood smoke curling from the censer—like a sprig of flowers that has fallen with the passing of spring, but the person beneath the curtain is still fast asleep.

Lightly red, and shallowly fragrant.

Thank you for sharing with me this long dream.

FEI WO SI CUN is a bestselling novelist and screenwriter who is known for crafting emotionally compelling, female-driven narratives. Since her debut in 2005, she has written twenty-three books, many of which have been published internationally and in Traditional Chinese, and nearly half of which have been adapted for screen. Her best-known works include *Goodbye, My Princess*; *Girl in Blue*; and *Sealed with a Kiss*, among others. She is also a producer for television.

TIANSHU is based in New York City, where she lives with a small cat and a large collection of unfinished knitting projects. Her dream is to be a Jin Yong heroine, but in the meantime, she's happy to daylight as an editor of award-winning and bestselling children's literature. Find her online at liutianshu.com.